I0678075

The Haunting of Nickelville Academy

The Nickelville Novels

Book One

Tom Barnett

Copyright © 2024 by Tom Barnett

All rights reserved.

No part of this publication may be reproduced, distributed, or transmitted in any form or by any means, including photocopying, recording, or other electronic or mechanical methods, without the prior written permission of the publisher, except as permitted by U.S. copyright law. For permission requests, contact tom.barnett@nickelville.com or visit www.nickelville.com.

The story, all names, characters, and incidents portrayed in this production are fictitious. No identification with actual persons (living or deceased), places, buildings, and products is intended or should be inferred.

Book Cover and Illustrations by Tom Barnett with the aid of Midjourney.com

First edition 2024

For my wife, Brandy,

Who has explored Nickelville and Guarded Wood with me since Megan

and Bruce first began to whisper in my ear.

Books by Tom Barnett

The Nickelville Novels

The Haunting of Nickelville Academy

The Goatman of Guarded Wood

Within the Silver Mirror

The Children of Nyx

Table of Contents

Prologue

Megan McGeehee, a girl who often sensed something hungry within the shadows around her, rose up through troubled dreams, fearing what the days ahead might bring. Sleep had been scarce in the weeks since she and her mother, Emelia, had taken shelter in the bowels of this derelict apartment building, and she desperately needed rest. But in the last few seconds, something had changed, bringing her awake with a lurch that made her empty stomach clench. She didn't think that the Wild Hunt had caught her scent yet, but the same things that made it hard for them to find her here made it difficult for her to sense her pursuers without leaving the protection of the building.

A rotten, earthy odor filled her senses, just as strong as it had been when they'd first arrived. Even after all of the hours she'd spent scrubbing the dingy walls and floors, that smell seemed to coat everything in a greasy film.

She peered through the damp strands of her hair into the dimly lit room. Although the scant light cast by the naked bulb overhead did little to dispel the shadows she felt closing in around her, it still made her head throb.

Angry voices bled through the thin walls, but they'd grown so commonplace that they no longer held any power to affect her. Fear and anger erupted so often in the nearby apartments that the echoes of one met the next like old friends when another outburst began the cycle anew.

The wool upholstery of the armchair pricked through her t-shirt and made her pale skin itch. Her whole body felt as if the damp air had left an invisible shell over her, and it hurt to move even more than it did to remain still. But she still straightened her stiff legs, trying to ignore how weak she felt. She knew she should eat, but even the thought turned her stomach. Placing her feet on the rough floorboards, she rested her elbows on her knees until the world grew still beneath her.

No matter how many showers she took, she still felt grimy. More than that, she felt *contaminated* by this place in a way that had nothing to do with dirt or even mold. And even if the ancient water heater had been sufficient to provide the scalding storm she craved, she doubted any amount of scrubbing would free her from this stain.

For as far back as Megan could remember, she'd sensed the feelings of the people around her. At that moment she could feel the anger of the man in the apartment above them whose money always ran out before the bills did. The woman next door grieved for a daughter who'd left to buy food and never returned.

Megan wasn't the only one hiding here. Terror washed over her from the little boy who hid in the closet across the hall with his sister, praying for their mother to pass out from the pills before she found them this time. But as bad as that was, it was the man in the apartment below that she'd have given anything to block out, as he gazed dreamily at the contents of the wooden box before him, reliving his crimes through trophies he'd collected from his victims.

She felt many others, and even though their hearts sung different tunes, the melody remained the same. They sang the lament of the forgotten, the ones who'd lost hope as they circled the drain one last time. Her shields blocked out the worst during the long hours of wakefulness,

2

but when she slept, an emotional pestilence oozed past her defenses, cutting off her air and threatening to drown her.

She couldn't remember which of her teachers had taught the lesson about chemotherapy. There had been so many men and women over the years that even the best and worst merged in her memory. At the time she hadn't understood how exposure to something so toxic could save a person's life. But what was this if not chemo? As long as she stayed hidden deep within the iron-laden bowels of this building and submerged in the noxious emotions of those around her, she'd be safe, protected from the faceless men who had followed her since birth.

It wasn't as if she or her mother had ever lived in a castle. In fact, running water and electricity put their current hiding place far ahead of many of the others in terms of physical comfort. But she preferred even the ones that had never been intended for human habitation to the emotional stench of this place. At least in those secluded places she'd felt free.

She wasn't like other teens, and not just in the stark contrast of her ebony hair and alabaster skin. Her freshman year in high school had brought an end to most of the childish name calling, but they still sensed something alien in her, something terrible. No matter how often she tried to fade into the background, no matter how hard she tried to pass unnoticed beneath the surface of their thoughts, they still caught her scent and banded together against her. But even so, right now she'd eagerly go back to school just to get out of this apartment.

In the past she and her mother had been able to live fairly normal lives for as much as six or seven months at a time before the Huntsmen found her again. Then the pressure would take root at the base of her skull, easily mistaken for the sort of stiffness she developed when sleeping in the front seat of the truck. But as the Wild Hunt drew nearer, discomfort grew into pain and eventual agony if she didn't escape quickly enough. Only two things could hide her from them: distance and iron.

But something had changed. Instead of months, the Wild Hunt now needed less than a week to find her, robbing her and her mother of the time they desperately needed to rest and gather the resources they'd need to run again.

Which was why they'd finally come here. Hoping that the iron skeleton of the old building would mask her magic from those who followed, her mother had rented an apartment deep inside where layer upon layer of the destitute would disguise her psychic scent. It had now worked for nearly a month, but not without cost. For the first time Megan could remember, her mother had fallen physically ill, making it difficult to find work. As for herself, the strain of living in such a place had begun to drive her insane.

She hadn't bothered to unpack her posters this time, fearing that she'd have to leave them behind as she'd been forced to do before. As childish as it seemed, she still missed the Kermit the Frog doll she'd left behind when the Huntsmen had come upon her too quickly to pack. Aside from the voice that sometimes spoke in her thoughts, and the magical creatures she occasionally found in forgotten places, that doll had been her only friend throughout childhood.

Megan felt her mother's approach an instant before the woman threw open the door, frightened enough to open the locks without even pulling her keys from the pocket of her coat. As usual, Emelia had her own long dark hair pulled back, and she was dressed warmer than the season seemed to dictate. But as soon as Megan saw her, she knew two things from her mother's disheveled appearance. Emelia's sickness had grown worse, and contrary to what she'd believed, the Wild Hunt had indeed found them again.

4

Megan snatched up their duffle bags and dropped them next to the door before rushing to the rusty refrigerator and scooping its meager contents into their battered cooler. Within minutes, she'd loaded the entirety of their possessions into the nearby elevator and was descending toward the parking garage where their old, questionably reliable, and most importantly iron laden truck waited.

"It's a good thing I went out when I did," Emelia said wearily. "Otherwise we'd have had no warning at all."

"How did they find me?" Megan asked while they waited for the doors to slide open.

"I don't know," Emelia whispered, steadying herself by holding onto the graffiti covered wall of the elevator. "I thought for sure that they wouldn't be able to feel you here."

Her mother's gray eyes looked sunken in the washed out light and frightened Megan even more than the rapid approach of the Huntsmen. The small woman shivered in spite of her jacket, and Megan worried that she might need more help than they could expect from one of the clinics. But even those cost money, and they had almost none left. The elevator lurched, and for one horrified second, she wondered what would happen if they actually got stuck now. With a sudden drop of several inches, it continued its downward descent.

As soon as the doors opened, Megan could hear the roar of the rain from the entrance of the parking garage. Even though it stank of booze, exhaust, and vomit, it felt like a paradise compared to the hole from which she'd finally been freed.

"I've got this," Megan said, guiding her mother toward the driver's side of the truck. It was a testament to how far the woman's health had deteriorated that she didn't argue. With the speed and accuracy born of perhaps a hundred such escapes, Megan slid the boxes and bags across the worn wooden boards of the truck's bed, each finding its way to the appropriate spot as if by magic. She tarped the bed of the old green Ford before her mother managed to get the engine to catch.

"Want me to drive?" Megan asked, taking her seat and watching as her mother steadied herself by holding onto the steering wheel.

"I'm okay," the stubborn woman whispered. "Just tell me where they are when you start to feel them."

According to her mother, once the Huntsmen laid eyes on them, it would be impossible to lose them again. As for what would happen if they were caught, her mother would only say it was the worst of their possible futures.

Emelia accelerated through the stop sign at the entrance to the parking garage, and the pressure at the base of Megan's neck tightened like a vise. She winced and held onto the armrest in white-knuckled anguish.

"How many?" Emelia asked when they cleared the gate.

"I don't know," Megan whispered.

"Any openings?" she asked.

Megan cleared her mind as best she could and found the ghostly images of the ones who sought her. Although they remained indistinct, like faint signals just out of sync on the radio, they were much clearer than she'd ever felt them before.

"That way," Megan said through clenched teeth while pointing west with the beginnings of a migraine blinding her to her surroundings.

"We're going to make it," Emelia assured her, exhaustion making her voice husky. "This isn't the time or place when they find you."

"How do you know?" Megan asked, nauseous with pain.

"I just do," her mother answered, turning the battered Ford west. "I've got it from here, get some sleep."

Even though the unusual girl didn't want to leave her mother to drive by herself, the pain and sleep deprivation of the past weeks soon stole her away while the storm raged on.

Chapter I: The Fall

Bruce Grimble resisted the rhythmic thump of the printing press as it fought to guide his steps while the morning edition of the *Nickelville Tribune* neared completion. While that sound might indeed be the heartbeat of the newspaper, it still made for a funky walk, and he didn't want to look like a kid when he entered Heather's office.

She was one of the college interns who sometimes worked at the *Tribune* for journalism credit. She was pretty, had a warm smile, and treated Bruce like a little brother. Not the treatment of his actual sister, which involved a lot of punching and tackling, but the sort of treatment he thought normal families probably experienced.

His mother thought he had a crush on Heather, and he suspected the young woman did as well. But even though he found something alluring in her dark hair and brown eyes, attraction had nothing to do with why he sought her company. She was an outsider, one of those lucky enough to have been born somewhere outside this claustrophobic town. It was her knowledge of places beyond that drew him into her tiny office day after day to hear stories of where she'd been. He came to her because somewhere out there, beyond the trees that encircled Nickelville, something had been calling to him for as long as he'd been old enough to notice such things.

"Here's the package you've been waiting for," he said as he laid it on the corner of Heather's desk. "Need anything else?"

"Thanks," she said and rewarded him with a smile. "I don't know what I'm going to do when you're gone."

"What do you mean?" he asked.

"I heard some of the staff talking about your asthma at lunch."

"Oh," he mumbled, turning back toward the door.

"So you'll stop coming in after the weather changes?" she asked.

"Yeah, probably," Bruce answered. "I'd better get going." He sped off without waiting for her reply.

Each year brought with it a single moment when he was no longer able to ignore the arrival of autumn and the restrictions it would place on his freedom. This year that moment had come earlier than expected and from someone he'd trusted. He knew Heather hadn't meant anything by it, but it still felt like a betrayal.

His feet carried him to the window where he'd spent so many of his best childhood days. As usual, it stood open to the predawn air, venting smells of machinery and newsprint, smells he'd always associated with happiness.

He still remembered the first time his mother had placed him there. His daycare had been closed for some reason, and his parents hadn't been able to get a sitter. Luckily his sister had been in school by then since she'd already been banned from the newspaper after throwing a rock into the printing press and jamming the equipment for several hours. His younger brother, Paul, had spent the afternoon with a friend since the loud sounds of the machinery gave him headaches.

It had taken Bruce a while to figure out exactly why his mother had chosen that spot for him. Although in hindsight, it was as well thought out as everything else that she did. Yes, it was an open window, but it was only about three feet to the ground outside should he fall. The air was fresher there than anywhere else in the building, which made it less likely that the

9

industrial fumes of the place would interfere with his asthma. It marked the furthest point from machines dangerous to small hands. And it was clearly visible from almost every point in the *Tribune*, which meant his mother could keep an eye on him even if she weren't within arm's reach.

He remembered the way the cracked paint on the sill had felt under his hands while he watched the *Tribune's* staff scurry from one place to another. To his young mind they'd resembled some enormous insect colony over which his mother reigned queen. That always made him smile, because if she was a queen then he was a prince.

The paint on the sill had flaked away long ago, and the wood beneath had been worn smoother than any sanding could achieve. At first, he'd been content to watch in wonder as common paper was transformed into the county's only newspaper. But as time passed, the staff became a second family to him. More so, in fact, than his own brother and sister whom he'd never really understood. Were it not for his parents' assurances that no one had been adopted, he'd have suspected that the differences were more than coincidence. And yet, the fact that he felt this way puzzled him as well, because he'd never been able to understand its cause. He loved his family, brother and sister included. He'd do anything for them, but that just wasn't enough. Something was missing, something he needed almost as much as the air his sickness would deny him in the months to come. Until he found it, something that remained dormant within him would continue to sleep.

Outside the window, past a field of corn stalks almost ready for harvest, something caught Bruce's attention. At first, he thought it was a voice, but then he realized it wasn't a sound at all, but rather something more akin to the feel of an approaching storm.

His heart rate soared and his face felt hot. The *Tribune's* machinery took on distant, muffled tones and his vision narrowed to a point of light.

10

A shadow passed over him and into his mind, settling like fallen leaves yet illuminating the dark places within him. His eyes lost their focus on the *Tribune*, and other images began to rush in:

He was falling over a vast ocean with the water rushing up from below. The biggest cliff he'd ever seen stretched out in a massive wall of rusty stone, connecting one side of the horizon to the other...

Bruce felt himself begin to fall out of the window.

A cottage made of black stone rose against an open field full of wildflowers. As he watched, flames began to billow behind the darkened panes of glass and then they exploded outward toward him.

He tried to catch the edge of the window, but it slipped through his numb fingers.

A huge bird, a raptor of some sort, rose into the sky where its immense size blotted out the sun. Then, with a mournful cry that threatened to drown Bruce in despair, it began to fall. He tried to run toward it, but two fair-skinned boys with eyes so dark that they almost looked black held his hands.

With a jarring crash he hit the ground and slammed his teeth together over the tip of his tongue, flooding his mouth with the metallic taste of his own blood.

The small hands still held his own, but the scene had shifted into the nightmare that often left him drenched in sweat in the deepest hours of the night when the house was still and even his siblings slept. The light was dim and his nostrils stung with the bitter tang of sulfur. It was hot and hard to breathe. Bruce wanted his inhaler, but he didn't have it with him. He wasn't alone. Packed into the tunnel where he and the two boys ran were

11

dozens of children, all of them tired and scared. Behind them,
something followed...

How embarrassing, he thought before he lost all sense of his
surroundings.

Bruce woke to find his mother and several of the *Tribune* staff
gathered around him. He'd only fallen a few feet, but he'd managed to land
on his head and could feel a trickle of blood working its way down from
the corner of his mouth. *At least Heather didn't see me fall*, he thought.

"She's coming home," he mumbled for no apparent reason. The
people clustered around him looked at each other uncertainly.

"What's that?" his mother asked with concern.

"Nothing," he answered.

"Your father will be here in a minute," she said, wiping at the blood
with a tissue.

"I'm fine," he said, trying to rise up to his elbows. A wave of nausea
washed over him and he lay quickly back before he could vomit. "It was
only a few feet."

"I'm sure you are," she answered, "but we'll see what his
professional opinion is just the same."

The siren from his father's ambulance could now be heard above the
ringing in his ears. *Great*, he thought, *Jade and Paul are going to have a
blast teasing me about this.*

"Paul really hates sirens," Bruce whispered, once again wondering
where the words he spoke were coming from.

12

Chapter II: Among the Old Ones

A single fluorescent light lit the gas pumps in a flickering strobe that made the shadows move of their own volition as Megan unbuckled her seatbelt and waited for the truck to roll to a stop. It had only been a few minutes since the presence of the Huntsmen had faded from the edge of her awareness. But Oscar, their grouchy green truck, was running on fumes, and they needed to be moving again as soon as his greedy tank was full.

With the last of the emergency money in hand, Megan hurried toward the station's entrance. Behind her, the truck gave an ominous rumble and backfired.

The attendant glanced back at the clock which read a few minutes past five in the morning and frowned at her when she approached.

"I need to put this much into pump five," Megan said quietly, trying not to think about how much she hated to give it to him. She didn't know what she and her mother were going to do when the gas ran out.

"Odd time for someone your age to be out, isn't it?" he grumbled, looking her up and down for several seconds before slowly counting the bills, stopping to scrutinize one against the light before finally flipping the pump switch.

She shrugged in reply and walked quickly back to the door with his eyes on her. She concentrated hard to keep his thoughts out of her head. Her clothing marked her as only slightly on the prosperous side of homelessness. Even though kids never let her forget, the adults were worse, watching her in places like this to make sure she didn't steal anything.

As the distance from that horrible apartment grew, Megan's appetite slowly returned. Maybe she'd get something out of the cooler while the gas pumped. Maybe she could get her mother to eat something too.

She felt the attendant move to better watch as she pumped the gas. She missed the anonymity of childhood. Before the scars from her skinned knees had faded, it had been much easier to blend into the background. But now she'd lost the ability to pass invisibly through the adult world. And while she disliked the mistrust she saw in almost every adult gaze, it was the strange feelings that sometimes came with them that left her feeling unclean.

Emelia smiled weakly through the cracked window of the truck, closed her eyes and leaned against the window to rest for the few minutes it would take to pump the gas. The glass fogged from the heat of her fever.

Megan unscrewed the cap and started to pump the gas. Still thinking about her mother's gray eyes, she forgot about the food and was again struck by how different they were from her own. She wondered if her father's eyes had been brown, and if, like her own, they could shift to an unnatural shade of violet when he became angry or frightened.

The weight of the Wild Hunt's focus bore down on her again, a physical weight that nearly drove her to her knees. She fought to keep the last of the gas flowing into the tank, forcing herself to breathe. After a short eternity, the pump shut off and she pulled the nozzle free. Pain throbbed in the pit of her stomach as she steadied herself against the side of the truck. When the hose stopped her short of the door, she dropped it on the ground and climbed into the cab where her mother was already cranking the engine over and over in unproductive lurches. At last the fuel ignited and the engine rumbled uncertainly beneath the hood.

14

"Damn," Emelia whispered groggily. "I don't understand what's changed. How are they finding us so quickly?"

The truck backfired and died when she coaxed it into gear, taking two more agonizing attempts to start before they finally left the frowning attendant behind. Back on the highway, they sped as fast as the truck would go for the better part of two hours in silence.

Then the engine gave a loud clunk and the truck shuddered. Worse yet, in spite of the pressure her mother applied to the pedal, the truck began to slow.

"Come on Oscar...just a little further," Emelia whispered, sounding more like a prayer than a plea.

"A little further until what?"

"Nickelville," Emelia answered, her words barely loud enough to hear over the rumble of the engine.

Megan stared at her mother, torn between curiosity and the need to let the woman conserve her strength. They'd never been to this part of the country before, and she had no idea of where to start looking on the faded map in the glove box. What she would have given to be able to use a phone without frying the circuitry!

They left the highway shortly after the sky began to brighten, and turned onto an unmarked farm road with more patches than pavement. Corn stalks stretched out on either side, deceptively peaceful against the knocking beneath the hood as they struggled to keep moving.

"Do you want me to drive?" Megan offered after Emelia finished a coughing fit that left her gasping for breath. "I know I don't have my license, but I can do it."

Emelia shook her head, scanning the semi-darkness ahead. Then a side road appeared, an imperfection in the otherwise perfect expanse of corn. She slowed just enough to make the turn and then sped on. The sensation at the back of Megan's neck tightened like a hand gripping her spine. The truck began to shudder.

Pain blurred her vision, twisting the trees that rose at the edge of the horizon into mountains on the otherwise flat terrain. But that couldn't be right. This was Texas, after all. As they drew nearer, she realized that these were some of the biggest trees she'd ever seen. Maybe not as big as the redwoods of California, but close.

Sunlight touched the uppermost branches and lit them in golden green fire. The road led directly toward their center.

Megan could feel the Huntsmen from all directions, and their presence became too painful for her to concentrate on her surroundings. She began to black out.

A sense of resistance built before them as if some sort of barrier blocked their path, a bubble of force that stretched thin before granting them admission. Then the first branches blotted out the view of the sky and the presence of the Wild Hunt fell away altogether. It didn't fade as the distance between her and the Huntsmen grew. It just ended as if a gate had been slammed shut behind her through which her pursuers could not follow.

Emelia exhaled a raspy breath and let off the accelerator. The engine coughed and died. Momentum carried them to the top of the hill, and then the truck rolled quietly down into a deep valley revealed on the other side.

Megan looked over at her mother and found Emelia swaying in the seat, the lids of her eyes half-closed. Picking up speed as it went, Oscar continued to roll down past towering giants.

"Mom," Megan called, placing her hand over the hot skin of her mother's hand.

Whether Emelia couldn't hear or just didn't have the strength to answer, she didn't respond. But she did continue to steer the truck past the trees and deeper into the protective woods.

At last the road leveled out. Emelia brought them to a halt in the parking lot of an abandoned building that stood at the edge of a small lake. The building itself sat at an odd angle, nestled between the trees and the cracked blacktop that surrounded it. Tendrils of mist rose from the lake like the monstrous sea serpents Megan had read about as a child. The silhouettes of yet more trees could just be seen on the opposite shore in the dawn light.

Emelia fell back against the seat and closed her eyes, hands sliding limp down the sides of the wheel. When they came to rest in her lap, Megan could see the scar that covered most of her left ring finger.

The engine clicked and popped in the cool dawn air, slow against the tempo of her heart in her ears. What was she supposed to do now? Her mother was unconscious, the truck was dead, and they were stuck out in the middle of nowhere without a single cent.

"Mom," Megan repeated, shaking the sick woman gently.

Emelia didn't stir, and Megan didn't know what to do now. If she left the iron shell of the truck so soon after breaking the connection with the Wild Hunt, they might catch the scent of her magic once again. But she'd never seen her mother like this before and feared that if she didn't find help for her soon, it might be too late. Megan reluctantly turned the door handle and slid out into the cold dawn air.

A quiet that had nothing to do with her sense of hearing filled her mind, and the silence of this wooded lake roared by comparison. The smallest movement of her worn shoes ground into the gravel so loudly that it echoed across the still water of the lake. She froze, afraid that the Huntsmen, who surely lurked nearby, might hear.

The interwoven branches stole away the light of the dawn sky and pulled the curtain of night back over her. Even in the hush where her extra senses had so recently resided, she could feel the presence of these giants as if they filled the world around her more completely than the rest of her surroundings.

She made out faded letters on the side of the building that read, *Carson's Bait Shop.* A breeze stirred the surface of the lake and whispered through the leaves.

Go to the other side of the building, a familiar voice whispered through her mind, not unlike the sound of the wind around her. She welcomed this figment of her imagination. It had been a while since her childhood companion had spoken to her, but at least it made her feel a bit less alone.

She cringed with each footstep, still worried by the sounds that echoed off the trunks around her. Maybe it was nothing more than a trick of the woods, but what she heard held more than evidence of her own movements. Shapes and shadows lurked in the corners of her vision, but disappeared when she turned her head to look.

They're nothing you need to concern yourself with, the voice whispered.

"What are they?" Megan whispered.

Leftover bits of what once was, it answered. *Survivors of another age.*

Sheltered under the overhang of the building's roof, she spied an old payphone.

Pick up the receiver.

"There's no way that thing still works," Megan whispered in confusion, yet doing as it asked anyway. "And who would I call if it did?"

18

The dial tone sounded strange, and she half expected it to cut out the way cell phones did when she touched them. When it continued to hum in her ear, she pressed the zero on the worn keypad.

"Nickelville operator," a man's voice drawled through the line. "What can I do for you?"

"I need to place a collect call to the McGeehee residence," she heard the voice say through her mouth. It was the first time it had ever done such a thing.

"Who shall I say is calling?"

"Emelia," it answered.

The phone began to ring, and a detached part of Megan's mind screamed with excitement. Yet this unexpected turn of events also terrified her. Surely this was a mistake. Surely the man would come back in a minute and say that no one lived in Nickelville with such a strange name.

"Hello," a deep voice answered.

"Azarich, you have a collect call from Emelia," the operator's voice announced. "Are you willing to accept the charges?"

"Emelia?" the new voice exclaimed, "Of course I'll accept the charges. Put her through."

A moment of awkward silence followed during which Megan waited for direction from the calm presence that had taken her thus far. When she realized she was on her own, she struggled with what to say.

"Emelia, is that really you?" The man's voice pleaded. Whoever he was, he really wanted to talk to her mother.

"Sort of," Megan finally managed to say, "I'm her daughter, Megan. She's very sick and our truck just broke down at an old bait shop at the edge of Nickelville."

She wanted to add that there were people following them, people she'd never seen but could feel from miles away. However, she doubted that would go over very well. Either this person knew about it already or needed to remain ignorant.

"Is it Carson's?" the man asked.

"Yes," she answered, "Can you help us?"

"I'll be there in ten minutes, fifteen at the most."

She placed the handset on the cradle and started back the way she'd come. Her eyes drifted to the lake where a huge bird with a crest of red feathers swept down and snatched up a fish before carrying it out of sight.

When she cleared the corner and the truck came back into view, she found it cloaked in a mass of questing shadows, pressing in on the place where her mother remained unconscious. Oblivious to her exhaustion, Megan broke into a run, afraid this might be the physical manifestation of the Wild Hunt as it caught their scent.

They're just curious about her, the voice whispered. *They haven't seen her in a long time. They're curious about you as well.*

Relief flooded her when the shapes dispersed. She found that without the adrenaline of the chase, she could barely remain standing. The sleep she'd managed in the truck since they'd left wasn't nearly enough to replace what she'd lost back at the apartment. She wrapped her arms around herself against the morning chill, even though she'd never been particularly affected by cold, and tried in vain to sort out the maelstrom of conflicting emotions that threatened to tear her apart.

She wished she had an explanation for how the surrounding trees hid her from the Huntsmen. Although thankful for this safe haven, she worried that their camouflage might not be enough if the ones who'd followed them all the way from the apartment stumbled across her now by accident. Her mother had come here on purpose, apparently knowing about the strange trees. But if that was so, why hadn't they come before now?

Who was this Azarich McGeehee? She knew who she wanted that voice to belong to, though she kept that hope down in the murky depths of her subconscious along with all of the other things she'd long since given up on. She simply felt too emotionally frayed to let her mind build the possibility that the owner of that deep voice might complete the equation of which her mother was the beginning and herself the result.

When the sound of a distant engine whispered beneath the rattle of the leaves overhead, she wondered if it was this Azarich or the Huntsmen. She couldn't, however, gather enough strength to care anymore.

Strangely enough, the truck that circled round from the opposite side of the bait shop could have been the twin of Oscar, except that it was in much better condition and blue instead of green.

The hope that Azarich might be her father died when she saw his short white hair. He looked at least eighty, but moved like a young man when he threw open the door of his truck and hurried over to where she stood. The look on his face was a mixture of excitement and awe.

"She's in the truck," Megan said, motioning unnecessarily toward the driver's side. "She has a bad fever and won't wake up."

He stared at her as if he hadn't understood what she'd said. She was about to repeat it louder in case he was hard of hearing when he broke from his shocked inaction on his own and rushed to the truck. He opened Emelia's door and brushed the back of his fingers across her forehead, wincing at the heat before shaking her gently.

"Emelia," he said softly, "I don't know if you can hear me, but everything is going to be okay. You're home now."

The tenderness he showed her mother touched Megan and made her want to trust him. But that was a lesson she'd learned early and learned well. She couldn't trust anyone. He looked up and caught her staring at him.

"I called the doctor on the way over. He'll be here with the town ambulance as soon as the driver is finished checking up on his son. We don't have a hospital, but we can set her up in her room like we did when she had pneumonia as a child."

Now that she was expecting it, she could hear an ambulance siren drifting up from the valley below.

22

"I don't know how to thank you," Megan said, so relieved that she could feel hot tears threatening to spill down her cheeks. She never let anyone see her cry, and she didn't want to start in front of Azarich.

"What kind of a father would I be if I didn't do everything in my power to help her?" he asked.

"You're her father?" Megan asked quietly, letting the information sink in. There were similarities in their expressions and a quality to his voice that she recognized from her mother.

"Which means I'm your grandfather," he added, gently closing Emelia's door to protect her from the cool morning air, "although I didn't know about you until you called."

"I didn't know about you either," Megan replied. Why hadn't her mother told her about this man? Could he be trusted, or was there a reason why they'd never come here?

As the ambulance pulled into the parking lot, Megan closed the distance to her grandfather and gave him an awkward hug. It wasn't an easy thing to do even though she wanted to do it badly. But she'd always dreamed of having a grandparent, and if this was some feverish dream while she slept back in that horrible apartment, she wanted to hug him before he was gone. Within moments of sitting down in her grandfather's truck, the exhaustion claimed her again and she slept.

Chapter III: Prodigal Return

Megan woke to the sort of panicked confusion she felt on nights when the power shut off and the silence screamed at her. But instead of waking to a darkened apartment, she woke in a pool of warm light that streamed in from a lace-trimmed window. Rather than a lumpy thrift-store mattress that rested directly on the floor, she found herself lying on an old four-poster bed with an antique bedspread. A watercolor hung on the wall directly across from her in which a dark-haired woman played the violin. Even though it portrayed a frozen instant of time, the olive-skinned musician somehow conveyed energetic movement that contrasted with the sadness in her eyes.

The silence created by the trees that surrounded the town reached all the way here into her mother's childhood home. She could hear, quite clearly, the faint popping of the window glass as it warmed in the sun. Leaves rustled in the wind, and a nearby wind chime danced on that same breeze. The silence, she realized, was within her mind. The part of her that could sense the world around her, that sixth sense her mother often acknowledged but refused to explain, had fallen utterly silent. For the first time in her life, Megan knew what it felt like to be normal.

With the grace of a cat, she went in search of her mother. She eased the bedroom door open and slid out into the hall, little more than a wraith in an old tee-shirt and threadbare jeans.

Dark framed photographs lined the hallway, and a worn but intricate rug covered the floor all the way to the staircase. She noticed these things, but her attention narrowed to the next doorway down the hall from which faint, rhythmic tones drifted.

She crept to the door, unsettled by her inability to feel what lay beyond and peeked inside her mother's childhood room. Posters of unicorns and castles covered the walls. Two bookshelves stood against one wall, filled to bursting with paperback books and a dollhouse sat on a table in the corner. Everything was pink, purple and frilly: completely the opposite of what Megan would have expected.

Emelia lay in a four-poster bed like the one where Megan had woken. Azarich perched on a chair next to her, and an IV bottle hung from a stand that also held the heart monitor Megan had heard from the hallway. The normally fierce woman looked small in the large bed, and were it not for the slow rise and fall of her chest, she might have been dead.

It took Azarich a while to notice his newly-discovered granddaughter in the doorway, so she took advantage of the situation to watch as he gently stroked his daughter's hand. Megan wondered about his age. Most of the old people she'd encountered had been homeless and crazy, so she wasn't sure how to approach him. When he did look up, his face lit with a genuine smile that made him look much younger.

"Well, good morning Sunshine," he said.

"Good morning, Grandfather," she responded, trying not to enjoy the way the word felt on her tongue. "How is she?"

"Her breathing is better," he said, "or at least I think so. Doc Soames left a little while ago, and he said he thought she'd be okay in a week or two. He treated her the last time she had pneumonia."

"She's had this before?" Megan asked.

25

"When she was about ten," he answered. "She never got sick often as a child, but pneumonia caught up to her one winter, and it took her a while before she completely recovered."

Megan's stomach betrayed her and growled loudly.

"Why don't I go make some breakfast," Azarich said with a grin.

"Sorry," Megan mumbled, embarrassed.

"No reason to be sorry," he said, standing. He walked around the bed and gave Emelia one last pat on the shoulder through the bedding. "We'll be back in a little bit," he told her.

Megan followed him down the stairs and found all of the boxes that had been in the back of their old truck waiting by the front door. It shocked her that she hadn't already thought about their possessions. Exhausted or not, she needed to keep her wits about her better than this.

"Ben Grimble unloaded these from your truck after the tow truck brought it here," Azarich said when he noticed where she was looking. "Good man," he continued, "He and his family live next door."

"Would you mind if I changed clothes?" she asked, feeling self-conscious about being in the same ones that she'd been wearing at the apartment before making an eighteen-hour drive across several states. Although she never sweated, she could still feel the corruption of that place clinging to her skin.

"Not at all, take your time. It's going to take me a bit to get everything together. The bathroom is across the hall from your mother's room if you'd like a shower. I know I always do after a long trip."

"That would be wonderful," Megan said with a grateful smile. "Are you sure you don't need help with breakfast? I don't mind."

"I've got this under control," he said. "I'll make your mother's favorite. Pancakes, right?"

"That would be great," she answered, already on her way up the stairs with her duffle bag in her hands. She relaxed a little more after hearing him say something about her mother that she could confirm.

After a scalding shower that would have likely burned anyone else, Megan checked on her mother again. The monitor continued to chirp at reassuring intervals, and she discovered that her mother had changed positions. Hopefully that meant she was regaining some of her strength.

Emelia mumbled something that sounded oddly like silly boy and trees.

"Everything will be okay now," Megan whispered, echoing her grandfather's words earlier. She kissed her mother softly on her forehead which still burned to the touch.

The house held a living warmth that Megan had never experienced before. She'd been in places far older, but they'd all reeked of mildew and decay. The photographs she'd noticed earlier drew her in, and she stopped at each one, devouring them with hungry eyes. Until now, she'd never known what her mother had looked like as a child. Given how little Megan's reflection resembled the girl she saw before her, she doubted she'd look anything like her mother in the future. Most surprising of all was a tall, Native American boy present in the pictures with her mother. Had her mother actually had friends?

She followed her nose downstairs to the kitchen, but stopped by the living room when a picture on the fireplace mantle caught her eye. She moved closer, dimly aware of the way the floorboards beneath her feet creaked with each step.

In a gold gilt frame no bigger than a paperback novel, a familiar face looked back at Megan in shades of light and shadow. It reflected almost perfectly what she saw when she looked in the mirror. With laugh lines at the corners of the woman's eyes and a few other differences that Megan suspected she'd develop herself in the next few decades, the frame might well have held a window into her own future.

"So, you found her," Azarich said from the kitchen doorway.

"Who is she?" Megan asked. Her fingers traced the contours of her own face to reassure herself that she hadn't somehow been transported into the frame.

"Your Grandmother," he answered. "We met on the first day of school at the Academy when we were about six, and she stole my heart. From that day forward, she was the only one for me."

"Was?" Megan asked, unsure how to ask if her grandmother was still alive.

"Yes, she passed away when Emelia was born," he answered, echoes of old grief still rippled through his gray eyes, which closely resembled his daughter's.

"I'm sorry," Megan said, staring again at the picture. "But we look so much alike."

"I'd be lying if I said my old heart didn't seize up for a moment when I saw you there at Carson's," he added. "When you get old like me, it's sometimes a little hard to separate the past from the present. I'm still afraid that I might be lying in my bed, and that I'll wake up to find that this has all been a dream."

"I thought the same thing when you picked us up," Megan said, nodding toward the picture. "I didn't see her in any of the pictures in the upstairs hallway."

"I'm greedy about my Josie," he admitted. "Our childhood photos are in an album next to my bed along with my favorites of Emelia. I'm usually more concerned with watching where I'm walking next to the stairs, so I don't put my favorites there."

"I never knew we had any family," Megan said softly, trying as hard as she could to keep the bitterness from her voice. "Grandma's name was Josie?"

"Yes, although she went by Josephine when we were younger. Today is the first time I've seen or heard from Emelia in thirty years," he said, and Megan could hear pain to match her own in his voice. "But I've got you both here now, and I won't let you starve in front of me. Let's go dig into those pancakes."

Megan felt both nauseous with hunger and excited by the prospect of questioning her grandfather about forbidden subjects. But alongside those healthy feelings, a pool of guilt gathered in the pit of her empty stomach. Emelia wouldn't approve of her asking about the past, and taking advantage of her mother's illness felt wrong. But what if this was the only chance she'd ever have to find out what her mother refused to tell her? Surely, she was old enough to know.

"Grandpa," she said, still trying to figure out what to call him.

"Yes?" he said, looking up from where he was pouring syrup on his pancakes.

"Did you know my father?" she asked in a rush, then held her breath lest she miss the answer.

"I met him at their wedding," he answered, putting down the bottle so he could better focus on her questions.

"What was he like?" she asked, afraid that her mother might somehow wake up and storm down the stairs to stop her.

"He was very charismatic," he answered after thinking for a moment.

"Charismatic?" she asked, "Like a strong personality?"

"Yes," he answered. "Seemed like a good enough person for the few hours I was around him. A bit eccentric, though."

"Eccentric?" Megan asked.

"The way he and his family dressed was strange, and they had an odd quality to their speech I couldn't place. Even though I could understand their words, I never could seem to understand what they were talking about."

"Did you like him?" Megan pressed.

"Not particularly," he answered. "But you have to realize that I hadn't heard from Emelia in months when she called and told me that she was getting married. I'd been worried sick about her, and I thought she was rushing into the whole matter."

"Then what?" Megan asked.

"Then she disappeared from the face of the earth," he answered, staring at his plate.

"Oh," she said, sadly realizing that he was as ignorant as she was about the information she wanted most to know. "What did he look like?"

"You've never seen him?" Azarich asked in surprise.

"No," she answered. "I always assumed I must look like him since I don't look anything like Mom, but now that I've seen that picture of Grandmother…"

"I've got a picture that I took at their wedding somewhere," Azarich said. "I'll look for it later and let you have it. He had black hair and pale skin like yours, and all of the people with him had unusual eyes."

"Unusual how?" she asked, suspecting she already knew.

"They were an unusual shade of purple," he answered. "It sounds strange, but it really was quite striking. I've never seen anyone else with that color since. That's about all I could tell you about them."

Silence hung between them, and Megan wondered if she'd asked too much, too soon.

"Why doesn't mom ever talk about him?" she pressed, finding that she couldn't let it end there. "I didn't even know that McGeehee was her maiden name before today."

"I don't know, but I'm sure she had her reasons," he answered, clearly troubled.

Megan realized she was putting him in an awkward position. No matter how cheerful and girly her mother's old bedroom might look, she doubted the woman's temper had been any less daunting when she'd been younger. The promised picture of her father was enough to keep her satisfied for the moment. She took a bite, and the hunger took over.

Throughout the rest of the meal, Megan devoured both food and stories of days long past with equal appetite. As one story gave way to the next, and the stack of pancakes disappeared, something happened of which she doubted her mother would approve. The circle of Megan's trust, which had always been restricted to her mother and herself, opened to include this man who should have never been a stranger. Megan wasn't sure if it was the pancakes or the growing knowledge of where she'd come from that left her more content. But she did know that she worried about him. When she and her mother left, as she knew deep down they would, the people who searched for her would pass through the sleepy little town of Nickelville. What would happen when her trail led the Wild Hunt to Azarich?

Chapter IV: The Forgotten

Bruce muttered under his breath, slung his backpack over his shoulder and walked down the deserted hallway to an unused classroom. He slipped inside, resisting the urge to glance back and see if anyone else had noticed.

One of the few benefits of being an honor-roll student who never got into trouble was that no one ever expected him to break the rules. If someone like his brother or sister had strolled up to that particular door and walked inside, any witnesses would have told a teacher. But since it was Bruce, no one would think anything of it.

There had never been enough students in Nickelville to fill the Academy, and this room had never been converted into a classroom. Its hardwood floor remained pristine under its layer of dust. *And beneath that, a foundation of black stone sits directly atop the limestone below.* He paused, wondering where that stray thought had come from. Ever since he'd fallen out the *Tribune* window, he seemed to know a lot more about such things. The door at the back of the room opened with a disused groan, and he slipped outside.

He sprinted past swings, seesaws and the two massive ash trees that dominated the center of the courtyard to the hidden corner. If he was lucky, his reputation would continue to protect him from wandering eyes. But that's where his plan ended. Before him stood a massive wall of tightly wedged wooden timbers. The roughhewn posts rose several feet above his head and disappeared into the ground beneath his feet, each one as big around as a railroad tie.

No one knew what lay behind the courtyard wall. Whole generations of Academy students had stood in its shadow. Their attempts to explain its presence had grown into legend, of which Nickelville had many. In contrast to the rest of the Academy's ornate and deceptively delicate architecture, the wall looked as if some long-forgotten giant had thrust whole trees into the ground.

Earlier that day, Chuck Baker had snatched Bruce's new book and thrown it over the wall. It would have been gone forever had it not landed precariously on the top of a post.

Bruce thought he might be able to reach the top if he jumped, but feared it might shake the book loose. A quick glance at his phone told him he didn't have time to think of something better, so he dropped his backpack and stepped reluctantly into the wall's shadow.

As gently as he could, he jumped up and gripped the tops of the posts. He worried at first that he wouldn't be able to hold on, but his fingertips managed to grip the very edge. He didn't weigh much, and he could normally pull himself up with ease. But the awkward angle and need to keep from shaking the wall made the muscles in his fingers and the backs of his hands tremble before his nose rose level with the top.

The courtyard changed, as if someone had become aware of his presence and the fact that he shouldn't be there. With a flutter of pages, the book fell the rest of the way down to the other side just as Bruce caught a glimpse of what lay beyond.

He gave up his cramped hold and slid down, catching his elbow on a jagged knot. With a defeated sigh, he turned back toward the door he'd left open.

Something huge passed overhead and into the forbidden corner of the courtyard. A second later, the tall grass he'd seen on the other side rustled as if something were moving through it.

"Hello," he called, "is someone there?"

The sun passed behind heavy clouds, and the air turned bitterly cold, even though it had been warm only moments before.

"Is anybody there?" he called louder, taking a step closer to the wall. "Can you throw my book back over?"

An enormous bird that looked like an eagle but had a wingspan close to ten feet, burst over the wall, dropping Bruce's book at his feet as it passed overhead. The courtyard exploded into movement around him. Wind howled through the courtyard. Swings clanked their chains, and seesaws pistoned like the arms of an engine. The wall shook as if hit over and over again with a truck from the other side. Lightning split the air so close overhead that the ground lurched beneath his feet.

Pausing just long enough to snatch up his book and backpack, Bruce raced toward the open classroom door, sure that he could feel something coming over the wall after him. He almost made it to the massive ash trees before the heavens opened up and poured down on him. Wind twisted the branches of the ash trees until one massive limb cut loose with a deafening crack and fell directly in his path. Sure that whatever he'd woken behind the wall followed too closely to risk going around, Bruce hurdled the branch, catching his foot and nearly falling. Although a part of him burned to look back at what followed, he feared his sanity might not survive the confirmation of his worst nightmares.

His wet shoes turned the layered dust of the unused classroom into mud, which he tracked onto the polished floors of the hallway beyond. Believing himself safe from whatever he'd woken behind the wall, he slowed his pace enough to catch his breath. But when the lockers began to rattle and lurch, he sprinted the rest of the way to the cafeteria, and through the front doors which lay beyond.

"Please be there, please be there, please be…" he panted, launching himself out the front of the school. The damp air burned his lungs as he flew down the stone steps toward the bus which, to his horror, had already pulled away from the curb. He reached deep and found the strength to put on one last burst of speed to catch up.

"Hey," he shouted, banging on the door.

The driver saw him and brought the bus to a stop.

"Lucky I saw you, Bruce," she said and closed the door behind him as he jumped aboard. "It would have been a long wet walk if I hadn't."

"Thanks," he panted. Safe on the bus, he finally looked back to find that nothing looked out of the ordinary. He scanned the sky for something dangerous, something amazing…something he could no longer recall.

"You've got a nasty cut there," the bus driver said, looking at his elbow. She took some tissue from the holder on the dash and pressed them into the hand not holding his book. "Put some pressure on it with these and get your dad to look at it when you get home."

"Thanks," he repeated before walking down the aisle, looking for a place to sit. As usual, his brother and sister sat together in one of the back seats, talking about rocks. He doubted they'd even noticed he was missing.

Chuck and Glenn, the boys who'd thrown his book over the wall, laughed while he made his way toward the back of the bus, leaving wet footprints in the aisle.

"Uh-oh," Glenn taunted in a thick drawl, "Looks like Wheezy almost drowned again."

"Get some new material," Bruce shot back. He held the book close to his chest and made sure they didn't have a chance to throw it out the window.

He found a seat next to a kindergartner who smelled like sour milk. He lowered himself next to the window and watched the rain slide down the glass while he tried to catch his breath.

In his mind he replayed that second's glance over the fence where the weeds were at least as tall as he was. Some sort of stone pillar had stood in the center of the hidden space, covered with vines. He looked down at the wet book in his hands and doubted that he'd feel much like reading when he got home. How had he gotten it back? He seemed to remember it falling over the other side.

What was back there? Was it whatever had chased him? Was it the thing under the vines? And what about the lockers inside the Academy itself? He thought about what had happened the rest of the way home. He thought about it while his father bandaged the cut on his arm.

One thing stayed on his mind when he couldn't sleep that night: he'd always assumed the wall was there to keep the kids out of the corner. But he'd been wrong. It had been built to keep something in that corner away from the kids.

Chapter V: Nickelville Academy

Diffuse sunlight filtered through her mother's window, bathing Megan in a warm glow. The air smelled fresher here than in her own room, leading her to wonder if Azarich had still visited this room regularly even before the return of his daughter. And although Megan's eyes were closed, her thoughts stretched outward, trying to find the men who searched for her. No matter which direction she turned, she felt nothing.

In the midst of that silence, the world suddenly flared around Megan, and she could sense every aspect of her mother's bedroom through her closed eyelids. It was as if the entire room were outlined in flame. She whirled, eyes opening as she turned, to find her mother awake for the first time since their flight. The sensation faded just as quickly as it had come.

She thought she saw a hint of something dark on her mother's arm where the covers had slipped down before the woman pulled them back again.

"We made it…do you feel anything?" the tired woman asked, her voice cracked with lack of use.

"No, but I felt something weird just a second ago," Megan answered, wondering if her mother was the source of the strange sensation. "How do you feel?"

"Weak, but not as bad as I felt on the road," she answered. "How long have I been out?"

"We got here two days ago."

"Where's your grandfather?"

"Cooking breakfast."

"Good. We need to talk." Emelia's eyes flitted shut as if she were only just clinging to consciousness.

Megan had expected these words. Even though she felt relieved beyond measure to see her mom awake, she knew this meant that Nickelville might soon be behind them.

"I can't feel them at all," Megan said hopefully.

"That's good," Emelia replied, opening her eyes again, "That means they can't feel you, either. We're safe for the moment."

"Is it the trees?" Megan asked.

"Maybe," Emelia answered. "They're unlike any I've encountered anywhere else. They seem to absorb the energy that we use, making everything seem quiet."

"So, they make us normal?" Megan asked.

"No, they just mute most of our extra senses," Emelia answered wearily, closing her eyes but continuing to speak in a quiet, measured voice. "Think of it like being in a room with almost no light. After a while, your eyes adjust, and you can see again. It will be like that here for you. I know it's uncomfortable, but remember that it's protecting us while I get better."

"Then we can stay?" Megan asked, hope battling with the discomfort.

"I'm afraid not."

"Why?"

"We just can't," Emelia answered.

"But if they can't find us here," Megan said, pressing the issue further than she would normally have dreamed of doing, "doesn't that mean that we could stop running?"

Emelia opened her eyes and gave her a long, hard look that Megan couldn't read. Was there a chance that they could?

"Grandpa seems really nice," Megan added. "I think we can trust him."

"He's one of the best people I've ever known," Emelia agreed. "I'm glad you finally got a chance to meet him."

"Can we stay here with him?" Megan begged. "Please?"

"Nickelville has its own dangers," Emelia answered after a long pause, "worse than the Huntsmen. Things that we can't sense from a distance."

Too shocked for further questions, Megan stood in silence. *Something else? Something worse?*

"I love you, Megan," Emelia said, reaching out to hold her daughter's hand. "You're going to have to trust me on this one. There's nothing I'd love more than to let you finish growing up here, but we just can't. There's too much at stake."

Megan sat on the edge of her mother's bed long enough to watch Emelia drift away once again. She felt guilty for being angry with her, but she couldn't help it. Was it possible that they could have had a normal life? One filled with friends and family instead of motels, run-down apartments and an endless flood of strangers? Something about this place spoke to her. It lifted her up and wrapped her in its warm embrace. Surely her mother was wrong about Nickelville.

Megan realized that she hadn't told her mother that she'd be starting school at Nickelville Academy that day, but doubted that her mother would care. After all, hadn't Emelia gone there herself?

Fog swirled around Bruce, Jade and Paul Grimble in the dawn glow while they waited for the bus, making it difficult to see more than a few feet in any direction. Even the outline of their house faded from view halfway down the driveway.

Bruce's imagination formed the mist into shapes that hovered along the edges of his vision, which was why he'd called his brother and sister outside early. He usually liked to keep such mornings to himself, but the experience at the wall still had him spooked. He wasn't at all thrilled about going back.

His sister's short hair was roughly the color of a standard fire engine this month, which was a definite improvement over the sickly green it had been a few days ago. And though his brother was practically her twin in his desire to study and explore just about anything that could be found in the ground, his appearance was as conservative as hers was disturbing.

"You won't believe what I found online last night," Paul said, running his hand through his short brown hair.

"What?" Jade asked.

"There was a geological map published here about fifty years ago."

Bruce tuned the rest of the conversation out. The world of rocks and fossils lacked the charm for him that it held for his siblings. In fact, were it not for how much he and Jade looked alike, he might think that his parents had lied about the adoption thing.

At last the rumble of the bus drifted closer. Lights pierced the swirling air around them, and the bus came to a stop. The doors creaked open with a familiar squeal of badly aligned metal.

"So, what are the rock hounds plotting today?" The bus driver asked, ignoring Bruce even though she had to peer around him to talk to Jade and Paul.

Chuck Baker, who had all the charm and appearance of wolverine with mange, made gasping noises when Bruce passed, and his slightly built friend, Glenn Floyd, acted as if he were drowning.

"Would you two grow up," Jade snapped. They might make Bruce's life miserable when he was alone, but they knew better than to cause more than minor mischief when his sister was around.

Today Bruce found an empty seat halfway down the aisle, and he bypassed the usual routine of asking to sit down and being refused. More often than not, he sat next to the sour-milk kid.

Jade and Paul made their way to the back where his sister discovered a boy from her grade sitting in her seat. As soon as she made eye contact with him, he moved to another, and the two continued their plans for turning the backyard into a rock quarry.

The bus lurched, and Bruce held on for the bus driver's trademark turn in the Grimble driveway. When it didn't come, he looked toward the front of the bus.

"Where are we going?" asked several voices in unison, peering into the fog ahead.

"I'm kidnapping you and turning the lot of you over to Old-Man Biggerstaff," the driver cackled.

The younger kids looked worried. After all, the road did indeed end at the woods where the recluse supposedly lived.

Waiting for a school bus filled with strangers always unsettled Megan. At least with public transportation, no one else knew each other either. But school buses felt completely different, as if each one was an organism and she an invading virus it sought to eradicate.

41

The fog made the waiting worse, distorting sounds and cloaking the world around her in a dreamlike shroud where she might be only feet from the Wild Hunt, or maybe even the last person left in the world.

Every once in a while, she thought she could hear voices coming from nearby, but sound moved strangely through the fog, and she wasn't entirely sure from which direction they came. Then the unmistakable rumble of a motor broke the silence and lights pierced the mist just before the bus pulled alongside of where she waited. An older woman smiled down from the driver's seat and beckoned her to climb up the steep steps.

Then began the all-too-familiar routine of asking people if she could sit with them. Her quick scan of the aisle revealed a sea of curious faces, but no empty seats. Each of the riders glanced quickly down at her second-hand clothing and shook their heads, not wanting to be associated with her. About halfway down the length of the bus she came upon a tall, gangly boy with chestnut hair and an awkward but eager smile. He turned his knees toward the aisle and gave her the window seat before she even asked.

"Hi," he said with a pleasant smile, "I'm Bruce."

"Hi," she replied, taking the offered seat, "I'm Megan."

"How's your mom?" he asked, taking her by surprise.

"How do you know about my mother?" she asked with an expression of concern.

"My dad's the town ambulance driver," he answered with a smile that put her more at ease than it should have. "He told me that Mr. McGeehee's daughter was sick with pneumonia, and that she had a daughter. I assume that's you."

The bus lurched ahead with a groan and turned around in her grandfather's driveway. It wasn't a very easy maneuver for the driver, but Megan doubted the woman wanted to go all the way to the end of the road

42

to the overgrown house that stood there. The bus remained quiet while they drove, each of the riders straining to get a better look at her.

"She's awake now, but still really sick," Megan answered, looking around uneasily. "Why is everyone staring at me?"

"We only get new kids every three or four years," he answered. "Just wait until you get to the Academy."

"Great," she said, trying to ignore the whispers around her. This was the first time she'd been around so many people since leaving the apartment, and her shields were hard pressed to block them all out. She could feel the desire to talk from the boy next to her, but he was trying to be polite.

"So, Megan McGeehee," he said when he could no longer hold back, "Where are you from, and what brings you to the official armpit of the state of Texas?"

She didn't want to be rude, but she had little in common with normal people and never knew how to hold a conversation. But this boy possessed some quality, some unidentifiable thing that made her want to try.

"Lots of places," she answered, "My mom and I move around a lot."

"Will you be staying long?"

"I don't know," she answered, "but I'd like to."

"Why would anyone want to stay in Nickelville?" he asked, motioning out the window to where only a few stores remained open among the derelict husks on Main Street. "I can't wait to get away from this town."

"My grandfather's here," she answered with a shrug. An old movie theater crept past, and she strained to catch a better look. But the fog still cloaked the morning in twilight, and she couldn't tell if it was still open or not.

"Yeah, Azarich is a great guy," he replied. "I mow his lawn during the summer. You'll probably put me out of a job."

"If we're here that long." she said absently. She'd never used a lawnmower before, and the thought of doing something so mundane made her smile.

A huge building rose from the fog, climbing high above the neighboring shops. Unlike the simple country architecture of the surrounding town, this thing would have looked at home in the middle of New York.

"Baker Hotel," he said without needing to look back. "It's been abandoned almost since it was built."

Rising several floors before it disappeared into the low hanging clouds overhead, its steps led to several stone arches. The sides of the building angled off like the wings of an angel, and the whole thing looked larger than it could possibly be.

"That thing looks more like it belongs on Mount Olympus than in this little town," she said in awe.

"If you like the Baker, you'll love the Academy." Bruce added.

"Is it like that?" she asked, motioning toward the hotel that was already returning to the fog as the bus bumped along the poorly maintained road.

"Nothing is like the Academy," he answered ominously.

Main Street gave way to a hard-packed dirt road that cut through vast fields of corn. In the distance, Megan could see trees.

"We're not leaving town, are we?" she asked, afraid that her decision to go to school might inadvertently cause her to leave the town's protection.

"Huh?" Bruce asked, not following.

"I remember coming through trees when we came into town."

"Oh, no," he answered. "The Academy sits in the middle of its own set of woods. There's a band of trees that encircles the whole town, but this isn't it. Trees are one thing that this town has never had a shortage of."

She still watched the approaching tree line, unsure if she should be worried. After all, she had no idea how any of this worked. She held her breath, ready to sprint down the aisle to the back exit of the bus at the first hint of the Huntsmen.

The bus hit a pothole and the window next to her dropped open with a crash. She nearly screamed.

She had no idea what Bruce might have said before they reached the treelined, but when they entered without mishap, he had to have noticed the way she sagged back into her seat in relief.

Something brightly colored sped past the window on the other side of the bus, drawing her attention away from her new friend. Her eyes tracked its movements as it flew, beating its wings hard to offset the drag of its plumage. She'd never seen anything quite like it, and wondered how it could even fly with that much weight. Beyond it, an impossible conglomeration of long spindly legs and white fur moved slowly through the trees followed by two smaller creatures just like it.

Everywhere she looked she found movement. Odd troll-like creatures the size of cats gathered on branches, one of which snatched a brightly colored insect as it flew past and greedily shoved it into its mouth. Something vaguely fox-shaped leapt from the foliage, chasing a common squirrel until it scrambled up a tree and out of reach.

"Sorry," Megan said when she found Bruce staring at her, clearly expecting a reply to something he'd asked. She hastily ripped her eyes from the scene behind him and tried to cover the strangeness of her actions. "I'm still trying to get the layout of the town."

45

Something landed hard on the windowsill next to her, making her jump. There she found a frog-like face peering at her. The rest of the thing defied identification. Possessed of not only four sets of legs and a weather-vane tail, its gossamer wings buffeted the air that flowed over the bus as they drove. It had several vines wrapped around it that hung down onto her seat as she looked at it. She held her breath as it gazed directly into her eyes before throwing its head back and screaming one long note of alarm.

"Megan," Bruce said in concern. "Are you okay?"

"I'm fine," she stammered quickly, unable to take her eyes off of the thing as it launched itself from the bus and flew deeper into the trees.

As if answering the call, a whirlwind of leaves and ground clutter rose beside the bus. Within it, a woman's face formed. There for only an instant, its features twisted into a grimace of fear before losing cohesion and falling back to the ground. By the time the last leaf fell, the rest of the strange creatures faded from view as well.

Megan stared in disbelief, waiting for them to return as the bus bumped along. Then they cleared the trees, and she felt a strange sensation, almost like passing through a wall made of static electricity. She shuddered, feeling the downy hairs on her arms stand up. Bruce didn't seem to notice. Glancing back, she noticed a shimmering disturbance in the air that traversed the length of the woods on either side.

Had there been something like this barrier when she first entered Nickelville? She'd been in such pain that she could have easily missed it. Strange as it seemed, she hoped that this sensation meant her extra senses were adapting to the town like her mother had predicted they would.

"Well," Bruce said when they pulled into a large clearing, "There it is: Nickelville Academy."

Two stories of black stone rose from the misty field, trailing lingering wisps of fog all the way to its gray slate roof. Stone gargoyles peered down

46

from the heights and bracketed two bell towers. Stained glass windows ornamented the fortress-like walls in geometric patterns similar to those she created in her own art. Steep stone steps climbed to a pair of massive wooden doors, each one easily ten feet tall.

Leaning almost out of the window to get a better look at the school, she noticed a line of small clear windows set into dormers along the length of the roof, looking out across the clearing from which the bus had come.

"I've been to tons of schools," she whispered when the bus came to a stop at the edge of the steps, "but never one like this."

"I know what you mean," Bruce said, slinging his bag over his shoulder and waiting for her to join him in the aisle of the bus, "Just think about what it was like for me as a kindergartener. I just about wet my pants the first time I saw it."

"Can you show me where the office is?" she asked when they reached the top of the stone steps. The iron-bound wooden doors towered over her, reminding her of the stories her mother had read to her when she was little. A faint sense, much like the one that warned her of pursuit, awoke at the base of her skull.

Here there be dragons... her imaginary friend whispered through her thoughts.

"Sure, it's just inside on the left side of the foyer," he said, guiding her through the crowded entrance with a hand on her elbow.

As soon as he touched her, there was a sense of familiarity about him, a sense that she knew him from somewhere other than Nickelville. But before she could think about it too deeply, it faded from her mind.

"Thanks," she said, noticing that the sense of pressure disappeared as quickly as it had come.

"What grade are you in?" he asked.

"Ninth."

"Cool, I'll see you in class then," he said with a reassuring pat on the shoulder before leaving through another door at the end of the foyer. A tingling sensation lingered where he'd touched her for a moment after he'd gone.

Inside the office, an aquarium spanned the front counter, distorting Megan's view of what lay beyond through a myriad of brightly colored plants and fish. The biggest black cat Megan had ever seen prowled the length of the lid, pausing from time to time to reach over the edge and swat at the fish that passed.

A pretty young woman with auburn hair sat at the open end of the counter, busily dividing one stack of papers into two. When she noticed Megan, her face lit with a smile.

"Hello, Megan," she said.

"How do you know my name?" Megan stammered. After a life of secrecy, it unnerved her to have so many people call her by her real name. It felt like something that could spiral out of control at any minute. The aquarium light flickered as her worry began to manifest itself as energy, and the cat stopped his stalking, laid down on the lid and gazed down on her with interest.

"I was expecting you because your grandfather just called."

"Oh," Megan responded awkwardly, "What do I need to do?"

"Azarich said he'd come by later and sign the necessary forms, so you just need to give us a history of your previous schools so we can request records. After that, go to the library, pick up your books and then to Mrs. Jones's room, number twenty-two."

Megan took the offered clip-board over to a chair and filled in the familiar blanks with the same bogus information she always provided. She had in fact gone to the schools she listed, just not under her true name. There weren't any records for Megan McGeehee at any school, or in the unlikely event that there were, they referred to someone else. Most of her learning had been guided by her mother, and the schools Megan had attended were chosen primarily for the fact that they weren't terribly good at record keeping. More than likely, they'd fabricate something rather than

49

admit that there was something amiss. By the time most schools realized that something was wrong, she was long gone. Hopefully her mother wouldn't mind the use of her real name just this once, since there hadn't been any way to explain the need for secrecy to her grandfather. When at last she'd filled all of the blanks, she returned to the counter and waited while the cat looked on with its enormous green eyes.

"Where's the library?" Megan asked.

"Go out the door and turn left," the woman said while making motions with her hands for each direction. "You'll see a big wooden door. Go through that and you'll find the cafeteria. On the right side of the stage there will be a door leading to the middle school hallway. Directly across from it you will see two beautifully carved wooden doors. That's where you want to go."

"Um," Megan said, "I'm a freshman. Isn't that high school?"

"Technically yes," the young woman replied. "But for some reason it's in the middle school hallway."

"Okay then, thanks, Mrs...." Megan said, trying to remember the directions and realizing that she didn't know the woman's name.

"Millie," the pretty woman said. "Just call me Millie, and say hello to Azarich for me."

Now that the fog had begun to lift, sunlight spilled through the cafeteria's stained-glass windows. It painted the old tables in garish hues that evoked strange emotions in Megan, almost like the way open flames drew her into a trance-like state. Although the windows near the roof had been curtained, they still allowed errant beams of sunlight to converge upon a single spot near the small stage.

How is it doing that? Megan wondered. *The windows open from different angles, so they shouldn't all land in one place.*

Although it puzzled her, it paled next to the magical creatures that lived in the woods outside. She hurried toward the right side of the stage

51

with its threadbare curtains and found the door Millie had mentioned. Her footsteps echoed off the walls of the large room.

Megan.

She looked back over her shoulder, but found no one there. From this angle, the cafeteria looked like something else, something not quite a school. She shook her head, deciding that she still needed more sleep.

"From here I should be able to see…"

Elaborate wooden doors towered over her, carved in such realistic detail that she had to touch them to see if they were real. Together the doors showed a scene in which a female angel emerged from a cave holding a cherub on her hip. With one hand and raising three keys above her head in the other. The door handles were worn smooth from generations of young hands, but the carvings themselves remained as crisp as when they'd been made.

Something as intricate as those doors would have been vandalized in seconds at most schools she'd attended. The fact that anything so beautiful could endure without some jealous fool destroying them gave Megan hope for Nickelville. She expected the hinges to creak when she pulled the handle. They didn't.

Inside, she found the first place at Nickelville Academy that didn't remind her of the set of a vampire movie. The same dark paneling covered the library walls as the rest of the school, but it had the warm glow that comes from being polished by someone who cares. Posters of popular books and movies hung on the ends of the bookshelves and brightened the otherwise dark walls. An old man with short white hair, glasses and a neatly trimmed beard sat at the corner of one of the tables, lost in thought as he stared off between the shelves. He had a reminiscent grin on his lips, and she hated to call him back from whatever memory or daydream he visited.

"Excuse me," Megan said quietly, not wanting to startle him.

He turned to look at her and his eyes widened for a moment.

"I'm sorry to bother you, but Millie told me to pick up my textbooks here."

"Dear God," he said, "Azarich must have thought he was dreaming when he saw you."

"Excuse me?" she repeated, unsure what he meant.

"The resemblance between you and your grandmother is uncanny," he replied, rising from his chair and moving over to stand in front of her. His clothing was of an older style, but well kept. His slacks were pressed, and he wore a vest with a watch chain that disappeared into his pocket. He extended one big hand toward her. "I'm Tom Harris, the school librarian and long-time friend of your grandparents."

"You know my grandfather?" she asked nervously, although she did remember this man's name from the stories her grandfather had told her.

"We all went to school here," he answered with a warm smile that reminded her of the way Santa looked in a book her mother had read to her once. "Azarich went on to become a lawyer, but Mr. Green and I just couldn't stay away from this place," he said, happily patting the check-out counter as he passed it. "The Academy always calls me back when I'm away for too long." He motioned for her to follow and lifted out a stack of books.

"Are those mine?" she asked.

"I picked out the best ones in the book-room just for you."

"Thanks," she said, noticing the scent of cinnamon in the air. "Someone's cooking apple pies. Maybe this will be one of those rare cafeterias with edible food."

The librarian looked puzzled. He sniffed the air and shrugged. "I guess my nose is getting as old as the rest of me. Say hello to your grandpa for me, ok? And give your mom a hug. I haven't seen her in years."

"I will," she said after loading as many of the books as she could fit into her backpack and carrying the rest in her arms. Then she slung it over her shoulder and returned to the garish light of the hallway.

Megan, the unfamiliar voice whispered again.

While looking behind her for the next person who seemed to already know her name, she ran into an older man wearing coveralls.

"Whoa, slow down there little lady," he said with a mischievous smile.

"I'm so sorry," she said. "I thought I heard something back there, and I turned to look."

"That's all right," he said. "This old building talks in a language of her own if you learn to listen. She's been whispering to me for years. I'm Alan, the school janitor."

"And one of my grandfather's school friends," she added. "I just met Mr. Harris, too. Can you help me find room twenty-two?"

"That's Mrs. Jones's room," he said with a grimace, all signs of his previous good mood gone. She noticed that he wasn't as neatly groomed as Mr. Harris, and although his coveralls were clean, they were stained and threadbare in places as if he'd worn them for many years.

"Is that bad?" she asked.

"Sometimes the truth has a way of coming back and biting you in the tender parts just as badly as any lie ever could. I'm sorry, but I'm going to fall back on one of the only benefits I've discovered in getting old. I'm going to pretend I'm hard of hearing and ignore that question. But I will say that I'm glad it's you and not me going in there." With that he turned and beckoned for her to follow with a contagious grin. Although she

54

wouldn't have admitted it to her mother, her feelings about being recognized and included had already begun to change. She'd never been part of anything before, and to a certain extent, it felt like this place had been waiting for her to show up.

She followed her grandfather's friend down a narrow hallway lit by a few scattered light bulbs and more of the garish windows. He had the sort of limp that came from an old injury even though he did his best to hide it. When they came to room twenty-two, it was so quiet inside that Megan first thought it was empty.

The teacher looked up from a magazine when Megan passed through the doorway, and every head in the class turned toward her. The large woman's stylish dress looked like something that Megan would have expected to see on a celebrity at some opening event. But the layered makeup she wore suggested that she had yet to accept the fact that she was no longer young.

"Who is this?" the teacher asked from her desk in a voice that had the shrill huskiness of someone who'd been a lifetime smoker.

"New student," Mr. Green answered.

"No one told me about a new student," the woman complained.

"I don't know nothin 'bout your end of the job," he said. "I just showed her how to get here."

The floor vibrated beneath their feet, and a musty odor belched from a grate on the floor along with a warm rush of damp air. For a few heartbeats it reminded Megan so much of the smell in that last apartment that she gripped her textbooks in white-knuckled panic.

"And I suppose you don't know anything about that side of the job either," the sour woman added.

"When the school board finally decides we need a new heating system, I'll be able to do something about the smell," he muttered under his breath and gave Megan a sympathetic shrug before he left the room.

Megan stood there, unsure of what to do. The class remained silent while the teacher continued to look her over from neatly braided hair to shabby sneakers. Megan stepped up to the desk and handed over the piece of paper from the secretary.

Something dark moved through the edge of Megan's vision while she stood there, and the strange sensation she'd felt at the front of the school returned. She wanted to turn and look, but the teacher already seemed irritated and Megan thought she should give the unpleasant woman her complete attention.

"Your name is McGeehee," Mrs. Jones said, her voice rising to a pitch that made Megan wince.

"My grandfather says it's Irish."

"Does your grandfather live here in Nickelville?"

"Yes, his name is Azarich."

"Ah," Mrs. Jones said with a gaudy red smile that didn't reach her eyes, "I know Azarich McGeehee. You may take the empty seat in the second row."

Megan clutched her books to her chest and walked past the staring children, trying to find whatever had caught her eye earlier. Bruce smiled at her when she passed him and she felt a bit better.

She'd never seen desks like the ones in Mrs. Jones's classroom. Each was made up of two cast iron frames onto which a curved wooden seat had been bolted. The writing surface had been mounted behind the seat so that each student actually used the back of the seat in front of them when they worked. And because the desks had been bolted to runners that ran the length of the aisles, the passage of untold feet had worn through the finish of the walkways until it was little more than bare wood.

A bookshelf stood almost empty next to the teacher's desk, holding only a faded globe and a stack of magazines. Just as Megan slid into her seat, Mrs. Jones closed the one she'd been reading and tossed it on the shelf with the others before picking up another.

The wooden surface of Megan's desk sported a wealth of drawings and inscriptions. More than a few had been dated well into the previous century. The sensation that she was being watched grew stronger, and she scanned the room again when the sour woman was too engrossed in her magazine to notice.

Although nothing in the room seemed amiss, a man walked past the open classroom door. The scent of cinnamon returned, sickening in its intensity. She brought her hand to her nose, glancing around to see if anyone else seemed affected. Then the man returned, stepping into the doorway. He wore a black shirt that buttoned at the collar, a pair of black pants and riding boots like she'd seen in movies. Nasty cuts covered his arms and face that looked only partially healed. A gauzy film covered his unseeing eyes, but he scanned the room anyway.

For the space of a few heartbeats, Megan worried he might be one of the Huntsmen. She had no idea what they looked like, but surely she'd feel one of them standing in the room with her. She hastily dropped her eyes back to her desk and tried to clear her mind of any thoughts that might betray her. She hardened her shields and wished everyone would stop staring at her. She needed to think. Then she realized that the fact that they weren't staring at him meant he wasn't new to them. If he was normal for Nickelville, then he couldn't possibly be what she'd feared. When she glanced up, he'd gone.

Since the teacher hadn't bothered to tell her what to do, and the class appeared to be reading, she flipped absently through the textbooks she'd gotten from the library and thought about what she'd seen since her arrival at this strange place.

Having slept through her first trip through town, Megan realized she'd been wrong to base her opinion solely on her grandfather's house. Not only was Nickelville run-down to the point of decay, but strange forces concentrated within this place, particularly at the school and that deserted hotel. In spite of the silencing of her extra senses, she could feel something powerful moving beneath the surface of this dying town and suspected that whatever it was could shed light on the mysteries in her own life.

Somewhere nearby, the loud, clear tones of a bell rang through the Academy and the students gathered up their books and started for the door.

Shaking her head, Megan did the same and realized that it might be the town itself that her mother had been running from. *Nickelville has its own dangers*, she heard her mother whisper.

When she gathered her things and followed the others toward the door, Megan saw the man in black pass by the outside of the classroom with his cloudy eyes focused on something further down the hall. But when she reached the corner and looked down the long hallway, he was nowhere to be seen.

Chapter VI: African Violets and Dancing Lights

Later that night, Megan twisted a damp lock of her hair around her finger as she stared up at the lace canopy that covered her bed. How many times had she wanted a bed like this one? How many times had she wanted to find family and a place she could call home?

Too restless to lay there any longer, she explored the rest of the hallway, looking at the pictures as she went. None of them stood out from the ones she'd already seen, but she still filed them away in her memory for when she could no longer see them in person. All too soon she'd be back on the run, and it would be nice to have these images tucked away in her mind as proof that she actually did come from someplace normal, even if Nickelville did push the limits of that word.

She wasn't sure what her mother had meant about the dangers of Nickelville. She'd seen creatures similar to those in the woods surrounding the school before, but it did surprise her to find them within the boundaries of a town. On the few occasions she'd encountered them before, it had been deep in the wilderness where few but she and her mother dwelled. But the man with the strange eyes? She'd happily never see him again.

She could easily put those things behind her. She could easily withstand the strange and slightly creepy for an opportunity to stop running, and to feel the thrill of people calling her by her real name.

Her mother's childhood home was not what Megan had expected. She walked into the other guest room and wondered again how large the McGeehee clan had once been to require a house this big. Floorboards creaked beneath her feet as she tried to fill in the empty space within her senses with the ones that still remained.

She took a seat at a window bench like the one in her own room and stared out into the fading light. She wondered if Bruce was looking out a window next door. Lights danced through the darkening trees, too dim to be flashlights. *That's odd,* she thought, *it's late in the year for fireflies.*

She stood, not wanting these strange lights to remind her of her inability to sense them, and went in search of her grandfather. Maybe he'd fill her troubled mind with more stories of the past.

Light from her mother's room spilled out into the hall where she passed. The heart monitor had been disconnected after her mother's return to consciousness, but the IV was still hooked up. She wondered if Bruce would come with his dad when it was time to change it.

Why did she keep thinking about him? Sure, he was cute in a completely awkward sort of way, but that didn't account for the way so many of her thoughts strayed toward him.

Her mother stirred in her sleep then settled again, hopefully not having one of her frequent nightmares. Megan told herself she didn't want to disturb her mother's rest, but in truth she didn't want to talk any more about leaving Nickelville.

The banister gleamed in the golden glow of the setting sun that shone through the high window on this side of the house. Worn smooth by the hands of who knew how many long-gone ancestors, its presence gave her a thrill of wonder at the realization that she, just like everyone else, had history.

The living room and kitchen were empty, but she found Azarich out on the back porch which had been screened in to keep out the mosquitoes and flies that were so common in the South. Plants and miniature trees filled the many shelves and ledges.

Her grandfather stood next to a workbench at the far end of the porch where the light was best. An open bag of potting soil had spilled across the surface where he was repotting a plant. He noticed her almost as soon as she stepped up to the door and motioned for her to join him.

"Emelia was always partial to African Violets," he said with a smile. "I thought a few might cheer her up."

"Wow," she said, looking around after she'd opened the door. "Where did you learn to do all this?"

"Japan," he answered absently.

"You've been to Japan?" she asked, surprised he would have traveled so far away.

"I fought in the war," he answered, going back to the plant.

"World War II?" she asked. She hadn't realized that he was that old.

"Tom, Alan and I all did," he answered.

"Wow," she said again, not sure how to continue.

"Makes me quite the fossil, doesn't it?"

"No, I was just wondering what it must have been like."

"Bad," he said without hesitation. "War is always bad. But I probably wouldn't be the person I am now if I hadn't gone."

"What do you mean?" Megan asked, curling up on the porch swing to listen. This was what she'd come looking for.

"I still can't get over how much you look like your grandmother," he said, pausing to stare at her over the top of his glasses. "She used to sit there exactly like that and watch me putter around out here when we first got married." It took him a few minutes to continue. "The fighting didn't

61

teach me anything, except that there are better ways to solve a problem. War always seems to boil down to the leaders in one country making decisions that annoy the leaders in another. Both sides do things they shouldn't, and a lot of people who had no part in the making of those decisions die."

"I don't think I could ever kill someone," Megan said with a shudder.

"I didn't either," Grandpa replied softly.

"Is that a bonsai?" Megan asked, gesturing toward an ornate pot with a beautiful miniature tree in it.

"Yes," he answered, looking grateful that she'd changed the subject. "I've had it for a very long time. It reminds me of the time I spent over there."

"But if the war was so bad," she said, puzzled, "why do you want to remember it?"

"After our side dropped the bomb on Nagasaki, it turned out that I could pick up languages pretty quick, and they needed interpreters. I was stationed in a remote village near the coast."

He finished with the pot at the table, took his gloves off and came to sit with her on the swing.

"There was an old man in that village who passed by me every morning on his way to the dock. He'd yell at me in Japanese, and from the reactions of the people around us, I could tell that what he said wasn't good."

"Did you ever find out what he was saying?" Megan asked. Azarich chuckled.

"Why don't we just say that every curse word I know in Japanese I learned from that old man," he said with a faraway look for a moment before continuing. "You know, it's funny. I call him old, and that's certainly the way I saw him at the time, but I'm about thirty years older

62

now than he was then, and with the exception of aches and pains when the weather changes, I still don't feel that old."

"So, you ended up being enemies?" she prompted.

"At first," Azarich mused. "But after a few weeks of yelling, I stopped him and asked him what his problem was with me."

"And?"

"He lost his wife in the fighting," Azarich said quietly. "He assumed I had something to do with it because I was an American soldier."

"Did you tell him you didn't?" Megan asked.

"That didn't really make much difference to him at first," Azarich said, standing up from the swing and motioning for her to follow him back into the house. "I have to admit, I've yelled at a few people myself when I was hurt or scared."

Azarich poured them each a glass of cold, sweet tea before sitting down at the kitchen table.

"I felt bad for him," Azarich continued when he'd had a drink. "And it probably helped that I couldn't understand all of the things he'd been yelling at me. Japanese is a very creative language."

Megan laughed.

He paused for another drink, collecting his thoughts. Megan wondered what it would be like to have so many memories.

"I did everything I could to help the people of that village," Azarich continued. "There were a lot of places that didn't recover as well under the Americans. Many of my fellow soldiers held the Japanese people as a whole responsible for Pearl Harbor. You know what that was, right?"

She nodded. "Surprise attack that brought us into the war." He seemed pleased that she knew. Although her education had been sporadic at times, her mother had never let her fall behind.

63

"You have to realize that it came as a real shock to the American people when that happened. In many ways it was like what happened at the World Trade Center, which also doesn't mean much to you. Or maybe Covid."

She nodded and waited for him to continue.

"But just like I had nothing to do with that man's family in Hiroshima, the typical Japanese citizen had nothing to do with Pearl Harbor. One night when I had all but given up on ever making peace with him, he came to the house where I was staying with a bottle of sake."

"So, he forgave you just like that?" she asked.

"No, there was still a great deal of yelling as that year went on. I found out later from the people in the village that he'd always been quick to anger. Some people are just built like that. But I came away from it with a better understanding of the difference between holding someone accountable for their own actions and holding them accountable for the actions of the group to which they belong. Well, that plus a love of rice wine and bonsai."

"How does the tree fit in?" she asked.

"He gave me one when I left to come back to the states. It was beautiful."

"You've had that tree since World War II?" she asked, looking out the window at the tree in the ornate pot with newfound respect.

"Nope, he didn't tell me how to take care of it and it was dead before the month was out," Azarich laughed. "I've learned a lot since then, and this one is in the same pot."

Megan thought she should tell him about something from her past, but couldn't think of anything that wouldn't sound crazy.

"You know," he said after a moment, saving her from the awkwardness of the situation. "That room you're in is yours now. Even if you leave, it will still be yours. So, feel free to decorate it any way you'd like."

"Really?"

"Absolutely," he answered with a grin. "There are some department store catalogs in that chest next to the fireplace in the living room. Why don't you get them and pick out curtains and linens for your bed? And while you're at it, get a few new outfits for school."

"You're the best," Megan squealed and hugged him before running off in search of the catalogs. It had been a long time since she'd been able to wear something that no one else had worn before her.

The doorbell rang and Megan listened to see if Bruce might have come with his father, but he hadn't. She flipped through the catalogs and found exactly what she wanted.

First, she unpacked the contents of her big duffle into the closet and dresser. The clothing she owned didn't come close to filling either. She then took out her thrift shop radio and plugged it in. It took her a moment to find something she liked, and kept the volume low so as to not disturb the rest of her family. She thrilled at the thought...*her family*. She would have loved to have had something more modern to listen to, but nothing electronic lasted for long around Megan. The more complex the device, the quicker it fried.

She tucked her photographs around the edge of the vanity mirror. All of them were from a handful of disposable cameras back when they could afford to waste money on such things. They were all of her and her mother and represented the only record she had of her life before Nickelville. Then she studied them for a moment and rearranged them.

Watercolors normally held no appeal for her, but when she noticed that each of these carried the McGeehee name in the corner, she decided her style would just have to open up and let them in. She loved the one with the violin player, but didn't care much for the one of a stern looking woman. So, she swapped it out for a picture of an eagle on a tree branch that she'd noticed in the other guest room when she was exploring the house. For some reason it looked familiar, as if she'd seen something like it recently.

Normally she used her posters to cover gaping holes in the walls of the places where they stayed. Here she had the opposite problem. She couldn't see a single pinhole in the pristine plaster and wondered if she was allowed to use her thumb-tacks. Then again, her mother's walls were covered.

"Better ask," she said to herself before walking out into the hall.

Megan heard her mother and grandfather speaking in hushed whispers before her socked feet took her around the corner. She wasn't prone to eavesdropping, particularly since her mother could normally sense her from a distance and simply wouldn't talk if she was near. But Megan could tell from their tones that they must be discussing something she wasn't supposed to hear. Given that these two people held the greatest likelihood of knowing the things she most desperately wanted to know, Megan decided that some higher power must have meant for her to hear.

"We have to leave as soon as possible," Emelia whispered. "Is there any way you could get the truck fixed, and I'll pay you back when we have the money?"

"Of course, I'll get it fixed, and you most certainly will not pay me back," he answered, "But you're in no condition to go anywhere. I doubt you'll be able to get out of that bed for at least a week. Stay here and get well, Emelia. You will always have a home here," he paused, "if you want it."

There was a moment of silence in which Megan would have given anything to see their faces and cursed her inability to sense what was going on.

"After all, Nickelville is a great place to raise a teenager," he continued, likely hoping that he could change Emelia's mind. "Great scores on tests, no gang problems. It's not like the cities where kids get shot every day or die of drug overdoses."

"We'd stay if we could, Dad," she said with such profound weariness that Megan wanted to go to her side, "but I don't want Megan going back to that school."

"Was it really that bad?"

"You know it was," she said bitterly.

"Surely you don't still fear the Dark Man," he said with a combination of sadness and worry in his voice.

"He wasn't a figment of my overactive imagination. No amount of medication can protect her from him. She's like I was, Dad. It's only a matter of time until he wakes up and realizes that she can see him."

"Your mother only saw him once," Azarich said hopefully. "Maybe it skips a generation."

"I'm not willing to take that chance with Megan. As soon as I can travel again, we'll leave Nickelville. Please get the truck repaired so we can leave quickly when we need to."

How much did he know? Megan wondered.

"If you're in trouble," he said, changing arguments.

"The days when you could bandage all of my hurts have long since passed," Emelia whispered groggily. "But in my dreams, I never left this

place. In that world Megan and I live happily ever after with you and…"
Her words trailed off as she drifted back to sleep.

Megan crept quietly away, afraid that her grandfather might hear.
When she got back to her room, she brushed all of her posters to the side of
her bed and laid down. Once again, she twirled her hair about her finger
and chewed on it as she had when she was a child.

The man in the classroom doorway hadn't been a man at all. At least
he wasn't one any more. He hadn't gone into another room like she'd
thought when he'd walked around the corner. He'd disappeared into thin
air. She looked around the room. *Where was he now?*

Chapter VII: Furball Invasion

"Why is there a teenage boy standing in the driveway?" Emelia called down the hall.

Megan hurried to her window and found Bruce waiting for her by the curb. She could tell by the way he fidgeted with his backpack that he wasn't sure he should be there. But she already knew that because she could feel his emotions if not his thoughts all the way from the road. Now that she thought about it, she'd already known he was there before her mother had called out. At some point over the past day she'd become aware of his presence at the edge of her senses even when he was all the way over at his house. That wouldn't have been unusual before she came to Nickelville, but with her extra senses muted by the trees that grew here, it was rather impressive. Maybe that was why she'd been thinking about him so much. But why was it just him? She could barely feel her mother in the next room and her grandfather not at all.

"That's my friend, Bruce," she shouted down the hall, ignoring the stack of posters at the foot of her bed. "He's in my class at school."

"Just a friend?" Emelia asked when Megan came in to hug her goodbye.

"It's only my second day at the Academy," Megan replied, noticing the way her mother grimaced at the name of the school. "Of course, he's just a friend. Already a good friend, but just a friend."

"You haven't seen or felt anything there in the school, have you?" the frail woman asked, no longer feverish, but looking mildly deranged just the same.

"Aside from the full-fledged zoo of weird creatures that live in the woods around it?" Megan quietly evaded.

"They're harmless," Emelia said dismissively, leaning back into her pillows.

"Like the ones at the edge of town near that lake?" Megan asked.

"I'd forgotten about those," her mother said with the hint of a smile. "They're much braver than the ones at the school. They actually show themselves. How did you know about the ones at the school?"

"I could see them at first," Megan said, remembering the way the woman's face appeared alongside the bus. "Then they noticed me and hid. But how did you know about them if you couldn't see them?"

"I had a friend who could," she yawned.

"You knew someone else like us?" Megan asked eagerly.

"You'd better get going. Don't get too comfortable here," Emelia whispered into her ear when she hugged her. "Don't let this boy make it harder to leave than it has to be. We're not like normal people."

"I won't," Megan whispered back, wishing that her mother would just let her be a teenage girl for a little while. "He's just a really nice guy."

"Be careful," her mother added.

"I will," Megan called back, stopping only to hug her grandfather on the way out.

Her mother's words chafed at her and added even more uncertainty to the whole subject of Nickelville. As much as she'd have liked to say that it was the knowledge of where she'd come from that made her want to stay, she hadn't jumped on the chance to be homeschooled by her mother. She'd

70

chosen to return to the Academy, to a teacher who clearly hated her, a ghost that wouldn't leave her alone, and...Bruce.

"Hey Megan," he said, eyes sliding past her tattered clothes and locking on her eyes as if already judging her mood by their color even though he hadn't witnessed them change yet. "I hope you don't mind if I catch the bus with you."

"Not at all," she said, casting an uneasy glance back at her mother's window.

"I hear your mom's really surprising the doctor," he said.

"Yeah, Grandpa's having a hard time keeping her in bed," Megan replied, aware of her mother's presence behind them, likely listening to their conversation from a distance. It occurred to her that if her mother knew Megan's extra senses would adjust, that probably meant that her own had already done so. She had, after all, grown up here.

"I wouldn't count on her getting up too soon," Bruce said. "Pneumonia really takes it out of you."

"You don't know my mom," Megan replied. Like the subject of Nickelville, she had mixed feelings about Emelia getting better so quickly. She didn't want her to be sick, but this miraculous recovery threatened to take her away soon, and she wasn't at all ready to go.

In the silence that followed, Megan thought she heard a woman's voice from the direction of the abandoned house she'd noticed at the end of the street. Then the bus rumbled in the opposite direction, sounding much like Oscar during his last hours. Megan wondered how many more miles it had in it before it suffered a similar fate.

"Let's sit close to the front if we can," Bruce said as the bus stopped alongside them and the door opened.

"Sure," Megan said, wondering why he didn't want to sit at the back.

As it turned out, there wasn't a completely empty seat anywhere, but there were two empty spots across the aisle from each other.

"Have you always lived in Nickelville?" Megan asked.

"I was born here," he said, shaking his head in disgust. "What I wouldn't give to get out of this town."

"You said that the other day. But I think it's kind of cool..." Megan trailed off at the look of horror on his face.

"Seriously?" Bruce asked.

"In a creepy horror movie on steroids kind of cool," she admitted.

"That's more like it," he said, nodding. "Don't get me wrong. There's all sorts of interesting stuff you can find out about Nickelville. I can see how it might seem cool at first."

"But it gets old after a while?"

"You have no idea," he answered, glancing toward the back of the bus. "You said you and your mother moved around a lot."

Megan nodded.

"So where have you been, and don't skimp on the details. Remember, you're talking to someone who hungers for more travel than he gets on the occasional summer vacation."

"Pretty much everywhere," she said uncomfortably, knowing that he'd eventually ask why she moved around so much. For some reason, it was important to her not to lie to him if she could help it.

"Details," he prompted with such rapt hunger that she laughed.

"I think I've lived in every state except Hawaii," she said.

"Even Alaska?" he asked, impressed.

"Yes, but my mother hates the cold, so it wasn't one of our favorites."

"Which one was?"

"Probably Maine," she said after a moment.

72

"Funny," Bruce said, "I wouldn't have thought Maine would be terribly warm either."

"It was cold there too, and my mom didn't like it, but we lived in an apartment close to this huge old library," she explained, intentionally leaving out that the apartment building had been condemned and lacked running water or heat. "It had fireplaces in it, and there was a corner with an old, worn armchair where my mother would read to me. I wasn't very old. It was like being in one of the old castles from the books she usually read to me. She also told me stories about a fairy castle like it was a real place. Sometimes we'd stay in that library next to a fire until it closed and then she'd carry me home."

"I'd love to visit a castle someday," Bruce said.

"I'm sure you will then," Megan said.

"Want to come along when I do?" he asked.

All at once she understood what her mother had meant. For just a second, she'd entertained the possibility before remembering the way this had to end. What was she doing? Yes, it was really nice to be accepted for once, even if he had no idea what she really was. But try as she might, she couldn't distance herself from him. There was a familiarity about his presence that nagged at her, bringing her thoughts back to him over and over in a way that confused her.

By the time the bus passed the deserted hotel, Megan had lost herself once again in the ease with which they talked. She still noticed things like the cargo truck that was parked at the hotel loading dock and the faded letters on the theater marquee, but they remained distant and unimportant.

She didn't notice how close they'd come to the Academy until they entered the small band of woods that surrounded the school grounds. Although she strained her eyes and tried to stretch her senses out past the

73

confines of the bus, she found no sign of the magical wildlife that she knew lived there.

She was ready for the shimmering barrier that separated the woods from the school grounds and felt the same current of static pass over her skin that she'd sensed the day before. Apparently, it wasn't a singular event.

"What was that?" Bruce asked, eyes wide.

Surprised, she gave him an inquisitive look.

"It felt like someone just ran about a hundred balloons over my head."

"I felt something like that yesterday," she said, scanning the bus to see if anyone else had reacted. "I thought it was weird too."

"You don't think lightning is going to strike, do you?" Bruce asked, leaning across his seatmate to look at the sky.

They rode on in silence with Bruce likely thinking about what had just happened, and Megan wondering why he'd felt it now and not the day before. Had the disturbance started when she first came to the school? Even if that were so, it still didn't explain why Bruce had become sensitive to it now when he hadn't been before.

She didn't particularly want to go into the building that now rose before her. It still reminded her of something she couldn't quite identify, like the visual equivalent of that word on the tip of the tongue that wouldn't come out.

"Are you okay?" Bruce asked when she paused, looking up from the steep stone steps. Another bus had pulled up after them, and the passengers looked at her with a mixture of irritation and curiosity as they were forced to walk around the two of them to enter the school.

"Sure, why?" Megan asked, surprised that he'd noticed her distress in the midst of the bustle of students vying to get to class.

"You looked spooked," he explained as he held the cafeteria door open for her.

"Just looking at the…" Megan broke off abruptly when a horse came galloping down the hall directly toward them. She knew it must be an illusion even as she shoved Bruce out of its path. This was, however, a country town in which there were likely many horses. Then she dove the other direction…right into the girl next to her.

Papers flew everywhere when the red-haired girl tripped over her and fell.

"Watch where you're going," the girl snarled with such hatred that Megan took an involuntary step backward into Bruce. The horse was gone.

"I'm…I'm sorry," Megan stammered as she and Bruce both bent to help the girl pick up her papers.

"I don't need your help!" the red-haired girl shrieked and snatched the papers from Megan's hand. The light cast by the morning sun through the stained-glass window gave the girl a demonic glow, and Megan felt her own temper flare.

Drawn by the sound of the girl's anger, students gathered around them, momentarily pushing Bruce away. Their cheers and taunts blended with the strange light from the windows, and Megan felt the world shift slightly around her.

Then the girl closed the distance between herself and Megan, shoving with all of her might. Megan would have fallen if not for the wall of students behind her.

"What's going on here?" a voice boomed.

The students parted before a tall, balding man in a suit. His bushy eyebrows almost met in the middle of his frown as he looked from the red-haired girl to Megan.

75

"This clumsy twit knocked me down," the girl snarled, pointing a well-manicured nail at Megan.

"It was an accident," Megan said defensively, relieved that the fight had been averted, but still angered by the girl's outburst. "I said I was sorry."

"Watch where you're going," he said pointing at Megan before turning toward the other girl, "and you stop screaming in the halls. This school is not your personal stage."

The girl rolled her eyes at him and looked back at Megan.

"You'd better watch your back," the redheaded girl spat as if the man hadn't been there. "I *own* this school." Then she sauntered toward her friends and started to laugh.

"I should have followed your grandfather's advice and gone into law," the man grumbled to Megan and stalked sullenly away.

"Does everyone in this place know who my family is?" Megan asked Bruce, shaking her head in exasperation.

"Pretty much," he replied, finally making it back to her side. "Still okay?"

"It takes more than that to get to me," she said, trying to hide how badly she'd been shaken.

"What's up with your eyes?" he asked. "I thought they were brown."

"They change when I get mad," Megan mumbled as she hurried to class.

"Like the Hulk, huh?"

"What?" she asked, scanning the hallway irritably for the Dark Man.

"His eyes always changed that weird color of green when he got mad and turned into the Hulk."

Megan stopped in the middle of the hall and stared at him. She could tell by the way his eyes kept searching hers that they must be going back to their normal color.

"Bruce," she said.

"Yes?" he replied, looking worried.

"Don't take this the wrong way."

"Uh oh," he said, still staring at her eyes.

"You are one of the strangest people I've ever met."

"Right back at ya, babe," he grinned.

"Glad we cleared that up," she said. "Let's get to class before I get into any more trouble."

"Can't argue with a plan like that," he said. "But I've got bad news."

"What now?" she groaned, starting to suspect this wasn't going to be a good day.

"That girl you knocked down," he began.

"Yeah?"

"Mrs. Jones's daughter, Allison."

"Suddenly I'm not so eager to get to class," she groaned, slowing her pace. "I don't suppose you want to skip class?"

"What?" he said with such innocent shock that she had to laugh.

"Just kidding, she said. "Let's get this over with."

"MISS MCGEEHEE," the teacher bellowed as soon as Megan walked through the door, "I don't know what was appropriate at your previous school, but running in the halls is not accepted here."

"But I wasn't running," Megan said.

"Don't talk back to me," Mrs. Jones's voice dropped to almost a whisper, and the class went silent.

Megan kept her eyes low where no one could see them.

"Write your name on the board," the teacher ordered, pointing a blood-red nail at the corner of the board where she'd written the word "DEVIANTS" so many times that it was carved into the faded brown paint.

Megan's face burned as she walked over to the board, picked up the chalk and started to write. Most of the school's she'd been to used dry erase boards, and it felt weird to be writing this way.

"Sometime today, McGeehee," the teacher snapped. "I see penmanship wasn't stressed at your last school either."

Megan flushed deeper and tried not to let her letters slant upward the way they always did when she wrote on the board.

"You do know how to spell your own name, don't you Miss McGeehee?"

Megan knew this game too well to be baited by Mrs. Jones. The old bat was trying to make her angry enough to yell or cry. She doubted the ugly woman cared which, so long as it proved her power. Without any outward sign of what she felt, Megan placed the chalk back on the ledge and walked to her seat.

Allison sat on the front row, gloating. She gave the girl next to her high-five when Megan passed, and several students broke the silence by laughing.

Megan chanced a quick look at Bruce. She worried that this might prove too much for their fragile friendship. But when she felt his anger at the way she'd been treated, her own slipped away.

Mrs. Jones, like many bad teachers, let a combination of textbooks and videos teach the class for her. The day dragged by until the cat from the office sauntered in through the open door, crossed the room and jumped onto Megan's desk.

She glanced at Bruce who smiled and shrugged. Apparently, this was another of the strange things considered normal in Nickelville. She hadn't truly realized how big the cat was until he was on her desk. Reluctantly she ran her hand over his back, then just below his chin and noticed a white starburst pattern on his chest.

In hindsight, that's when all of her problems with the cat, whom she later learned was named Mr. Bob, began. From that moment on he wouldn't leave her alone. With a contented purr he stretched across her book and lay down. No matter how hard she pushed or shoved, he just purred louder and stuck to her desk like a big furry parasite. Even Megan's childhood companion, the voice that sometimes spoke in her thoughts, seemed surprised by the cat's tenacity. It whispered at the edge of her awareness as if talking to itself just out of hearing.

"Close your books and take out a piece of paper for a quiz," Mrs. Jones said, looking directly at Megan.

Having given up any attempt to be nice to the cat, Megan pulled her book out from under him, closed it, and put it under her desk. She then pulled out a piece of paper and shoved him over far enough to have a corner of the desk to write on.

None of the questions proved difficult for Megan, though she suspected Mrs. Jones to be the sort of teacher to count them wrong anyway. Halfway through the test the ceiling above her head began to creak as if someone were walking on the floor above. Out of curiosity she looked up.

"You won't find the answers up there, Miss McGeehee," Mrs. Jones's voice squealed in glee.

Megan *definitely* didn't like the way the woman pronounced her name.

An overwhelming stench of cinnamon filled the air. Her gaze swept toward the open door and the hallway outside before she remembered that Mrs. Jones was looking for a chance to target her again. The cat stood, stretched lazily and then jumped down from her desk before padding out the door.

She took a steadying breath, flattened the edge of her paper where the cat had rumpled it and finished her test. A haze filled the air, giving the room a dreamlike distortion much like looking out through partially closed eyes. Then the presence from before oozed through the open spaces between the desks. She dared not look at Bruce, though his presence proved a life-line in the dark waters through which she swam.

Alien thoughts and images flowed around her, each of them tugging at her sense of self. But none of them made any sense, as if she'd been submerged in the dreams of a madman.

Megan closed her eyes and held her breath, tightening her shields until she couldn't even feel Bruce seated nearby. But even that seemed to draw the attention of whatever force it was that surrounded her. She felt as if she'd been caught up in the mouth of some vast beast, and now it was probing the numb spot her shields created with its tongue.

She passed her paper to the front when asked, and Mrs. Jones scanned it with a grimace that told Megan all of her answers had been correct. She would have smiled if she hadn't been so frightened.

The bell rang through the building, and the presence lurched unpleasantly, knocking pens and pencils from desks and making one of the teacher's magazines slide to the floor.

"Leave your things and let's go outside for break," Mrs. Jones said, tossing the quizzes into the trash.

The class lined up obediently at the back door to the classroom. Although Megan wondered what was going on, she was more than happy to leave the classroom behind. Bruce slipped into line behind her.

"Surely we don't have recess," she whispered back to him when Mrs. Jones looked away.

"Our new principal thinks we should have time to let off a little steam when the weather is nice," Bruce answered. "It's not very long and technically not a recess, but we do go to the courtyard. Mostly people just stand around and talk or play cards."

"Why didn't we do it yesterday?" she asked, not caring what he called it as long as they left the room as soon as possible. "The weather was nice then too."

"The courtyard was still wet from the rain," he answered.

"What rain? It hasn't rained since I got here."

"It poured at the Academy the day before you came to school," he answered, shifting his weight from foot to foot uncomfortably.

"Yeah," a boy said from behind Bruce, "Wheezy don't like the rain, does he?" Then the boy shoved Bruce out of his way to move closer to the door.

Mrs. Jones watched him do this, but didn't seem to care.

Bruce might not like to call it recess, but the class acted exactly like Megan remembered from elementary school. Some of them chased each other in a spontaneous game of tag. Others grabbed a basketball and started to shoot hoops. A few even sat on the swings, though no one actually swung.

Out in the warm sunlight Megan chided herself for being so frightened. Sure, it was weird. But for someone who'd been chased across most of the continent by supernatural hunters, this wasn't exactly mind-breaking. Besides, her mother had made it through her entire childhood

81

without being harmed by the ghost. Maybe Megan could just learn to ignore it. She'd have to if she wanted to stay.

Unlike the playgrounds she'd seen in large cities, the courtyard sported a collection of homemade equipment that looked as if it had been repaired and added to by generations of Nickelville parents. At the center of the courtyard stood two enormous trees that spread their branches almost to the walls on either side. Beneath them, Mr. Green stood in his stained coveralls, having just finished cutting up a huge branch that had fallen from one of the otherwise majestic trees. He waved when he saw them, and she happily waved back.

"So, what do you usually do out here?" Megan asked, finally relaxing her shields again.. Bruce smiled as if he could feel the difference as well.

"I read," he answered without hesitation, but his eyes clouded again, and she knew that something bothered him about that answer.

"Any particular spot?" she asked. Maybe there was room for two, and she could find a good book next time too.

"Well," he hesitated, "There's this one spot I like to go to because it's hidden."

"Why do you need to be hidden?" she asked, wondering if this had anything to do with the boy who'd shoved him.

"Chuck Baker and Glenn Floyd," he said with a sigh, confirming her suspicion.

"The guy that pushed you?" she asked.

"Chuck," he said, looking around the courtyard, then pointing to another boy that was now talking to Chuck. "Glenn is the one with the long nose and the beady little eyes."

"He looks a lot like a ferret," she observed, making him laugh.

"Don't be insulting ferrets now," he said, smiling at last. "I happen to like ferrets. Any pet for that matter."

"So where is this hidden place?" Megan asked, scanning the courtyard. "It all looks pretty out in the open to me."

"You sure?" he asked. "It's close to the wall and we're not allowed to be over there.

"Point me toward danger," she said, linking her arm through his. "Onward to adventure!" Once again, she noticed that there was something when she touched him, something she couldn't define. It was a little bit like the memory of a smell or taste, fleeting and impossible to hold onto before it was gone again.

With a foolish grin, he led her across the courtyard toward a corner that was walled off with crude wooden timber. Without needing to be told, she knew he'd had just as little experience with friendship as she had.

"Can we get behind that thing?" she asked, not sure she wanted to go back there. Something about it felt wrong, and her diminished extra senses slid off of it without giving her any hint at what might lay on the other side. Furthermore, if this was the place where the Dark Man kicked back and caught some rays, she didn't think she wanted to intrude.

"No," he said, and his steps faltered. "I mean…there isn't any way back there. Not even the teachers know what's there. Or if they do, they aren't talking."

"Good," she said, relieved. "So, where's this hiding place?"

"Just stand next to the opening in the bushes and look casual," he said, and glanced over his shoulder toward the rest of the courtyard.

"How am I supposed to look casual?" she asked.

"Quick, while no one's looking, he said, getting down on his knees and crawling behind the bushes. "Follow me."

It was hard not to laugh at the seriousness with which he'd suddenly disappeared, but she managed. She had no idea if anyone had seen her, but she was happy. She'd done things before that broke the rules. After all, in many ways her entire life seemed to break one rule or another. But she'd never had a partner in crime before, and she liked it.

It surprised her to find that the old bushes, which had probably been planted decades in the past, formed a sort of tunnel where they met the wall. It was easy for her to crawl without touching anything, but she noticed that Bruce's long limbs made it necessary for him to stoop while he did so.

"Pretty cool," she whispered, wondering if this was what her childhood would have been like without the Wild Hunt. "I would have thought it would be wet back here."

"The ground is higher under the bushes and the roof comes out far enough to protect it from most of the rain. It doesn't get wet very often, but it takes a long time to dry out when it does."

They came to a larger opening against the wall where the bushes were thinner. Bruce put his back against the wall and gave a "What do you think?" gesture with his hands.

"How long have you been coming here?" she asked, sitting next to him. It was cramped for two people, but she didn't mind. With her shoulder resting against his, she could feel contentment from him that mirrored her own.

"I found this place when I was in the second grade," he said. "I've been coming in once or twice a week ever since."

"Afraid they'd notice if you did it too often?" she asked.

"Yeah, not that anyone usually looks for me when we're out here, though," he glanced at her anxiously, and she knew he hadn't meant to say that last part. "Chuck and Glenn have short memories," he added hastily. "If they don't see me they usually forget I'm around."

"No other friends?" she asked.

84

"Not really," he answered. "I just never had much in common with the kids here in Nickelville."

"Well, now you've got me," she said. "But since we're friends, can I ask you something?"

"Sure."

"What is it out here that worries you?" she asked, turning around so that her back was to the bushes, and she could see him. The look that crossed his face told her she was right to think so. "I thought it was just Chuck and Glenn, but it's something more, isn't it?"

"I'll tell you if you tell me what made you run into Allison this morning when we got to the Academy."

"Touché," she said out loud.

Just then Megan felt the bushes move at her back. Her head jerked backward as something snatched her hair, dragging her away from Bruce.

He grabbed her hand and tried to pull her back, but whatever had her was stronger than he was. Her fingers started to pull loose from his grasp and the pain in her scalp brought tears to her eyes.

"Bruce," she cried, "Please don't let him take me!"

Then he lost his grip and fell hard against the wall as she disappeared through the bushes. As he did so, she had a clear vision of massive talons reaching for her and the entire courtyard moving as if in the midst of a tornado.

Chapter VIII: Terrible Trio

Bruce watched helplessly as Megan's feet disappeared through the tightly interwoven branches. He wasn't sure what had her, but with the wall looming nearby, he feared they might have stirred up something from the other side. Heedless of the branches that tore at his face and snagged in his clothing, he launched himself through after her.

"What do we got here?" an all-too-familiar voice bellowed just as he ripped himself free. For the first time in his life, Bruce was happy to hear Chuck Baker's voice.

"They're over here," Allison squealed in glee as she dragged her mother to where Chuck still held a struggling Megan by the hair.

"Let her go," Bruce demanded, stepping toward the large boy.

"Or what?" Glenn laughed.

"Get lost or you'll be next," Chuck growled, shaking a work-calloused fist at Bruce's face.

Bruce grabbed the outstretched hand and twisted it behind Chuck's back, lifting it toward his shoulder blades as his sister had taught him to do.

Something popped in Chuck's shoulder, making him howl in pain as he turned Megan loose. When he did, Bruce released his own hold and stepped between the new girl and her attacker.

The class stared on in silence as Bruce stood his ground against the school bully. Until that moment, Bruce had ever realized that he was as tall as Chuck, though not nearly as heavily muscled.

86

"Why am I not surprised to see Miss McGeehee behind this?" Mrs. Jones said, making Megan's name sound like a curse. "You certainly don't waste any time getting into trouble or taking good students down with you."

Bruce couldn't see Megan's face since she was still behind him, but he knew she was looking at the ground again, trying to hide her eyes.

"They were in the bushes," Glenn said, his voice less certain than it had been moments before.

"Chuck pulled Megan out of the bushes by her hair and wouldn't let go," Bruce said, his voice surprisingly steady. He'd thought being in trouble would be worse than this.

"I don't care who did what," Mrs. Jones said. She studied Bruce, clearly not liking this development. "You knew the bushes were out of bounds, yet you chose to go there anyway. You two will sit out the rest of the break on the steps behind the bench."

"What about Chuck?" Bruce demanded.

"What about him?" she asked with the hint of a smile.

"What is his punishment?"

"Punishment for what?" she asked.

"For hurting Megan," Bruce said loud enough for the entire courtyard to hear.

"Nothing," Mrs. Jones said, turning away. "She looks fine to me."

Bruce watched her go, ignoring the way Chuck glowered at him while massaging his sore shoulder.

"Are you okay?" Bruce asked, turning to look at Megan.

"I'm fine," she said, looking him in the eye and not trying to hide their strange violet color. "Thanks."

"Any time," he said, reluctantly following Mrs. Jones across the courtyard.

"Is she actually putting us in time-out?" Megan asked.

He nodded.

"What does she think we are? Five?"

"Mr. Danders won't let teachers send students down until they've acted up several times and had their parents contacted," Bruce explained quietly. "This is the best she can come up with for a first offense."

Students watched them pass, many looking at Bruce as if seeing him for the first time. Maybe some of them were. He'd made such an art of blending into the background that he was easy to overlook.

Megan suddenly lurched to one side, narrowly missing him as she walked. A wave of fearful revulsion washed over him, making him wonder if it somehow came from his new friend. She spun on the spot as if watching something he couldn't see and stared back toward the walled-off corner of the courtyard.

"What's wrong?" Bruce whispered, careful not to draw Jones's attention.

"Nothing," she whispered back, still looking back toward the corner.

"What are you looking at?" he pressed.

"Seriously, it's nothing."

"Megan," he said quietly, putting his hand on her arm to make her look at him, "you're looking awfully hard at nothing back there."

She shrugged and started back toward the bench. Allison, Chuck and Glenn were now entertaining a large group of boys and girls. The entire group would periodically turn to look at Megan before bursting into laughter. Even from where he walked, he could hear them talking about his friend's clothes. He hoped she hadn't heard them, but somehow knew that she had. Why should any of that matter? Allison had the nicest clothes in school and she was by far the vilest.

88

Mrs. Jones plopped her large frame down onto the bench and picked up the magazine she'd been reading for most of the day.

"Bruce, you sit on that side," she said, motioning toward the porch that opened from the next classroom. "McGeehee will sit over there." She took off her watch and rubbed the pinched skin underneath. She laid it on the bench beside her before returning to the magazine and likewise resumed ignoring her class.

Mr. Bob sauntered up as if summoned from the bushes nearest the steps, stretched and crawled onto Megan's lap. Bruce never had figured out how the cat got outside, but he often showed up during break.

Megan tried to push him away, but soon realized the futility of her efforts. Resigned to his presence, she absently petted him while she stared out across the courtyard, lost in thought.

Bruce stared at her while she did this, trying to make sense of what had just happened. Had he really just stood up to Chuck Baker? Had he really questioned Mrs. Jones's authority in front of the class? What was wrong with him?

"I'm going to the restroom," Allison said, startling Bruce from his contemplation of his friend.

Mrs. Jones grunted in reply.

He glanced back at Megan, but made sure he didn't stare at her this time. He didn't want to think that she was crazy, but she acted like she saw and maybe heard things that weren't there. And what was up with her eyes? Eyes didn't just change color like that. Sure, a person with hazel eyes might change from green to blue depending on what they were wearing, but from brown to violet? He'd never even heard of violet eyes. Something caught his attention from one of the classrooms that opened into the courtyard.

In the window across from where he sat, his sister Jade stood, laughing at him. One of the reasons he hadn't been worried about getting into trouble was that he didn't think it would reach home. But now Jade knew that he'd been in trouble.

He motioned for her to go away before she got him into more trouble, but she only laughed harder. He sighed and wondered yet again if he was adopted.

"Stop petting that foul thing," Mrs. Jones snapped, "I can hear it purring from here."

He turned to find Megan looking at him.

She pointed to her own eyes, then to his and finally to the window where Jade was still taunting him. He doubted she could see his sister and didn't know how to explain the problem in pantomime.

The bell sounded, students began to line up, and Mr. Bob bounded over the bench where Mrs. Jones sat, making her fall to the ground with an audible thump. Glaring at the two of them with utmost contempt, she levered herself to her feet and opened the door to the classroom while Bruce and Megan went to the end of the line.

"What were you looking at?" Megan asked, when they were safely away.

"Have a look for yourself," he said grimly, pointing toward the window, where Megan could now clearly see Jade, still pointing and laughing.

"Who is she?" Megan asked, "Friend of the Terrible Trio?"

"Terrible Trio?" Bruce asked.

"Allison, Chuck and Glenn," she whispered.

"Nope," he muttered, glancing over at Jade. "Worse."

She looked back at him questioningly.

"My sister."

"Is there something the two of you would like to share with the class?" Mrs. Jones yelled.

"Nope," Bruce answered, making Megan giggle.

"Go to your lockers and prepare for math and science," the unpleasant woman ordered with a look of disgust.

The class passed through the room in single file and went to their lockers more quietly than they usually did. Everyone knew the teacher was in a mood, and no one wanted to become the focus of that anger.

Even though Megan had only been opening her locker for a few days, she still had it open before Bruce. She stiffened when she looked inside, and he was about to ask what was wrong when he noticed something black running out of the corner of his own. When he pulled the latch, all of his books, papers and backpack came tumbling out. Someone had dumped ink over everything. A quick glance at Megan told him that her locker was the same way, though her stuff hadn't fallen out.

Chuck and Glenn started to laugh first, but it soon spread to everyone around them. For most, the laughter was nervous, but some of them truly enjoyed the situation.

Bruce looked to see how Megan was taking this and found her staring at Allison with such anger that he felt an instant of fear before moving to her side.

He put his hand on her shoulder and with a lurch, he found himself looking at Allison through Megan's eyes. She'd seen thousands of girls like Allison, with their expensive clothes and their disdainful friends. They'd all laughed at her, thrown stuff at her and destroyed the few things she had to call her own. Bruce might have been bullied by the Terrible Trio, but he sensed that Megan had suffered at the hands of hundreds if not thousands of mean children, each of them seeing in her an unprotected, friendless victim.

He could feel her trying to hold something in check, but like the thing behind the wall, it was huge and hungry and sensed prey. She went rigid with the strain, and he felt her control slip.

In a blinding flash that he somehow knew only he and Megan could see, Allison began to scream and fumble with the pocket of her designer jeans. Smoke poured through the fabric as Mrs. Jones rushed to her daughter. At last the girl pulled her phone free, dropping it with a howl and watching as the screen split into a spider web of cracks before dying with a feeble croaking ring.

The quality of the air around them changed, as if the gravity of this one spot had increased, drawing in fumes from other parts of the building...*why did it suddenly smell like apple pies?*

"What's going on here?" a familiar voice boomed above the chaos. Mr. Harris, though as old as Megan's grandfather, gave a sense of profound strength as he surveyed the mayhem in the hallway.

"Someone dumped ink all over our books," Bruce told him, releasing his grip on his friend's shoulder in an attempt to shift attention from Megan as quickly as possible.

Mr. Harris glanced at the ruined books laying on the floor, over to Allison and then back to Megan who was now looking around her in mild panic. Before Mrs. Jones could recover, he took control.

"Dale," he said to the freckled boy next to Bruce, "Go get Mr. Green and have him dispose of these ruined books." Reluctantly the boy took off down the hall in search of the janitor.

"Gina," he continued, "Go and get the nurse for Allison. Tell her that she may have some burns from a defective phone."

"You two come with me and I'll get you new books," he said, using his long arms to cull the two stunned teenagers from the crowd and herd them toward the library. Megan was still staring back at the phone, but she allowed herself to be led down the hall at a brisk walk toward the library.

"Now tell me what that was all about," he said when the heavy wooden doors were shut behind them.

Chapter IX: Dear Delinquent Sib

Within the safety of the library, Megan let Bruce explain their problems to Mr. Harris. She didn't want either of them to see how badly the phone had shaken her, so she wandered between the shelves, careful to stay away from the computers.

You've got to get control of yourself, she thought. *Bruce is a smart guy. Between jumping at ghosts and blowing up cell phones, he's going to figure out something is weird about you if you keep this up.*

But people like Allison, who always had everything they could possibly want and more, would never understand that her mother had skipped meals so her daughter could have a new backpack. And as soon as she'd gotten it two years ago, Megan had spent hours sewing extra seams into it so it would last longer. It was the one thing she'd owned that wasn't from a thrift store or garage sale.

It had been a long time since she'd fried anything that badly. Worse yet, it was the first time she'd destroyed something without even touching it. She supposed the sheer strength of her anger might explain it, but that didn't feel likely.

She needed to distance herself from Bruce. It wasn't fair for her to cling to him like this. He'd have to deal with any trouble she started long after she and her mother moved on.

The anxiety she'd tried so hard to dispel surged at the thought of distancing herself from him. Overhead, the fluorescent lights hummed loudly as their ballasts attempted to use the energy she radiated.

She took several deep breaths the way her mother had taught her to do at times like this. It helped, but only enough to save the lights.

A display case held a big curling fossil and a picture of four young men digging it up. She was pretty sure one of them was her grandfather.

How can I be this attached to him after so short a time? It's not safe for him to be around me. What if I lose control and hurt him? I feel bad enough about Allison, and she deserved it.

What was she doing? She kept acting like she and her mother could make Nickelville their permanent home. As much as she might want that, in reality she'd probably have to leave in the middle of the night sometime soon without even getting a chance to say goodbye.

"Megan," Mr. Harris called.

She took another deep breath and went back to the front desk where the two of them had been joined by Mr. Bob.

"What is it with that cat?" she asked.

Mr. Harris looked questioningly at Bruce from where he sat on the stool behind the counter with the cat content in his arms.

"He was outside with us just a few minutes ago," her friend explained.

"He's been like that since he showed up here last year," the librarian said. "He seems to be able to go just about anywhere he wants. Anyway, Azarich, Alan and I have watched each other's backs since we were boys," he said with a frown. "Your grandfather even saved my life once, back in the war."

"Alan?" Bruce asked, confused.

"Mr. Green," the librarian answered. "What I'm trying to say is that there's nothing I wouldn't do to help Azarich or his family, but we've got to play this smart."

He rose from the stool and put Mr. Bob down on an empty shelf in the garish light from the window. The cat stretched out happily in the warm sunlight and promptly fell asleep.

"Bruce, do you know to whom Mrs. Jones is married?" he asked.

"How could I forget with Allison in our class?" Bruce answered, looking disgusted. "She reminds someone almost daily that their parents work at her father's factory."

"Did you know that Allison's father also heads the school board?" Mr. Harris asked.

Bruce nodded.

"There's nothing I can do that would make Mrs. Jones leave Megan alone. She's an evil woman, and I don't say that lightly. Most of our problems here in Nickelville can be traced back to that family if you're brave enough to look closely. If I interfere here, things will become even more difficult for you than they are now, and the Academy will have a new librarian next year."

"That's okay," Megan said, trying to hide her disappointment. "It's a good thing you came along when you did though. I was starting to think about how much better Allison would look with a few teeth knocked out."

"You're sure she's the one who vandalized your lockers?" the librarian asked.

"She had ink all over her hands," Bruce replied. "Mrs. Jones knows too. She'll probably buy her a new phone that's twice as expensive as the last one."

"And neither of you know what happened with the phone?"

"No," Megan and Bruce said together with such force that Mr. Harris looked at them suspiciously before continuing.

"Well, I'd better get you some new textbooks," he said, moving toward the bookroom. "Bruce, I'm behind on my shelving. Would you mind taking care of it while I get these together?"

"Sure," Bruce said.

"Did you finish your book yet?" Mr. Harris asked from inside the book room.

"No," Bruce answered, shooting a troubled look at Megan as he moved quickly toward the shelving cart.

"Slowing down?" the librarian asked, surprised.

"I guess so," Bruce answered.

"I think Bruce has read just about every book in the place," Mr. Harris said when he'd collected two identical stacks of books on the counter. "He comes in here a lot during the spring and fall when his asthma acts up. He and his siblings make up a large part of my patronage. Jade has read every book we have on geology and her brother Paul has checked out and lost almost every book we've ever had about fossils."

"So, his brother's the irresponsible one?" she asked.

"Only with books," the librarian answered. "He always has a good story about what happened to them. I believe he said the first one was stolen by an eagle."

"Do you even have eagles around here?" she asked, the hint of a memory trying to stir at the back of her mind.

"Not that I know of," he said. "Which is why he isn't allowed to take any new books on the subject out of the library."

"Do you have any books on the supernatural?" Megan asked on a whim.

"Like what?" Mr. Harris asked.

"Ghosts," she said simply.

"Ah," he said, rubbing his hands together enthusiastically. "That has always been a favorite subject of mine as well. Although my wife knows a surprising amount about such things for a nice old church lady. We have several books on ghosts. Would you like to see them?"

"I would," Megan answered, enjoying his eagerness as she followed him into the shelves.

"Do you want ghost stories or actual books on the phenomenon?"

"Actual books," she answered as he scanned the shelf, looking for just the right one.

"Here we go," he said, handing her an old book. "It probably won't have the most modern information on it, but should still have some good stuff. I wish we could buy new books more often. But budgets are thin and let's face it, these never get read anymore unless one of the teachers brings their class down and makes them check something out. Even that seldom happens anymore."

"Why is that?" Megan asked. "I love books."

"You're a dying breed my girl," he said sadly. "Kids your age prefer the instant information of the internet to searching through books."

"Well I promise I'll be here often," She said, taking the book from his hand and flipping through its gilded pages. "Computers don't like me, so I prefer to do things the old-fashioned way."

While she checked it out, the now familiar sound of footsteps crossed the ceiling above. Neither Bruce nor Mr. Harris heard it, but Mr. Bob jumped down irritably from the shelf where he'd been napping and sauntered over to an old wardrobe behind the counter before squeezing his considerable mass behind it.

"What's up with him?" Bruce asked, shelving the last book.

"I don't know," the librarian said with a dismissive shrug. "He comes through here a few times a day and climbs into that old wardrobe. I lost the key years ago, but he seems to have found a way in."

The bell-tower chimed for lunch.

"Thanks, Mr. Harris," Bruce said and headed toward the carved wooden doors. "I don't know what we would have done without you."

"And for the book," Megan added.

"Come back any time," he said. "And enjoy your lunch. Hopefully the rest of your day will go better."

Lunchtime was chaotic at Nickelville Academy since all of the grades, Kindergarten through twelfth, ate at the same time. Mr. Danders patrolled the tables to make sure that order was kept. He seemed to take any horseplay personally and yelled entirely too much.

The class was already seated when they arrived since Megan and Bruce had to return to Mrs. Jones's classroom to get their lunches.

"I'm glad the ink didn't get on the food," Bruce said, opening his.

"It's kind of funny," Megan said. "Grandpa is a great cook. So, when he asked if he could make my lunch in the mornings while we were here, I said yes. But he insists on making my mother's favorite sandwich. The problem is, I hate grilled cheese, and now I don't want to hurt his feelings by telling him so."

"Have one of mine," Bruce said, passing over a ham sandwich. "My parents seem to think that packing a huge lunch for me will somehow make me outgrow my asthma faster."

"Are you sure you still have enough?" Megan asked.

"Sure, I never eat more than half of the stuff they put in here." He looked up over Megan's shoulder and groaned.

She turned to find the girl who'd laughed at them through the courtyard window. Megan hadn't been able to tell before, but the girl had unnaturally red hair with hints of purple running through its short length. She was about Megan's height, but had the muscular build of a dancer or maybe a gymnast. In short, she looked like she belonged in Nickelville about as much as Megan did.

"Greetings my delinquent sib," the girl said and took the seat next to Megan. "Hi, I'm Jade," she said, offering a friendly smile and a very calloused hand.

"Hi," Megan said, liking the other girl immediately. "I understand we're neighbors."

"Yep," Jade said. "Your grandpa's a great guy and a great cook, so I'll be taking that grilled cheese you're not eating. And best of all, Azarich lets Paul and I search his property for rocks any time we want."

"Paul?" Megan asked, happily handing the sandwich over.

"Our younger brother," Bruce said, clearly not liking this turn of conversation. "He's into paleontology, and she's into mineralogy. They're complete fanatics over just about anything you can dig out of the ground."

"Sounds cool," Megan said.

"And now, for the million-dollar question," Jade said with relish as she turned from Megan to Bruce, "What did my perfect brother, who would rather have someone call him the wrong name for a solid ten years than correct them, do to end up in trouble with the wicked witch of Nickelville?"

"None of your business," Bruce said pleasantly, taking a bite of his sandwich. "You know, you don't have to start eating lunch with me just because Megan is here."

"Perhaps you'd rather I find out when Mom does?"

"That's cold," Bruce said. "I never rat you out."

"It's my job as big sister to make sure that my brother stays on the path of the do-gooder, or at least steps off with style."

"What's going on?" a new but strangely pleasant voice asked. "Are we sitting with Bruce now?"

Megan turned to find a boy who looked almost nothing like his brother and sister. Even though he was younger than Bruce, it was already apparent that he'd grow to be far more muscular. Furthermore, he had chiseled features that would have looked more at home in one of her mother's black and white movies than Nickelville, Texas.

"Our dear delinquent sib got into trouble with Jones during recess," Jade said, pointing a carrot stick from her own lunch at Bruce.

"It's break, not recess," Bruce mumbled.

The boy, who Megan assumed to be Bruce's younger brother, grabbed his chest in shock.

"You must be Paul," she said. "The one who loses library books."

"And you're Mr. McGeehee's granddaughter," he said, extending a hand almost as calloused as Jade's. "And on the subject of library books, I was framed by an evil force in Guarded Wood that wishes to tarnish my spotless scout reputation and eat my soul."

"Megan," she said, trying to figure out exactly what it was about his voice that she liked. "It's good to meet you."

"Bruce was just about to share his deviance with us," Jade prompted, "on pain of us telling Mom."

"All right," Bruce said with a defeated sigh, "Megan and I were caught in the bushes. Then Chuck pulled her out by her hair and I put him in the arm bar you showed me."

"In the bushes?" Paul asked, looking from Bruce to Megan in confusion.

101

"And just exactly what were you doing in the bushes?" Jade asked, her eyebrows disappearing beneath her bangs.

"There's a spot over by the fence where you can sit, and no one can see you," Bruce answered, leveling an irritated glare at her as he spoke, "I go there to *read*."

"That's it?" Jade asked, disappointed. "I must say, Bruce, I'd hoped for something better. At the very least I'd hoped that you'd put hair remover in Allison's suntan lotion or something. Good job with the arm bar though. I told you he'd back off if you stood up to him."

"Suntan lotion?" Megan asked, enjoying the unfamiliar ease of their banter but not understanding.

"You see, her lily-white skin burns easily," Paul said, dropping effortlessly into a feminine southern drawl that sounded eerily like the girl of which he spoke, before looking back at Jade and returning just as quickly to his own voice. "The hair-remover's a good idea, now that you mention it, Sis."

"Why don't you come over to our house to catch the bus in the morning?" Jade suggested.

"I'd love to," Megan replied.

"I've got an even better idea," Bruce cut in. "I'll walk over to your house like I did this morning, so I can get away from their endless rock-talk."

"Have it your way," Paul said. "We're more than capable of amusing ourselves without you, my recently fallen brother."

Megan spent the rest of that short lunch talking with Bruce about more of the places she'd been and listening to the other two talk.

The rest of the day passed in a flow of thinly disguised insults from Mrs. Jones and snide remarks about Megan's appearance from her daughter, but Megan found it easier to bear than it had been before meeting

Jade and Paul. Still, she was glad when the end of the day came without any more ghostly manifestations, and she could ride home on the bus with the library book safely hidden in her ink-stained backpack.

Chapter X: The Last of Her Kind

When Megan got off the bus, still basking in the energy of being with the Grimbles, she found her grandfather crawling around on the ground under a tree. He had a bucket of the sort one would buy from a home improvement center next to him.

"Hey Grandpa," Megan said, walking up to make sure he was okay. "Did you lose something?"

"I'm picking up pecans," he answered. "Your mother was always partial to pecan pie."

"I didn't know that," Megan said, putting her ink-stained backpack down on the ground next to her. "Want some help?"

"My old knees would greatly appreciate it," he said with one of his infectious grins. "What happened to your book bag?"

"Allison Jones," she answered, making him frown. It was clear he knew the name. "Do your knees always hurt?"

"Not really," he answered, still frowning at the backpack. "Alan, Tom and I lucked out with the whole arthritis thing. With the exception of Alan's knee, we all still get around pretty well."

"What's wrong with his knee?" she asked, remembering the janitor's limp.

"He was hit by shrapnel in the war," Azarich answered, returning to picking up pecans. "It damaged some of the nerves."

"That's awful," she said, starting to add some to the bucket.

"Compared to what happened to so many others," he said, glancing again at her bag, "We were all lucky. Well, except for Carl."

"Who is he?" she asked.

"He was a friend who left with us but didn't make it back home," he answered sadly. "He disappeared while on patrol. His body was never found."

"I'm sorry," she said. "That must have been hard on you guys."

"Not as hard as it was on Elizabeth," he said, sitting back on his heels. "He asked her to marry him right before we left. She was never really the same as she'd been before. We'd all been so close, my Josie and me, Tom and Esther, Carl and Beth, and of course Alan. We were inseparable before the war, but I think it hurt Beth too much to be around us without him. She passed away a few years back. We all went to the funeral even though none of us had spoken to her more than a few times over the years. But we all knew Carl would have wanted us to."

"So how many pecans do we need to make a pie?" she asked, noticing that he already had three full buckets in addition to the one they were filling.

"Not too many," he said, following her gaze. "I'll freeze the rest for later. There's a man in town who has a cracking machine. I'll take these to him to speed up the shelling process. Want to come?"

"Sure," Megan answered. "Let me go put my stuff inside and see Mom."

"I'll put these in the truck while you do," he said, climbing to his feet.

Megan ran up the steps and then up the stairs inside, hoping her mother wouldn't see her backpack before she got it to her room. It turned out that she had no need to worry since Emelia was out of bed and currently enjoying a long hot soak in the bathroom's claw-footed tub. It

105

had been a long time since they'd stayed somewhere clean enough to safely take an actual bath instead of a shower.

"Hey Mom," Megan called through the door.

"Yes, Dear?" Emelia answered happily.

"Grandpa and I are going to get the pecans cracked," she said. "We'll be back soon."

"Okay," her mother answered. "Have fun."

"I'm sure we will," Megan called through the door before running back down the stairs and out to the truck where her grandfather waited.

A short while later, they pulled up to a farmhouse that had, like most of Nickelville, seen better days. An old Jeep sat in the grass on one side of the gravel driveway. She noticed that the driver's seat was missing and that a lawn chair sat in its place.

"Hey Azarich," an old man called from the open shed door. "What brings you around?"

"I hate to bother you," Azirich called back, "But it's pecan season."

"I knew you weren't here to admire my good looks," the man said with a good-natured laugh. "How much you got?"

"Twenty gallons," he answered. "But ten of that's for you. I remembered that you said your tree died. You're welcome to more, but you'll have to come up and pick them yourself."

Megan helped carry two of the buckets toward the shed, noticing that the property backed up to the trees like the houses on Beverly Road.

"You must be Emelia's girl," the man said, taking the buckets from her.

"Yes," she answered, still a little bit startled by strangers knowing who she was. "I'm Megan."

106

"And I'm Hubert," he said. "This shouldn't take long, but if you want, you can go see the baby goats. They're cute little things, and they just can't get enough petting."

"I think I will," she said. She'd never seen a baby goat in person before.

She followed a worn rut in the grass around the house and came to a large pen where several goats ran up to the fence when they saw her. She petted the two young ones over the side, laughing at the way they'd bound away only to come straight back. But as cute as they were, she felt drawn to the back of the property.

Megan could hear water ahead and didn't notice the old woman at the edge of the fast-moving creek until she was almost on top of her. She had a bamboo fishing pole in her hand and a hook in the water. Tattoos covered her exposed skin in a web of what looked like scales.

"Hello there," the woman called, apparently hearing Megan approach since she never turned to face her. Her words paused in a lisp, almost as if her mouth wasn't designed for human speech.

"Hello," Megan replied. "I'm sorry if I bothered you."

"It's never a bother to meet one of you," she answered. "There's not much biting this afternoon, and the water has a strange smell to it. Are you enjoying your stay in Nickelville thus far?"

"For the most part," Megan answered, assuming the woman knew who she was already.

A slight movement drew her eye to a tree branch on which perched the biggest eagle Megan had ever seen. It was far larger than the bald eagle she'd seen at the zoo once during a school field trip.

"Don't worry about her," the old woman said. "She's the last of her kind."

"That's sad," Megan murmured. "She's beautiful. I think my grandmother painted a picture of her."

The great bird dipped her head as if thanking her for the compliment.

"Have you been posing for portraits?' the woman asked.

The bird cocked its head as if to say, *what if I did?*

"You naughty thing," the odd woman cackled with glee.

"Megan," she heard her grandfather call. She turned her head to look back toward where she'd left him.

"I have to go," Megan said, turning back. "but it was nice to meet you."

Both the woman and the bird were gone.

By the time she reached her grandfather, she remembered the woman, but could no longer remember what they'd spoken about or what she'd seen. She was still telling him about the baby goats, however, when they stopped at a feed store that oddly enough sold a small selection of backpacks.

Chapter XI: French Fry Fiasco

The faint glow of the coming day lit Bruce's bedroom while the sound of his father humming in the kitchen drew him unwillingly up from some dream he couldn't quite remember. It had been a good one this time, of that he was fairly certain. He tried without success to return to it for several minutes before finally untangling himself from the twisted sheets.

His stomach gave an impatient growl, and he reluctantly surrendered to the aromas that drifted down the hall from the kitchen. Unlike Paul, Ben Grimble was by no stretch of the imagination a musical genius. However, he more than made up for the lack of talent by being such an amazing cook. By the time Bruce reached the kitchen, he wasn't even irritated about being woken up any more.

His father had already placed a cup of coffee on the edge of the counter for him when he crept in, frowning at the bright kitchen lights. He took it with mumbled thanks and took his place at the table.

Mr. Grimble took out two more mugs and filled them with hot water from the brass kettle he'd been heating on the stove. To those he mixed packets of cocoa and set them on the edge of the counter just before Jade and Paul entered and took them to the table.

As energetic as Jade might be during the later hours of the day, she seldom spoke when she first woke. Her shock of two-toned hair stood out from her head in uneven clumps, and she wore one of their father's old concert t-shirts. But the crowning piece of her wardrobe was the latest in a long line of Elmo slippers. The current pair sported bloodshot eyes drawn in with permanent marker, and as usual, Jade had cut off their noses. Bruce never had figured out why the noses seemed to offend her so.

Paul, on the other hand, woke up looking like he'd just combed his hair and brushed his teeth. He wore what Jade referred to as his "old man" flannel pajamas, and he was as alert as his sister was grumpy when he settled happily into his seat.

"Thanks Dad," he said when he had the steaming cup in his hand. "Need help with anything?"

"I've got it," their father answered, ruffling the youngest Grimble's hair affectionately. "Any signs of the Boss-Lady?"

"Something was growling in there," Jade mumbled, waking to the familiar words of their morning ritual. "Better forget the coffee cup and get the funnel."

Bruce's mother staggered into the kitchen a few minutes later. Like her daughter, Mrs. Grimble's hair was a two-toned and tangled snarl, though hers was a mixture of brown and gray. Her eyes narrowed to slits in the bright light.

Mr. Grimble took her by the hand and led her to the table, still humming. When he left her, she too had a steaming cup in her hand.

"Stop that," she said irritably.

"Stop what, oh great love of my life?" he sang tunelessly.

"Stop being so annoyingly happy, " she said, glaring around the table. Although she tried to look stern, her eyes twinkled the way they always did when her husband was home. "That goes for you lot as well. You know the rules, no happiness until after I've had my first cup of coffee."

Now with the whole family seated, Mr. Grimble began to place omelets before them, along with a plate of biscuits and bacon in the center of the table. It was quiet as the first bites were eaten. But as usual, now that she'd fully woken, it was Jade who started the conversation.

"I'm so glad your shift is over for the week," she said around a mouthful of omelet.

"There's no telling how much we'd weigh if he cooked every day," Paul chimed in cheerfully.

Jade tried to kick him under the table and hit Bruce instead.

"Hey," Bruce complained. "You can't kick me for what he said."

"Sorry, Del…," she said before catching herself and shoving another bite into her mouth to cover her slip. As much as she might enjoy teasing Bruce about telling their parents about his problem with Mrs. Jones, she'd never intentionally rat him out.

"Are you going to walk over to Megan's again this morning?" Paul asked after he'd carefully cut his omelet into identical pieces.

"Hmm, let me think," Bruce said absently while taking a drink of his coffee. "Listen to rock talk or see if I can get Megan to tell me more about New York…"

"Megan's been to New York?" Mrs. Grimble asked enviously.

"I think she's lived just about everywhere from the sound of it," Bruce answered. "But you know what's weird?"

"What?" Mr. Grimble asked, sipping his own coffee.

"She says Nickelville is her favorite place so far."

"I didn't realize she was mental," Jade said between bites. "It's always the quiet ones you've got to watch out for. Next thing you know she'll be taking Bruce away to some sort of commune up in the mountains."

"Be nice," Mrs. Grimble said. "Your father chose Nickelville over the other places he could have lived."

112

"That's because you lured him here with your Voodoo magic," Jade said. "Who in their right mind would like Nickelville more than all of the other places she's lived?"

"She's even been to Canada and down into Central America a few times," Bruce added.

"Impressive," Mrs. Grimble said, completely awake now and fondly patting the back of her husband's hand when she found him looking at her. "I wonder what Emelia has been up to that takes her so many places."

"Emelia?" Paul asked.

"Megan's mother," she answered. "We were in the same class together at the Academy."

"Megan never said what her mother does," Bruce said, surprised to find that he'd almost eaten the enormous portion his father had put on his plate.

"Well, she won't be doing much of anything for a while," Mr. Grimble said. "She's recovering quickly, and from what I saw, I doubt Azarich will be able to keep her in bed much longer. But she was close to death when we found her. I have no idea how she drove here in that condition."

"Good," Jade said, happily taking another bite.

"Jade Grimble!" her mother scolded.

"Huh?" Jade looked confused until she realized how she'd sounded. "Oh, I don't want her to be sick, but I like Megan. I hope they stay."

"Me too," Paul said when he'd finished chewing.

Conversation continued, mainly among the Grimble children. The adults watched them while they ate, and Bruce could tell they'd noticed he wasn't reading. Thinking about the book gave him just an instant of panic, but he quickly pushed it from his mind. He'd become much better at not dwelling on things that bothered him since Megan's arrival. His siblings

113

even bothered him less since they'd stopped talking about rocks in favor of their neighbor. In fact, now that they had something in common, they got along pretty well. Maybe he wasn't adopted after all.

Bruce noticed a woman watching him from the upper floor of the McGeehee house as soon as he walked up. She didn't look anything like Megan, and he somehow knew that she didn't like her daughter hanging around with him. No, that wasn't quite right. Something about them being together worried her... something about someone promising something. *How could I know that or that she likes the potted plant on the windowsill?* he wondered, *I haven't even met her.* But the feeling persisted anyway. He was pleased when Megan's face appeared in the next window shortly afterward. She opened it with a little effort and stuck her head out.

"I'll be out in a minute," she yelled.

"Okay," he yelled back with a cheerful wave and then put his hand back down awkwardly when he realized it was still hanging up there.

A short time later, the front door opened, and Megan rushed across the lawn to him. The smile on her face drove away any worries and replaced them with the peaceful agitation he always felt with the arrival of his dark-haired friend. She was wearing new clothes, or at least clothes he hadn't seen her wear before.

"Is that the top of the Baker Hotel?" she asked, pointing toward town.

"I think so," he said. "I know you can see it from our roof and probably your bedroom window if that's the one you were looking out of just now. Ready for another day with Mrs. Jones?" he asked.

"Is anyone ever ready for a day with that woman?" she asked.

"Probably not," he conceded. "Now that I think about it, I don't even think Allison likes her. You look really nice today, by the way. I've never seen you wear your hair down before."

"Thanks," she said shyly. He sensed that she didn't want to talk about the clothing, and he was happy to oblige.

By the time the bus pulled up, Jade had cleared the seat in front of the one she shared with Paul so that the four of them could sit together.

"What are you looking at?" Megan asked Paul, noticing that he'd grown quiet while staring out the window over her shoulder.

"That house is haunted," he answered.

Megan turned to look at a vine-entombed structure that marked the end of Beverly Road. Judging from its size, it had once been a grand mansion, but the flowering white vines made it impossible to be sure.

Their conversation flowed as they rode, easy and animated, flitting from subject to subject as the teens grew to know each other better.

Bruce had completely lost track of where they were when the static barrier crossed his skin. His eyes darted to Megan's, and she gave him a faint nod to show that she'd felt it too.

I wonder what it is, he thought. *Jade and Paul didn't seem to notice. Is it just Megan and I who can feel it? Does this mark the edge of the territory for whatever lives behind that wall? Did it become aware of me when the book fell over? If so, why can she feel it?*

Bruce shook his head, trying to keep his worries from spilling over into his expressions, which Megan had already shown an unsettling ability to read.

But she was leaning toward the window, looking closely at the school when it rose from the trees. She looked scared. When she noticed him looking at her, she shrugged, pulled the strap of her new backpack over her shoulder and followed the sour milk kid up the stone steps.

115

Mr. Danders stood at the door, glaring at the students as they passed. Bruce made a mental note not to break any rules today. It might bring him closer to his family, but Nickelville was a small town, and it was only a matter of time before bad news reached his mother.

"He looks like one of the gargoyles from the roof," Megan whispered in his ear after they'd passed the office.

"If you had to deal with the Terrible Trio and work with Jones, do you think you'd be smiling?" he asked. For some reason there were more than the usual number of eyes following the two of them as they walked through the cafeteria and down the hallway beyond.

"Probably not," Megan admitted. "Speaking of Jones, is it my imagination or is she watching me closer than usual?"

"This doesn't look good," Paul said, coming up behind the two of them. "An awful lot of people are saying your name right now, Megan. What's going on?"

"Not sure," Bruce said absently. "What do you think, Jade?"

"One way to find out," his sister said, grabbing one of the gawkers by the collar of his jacket. "What's going on here?"

"Allison told everyone that the new girl took her mom's watch," the boy squealed, terrified to be in Jade's grasp. "Please don't hurt me!"

"Why does everyone always think I'm going to hurt them?" Jade muttered, turning the kid loose. "Doesn't look like you two are going to have a good day," she added to Megan and Bruce. "At least it's Friday."

"Yeah," Bruce said without enthusiasm while he surveyed the crowd. "All we have to do is get through seven hours of purgatory."

"Just yell if you need me," Jade said, pounding him on the shoulder before heading down the hall toward her own class.

Class was strange, but not as bad as Bruce had feared. He'd expected some sort of confrontation with Mrs. Jones, but nothing like that materialized. Instead, they watched yet another movie. But rather than reading one of her fashion magazines as she normally did, Mrs. Jones did nothing but openly stare at Megan.

His new friend wasn't watching the movie and didn't seem particularly concerned about Mrs. Jones. Instead, she was reading that ghost book she'd picked up at the library. He wasn't much for the supernatural himself, particularly with the strange things going on at the Academy.

Wait a minute, does she think it's a ghost?

He thought over what he'd seen himself. It did make a certain amount of sense, now that he thought about it. But how would that explain the weird change in the weather? Changes like that would have had to take place far up in the atmosphere over the school. Could a ghost really do something like that?

Megan's calm was a sham. She'd read the same passage about ghosts with unfinished business three times, but kept getting distracted by strange surges of feeling that had nothing to do with anyone around her.

In almost perfect intervals of eleven minutes or so, an audible sigh passed through the very floor beneath her feet, bringing with it a psychic breeze like the exhaled breath of a slumbering giant…a giant with a serious addiction to red hot candies.

She glanced up when she felt someone watching her to find Allison looking her new clothing up and down with disdain. Refusing to acknowledge the redhead's dislike, she turned the page and continued to read. After all, it wasn't as if anything she wore would ever meet with the rich girl's approval.

If Bruce could hear or smell any of the odd manifestations, he never acted so in a way that she could recognize. As it was, she doubted she'd ever be able to enjoy the scent of cinnamon again. Her head ached from the strain of keeping out the alien emotions that traveled in on those breaths. It would be easier if they came all at once, but each new intrusion started as a trickle and grew over time, taking a few minutes to build within her before threatening to spill over into her thoughts. The current feelings of grief and loss left her weary but posed no real threat, unlike the anger that had surged through her half an hour ago and made her eyes change.

She took another deep breath and read: *Many believe that the apparitions of those who have been wronged or died before completing some task important to that individual can be helped to move on if one can find the source of their unhappiness. Once that link to the world of the living has been severed, the spirit should, theoretically, move on to the afterlife.*

What if she could find out what the Dark Man wanted? She'd been hiding the fact that she could see him from her mother, but it was only a matter of time before Emelia found out. Would it be possible for them to stay if she could get rid of the ghost?

Then came the heaviness of the Dark Man's presence as he wandered nearby. He hadn't paused to look in the doorway again since that first time, and for that she counted herself lucky. But his presence still flowed over the room occasionally like some sort of invisible organism, detectable only by her increased heart rate and the telltale rustling of papers or the unexplained fall of pencil shavings from the chalk ledge.

When it passed, she found Mrs. Jones watching her intently. Thinking that she might get in trouble for reading during the movie, she reluctantly put the book back inside her desk.

Outside, the bright sun hurt after the darkened classroom. But it also pushed back the shadows and gave her what she craved, a short time in which she could talk to Bruce. The Dark Man seemed less threatening when Bruce was near.

"Enjoy this weather while you can," her friend said. "We don't get much of a fall here. It pretty much goes from super-hot to cold without anything in between."

She needed to let off some steam.

"You're it," she yelled, thumping him on the back and running away. Sure, it was a kid game, but she'd never gotten to play it with a friend before. She suspected he hadn't either.

She almost made it three steps before he caught her.

"No, you're it!" he laughed and sprinted away. By the time she changed directions he was yards away from her, running backwards.

No matter how hard she ran, she couldn't get any closer to him. He slowed, letting her think that she had a chance from time to time before effortlessly dodging away.

At last she gave up and collapsed in the shade of the big trees at the center of the courtyard. He was next to her in an instant.

"That was fun," he said simply.

It took her several minutes to catch her breath. She'd never thought of herself as being in bad shape before, but he wasn't even breathing hard.

There's magic in moments like these, she thought, hardly able to believe she'd been slowly losing herself in that apartment just a little over a week ago. For that matter, she'd been in a similar state only a little while ago in the classroom. And this was only a glimpse into what she'd missed while being hunted for all of those years.

"Are you on the track team or something?" she asked as soon as she was able.

"Oh yeah, that would go over well."

"What do you mean?" she asked. "You're like the fastest kid I've ever seen."

"Until my asthma kicks in."

"You seriously have asthma?" she asked, still winded.

"Since I was born," he said, trying to sound casual, but she still felt how uneasy this subject made him. He didn't want her to think he was weak.

"You could have fooled me," she said.

"Trust me," he said without looking her in the eye, "in a few more weeks I'll barely be able to walk across this courtyard without resting."

"That's terrible," she said, placing her hand on his shoulder. She felt like she could get up now, but liked sitting under the tree with Bruce. "Is there anything I can do?"

"Just remember that I'm still the same person when it happens."

"No problem," she said, leaning back against the tree.

"You could do that?" he asked.

"Do what?" she asked, puzzled.

"Not think I'm weird when it starts."

"It's not like you have any choice about having asthma," she said.

"People here seem to think I do," he said. "The experts say that asthma is becoming more common. But here in Nickelville I seem to be the only one who has it."

120

"That's strange," Megan said, surprised. "I've been in classrooms where half the class had it."

"Cool," he said.

"Not for them, I'm pretty sure," she said.

"I mean it would be cool not to be an outcast," he said.

"Now that I understand," she said. "I get really tired of being the new kid."

"I'll bet," he said, rising to his feet. "Well, you will never be an outcast to me. And if there is ever a situation where you can't help but be an outcast, I'll just be one with you."

"And I will never think you are weird for something you can't help," she added, rising as well.

"Oh, and I'm sorry," he said with a grin.

"For what?"

"For this," he said, tapping her on the shoulder. "You're still it!"

A less stubborn person would have given up on chasing him long before she did. But like she'd thought before, there was magic in moments like these, and the world offered too few to let any go to waste. By the time the bell rang, she could barely walk, and she was happier than she'd ever been.

On the way into the cafeteria, Megan noticed a new poster on the wall. A group of students had gathered around it, talking in excited tones.

"What's that?" she asked.

"Nickelville Jubilee," Bruce answered with a sigh.

"What's a Nickelville Jubilee?"

"Big town festival," he said.

"And you don't like that kind of thing?" she asked, trying to puzzle through this sudden change in mood.

"I love festivals, just not that one."

"Why?" she asked.

"It culminates in a big town race," he said.

"You're like the town champion, right?" she joked, still a little winded from chasing him outside.

"I've never run in it," he answered.

"Why not?" she asked, surprised.

"It's too late in the year. My asthma will kick in by then," he said simply. "Want anything from the line?" he asked, handing her his lunch. "I'm getting some fries."

"No, I'm good," she said, watching him pass Jade and Paul on their way to the table.

"Howdy Neighbor," Jade drawled, sitting down next to Megan.

"Hey Jade," Megan said, still watching Bruce.

"Where's our recently fallen sib going?" Paul asked, sitting down next to Bruce's lunch.

"He wanted French fries," Megan answered, turning to face him. "How are you guys doing?"

"That's weird," Jade said, digging into her food. "He never gets food from the lunch line. Something about wanting to know what he's eating."

"We're fine," Paul answered, "But how are you doing? Is Jones giving you a hard time about the watch?"

"She hasn't said a word," Megan answered. "Which worries me." She dropped the extra sandwich she'd taken from Bruce's lunch in shock as a wet sensation flowed down her spine. To her surprise, her questing hand found the back of her neck dry.

122

The cafeteria erupted into laughter. Megan and the two Grimbles turned to find Bruce standing in the middle of the aisle with water dripping down his face and into the French fries he'd just bought.

"Oh no!" Glenn yelled in mock horror, "Wheezy's gonna drown!"

Jade was out of her seat and halfway across the cafeteria to help her brother before Megan had even processed what was happening. But before she got there, Bruce dumped the hot, though slightly wet container of fries down the front of Glenn's shirt.

Glenn yelped, trying to rid himself of the hot fries and slipped in the water he'd dumped over Bruce's head. He went down so fast that he hit the ground before he even realized he was falling. The laughter that greeted this turn of events dwarfed what had greeted Bruce's misfortune.

A new emotion filled the air before Megan could harden her shields against it. Irritation flowed over her, making the temperature in the cafeteria plunge several degrees. She gasped at the change, and the reek of cinnamon made her gag.

Chuck started to rise, anger cutting through his usual stupid expression, but stopped when he found Jade standing in front of him. The cafeteria went silent just as quickly as it had erupted into laughter.

"Go ahead," she growled. "I dare you."

The air in the room lost its chill, and the Dark Man's sleepy presence returned to the dark recesses from which it had come.

"What is it this time?" Mr. Danders bellowed from the cafeteria door.

Jade continued to stare Chuck down while Glenn made his way back to his feet. Megan and Paul finally reached Bruce's side.

"And to think I almost made it an entire day without having to deal with this kind of thing," the vice principal growled. "Baker, Floyd, and Grimbles. My office. *Now*. Ms. McGeehee, you might as well come too. I understand something of value is missing from your classroom."

123

Chapter XII: Old School Haunting

Millie had to pull up another chair when the four of them followed Glenn and Chuck into the office. Megan was struck again at how big the aquarium was that spanned the front of the counter. But too soon, her thoughts returned to what being in trouble at school meant where her mother was concerned. Emelia wouldn't be nearly as concerned about the fact that she'd gotten into trouble as for the attention she was drawing to herself.

Chuck and Glenn tried to look intimidating for the first few minutes, but soon withered under Jade's glare. By the time Mr. Danders walked stiffly past them and unlocked the door, the two boys were studying the gray carpet that had been laid over the wooden floor beneath.

"Floyd and Baker," the balding man said under his breath, before walking through the door without looking back to see if they followed.

"Great," Bruce whispered as soon as the door closed.

"What?" Megan asked.

"They'll give some bogus story that Danders will probably believe, and then we'll be the ones who get into trouble," Paul answered.

Mr. Bob sauntered into the office and jumped into Megan's lap, where he promptly went to sleep.

"Would you do me a favor and make sure that he stays away from my fish?" Millie asked, glaring at the cat from over her screen. "He has an uncanny ability to get the lid open when I'm not looking."

He purred deeply in response.

When at last the door opened, first Chuck and then Glenn strutted out with matching grins on their faces. Megan's stomach turned, and she deeply wished that she'd gotten to Chuck before Jade had.

"Miss Grimble," Danders called through the open door.

"Tell Mom not to sell my body to science," Jade told Bruce before walking in and closing the door behind herself.

"She's not worried?" Megan whispered.

"Not really," Bruce said. "She does stuff like this fairly often. Mom and Dad will be proud of her for sticking up for me. She didn't actually fight him, so I don't think she'll get suspended."

"What exactly did you kids do?" Millie asked, unable to ignore them any longer.

"Glenn poured a glass of water over my head, Jade threatened to shorten Chuck's life by several decades, and I dumped hot fries down Glenn's shirt," Bruce said, quite satisfied with himself.

"Paul?"

"I, my dear, am hopelessly and wrongfully accused purely for the accident of my ancestry," the youngest Grimble answered.

"Okay, and what did you do?" she asked Megan, trying to hide the smile that was playing at the corners of her mouth.

"Mrs. Jones thinks I stole her watch," Megan answered.

"Did you?"

"Of course not," Megan replied. "What would I want with that gaudy thing?"

"Then I'm sure you don't have anything to worry about."

The door opened again and Jade strolled out. She didn't look the least bit upset.

"Good luck my delinquent sib. Remember, you're representing our family in there. Make us proud."

"Miss Grimble, please stop filling my office with your witty repartee and send your brothers in."

Jade patted Bruce on the head, gave Paul a hearty punch in the shoulder and scratched Mr. Bob under the chin before walking back to class. Bruce stood up and walked into the office, his shoes squishing as he went.

"No!" a man's voice echoed through the office.

Megan jumped, startling Mr. Bob, who dug his claws into her leg before jumping down and walking out the door. She clapped her hand over the spot and thought she might be bleeding.

"Are you okay?" Millie asked, looking puzzled. "I wonder what spooked him this time."

"No! They can't be," a voice sobbed. No one else in the office reacted. The skin across her arms felt as if it had shrunk several sizes, drawing the downy hairs outward. She felt the Dark Man standing just behind her, leaning so close that she'd have been able to feel his breath on her neck if he'd still needed to breathe.

The plumbing rattled beneath the floor when someone flushed, and Megan nearly jumped out of her seat. Several lights burned out at once.

Trying to calm herself, Megan held her head in her hands and tried to center herself. It was difficult to do while listening to a man no one else could hear sobbing nearby.

At last the door opened, and the Grimble boys stepped out. Bruce didn't look very happy, but he didn't look terribly upset either. He squeezed her shoulder as he passed, and it made her feel much better.

"Just a warning," Paul whispered.

"Miss McGeehee," Danders called. It was a definite improvement over the way Mrs. Jones said it.

126

Her knees didn't want to hold her weight. She put her hand on the back of the chair where Bruce had been sitting a few minutes earlier to steady herself.

"...when it is complete, I will ask you to be my bride," the disembodied voice whispered in her ear.

"I don't have all day, Miss McGeehee." Mr. Danders called.

The dark wood paneling of Mr. Danders's office absorbed most of the light from the antique light fixture overhead. Thick drapes covered what was likely another of the stained-glass windows that surrounded the strange school.

Much of the office outside looked as if it had stopped changing sometime back during the sixties, but this room felt as if it had given up a century before that. In spite of the assistant principal's urgings for her to hurry, he seemed uninterested in talking now, choosing to read a memo instead.

So, she let her eyes drift over the contents of the bookcases which held titles ranging from educational law to the westerns her grandfather loved. An old manual typewriter stood on a small table in the corner and of course, several diplomas hung on the wall.

It was ordered and neat, without personal pictures or the sort of debris that normally spread from home to the workplace. Megan knew from the surface of his thoughts that even though it might look staged and artificial to some, this room did in fact reflect this man's inner self. And although he might not sleep there, the Academy was indeed his home.

"I understand that there have been some things missing since you started attending the Academy," he said at last without looking up.

"I'm not sure about anything other than Mrs. Jones's watch," Megan said, glad that he hadn't asked her to sit where she would have felt confined after waiting out in the main office. She needed to keep calm and

127

resist the urge to yell over sounds that only she could hear. Since she didn't know what to do with her hands, she put them behind her back and made them into fists so tight that they'd be sore the next day.

"So, you know about the watch?" he asked, at last looking up at her.

"Everyone knows about the watch. Allison told the whole school I stole it."

"Did she, now?" This seemed to surprise him. "What do you think?"

"I wish she'd searched me in the courtyard, so she'd know I didn't have it. That would have been the smart thing to do," Megah added.

"Are you saying that you are smarter than your teacher?" Mr. Danders asked, laying down the memo and folding his hands over it. His voice held an edge that put Megan on guard, as if he was trying to trap her into saying something that would get her into trouble.

The smell of cinnamon returned.

"No," Megan answered in a measured voice, choosing her words carefully as the smell overwhelmed her, "I would never say something like that. She's been to college and done all of the certification stuff it takes to be a teacher. I'm just a kid."

"Of course," he said, raising one end of his bushy unibrow, apparently finding something ironic in what she'd said. "Since there is nothing more than speculation at this point, I'm going to let you return to your class."

"Thank you," she said, turning to flee.

"I'm not saying that you did or did not take it," he added. "I'm just not going to punish you until I find out for sure."

Megan didn't know how to respond to something like that. She was angry and scared, and she didn't know how much longer she could keep from frying everything in the office. She took another step toward the door.

128

"Remember, Miss McGeehee," he said in a low voice that didn't carry out of his office, "I'll be watching you closely. If you step an inch out of line, I'll know."

How many times had she been in exactly this situation? How many times had everyone assumed she was a thief just because she was new and poor? She'd been foolish to think that a new outfit and backpack would change anything. It was all she could do to keep the angry tension from showing in her shoulders as she gently closed the door. She wanted to slam it. She wanted to hear the glass in the door shatter and cut gouges in the ugly carpet as it fell, but she walked away and didn't let anything show on the outside. Things like that would make them have to move away sooner, and in spite of this, she still didn't want to leave.

The foyer had emptied by the time Megan left the office. Beyond that, only one class remained in the cafeteria. Mr. Green whistled happily while he swept the floor, and she managed to smile at him even though dark thoughts filled her mind.

As soon as she entered the hallway that led to the classrooms, she noticed that the lockers had disappeared. Light no longer flowed in from the garish windows, and the electric light fixtures had been replaced with glass globes that each held a single finger of flame, casting flickering shadows across everything.

She'd thought the empty halls had been quiet before. Now she knew better. The hum of the electric lights, the murmur of children's voices, and all of the other sounds were absent in what she suspected to be a much older version of the school.

Through the roar of total silence, a faint sound intruded: a rhythmic beat that did nothing to steady her trembling hands.

A dark figure appeared at the opposite end of the hall, dressed in the same clothing as before. In his arms he carried a woman who wore a pale green dress, her head cradled against his chest. Her eyes were closed and one arm hung limp.

Megan wanted to believe that the woman with the long black hair and olive skin only slept, but she knew better. Her bare feet dangled above the floor as he walked.

"What do you want from me?" Megan asked in a quavering voice.

He said nothing, but continued to come closer, his boots echoing off of the bare walls.

"Stop," she ordered, knowing even as she did so that her words had no power here. This was *his* place. Megan was an intruder, and no one would be coming to save her.

When he was only a few feet away, he stopped.

The woman barely filled his arms. The long black hair, the angles of her face, and even the shape of her hands shouted at Megan that she should know her identity.

Then bells began to ring, louder than she had ever heard them. Unlike the usual one, there were at least two, and one of them must be huge to sing so deep. She clapped her hands over her ears and fell to her knees.

With each thundering reverberation it felt as if the protections that she and her mother had woven around her gave just a little bit, leaving small fissures in its wake. How long would she be able to withstand this before her mind was laid bare?

She became aware of two points of pressure just below her collar bones as the real world attempted to reassert itself over this one. Something soft nuzzled her jaw.

She opened her eyes to find herself bathed in the colored light of the window next to her. Nothing had ever seemed so beautiful. She wrapped her arms around Mr. Bob and stood up with him, holding him tight as if he were a talisman to ward off evil. It took her a while to stop trembling, but judging from how hard the cat purred, he didn't mind at all.

"I can't believe Glenn didn't even get into trouble," Bruce fumed while he and Megan walked out to the bus. He was angry enough that he didn't notice how quiet and withdrawn his friend had become.

"I can't believe *we* didn't get into any trouble," Jade said from behind them. Paul burst from the front doors and hurried to catch up.

"Was that my brother I saw dumping fries all over Glenn Floyd?" Paul asked in reverence, ruffling Bruce's hair as he passed. "Am I to believe, at long last, that my delinquent older sib has not only developed a taste for the forbidden fruit of our school's activities, but developed a backbone too?"

"Stop talking like that," Bruce complained, running his fingers through his hair to straighten it, "You sound like one of those Shakespeare in the Park people."

"Dear bro, mine heart breaketh to be the source of thine angst," Paul replied, flourishing an imaginary hat and bowing.

"Ladies first," Bruce said, moving out of the way and ignoring Paul.

"Then you and your brother should have been first to get on," Chuck taunted from further back.

"Glenn, Glenn, Glenn," Jade said, shaking her head sadly. "I've told you time and time again that it's against school policy to bring your pet to school," she said, nodding toward Chuck.

On the bus, the four sat together with Megan and Bruce once again in front of Jade and Paul. The air was filled with an energy that the four had never felt before. Megan noticed that she could see the top of the Baker Hotel over the tops of the trees.

131

"Hey Megan," Paul said, when almost everyone else had gone and they neared Beverly Road. "Why don't you come over to our place tomorrow? We can go into the woods."

"Yeah," Bruce said. "It would be great!"

"It'll be nice to have another girl around for a change," Jade said.

"Aside from Mom, we've never had one there before." Bruce said innocently.

Jade laughed even as she hit him so hard that he nearly fell into the aisle. She turned to Paul. "I take it back, maybe he wasn't switched at birth."

So even though Megan had no real desire to explore the woods near their house, she agreed eagerly. After all, what could possibly go wrong?

Chapter XIII: Jubilant Persuasion

Megan could no longer remember why she'd thought it would be a good idea to follow the Grimbles into the woods. Neither could she recall how she'd become separated from her friends.

She'd heard once that it was better to hug a tree and stay in one place than to chance wandering further away from help. But these weren't the sort of trees she'd have wanted to hug, even if she could find one that her arms could fit around.

She'd never seen so much green. From the moss-covered boulders that littered the sloping ground in tumbled heaps to the gnarled and twisted trees that spread their limbs in chaotic undulations, the world upon which she gazed had been painted by an artist with only the shades of green in her pallet.

She tripped on something hidden within the mossy undergrowth and came down hard on her knee. She was glad that she'd worn her oldest clothes, although she couldn't remember choosing to do so. When she knelt next to a small stream, she wasn't surprised to see that her eyes had changed.

Mist began to collect in the low places between the rocks. The sun would soon set, and she had no desire to spend the night there. The oddly shaped trees already teased her imagination in the light of day. What if they became more than imagination when the shadows spread and consumed everything?

"Bruce?" Megan called again, but the mist-shrouded forest swallowed her pleading voice, leaving nothing but the faintest echo.

She stretched out the extra senses that she and her mother possessed, knowing even as she did that Bruce was beyond her reach in a way that had nothing to do with distance. Below her, in the depths of the valley, something stirred in response to her questing thoughts.

Taking an involuntary step back toward the protective embrace of the trees, she discovered that the forest had disappeared. To either side, brambles barred her way, leaving only the way down clear. Suspecting that she was being herded like prey, she nevertheless began to descend. Boulders gave way to stone terraces and eventually ended in a large circular depression similar to the ruin of an overgrown amphitheater.

The mist climbed her body as she descended, enfolding first knees, thighs and hips. It parted before her and flowed seamlessly back into place, leaving no sign of her passage.

When the mist reached her shoulders, the path dropped away and left her teetering with arms flailing over a hidden drop-off. Unable to stop her forward momentum, she fell several inches until her toes found a stone step.

"Bruce," she called again, "Jade... Paul...I'm lost!"

No one answered.

The steps weren't level or evenly spaced, making the placement of each foot treacherous. She closed her eyes and opened her mind to what lay below.

All about her, the fog teased her senses, seeming to draw her eye one direction then another. With a shaky breath, she allowed herself to be swallowed by the mist.

As the meaningless blur of vision faded from her inner eye, she became aware of her surroundings and knew the last step before the ball of her foot touched it. To each side she sensed stone monoliths rising like the trunks of ancient trees toward the hidden sky above. Both bore intricate runes and overlapping circular patterns. The strangely familiar shapes caressed the questing tips of her fingers and grew warm at her touch.

Energy flowed up from the earth at her feet, passing through the standing stones and burning away her fear.

Taking three bold steps forward, she spread her hands upward and with a surge of elation, pushed outward with her mind. The mist grudgingly released its hold on the valley and revealed that the rune-carved monuments were only two of many that encircled the valley floor.

She knew the Dark Man stood before her even before she opened her eyes. As before, he seemed no less substantial than the rest of her surroundings. His presence burned into her senses like the dangerous appeal of roaring flames. Behind him, in the center of the circle, rose a stone cross.

"What promise was broken?" she asked, refusing to look anywhere but directly into the green eyes that regarded her with such interest.

He opened his mouth. She waited, gripped by dreadful curiosity. She concentrated hard on what might prove the key to giving him what he wanted and sending him on his way. Her hands clenched at her sides.

"Megan!"

She wrenched her head toward the sound of her name. Light blinded her to her surroundings, and her head spun with the sudden movement. Panicked, she lashed out instinctively with her mind, thinking that he'd somehow followed her.

Emelia gasped, then somehow shunted the brunt of her daughter's attack until it died away on its own.

Megan relaxed by degrees, settling fully into reality and leaving the vivid dream behind. The book she'd been reading before she fell asleep dug into the hollow beneath her arm. She hurriedly turned her thoughts from it.

"Bad dream?" her mother asked.

136

"Yeah," Megan answered, sensing her mother's questing presence overlapping the edges of her thoughts. She yawned and stretched, breaking the physical contact before Emelia found a reason to take them away from Nickelville.

"What was the dream about?" her mother asked as she ran her fingertips across Megan's forehead.

"I was lost in the woods," Megan answered, sticking as close to the truth as possible and allowing images of mist shrouded trees to drift across the surface of her thoughts.

"It was just a dream," Emelia said at last, "Come down soon, breakfast is ready. And before you get the idea to try and slide down the banister, don't. I bruised my backside on that knob at the end more times than I could count, and I never once got off before I hit it."

Megan waited until her mother's footsteps descended the stairs before she pulled the book from under her new comforter. She needed to figure out what the ghost wanted so she could make him go away. As it was, the strain of blocking him out at school and hiding her thoughts from her mother at home had begun to eat away at her, much like the apartment had at the end of her time there. But if she could just solve the problem of the ghost, life in Nickelville would be perfect, or at least as good as it could be with Mrs. Jones as her teacher. At least until they had to leave. But that was a thought with which she still couldn't come to terms.

Apparently, Grandpa thought Megan needed fattening up, judging from the full cast-iron skillet of scrambled eggs he'd divided onto three plates. His short white hair was ruffled, and he wore an unflattering orange shirt that was almost as bright as his smile.

Emelia watched her suspiciously.

"Wow," Megan said in her happiest tone while eying the eggs. "Are we having company? There's no way the three of us could possibly eat that much."

"Good morning Sunshine," Azarich said, reaching over with his free arm to give her a hug. "You're a growing girl, your mother needs to regain her strength, and I am a hungry old man this morning."

"Well, it smells incredible," Megan said, snatching a piece of bacon from the plate.

"As good as those apple pies at school?" he asked.

"What pies?" Emelia asked, reacting so violently that she sloshed some of her coffee onto the table.

"Tom Harris said she'd mentioned smelling apple pie the day she started school when I called to see how she was doing. His old nose didn't catch it though."

"You checked up on me?" Megan asked, both touched by his concern and annoyed by his lack of confidence in her.

"You didn't tell me you were smelling cinnamon," Emelia snapped angrily.

"What's wrong, Mom?" Megan asked, trying to seem surprised by the outburst.

"I knew this would happen," Emelia answered, shaking her head angrily.

"Should I not eat the apple pie at the Academy?" Megan asked, hating the way it felt to lie to her mother after all that they'd been through together. "It looked really good, and I don't think anyone got sick from it."

Emelia slumped back into her chair, and Grandpa gently placed his hand over hers.

"Have you seen or heard anything strange at the Academy?" Emelia persisted, pulling her hand away from her father.

"Mom," she said reassuringly. "I think just about everything in Nickelville is strange. I mean, have you ever taken a close look at that big hotel in the middle of town?"

The happiness that had animated her grandfather's face earlier was gone and her mother's eyes looked wary. They finished their meal in silence.

"Okay," Megan said when she'd finished, trying to sound baffled. "Since you guys clearly aren't going to tell me what that was all about, I guess I'll go get ready for my hike in the woods with the Grimbles."

"Are you sure you can trust them?" Emelia asked.

"Of course, she can," Grandpa said, trying to smooth things over. "I've watched those kids grow up since they built their house. You probably remember their mother, Doreen. She was the one who was always trying to get you to write for the school newspaper."

"Hmm..." was Emelia's only reply.

"She runs the *Nickelville Tribune* now," he added.

"Good for her," Emelia replied irritably, getting up to pour another cup of coffee.

Megan took the opportunity to hug her mom so hard that the sour look softened if only briefly.

"Be careful, and don't stray too far," Emelia said, echoing the words of Megan's childhood, but leaving the last sentence unspoken. *You never know when the Huntsmen will find us, and we'll have to run again.*

"I'll be fine, Mom... more than fine. I've never had friends as cool as these guys." *For that matter, I've never had friends before at all.*

She gave her grandfather a quick kiss on the cheek and ran up the stairs to get ready.

Why cinnamon? she wondered, *and what about that dream? Can he reach me here all the way from the school? I don't know if I'm going to be*

139

able to separate the real world from when I sleep if he can. But we have to
stay. I can't leave all of this behind and go back to what it was like before.

Megan felt awkward walking next door even though she'd driven by
the Grimble home many times. The lines and angles of its modern design
drew her eyes from one aspect to another as she walked across the well-
manicured lawn to the front door. The windows that flanked the entrance
gave her a clear view through the open layout of the house all the way to
the back yard.

She hoped Mr. and Mrs. Grimble liked her. Out of habit, she thought
about what she was wearing, and reminded herself to do nothing that could
make them think she was trying to steal anything. Before she reached the
door, she felt Bruce become aware of her. Seconds later, he opened the
front door before she had a chance to ring the doorbell.

"Cool place," Megan said, trying not to show how uncomfortable she
felt. For just a second, the years on the run almost made her turn around
and go back home. How could she trust him so completely after knowing
him for such a short time? In response, the presence at the back of her
mind whispered, and although Megan couldn't quite make out the words,
any doubts she might have had about the loyalty of the awkward boy
standing before her faded with them from her mind.

The Grimble home could have come straight from the pages of a
home improvement magazine. Megan saw nothing in the whole house that
looked as old as she was. White leather covered the living room furniture,
and what she saw of the kitchen would have made some chefs envious.

"Welcome to our humble abode," Paul yelled from somewhere
deeper in the house.

Bruce led her down the hall and into a small, but tidy office where an energetic woman was digging through a desk drawer and muttering about missing scissors and inconsiderate husbands. Were it not for the prominent streaks of gray that ran through her shoulder length hair, it would have been a perfect match in color to Bruce's.

"Mom, this is Megan McGeehee," Bruce said.

"Oh, hello Megan," the woman said, looking up from the drawer.

Megan knew that this woman and her mother had graduated from the Academy together, but her mother didn't have a bit of gray in her hair and looked ten or fifteen years younger.

"Hello, Mrs. Grimble," Megan responded, wanting this woman to like her.

When the woman smiled, the wealth of laugh lines on her face told a story far different than Emelia's. Her eyes held the promise of laughter, and in that instant she looked a decade younger than Megan's mother.

"I've been looking forward to meeting you," Mrs. Grimble said, "and there's no need to call me Mrs. Grimble. I'm Dora, and I went to school with your mother."

"Okay Dora," Megan said. "Grandpa told me that you wanted Mom to work on the school newspaper."

"She never did though," Mrs. Grimble said with a regretful sigh. "She was probably the best writer in the school, but the only reason I knew it was because I found one of her papers in the hall. Does she still write?"

"Not that I know of," Megan said, "but Grandpa has a short story framed on the wall that she had published before I was born."

"Really? I wonder if she'd let me read it."

"I'll ask her," Megan replied politely while Bruce dragged her off in the other direction. "It was nice meeting you, Mrs. Grimble... I mean Dora."

141

"Where are you guys going today?" Mrs. Grimble called after them.

"We're going to the woods," Bruce answered.

"Be careful, and don't go too far," Dora said, echoing Emelia's warning.

"Stay away from Old Man Biggerstaff, be back before dinner." Bruce mouthed in perfect unison with his mother's fading voice as he led Megan back toward his room.

"And don't do anything that Jade or Paul try to talk you into!" Paul added from somewhere deeper in the house.

Although the level of organized cleanliness didn't particularly surprise Megan, she hadn't expected it. She probably could have bounced a quarter off of his bed without leaving a mark like she'd once seen in an old movie.

The open page on his computer suggested that he'd been surfing when he felt her, and she wondered if he could feel her presence the way she did his. She made sure she stayed as far from his electronics as she could. Several bookcases lined the walls, each filled to capacity with novels.

"Okay," she said. "I'm starting to feel like a slob."

"I just like to know where everything is," he said defensively. "Besides, if you had to live with Jade, you'd want a little order in your life too."

"I resemble that remark," his sister said from the doorway. "Hey Megan."

"Hi," Megan replied without looking up from his books. "No way! They're alphabetized!"

"Scares me too," Jade said, leaning close and dropping her voice to a whisper that she knew Bruce could hear, "If you ever want to make him

142

mad, just sneak in here and move some of them. It takes him hours to get everything back in order."

"So, you admit it!" he yelled and threw a pillow at his sister.

"Stop giving away trade secrets," Paul said, finally making an appearance. "We'd better get going if we're going to get back in time for dinner. I packed four lunches and bottles of Gatorade in my backpack. I don't mind carrying it, but someone else will have to take over if I find something big that's worth keeping before lunch."

"I can live with that," Jade said. "I've got the geological map. It looks like there are some promising formations out past Miller's Pond, but we already know nothing ever matches what we actually find in Guarded Wood." She winked at Paul and held her finger to her lips to signal silence. "We think there's a cave out there," she whispered.

Megan had never seen a real cave and hoped they were right. Even Bruce perked up at the idea.

The four slipped out the back door, but not before Bruce put the pillow he'd thrown back on the bed. The backyard was neat and orderly, though not to the level of Bruce's bedroom. With Paul in the lead, they took a path that led from the back of their yard.

First, they came to one of the huge trees that surrounded the town, and Megan marveled again at the size of the thing. She doubted that the four of them would have been able to link hands and reach around the trunk, yet the Grimbles passed beneath it without an upward glance. Then they ran as fast as they could to the back of the Grimble property, laughing as they went. Just before they entered the tree line, she noticed the remnants of an old barbed wire fence. It had long since been cut and the posts looked rotten.

"Guys," Megan said, looking worried, "People don't usually put up fences like that unless they want to keep something in or out. I don't suppose you'd happen to know which?" Bruce jumped when she said this, and she had a fleeting flash of the wall in the courtyard.

"The previous owner used to have cattle," Jade answered.

"Oh," Megan replied, trying to figure out if the image had come from Bruce.

"Old Man Biggerstaff is the one we have to worry about," advised Jade. "He's an old hermit that lives out in the woods. We've never seen him, but everyone who has says he's old, creepy and possibly eats kids."

"No one ever says that," Bruce said, glaring at his sister.

"Come on," Jade complained, "How often do I get a chance to mess with someone who hasn't lived in this town their whole life?"

Tall grass gave way to a strand of saplings where the woods had begun to reclaim the field. Behind the saplings, older trees blocked most of the sun from the woodland floor and stunted the grass below. Jade led them to a path that twisted and turned through the sparse undergrowth.

"You guys know how to get out of here, right?" Megan asked when she completely lost all sense of direction. Flashes of her dream kept intruding on her thoughts as she followed them. And even though her rational mind understood she was perfectly safe with Bruce and his siblings, too much of her life had been anything but rational.

"Sure," Bruce assured her. "I know it well enough to get back from here, and they know Guarded Wood better than I ever will."

"We haven't been lost in years," Paul said, "It used to mess me up a little at first since you can't get a GPS tracker to work in here, and even compass readings are unreliable."

"Why is that?" Megan asked.

"There probably aren't enough cell towers around for my phone to triangulate, and this heavy cover makes it hard to pick up satellites with a tracker. As for the compass, I suspect there might be a big iron deposit out here somewhere."

"The Academy has something weird going on too," Bruce added. "You can't get a cell signal unless you're right by a window. The school has tried to install Wi-Fi several times without any luck."

"Paul's a scout," Jade added, returning to Megan's original concern. "He actually teaches classes on how to use a map and compass. We're not going to get lost."

"And why is it called Guarded Wood?" Megan asked, finding that asking questions seemed to help with her fear.

"You know," Paul said, pausing. "I've never even thought about that. I'll ask my scoutmaster the next time I see him. He's something of a local history buff."

His words failed to comfort Megan as they moved deeper into the woods. A wrongness she couldn't identify permeated these trees. It lacked the sinister intent of her dream, but there was something spread over this place like a shroud, hiding what really lay beneath. It wasn't like the woods near the school where she could sense the presence of hidden magic all around her. Here it felt like the woods in which they walked were nothing more than an illusion. Then a spot in the trail caught her eye, almost as if it were actively trying to avoid her gaze. She paused, squinting with the effort of trying to see beyond.

Movement drew her eye to the other side of the path. She expected some cute woodland creature like a squirrel or mouse since she hadn't heard the passing of anything large. What she found looked like a full-grown wolf. But even she, a city girl, knew that wolves were supposed to be all but extinct in this part of the country. This rude specimen obviously lacked the decency to die off with its kin.

"Bruce," she whispered.

He turned, followed her gaze and smiled.

"Hey Fang," he said, crossing the path to scratch it between the ears before kneeling down and giving the beast a hug.

"Is that a wolf?" Megan asked, still in a whisper.

"Wolf-dog hybrid," Jade answered, coming back down the path to see what was holding them up. She petted him affectionately and motioned for Megan to join her.

The hackles along the back of the creature's neck rose, and he bared his teeth in a deep growl.

"Maybe I shouldn't," Megan said, pulling her hand back quickly and edging away.

"That's weird," Paul said. "He's never done that before. Maybe it's because he doesn't know you. Just give him some time."

"We found him hurt about three years ago," Jade said. "The vet told us that he was a mix of dog and wolf."

"Cool," Megan said, not liking the way he watched her. *Oh my,* she thought while the Grimbles continued to greet the beast, *what enormous teeth and bad breath you have!*

Jade and Paul led the way while Megan and Bruce brought up the rear with Fang trailing last. She didn't like having the thing where she couldn't see it, and the longer they walked, the more she thought she could feel something behind the wolf looking out of its eyes at her. Furthermore, some of his movements looked almost human.

"What's that?" she asked nervously, distracted from Fang by a faint rumble ahead.

"Just the creek," Jade said. "We'll stop there and rest."

The woods had grown dense as they moved deeper. The trees here towered over them, interlocking their branches overhead and blocking out all but occasional glimpses of the sky. She felt oddly free, safe within the

146

towering trees that sheltered her within their ancient awareness. Yet she also felt like something else was closing in around her and closing her off from the world she knew.

"You've never been in the woods before, have you?" Bruce asked quietly.

"Not like these," she answered. "Even the deepest parts of Central Park don't feel like this."

"We come down here every chance we get," Paul assured her. "This is still practically our back-yard as far as we're concerned."

The trees ahead ended at a ravine through which flowed the stream she'd heard earlier. It made her remember the old woman with the bamboo fishing pole, which in turn made her almost remember something else as well.

A rope bridge spanned the thirty or so feet to the other side. Megan looked to Bruce for an explanation of the bridge's presence, but left the question unspoken when she saw the bulge of his jaw muscles.

"What's wrong with him?" Megan asked Jade, keeping her voice low enough to be lost in the roar of the creek below.

"He's scared of water," she answered.

Megan nodded, remembering the way Chuck and Glenn often teased him about drowning.

"My troop built that," Paul said, motioning toward the bridge. "It was a fun project even if it nearly bankrupted my parents. For some reason it took a lot more in materials than we estimated at first."

She crept forward and peered below. Although the water looked no more than a foot deep, it ran through a deep channel that cut through the white rock below. The bushes and trees that grew from the sides had been swept back in the direction of the current.

147

"It must flood sometimes," she said, finding it hard to believe that such a small creek could make such a deep cut through the rock.

Bruce shuddered.

"Want to see some fossils?" Paul asked.

"Oh no, it begins," Bruce groaned. In spite of his words, he looked happy to move away from the subject of the water.

"You mean like dinosaurs?" Megan asked.

"Kind of," Bruce answered. "This part of the country was underwater when the dinosaurs were around, but the stuff here was alive at the same time."

Jade and Paul looked back at Bruce, surprised.

"What?" he asked. "Did you really think I could live with the two of you and not pick it up?"

"Are you thinking what I'm thinking?" Paul asked, dropping the backpack on the ground.

"It must be an alien imposter," Jade yelled. "I'll hold him down while you pull his mask off!" She took off after Bruce with Paul close behind.

"Not this time!" Bruce yelled back. He spun on his heel and took off through the trees, leaving Megan laughing so hard that she had to hold onto a tree to keep from falling down.

The three of them darted around tree stumps and jumped over rotten logs. Bruce taunted them the whole time, letting them come within inches of him before leaving them behind. Fang barked happily now that Megan wasn't trying to touch him, wagging his tail and turning his body so that the children stayed in front of him. When Jade and Paul finally gave up and collapsed onto the ground beside Megan, Bruce walked up with his hands in the pockets of his jeans, grinning.

"I always forget how fast you can run," Jade panted. She looked over at Megan. "Hard to believe he's asthmatic, isn't it?"

148

"Yeah," Megan agreed. "I think he should run at the Jubilee."

Jade and Paul stared at her as if the meaning of her words had alluded them just as effectively as their brother had done moments earlier. Then they turned to look at Bruce, who was no longer smiling.

"It's too late in the year," Bruce said, suddenly sour, "I won't be able to run by then."

They continued to stare at him. Even Fang seemed to be encouraging him.

"It will start any day now," Bruce continued, averting his eyes and running his fingers through Fang's thick fur.

"But it comes on later every year," Paul said. "You were already starting to miss school by this time last year."

"And you have to admit," Jade added, "it would be the perfect way to kick dirt in Glenn's beaky little face."

"Come on Bruce, what do you say?" asked Megan.

Bruce looked at each of the three eager faces, frowned even deeper and walked away toward the ravine with Fang in step beside him.

By the time they caught up to him, he was standing on the top of a white boulder near the ravine.

"So, what exactly are we looking for here?" he asked, studying the rocks where he stood as Paul climbed up beside him. "I know I've heard you two talking about inocentimus or something like that in the creek."

"Inoceramid oysters," Paul answered without thinking.

"Don't change the subject," Jade said just loud enough to be heard above the water.

"Is that one there?" Bruce asked, pointing at a big swirl that stood out on the surface of the boulder he was standing on.

149

"Bruce," Paul said, ignoring a rock for the first time in his life and putting his hand on his brother's shoulder. Something in his voice demanded that his brother answer.

"Don't you think I want to?" Bruce asked at last. "Haven't you ever wondered why I don't go to the Jubilee with you guys anymore?"

"What do you mean?" Jade asked, confused.

"When was the last time I went with the family?" he asked.

"Didn't he go last year?" Paul asked Jade, sounding unsure.

"No, he didn't," she said quietly, understanding at last. "He said he didn't feel very well and that he wanted to stay home and rest. The last time I can remember him going was the first year that Glenn ran."

Bruce nodded.

"Maybe this year will be different," Megan pleaded. "You said it yourself. You've never made it this far into the year without getting sick. Will you run if you're still okay?"

"Sure," Bruce said, "but don't get your hopes up. Two weeks is a long time when you're talking about my asthma in the fall. One day I can be like this, and then I can spend the next week in the hospital."

Paul grabbed him in a bear hug, and Jade climbed up to hug them both. Megan watched them, wondering what it would have been like to be a part of a family like the Grimbles.

"Are you guys going to tell me what that thing is or not?" Bruce demanded when they finally let him go.

"Good eye," Paul said, looking down at where Bruce was pointing. "That's an Inoceramid oyster. And you're right, they did die out with the dinosaurs. It's not a bad specimen either, although Jade and I found one a few months ago that was about five feet across. I've found a couple of fossilized pearls from them too," he added.

"Pearls?" Bruce asked, looking up.

"Yeah," Jade said. "They're perfectly round black rocks. They're not really worth anything, but they're still kind of cool."

"I don't think I've ever seen a fossil that wasn't in an exhibit at a museum," Megan said, kneeling down to run her fingers over the swirls in the rock.

"Sure, you have," Bruce said. "Have you ever been to a playground that had gravel under the equipment?"

"Yeah," she said, "but what does that have to do with anything?"

"Did you ever notice those rocks that are cupped like little shells?" he asked.

"Yeah," she answered again, seeing where this was going.

"Those were fossils," Bruce said.

"You're kidding," Megan exclaimed.

"There may be hope for him yet," Jade said, slapping Bruce hard enough on the back to make him lose his balance and nearly fall off of the boulder into the ravine.

"Those are called *exogyra*," Paul added, "or Devil's Toenails."

"Speaking of toenails, Bruce," Jade said, "When are you going to start training for the race?"

"What do toenails have to do with the race?" Bruce asked, glancing at Megan. She pretended not to notice how badly the near-fall had frightened him.

"Nothing, but that's what we really wanted to talk about, so it sounded like a good opportunity to change the subject," Paul answered.

Bruce shrugged.

"Why not start training now?" she asked.

"What about the cave?" Bruce asked.

"If we're being completely honest, I've always thought caves were seriously creepy," Paul admitted.

151

"The cave's not going anywhere," Jade said. "Besides, I'm not positive that it's really there or that we could find it if it is. I just know that the surveys said that there was a good possibility of caves in the area."

"And given the geology of the area, it might be dangerous to go too far into one. You know, cave-ins," Paul added, "Besides, we're too worn out from trying to catch you to hike for the next several hours. Let's eat lunch and then head back."

So, the four of them shared their lunch with a wolf in the woods while Jade planned how to best train Bruce, and Megan tried to throw off the sense that she was being watched.

Chapter XIV: Glenn's Surprise

"I'm going to go turn this library book back in," Megan said, breaking off from the Grimbles when they arrived at the Academy that Monday morning. "I'll catch up with you in class, Bruce."

"Okay," he winced, limping along in the wake of his sister's brutal training regimen.

She reached for the surprisingly cold handle of the library doors. To her surprise, only a rough pencil outline marked where the elaborate carvings would eventually reside. But rather than the three keys that the angel held in Megan's time, it held a torch instead.

Then the doors were gone altogether, and she looked into a cavernous space she scarcely recognized. The chatter of the students behind her grew faint, and the sounds of hammering and sawing filled her ears. She smelled fresh sawdust and the coming of rain.

Light poured in through empty openings where the garish window glass had yet to be fitted, as well as down through the exposed rafters and joists that spanned the open sky above.

She clutched the ghost book to her chest, so taken by the realism of the vision that it actually felt like she was in the past.

A red-headed craftsman stood in the middle of what would eventually be the library. He wore a simple gray cap and blouse-like shirt with a bandana tied around his neck. Without the context of having just been in the present, Megan would have thought he was real.

"What are you gawking at, Seamus?" asked a man in similar dress, but sporting a vest and missing the bandana who walked into the open carrying some sort of ax-like tool.

"Nothin," Seamus answered, quickly looking down. "Looks like we're done with the roof supports."

"Tis' witchcraft," the newcomer said, crossing himself when he looked above. "Tain't no other explanation."

"We get paid to work," Seamus chided. "Not to stir up trouble. Don't be gettin' it into yer head to start accusin' good folk of bein' in league with the cloven hoofed one, Friedrich."

"Tain't natural!" Friedrich continued. "No man could lift them timbers into place by himself."

"Hush," Seamus scolded. "Didn't yer mam teach ya 'bout the gruagach?"

"Next ye'll be wanton to leave a saucer of milk out for the wee beasties," Friedrich taunted.

"I jus' might, mind ye," Seamus whispered. "Now shut yer mouth afore ye offend it an bring ill fortune down on us all. At this rate we'll be done ere the spring rains. Then ye be free to say and do as pleases ya."

"Easy to say now with his coin in yer purse," Friedrich spat, "but ye'll be singin a diff'rent tune when ye stand afore the gates accused o' witchcraft."

"I done nothin but ply me hammer and me adze," Seamus argued. "Me soul is safe. The good Lord won't hold it 'gainst me for taken honest coin for honest work. If'n he has a problem wit' what happens in this place under the light of the moon, he'll take it upon himself to pass judgement on them that does it. So you just leave the Reverend to himself and them three sisters as well. As for me, I'll be taking yer advice and leavin some milk

154

for the gruagach so we don't have to lift anything bigger than a bucket to the roof!"

Megan closed her eyes, reached out with her senses and anchored herself in the real world. When she opened them, Mr. Harris was snapping his fingers in front of her face.

"*Megan!*" he shouted.

"Good morning," she said hastily, pressing the book into his hand. "Thanks for letting me borrow this."

"I think you need to sit down," he advised, his face lined with concern.

"I'm fine," she lied, "Just a little tired. That was a really scary book, and I didn't sleep very well last night."

"Megan," he said, looking closely at her eyes, "that looked like a seizure of some sort,"

"No," she said hastily, moving toward the hallway. "I just get a little spacey when I'm tired. I'd better hurry, or Mrs. Jones will have an excuse to get mad at me."

She fled back into the crowded hallway, praying that he didn't call her grandfather.

Megan lurched back into the present when Mr. Bob dashed from the room. She wasn't sure what had changed, but she kept falling through holes into the Academy's past. Much to her relief, the Dark Man didn't materialize this time, but a rowdy class of high school kids went down the hall a second later. She never thought she'd miss the days when all she had to worry about was ignoring the ghostly presence. Although she wasn't entirely sure that her mother's tormentor had woken, it did seem at least that the incident in the cafeteria had brought him closer to full consciousness.

"Where did my glitter go?" the girl in the front of the room blurted out. As one, the entire class turned to look at Megan.

"Miss McGeehee," the foul teacher drawled.

Megan walked up to the teacher's desk, already beginning to drift back into the older version of the Academy. She made a great show of turning out her pockets while someone else searched her desk.

"Can we *please* get on with the lesson?" Bruce groaned, banging his fist on his desk. "We've been doing this every time something's been lost for a week."

"Mr. Grimble, come here," Mrs. Jones snapped.

Megan, though numb to this humiliating routine, managed to rise from the daze of construction sounds around her at the thought of anyone mistreating Bruce. She welcomed the anger. It cleared her head.

"Empty your pockets," Mrs. Jones ordered Bruce, who shrugged and started to pull out his empty pockets. "Denise," she said, still glaring, "go and get Mr. Danders, and let him know that there has been another theft."

The girl rose from her seat and disappeared out the door only to return a second later.

"Surely you remember your way to the office," Mrs. Jones snapped, swiveling her chair to face the startled girl.

"Um," the girl stammered, holding out something to the teacher. "This was outside the door."

It was the missing vial of glitter.

"Now, how did that get out there?" its owner asked, coming up to the front of the room. "I had it just a few minutes ago."

Somewhere nearby in the past, a baby started to cry weakly.

156

During break the next day, Megan sat next to Bruce on a bench by the swings with her shoulder resting against his. For a few moments now, she had been completely in the present. It felt like one of those mornings when she woke up after being sick and realized that she was finally well.

They watched Glenn jog around the courtyard. He wasn't going very fast, but that was probably because there was a group of kids following him, and he didn't want to leave his admirers behind.

"Is he really as fast as everyone says he is?" Megan asked, realizing that she had never seen Glenn run before.

"He's fast all right," Bruce muttered. "He's the only person here that I'm not sure I can outrun. I think I can, but I've never actually run beside him."

Ferret Boy didn't look like he could run as fast as Bruce. While she watched him strut around, Allison came running up from Mrs. Jones with a stopwatch.

"Hey Glenn," she gushed, "Let's find out how long it takes you to run from one side of the courtyard to the other!"

"Sure," he said, "Where do you want me to start?"

Bruce surprised Megan by standing up and walking over to where a small crowd had gathered. She followed him, wanting to be there if something bad happened. He stopped ten feet back and to the left of where Glenn made a show of assuming a starter's stance.

"On your mark... Get set... Go!" Allison screamed.

In a blur Glenn flew into motion, and Megan's heart sank. He *could* run. She might not like the bully, but she had to admit he shared Bruce's gift.

Bruce disappeared from her side. In the first few strides he left the crowd behind him.

At first no one understood what he was doing. Too much of the way they defined Bruce depended on his asthma, and they couldn't see beyond it to the talent he possessed.

Bruce matched the pace Glenn had set ahead of him in the first ten feet. In the second, he closed the distance. By the time Glenn became aware of his competition, Bruce pulled even with him.

Thirty feet left. Bruce led by three strides.

Twenty. Bruce started to sprint, making Megan realize that he hadn't even been running his fastest.

Ten. The whistle blew and Glenn turned toward the door to line up, leaving Bruce to finish alone.

Glenn rejoined the silent class. Megan ran out to meet Bruce and nearly knocked him over in her excitement.

"I wasn't really trying," the bully said when they walked up. "I've got to save myself for the real thing." His words, though smooth and only slightly winded, contradicted the way his eyes would burn into Bruce for the next two days.

Megan followed Bruce to the line, enjoying the way the other kids turned back to look at him. For the first time in weeks, everyone forgot about watching her. Then the sound of a chisel cutting into stone echoed through the empty courtyard. Try as she might, she couldn't tell if it was real. The construction seemed to be almost complete, but what was going to happen when it was finished?

Gym time greeted Bruce with something he'd never seen before: Coach Beates sitting down. After all, the seventy year-old prided herself on swimming the length of Nickelville Lake every morning, even in winter.

"Time to change things up today," she called as Mrs. Jones's class filed into the blue and yellow gym. "Can anyone tell me what a constitutional is?"

Either no one knew or no one felt like talking.

"It's a long walk outside for your health," the normally animated woman said wearily. "Today you are all going outside to explore the Academy grounds."

"But we just went outside an hour and a half ago for break," someone complained. "And we just ate lunch."

"Walking is excellent for digestion," Coach answered. "Now to make sure you all don't just take advantage of being outside to play with your phones, you're going to surrender them at the door."

Sounds of displeasure filled the cavernous room.

"Or if you'd prefer," she added with something resembling her normal iron, "You can all spend the next hour running laps around the gym."

Suddenly a long walk outside in the cool autumn air didn't seem so unreasonable to the class. The line to surrender phones went smoothly until it got to Megan.

"Do you really expect me to believe you don't own a phone?" the irritated woman asked. "Look, I don't feel up to arguing today."

"Seriously," Bruce said, handing his over. "She doesn't have one."

"She's too poor to own one," Allison giggled from further back in line. "Haven't you seen how she dresses?"

The class began to laugh, and Megan stiffened, but otherwise didn't respond.

"Okay," the coach said at last. "But I'd better not find out you're lying to me."

The only other person to refuse of course, was Allison, who claimed that her broken phone hadn't yet been replaced even though it could clearly be seen hanging out of her back pocket.

Outside at last, Megan took Bruce by the hand and led him straight for the woods that surrounded the Academy grounds. Although he'd expected her to be upset, it seemed that she just wanted to put space between the school and herself. As they approached the tree line, Bruce realized he could see a disturbance that spanned the entire boundary between the field and the woods.

He reached out and touched it just before they passed through. The now familiar static sensation passed over them as they did.

Megan giggled as if it tickled.

"I'm sorry she said that," he said when she stopped just within the woods.

"Why?" Megan asked, looking deeper into the trees. "It's true. I'm poor. When you get down to it I'm homeless. If it wasn't for Grandpa, we'd have been in real trouble with nowhere to stay."

"That doesn't mean she has the right to make fun of you for it," he said angrily. "You might not have expensive things, but you're the most amazing person I've ever met."

This drew her full attention back to him.

"That's seriously the nicest thing anyone has ever said to me," she said, looking at him oddly for a moment before placing a chaste kiss on his cheek. It wasn't much, but it was the first time anyone had ever done so, and he found that he liked it. In fact, he liked it a lot.

160

She looked into his eyes, and he saw a warmth there that made his heart sing. But then it quickly turned into confusion, as if she'd walked into a room and forgotten why she was there.

"These woods are different from Guarded Wood," she said at last. "They feel older than I thought they would."

"Yes," he agreed absently, trying unsuccessfully to think about anything but the fading warmth on his cheek.

They walked deeper into the shadowed interior where the leaves overhead still blocked most of the autumn sunlight. He'd expected it to be colder, but the trees blocked out most of the wind. And there was something more, he realized. Although no more than a hundred yards deep at most, he felt a vastness to the woods that defied explanation.

Megan released his hand and walked deeper into the trees, her eyes darting from place to place as if searching for something. He glanced back at the clearing, noticing that the two of them were the only ones making any attempt to leave the open lawn that surrounded the school. Something instinctive warned him that they shouldn't be there, but he followed her anyway.

Megan spent an inordinate amount of time staring into the darkened interiors of hollow trees and tracking the path of unseen things through the air as he followed her through the trees. Her reactions there could not have been more different than when she'd been in Guarded Wood. Here she acted as if she'd finally found a place where she belonged. Much like her behavior inside the Academy itself where he often suspected she saw things that weren't there, his friend was clearly interacting with this place in a way that he could not. But in the end, he decided it didn't matter if she did, because when she was thus distracted, it was much easier to admire the way she looked without having her catch him.

She was unlike anyone he'd ever met. And as much as he hated to take her away from something that clearly made her happy, they'd need to return soon or risk the wrath of Mrs. Jones for being late back to class.

He gently placed his hand on her bare arm, and for an instant, he thought he could see shapes moving through the foliage of the plants and trees around them. On a branch overhead, he thought he saw a monkey-like creature, but when he tried to focus, everything went back to the way it had been before.

Why are they hiding from me?

Had he just heard her thoughts?

"We need to head back," he whispered, superstitiously fearful of waking something with his voice. "We don't want to be late."

"It was nice to get away for a bit," she said, turning toward him and taking his hand once again. "Maybe Coach knew what she was talking about with this constitutional thing."

Maybe it was nothing more than the suggestion of what he'd thought he heard in her mind, but something felt different in the woods now. He heard things moving in the undergrowth and kept catching glimpses of movement within the canopy overhead. Something kept drawing his attention, but when he turned his head to look, he found nothing to explain it.

"You're seeing and hearing things, aren't you?" she whispered, close to his ear as if not wanting to be overheard. Although her breath was hot against his neck, the hairs on his arms rose in response.

He nodded, unable to hide it.

"It's like something is playing hide and seek with you, but you can only see it out of the corner of your eye," she added.

He nodded again in reply, holding her hand a bit more tightly.

162

"They're showing you more of themselves to you than they are to me," she confided, and somehow he knew that this was all she was going to say on the subject. "I'm not sure why they're hiding from me..."

When they left the trees, they passed by the Terrible Trio gathered around something on the ground. Allison was taking pictures of whatever it was on her nonexistent phone, and the boys were laughing.

On the way home from school that day, Bruce saw a woman standing far out in the thin band of trees watching them as they drove past. As he watched, she seemed to dissolve into a gust of leaves.

"Want to stay and help train Bruce?" Jade asked with perverse pleasure after the bus dropped the four of them off after school several days later.

"I'd like to," Megan replied, "But I promised my grandpa that we could spend some family time together this afternoon."

"We've been monopolizing you, haven't we?" Bruce said, disappointed that she was going.

"We'll see you tomorrow then," Paul said. "Take care."

As she walked the rest of the way home, she could hear Bruce trying to talk them into taking a night off from his training. She silently wished him luck with that. Jade was having entirely too much fun torturing him to let him off that easy.

She let the day drain from her as she walked. She might not be able to keep her visions of the past under control at school, but she was getting better at walling them off when she got home.

It took her a moment to notice their truck's absence from the driveway. When she did, her stomach lurched, and she badly wanted to break her promise and return to the Grimbles. The reassuring presence of the immobile hulk had meant that they couldn't leave Nickelville yet. But now that it had been taken to a mechanic, their days truly were numbered.

Inside the old house, the smell of meat roasting lifted her spirits until she remembered that good meals would be hard to come by after they left. Thoroughly depressed, she dropped her backpack next to the front door and went in search of her mother and grandfather.

"It's my money and I'll spend it on the two of you if I want to," Azarich said firmly, arguing with her mother when Megan came into the kitchen.

"What's up?" Megan asked, sitting down next to her grandfather at the table.

"Your grandfather wants to take us shopping," Emelia said irritably. "At the mall outside of town."

"Oh," Megan said, seeing the problem immediately. If they left town, they'd be exposed again. "I hate shopping, and so does Mom."

"I don't buy that for a second," he said, just as irritated as his daughter. "Why won't you let me treat you girls to a new wardrobe?"

"Dad, you don't need to buy our love," Emelia said.

"I'm not trying to buy anything but clothes," he exclaimed, stung that she'd even suggest that as his motive.

"Then why?" Emelia asked, crossing her arms.

"You want to know why?" he said, rising to look out the window over the kitchen sink as he spoke.

"Yes," Emelia answered.

"Your truck will be fixed sometime next week," he said, confirming Megan's suspicions.

"That's right."

"And you've never wavered in saying that you're going to leave as soon as it's ready," he said sadly.

164

Emelia had nothing to add this time.

"How long will you be gone this time?" he asked, his strong voice breaking. "I'm over ninety years old. There's a good chance that when you leave this time, it will be the last time we will ever see each other."

Megan rushed forward, wrapping her arms around him. Emelia joined the embrace as well.

"I'm an old man who had a good-paying job," he said, hugging them both to him. "The two of you are my legacy. Let me spoil you while I've still got you."

"Okay," Emelia said grudgingly, "But only from the catalogs. We really do hate to shop."

"That's fine," he sniffed happily. "Megan, you know where they're at."

"Sure Grandpa," she said, wiping the tears from her cheek.

On her way to the chest where the catalogs were stored, she thought about his age. Ninety? She knew he and his two friends at the Academy were old, but that still came as a shock. Maybe there was something in the Nickelville water supply that kept people young longer. That would have made him about forty-five when her mother was born and his wife died. People had children that late all the time now, but that was pretty old back in those days.

Catalogs in hand, she returned to the table, secretly delighted by the thought of getting rid of the last of her old clothes.

Chapter XV: Freaky Fortunes and Goth Girls

The second hand swung lazy circles around the clock while Mrs. Jones read yet another magazine. In less than a minute, school would dismiss for a three-day weekend to celebrate the two hundredth anniversary of both the town and the Jubilee.

The excitement of the night to come pulled Megan from the phantom world around her and allowed her to focus on the present. Bruce looked nauseous.

The bell rang through the halls of the school and into the woods and town beyond. In their excitement, they ignored Mrs. Jones's complaints that she hadn't dismissed them, and ran down the hall toward the front of the school.

"Good luck, Bruce," a group of his classmates called as he got on his bus with Megan at his side. He waved back, tripped over the step and nearly landed in the bus driver's lap.

"Careful," Megan said, following him down the aisle to the back of the bus, "we don't want you to break a leg before you have a chance to let Glenn eat your dust again."

When the bus pulled away from the Academy and entered the woods that surrounded it, the driver pulled aside and allowed several large trucks to pass, each bearing rides for the Jubilee.

"It's held out here?" Megan asked, craning her neck to watch as the pieces of a carousel disappeared into the trees.

"Yeah," Paul said, watching as well. "There are two other clearings beside the one the school's in. The town uses one for parking and the other for the actual festival."

"I don't envy those carnies for trying to get their equipment back there," Bruce said. "That road isn't much more than a goat-trail."

"Why don't they set it up somewhere else?" Megan asked.

"Town traditions," Jade answered, shuddering as another truck passed, this one loaded with giant teacups.

"What's wrong?" Megan asked.

"Jade's scared of the rides," Bruce answered with a grin.

"Am not," Jade said.

"Then why don't you ever ride?" Paul asked.

"Because I like the food, and as Paul can tell you from past experience, corn dogs and that teacup ride don't mix," Jade answered.

"Don't remind me," Paul pleaded with a grimace. "Just thinking about corn-dogs makes me want to puke."

The setting sun cloaked Megan's family in a soft glow as the three of them climbed into Azarich's old truck. The air had started to cool, and Megan wore a jacket to avoid the usual questions about why she wasn't cold.

"What's the story of that house at the end of the road?" Megan asked. "Paul says it's haunted."

"I don't know about haunted, "Azarich said, "But I'm pretty sure the vines are the only thing holding it together. One of these days, and if I was a betting man I'd say sooner rather than later, the whole thing is going to fall in on itself."

"You guys never explored it?" Megan asked, surprised. Neither of them sounded like they'd been particularly cautious as teens.

"Not that one," Emelia said, making sure that she made eye contact with her daughter. "And you don't need to either."

"Mom has made us stop at every carnival we've passed since I was a little girl," Megan told her grandfather, deciding to change the subject. "I doubt there's a ride they make that I haven't ridden."

"They're supposed to be making a big deal out of it this year," Azarich said.

The Grimbles were loading into their SUV when they drove past. Megan waved happily.

"Apparently Paul got really sick eating corn dogs once, and now he gets nauseous even thinking about them," Megan said. "Maybe I shouldn't either, just to keep him from being uncomfortable."

"That's one tradition I refuse to give up," Emelia said, looking out the window with a big smile on her face."

"Did you and Grandpa start it?" Megan asked.

"No," her mother answered after a moment's hesitation in which the smile left her lips. "I did that with someone else. You could always eat one while you're not with Paul. That way you get what you want and he won't get sick."

"So, Bruce is running in the race this year," Azarich said, turning onto the main road.

"Absolutely," Megan said, "Unless something triggers his asthma before then."

"Well, I hope Bruce wins," Azarich said fondly. "He's a fine young man."

"Yes, he is," Megan responded, then noticed the way her mother was looking at her. "What?"

"Nothing," Emelia answered with that mocking yet still slightly worried smile she reserved for discussions about her daughter's friend.

"He's *not* my boyfriend," Megan snapped, looking involuntarily back at the Grimbles in the rearview mirror.

"Whatever you say," Emelia replied.

"So, is the Jubilee why you've always loved carnivals?" Megan asked, trying yet again to change the subject.

"Yes," Emelia answered. "I have very fond memories of it."

Until now, Megan hadn't realized there were enough people in Nickelville to cause traffic, but they soon found themselves waiting in a line of cars that crept slowly toward the woods. When at last they approached a middle-aged woman with a wad of money in her hand, the sky was completely dark.

"It'll be three dollars, Azarich," she said when he rolled down the window.

"But it only cost one last year," he complained with an indignant stiffening of his neck and shoulders.

"Bicentennial Anniversary and all that," the woman said with the air of someone who'd heard the same complaint many times already. "Supposed to be the best one we've ever had."

Megan's grandfather grudgingly withdrew two more bills from his wallet then parked where the next attendant directed them, followed by the Grimbles a moment later.

It surprised Megan how dark the parking area had grown now that the sun had set. She wasn't particularly happy about their proximity to the Academy, but she did take a certain amount of reassurance that they were still outside the static barrier. She also remembered the strange world that

169

appeared to exist within that thin band of woods around the school and wished that she'd been able to share it with Bruce while they took their constitutional.

"Emelia," Dora greeted warmly when the families joined, "It's so good to see you again, although the years seem to have been kinder to you than they were with me! You don't look a day over thirty-five!"

"You too," Emelia said with considerably less enthusiasm.

"Do you still write?" Mrs. Grimble asked.

"Not since college," Emelia answered, starting to become irritated.

"Well," Mrs. Grimble pressed, "If you decide to start again, you can consider this a formal job offer."

"Oh," Emelia said, surprised. "I'll think about it."

"Good," Mrs. Grimble replied, rubbing her hands together happily. "That's the last bit of *Tribune* business that I want to think about for the night. Let's go have some fun."

"Now that's a parental command I can happily obey," Paul said, linking his arm through Megan's. "Shall we join the frivolities, my lady?" he asked.

"I've never understood why we can't see the lights through the trees," Mrs. Grimble said, eyes straining toward the calliope music in the distance.

"Me too," Emelia said, frowning as if remembering something.

"Ooh, a mystery" Jade whispered, taking Megan's other arm and leaving Bruce sulking behind them. "Time's wasting, food's waiting and there's money in my pocket that needs to be spent."

Giggling, the four young people entered the woods with their families following. Candles in multicolored paper bags lined the sides of the path, lighting the way through the darkness. But even though she watched closely, none of the creatures she'd sensed earlier remained. Maybe they were shy of large crowds.

When the path ended in a clearing, Jade and Paul let go of Megan's arms to pass through the narrow space between the trees, and Bruce took her hand in his. Torches lined the entire perimeter of the field like sentries, cloaking the festival in an otherworldly glow. Shadows danced across the field and all that it held, making her feel like she'd drifted into a dream.

Megan's extra senses came alive in a flood when she and Bruce entered the circle of torches.

"Looks like the fire marshal is still taking bribes," Mr. Grimble grumbled. "As if the candles in the woods hadn't been bad enough."

"They've always done it this way," Azarich said. "There were torches down the path when I was a boy as well."

"Some traditions die hard," Mrs. Grimble said, taking her husband by the hand. "You have to admit though, it does add a certain amount of drama."

He grudgingly allowed her to lead him forward.

"Wow," Megan said, trying to sort through this sudden surge of sensory input. Not only were her extra senses fully active for the first time since their arrival in Nickelville, but the normal five seemed stronger as well. The colorful lights of the rides shone too vividly to be real, the laughter and screams of children rippled across her skin in their enhanced clarity, and the mixed aromas of popcorn and alcohol overwhelmed her. The motion of the rides slowed as if her mind were working faster than normal.

She didn't have to look at Bruce to know that he was feeling much of the effect. She could feel his awe through the physical bond created through their linked hands. Reluctantly, she slipped her hand from his and felt much of her surroundings return to normal.

"Don't worry," Emelia whispered in her ear as she passed. "This place always makes us feel this way. We're still hidden."

With an unpleasant lurch of her stomach, Megan realized the possibility should have occurred to her the second her senses came alive. What was this place doing to her? Maybe the real danger of Nickelville lay in making her so comfortable that she would no longer be able to survive out in the real world when the time came to leave.

"They really did take out all the stops this year," Azarich said, scanning the rides before him. Everywhere they looked the strobing lights of spinning, twirling, swaying and plummeting rides merged with screaming laughter. In addition to the sorts of attractions Megan was accustomed to seeing, there were many she'd only seen in old movies. Several tents rose among the rides, games and food booths, each topped with gaily colored flags that moved listlessly in the night air.

"So, it's not usually so…" Megan said, unable to think of the right word to describe it.

"Nope," Paul answered, for once as lost for words as everyone else.

"Welcome to the Nickelville Jubilee," a deep voice boomed behind them, causing Mrs. Grimble to scream.

Megan whirled, noticing as she did that the space around her mother's hand was shimmering like the air above the blacktop on a hot day.

Standing behind them, somehow overlooked in the strange transition from woods to carnival, stood a man in an old-fashioned top hat and coat. His cheeks bore deep scars beneath a scrub of dingy stubble.

"I'm sorry to have frightened you," the unpleasant man crooned, clearly enjoying their reaction to him as he bowed deeply and moved on to greet the next family to arrive.

"Who is that?" Emelia asked, watching the man with more than her eyes.

"Don't know," Mrs. Grimble answered, still shaken. "But he's been lurking around town for several weeks now. He hasn't done anything wrong, but he doesn't seem to be particularly wholesome either."

Megan shot her mother an uncomfortable look at the timing of his arrival in the isolated town and noticed that Bruce was still staring at her mother's hand, eyes wide.

"I've been waiting a long time for this day," Mr. Grimble said, breaking the silence and ruffling Bruce's hair affectionately. "Tomorrow I get to watch my son put that arrogant little runt in his place."

"Hey," Bruce said, still frowning, "watch the hair, Dad."

"That's right," Mr. Grimble said. "You've got to look your best for the victory pictures tomorrow."

Megan slipped her arm through Bruce's, hoping that the sharpening of his senses would distract him from what she suspected he'd seen. The spongy sawdust beneath her feet gave off the strong scent of pine. The smoke from the torches filled her nostrils and tickled her throat.

A group of children raced past them as they stood there. Their shrill cries made Megan wince, but she was so happy that she felt like she could beat Bruce at a race.

"I see Tony Jones has taken over his daddy's business," Emelia said, eyeing a banner near one of the rides.

"His place on the city council and school board as well," Azarich added.

"That's not Mrs. Jones's husband, is it?" Megan asked.

"I'm afraid so," Jade answered.

"That's why she and Allison get away with so much," Bruce added. "No one wants to get on Mr. Jones's bad side. He might not officially run the town, but everyone who does is in his pocket."

173

"At least two thirds of the town works for Jones and Jones Industries," Mr. Grimble added.

"So, who finally caught Tony?" Emelia asked. "Most of the girls in our class planned to marry him."

"Your favorite," Mrs. Grimble said with a grimace.

"Favorite?" Emelia asked, confused.

"Paula."

Emelia froze in mid step, all traces of her previous good mood evaporated in spite of the festivities around her. Then she stepped toward Megan with a predatory grace that dropped the temperature of the group a good ten degrees. She wrapped her arm around her daughter's shoulders before she spoke again.

"Paula is Megan's teacher?"

"Wow," Jade said, "I take it we're not the only ones who wish someone would drop a house on her!"

"How does she treat you?" Emelia asked, turning her daughter to where she could look directly into her eyes.

"Horribly," Bruce answered before Megan could make it sound better than it was.

"What exactly has Paula been up to?" Emelia asked through clenched teeth.

"She has the whole school convinced that I'm a thief," Megan admitted. She feared that she might be giving her mother an excuse to pack up and leave, but oh, how good it felt to speak the words aloud!

"Is that so?" Azarich said angrily. "I can probably do something about that at least."

"Let me take care of it," Emelia said. "I think it's time Paula and I had a little reunion."

"Can I watch?" Jade asked eagerly.

174

"We can move away if you like," Emelia said with a mixture of hope and dread, echoing her daughter's feelings.

"No, Mom," Megan said, "I really like it here. I just wish there was some way to get away from Mrs. Jones. She's even got Mr. Danders convinced that I stole her watch."

"I was there the entire time," Bruce added. "There's no way that she could have stolen most of the things that are missing."

"Yeah," Paul joined in, "We've been having stuff disappear from our class too. You must be a really good thief to manage that, Megan."

"Ours too," Jade said thoughtfully. "Now that you mention it, it's really strange that there are so many things walking off these days."

"Do you have a new custodian, or someone else who has access to all of the rooms?" Mr. Grimble asked.

"No," Bruce said. "Mr. Green still takes care of the building."

"Well, I know for a fact that he wouldn't steal anything," Grandpa said. "I've known him since we were pups."

"The only new person we've had is the principal, Mr. Hamby," Paul said thoughtfully.

"And seeing as he never leaves his office," Bruce added, "I don't see how he could be the thief."

"Are you sure you want to stay?" Emelia asked again. "Is this why you've been so withdrawn?"

"Yes," Megan lied.

"Let's not let this spoil the Jubilee for us," Grandpa said, worried that this revelation might split up his family once again. "There's nothing to be done about this problem tonight. Why don't we let the youngsters go and make gluttons of themselves before getting sick on the rides?"

Both families murmured agreement.

"Be careful," Emelia said, hugging Megan tightly before letting her go.

"I will, Mom," she promised.

"How about the Ferris wheel at ten?" Mrs. Grimble asked, looking at her watch. Everyone turned to look at the giant wheel, which could be seen from anywhere in the carnival.

"Okay," Grandpa answered, slipping something into Megan's hand and giving her a big wink. "The Ferris wheel at ten. Here's enough money to have fun with without getting into trouble. Now I think your mother and I have quite a few years of carnival fun to catch up on."

"Thanks, Grandpa," Megan said, taking the money and standing up on the tips of her toes to give him a quick kiss on the cheek. The short stubble on his skin prickled her lips.

"Well now," Grandpa said, offering his arm to Emelia, "Shall we see if you can still beat me at the dart throw?"

"I'd love to, old man," she said and took his arm. "We'll make them wish they'd never laid eyes on the two of us."

Before anything else could happen to dampen the evening, the Grimble children swept Megan away from her own family and into the heart of the carnival.

"Where to first?" Megan asked.

"Food," Bruce and Paul said in unison. Each grabbing one of her hands and dragging her toward the smell of roasted meat.

"Typical," Jade said, falling in behind them. "Stomachs with legs."

On one side of the row, Megan saw a stand that, according to its illuminated sign, specialized in popped corn, cider and candy apples. It had a border of flashing light bulbs and a general sense of permanence that one usually only saw in fairgrounds that never moved locations. Further on, booths advertised cheeseburgers, corn dogs, French fries, cheesesteak and

176

Italian sausage. The unmistakably sweet aroma of funnel cake caught her attention, and her stomach decided that it agreed with the Grimble boys after all.

"So, what do you want?" Bruce asked.

"Corn dog," Megan said. "I've been craving one since Jade mentioned it on the bus."

"Ugh," Paul grunted, screwing up his nose in distaste and releasing her hand. "And here I thought we were friends."

"Sorry Paul," Megan laughed.

"Remember," he said, sliding back into accent again, "that this was the night when I forgot you and found some other bonnie lass to be my bride!"

"How about you guys?" Megan asked.

"Pizza," Jade and Paul said in unison.

"I'm with Megan," Bruce said.

"Now there's a surprise," Jade said with a knowing grin.

"I get pizza all the time," Bruce added, glaring at her. "But we haven't had corn dogs since the teacup incident."

"Looks like the corn-dog line is shorter," Jade observed, looking down the row.

"Of course it is," Paul said, already walking away. "What sane person would turn down pizza from Gordon's?"

"Gordon's?" Megan asked.

"Best pizza in town," Bruce explained. "But corndogs are a carnival tradition. We'll wait for you guys next to the stage under those big laurel trees."

"Feel free to eat them before we catch up," Paul called over his shoulder.

"Is it smart to eat right before the rides?" Megan asked as they waited in the short line.

"That's part of the fun," Bruce said with a wicked gleam in his eyes.

"Boys," Megan said, shaking her head in dismay.

"I've never seen some of these before," she told Bruce while they waited in line.

"Like what?" he asked.

"Candy apples," she said, nodding to the booth which, in spite of its oddity, had a line every bit as long as their own. "Cider? And it's funny that it says popped corn instead of popcorn."

"I never thought of that," Bruce said, ordering their food. "But then again the Jubilee is just about the only carnival I've ever been to."

True to Paul's suggestion, they didn't wait to start eating. As much as they might enjoy teasing him, they didn't really want to cause him any discomfort.

A stage stood beneath the two trees under which they'd decided to eat while they waited for Jade and Paul, and on it stood a battered old upright piano. A man, who looked almost as old as his instrument, sat next to it on a stool, nodding off with his weathered hands folded in his lap. A cello case sat nearby, though its owner appeared to be absent at the moment.

"This should be interesting," Megan said, pointing with her half-eaten corn dog at an older girl who stepped up onto the stage with a violin case. She had olive skin, long black hair, a dark red tutu and green combat boots. She gently shook the old man by the shoulder and he woke with a start, mumbling hasty apologies. Then she scanned the faces of the crowd and yawned as if she'd been the one who'd only just woken up.

"So that's who Jade goes to for fashion advice," Bruce whispered.

As they watched, the girl opened her case and pulled out a much-worn violin. She brought it to her shoulder, raised the bow to the strings,

then closed her eyes and waited for the pianist to begin.

His first notes were slow and measured, almost stumbling through the other sounds of the carnival around them. By contrast, when she joined him, hers sent a mournful sigh through the crowd, spinning a tale of loss without anything so clumsy as words, a tale of forbidden beginnings and lost chances. She did all of this with her eyes closed, as if after that first hopeful glance, she knew the world around her held nothing of interest.

"Didn't see that coming," Bruce said in awe.

"Better save a space for Jade and Paul," Megan said, "I bet it's going to get crowded quickly with her playing."

Megan barely finished her food before the other two returned. With her heightened senses, she thought she could sense something powerful beneath the surface of the melody, something less than the thickness of a violin string away from spilling over into true magic and bringing forth whatever the strangely dressed musician was attempting to summon.

"Wow," Paul said, staring at the eccentric performer, his pizza forgotten.

"No kidding," Jade added. "I wonder where she bought those boots."

Whether the sounds of the Jubilee stopped for the duration of her performance or if Megan's senses had focused on the girl to the exclusion of everything else, she couldn't be sure. But a part of her wished it would never end.

It was hard to tell how long they'd been lost in the music when, without warning, the girl packed up her violin and left.

"Sorry Megan," Paul said dreamily. "It's over. I've found someone else."

Bruce slapped him across the back of the head.

"Hey," Jade said, laughing along with Megan. "I'm the only one who gets to slap Paul."

"Sorry Sis," Paul said with a grin. "Goth Violin Girl can slap me any time she wants."

"Come on guys," Bruce said. "Let's see what's on the next row."

Megan followed, pleasantly full and still awed by the music that Paul's Goth Girl had played.

The carnies who ran the rides wore an assortment of old clothing to symbolize the age of the town. But while the Grimbles seemed to enjoy the costumes, they reminded Megan at times of the school's specter.

"Look Megan," Jade squealed, "a fortune teller."

"But you don't believe in that sort of stuff," Paul said, surprised by his sister's interest.

"It's a girl thing," Jade said, dragging Megan through the flaps of the tent and making her realize that even though Jade had always been close to Paul, she'd never had an opportunity to hang around with another girl before.

Inside, the perfumed smoke of two braziers drifted through the dim interior. A single candle burned in an iron stand next to a small square table where a woman sat, looking at them intently.

Megan's first thought was that she didn't look like much of a fortune teller. But once again, this wasn't something she'd normally encountered at carnivals. For that matter, now that she'd taken a moment to think about it, her mother had always steered her away from such people in the past. But even so, in spite of the way the candle had been positioned to cast the fortune teller's face in shadow, she looked like any other of the vintage-clothed carnies.

The sounds from the crowds faded as soon as the colorful canvas door dropped behind them.

"Welcome," the woman whispered, and though it in no way resembled the deep tones of the scarred man who'd startled them at the edge of the carnival, it nonetheless raised the downy hairs on the backs of Megan's arms.

"We would like to have our fortunes read," Jade said eagerly.

"But of course," the woman replied quietly. "You honor me with your presence."

Megan remained standing while Jade took the chair opposite the strange woman.

"Place your hands on the table," the woman said.

Jade complied, then the woman placed her own over them.

"I see both happiness and sadness in your future," the woman said in the oddly quiet tent. "In spite of your dreams to move away from this town, you will be bound by love to live out your days here. And although you are still young, you will hear your future calling soon and be happy to heed it. Although your husband has never graced your dreams, he already dreams of you." Then she paused, turning her head as if listening to something far away. "You will deliver a son and daughter in one birth, but you will have to give one up to keep the other."

The woman withdrew her hands.

"Thanks," Jade said, puzzling through the cryptic prediction. "How much does it cost?"

"I ask no coin for my visions," the woman said quietly. "Now send your companion to me."

Megan didn't want to sit in the chair, but found herself there anyway.

"How are you enjoying this unique little town?" the woman asked in that same whisper she'd used since they arrived.

"I'm sorry," Megan said. "I didn't realize you were local."

"I'm not," the fortune teller whispered, "but I've been returning to this festival for many, many years. There's something in the air here that keeps bringing me back."

"Then how did you know I'm not from Nickelville?"

The woman smiled in reply, though she still didn't look up.

Reluctantly Megan placed her hands on the table as her friend had done, willing her mind to settle.

182

Cold hands covered her own, drawing her senses away from the tent, away from the carnival and away from Nickelville itself.

"Your travels are not complete, though you wish otherwise," the voice whispered.

Mountains rose through the place Megan saw in her mind.

"You will not always be able to tell friend from foe," the voice continued.

A stone cottage materialized before her, nestled between a river and forest.

"You will find the key to the second promise only after the lock has been broken."

A city within a mountain. Gates sparkled in the morning sunlight, black stone absorbing the light.

"And only after you die will you finally be free to live."

The interior of the tent rushed back into Megan's vision, cementing her to the chair and table where the strange woman still gripped her hands.

"Megan?" Jade said, her voice tinted with concern.

The woman turned her face to better catch the light and for just an instant Megan found someone else looking back at her, someone with long black hair, pale skin and gently glowing violet eyes. Then this oddly familiar apparition faded into the features of the woman they'd seen when they'd entered.

"Thank you," Megan said, pulling her hands free.

"No," the woman whispered. "It is I who thank you for the chance to glimpse a life such as yours, Daughter of Crina."

"My mother's name is Emelia," Megan whispered, rising quickly to flee from the tent, dragging Jade with her.

"As you wish," the woman said, "Have you noticed how alive this clearing feels tonight?" The tent flaps closed before Megan could answer.

"Are you okay?" Bruce asked when he saw her, taking her hand in his own. "Why are your hands so cold?"

"That was so cool," Jade said. "Creepy but cool."

"Should Bruce and I go?" Paul asked.

"No," Megan said too forcefully, then took a breath before continuing. "There's so much to see and we only have until ten."

"Come and see the freak show," one of the carnies yelled from the front of a tent where a large crowd had gathered.

"I didn't think they still had those," Bruce said, disgusted. "And why am I not surprised to see them there?"

Megan followed the direction of his gaze and found the Trio staring back.

"McGeehee can just look in a mirror when she wants to see a freak," Allison yelled.

"Going to visit your mom at work?" Jade shot back. "Tell me, is she the bearded lady, the wench with two butts or the village idiot? They all fit her pretty well now that I think of it."

"Are you going to let her talk to me like that?" Allison snapped at Glenn.

"Have you ever seen her fight?" Glenn asked, shocked that she'd even suggested it.

"Come on," Paul said, dragging Jade away. "We don't want to get kicked out of the Jubilee over those rejects. Bruce will show them tomorrow."

"Hey, Megan," Bruce asked several booths further down, "Have you ever shot a pellet gun before?"

"I've never even shot a water gun before," she admitted.

"Well, here's your chance," he said, putting an air rifle into her hands and picking up another for himself. The carnie running the booth took two dollars from Bruce and stood back.

"How do I do it?" Megan asked.

"I'll show her," Jade said, moving Megan's hands to the proper places on the rifle. "Hold it against your shoulder when you shoot, even though it's not a real gun."

It felt familiar, almost as if she'd done this before. She looked down the barrel and found the smallest painted disk on the wall. Somewhere nearby a girl yelled at her boyfriend.

A loud ping sounded when she pulled the trigger and the disk fell backward.

"Good shot," Paul said, glancing over after looking across the crowd. "See if you can do it again."

One after another, five targets fell.

"Not bad," Bruce said after missing his last shot. "I'll bet you can't hit one of the moving targets on the top row."

She tracked one as it first appeared from the side of the booth and squeezed the trigger.

PING.

"One more and Little Anne Oakley wins a prize," the man behind the counter boomed. Bruce gave the carnie another dollar.

By the time they left, Bruce was five dollars poorer and several stuffed animals heavier. He shifted them for better balance and looked around, wondering how stupid he looked.

"It was your idea to have me shoot," Megan said with a wicked grin, "so it only makes sense that you should carry them."

"Hey," Bruce said, "I paid for the shots!"

"Actually, Dad did," Jade corrected him. "You spent all of your money on that book you were reading a few weeks ago."

Megan caught sight of her mother and grandfather walking arm in arm with a load of stuffed animals even larger than the one that Bruce carried. Mr. Green had joined them along with Mr. Harris and a woman who was probably the librarian's wife. They'd been smart enough to get a bag to carry their prizes in though. Megan watched Bruce struggle for a moment and decided this was too much fun to suggest getting one themselves.

When she looked back, her mother was *laughing*. Megan couldn't remember the last time she'd seen her mother look so happy.

"Was your mom serious about that job?" Megan asked Paul while Bruce transferred all of the prizes to Jade, who refused to climb into the seat of a giant spinning star.

"I think so," he said, still scanning the crowd. "She really liked your mom's writing when they were in school."

"You're looking for the girl with the violin, aren't you?" Megan asked.

His guilty look was answer enough.

"A job Mom likes might be the key to staying here," Megan said, her excitement growing. She didn't want to move away again, and she suspected her mother didn't either. The school year was almost halfway over, and she thought she could deal with Mrs. Jones for a few more months. But was it worth being stalked by a ghost? It was easy to say yes while eating corn dogs and walking down the fairway with the Grimbles as warm laughter surrounded her and the smell of turkey legs filled her nose. But how would she feel about it on Tuesday when they went back to the Academy?

186

"Hey Megan," Jade said. "How about we try the knife throwing next?"

Throughout the night, Megan noticed a pattern to her abilities. If something required a skill similar to fighting in any way, she mastered it no sooner than she tried. But she failed at everything else utterly.

As ten o'clock approached, they began to drift toward the Ferris wheel.

"Wait," Paul said, suddenly changing direction. "Don't the musicians all get together for a performance at the end of the night on that same stage?"

"I think so," Bruce said, grinning knowingly at his brother. "But that's nowhere close to the Ferris wheel."

"We can run back," Paul said eagerly. "Can we? Please?"

"Who are we to stand in the way of true love?" Jade asked.

Paul was already jogging in the direction of the stage before the last words were out of her mouth. They hurried to catch up to him, laughing at his sudden fascination with a girl he'd never even spoken to before.

When they reached the stage, it was already half full of performers, but none of them the elusive goth. Paul stood quietly, looking often at his watch as ten o'clock approached.

"We may not be able to stay long enough," Jade warned. "As much as I don't mind getting in trouble at school, I'd rather not get on Mom's bad side this close to a long break."

"Just a few more minutes," Paul begged.

The clear tones of someone plucking a violin stilled the crowd. Another joined in with a lively jig, weaving itself around the notes of the first and the goth girl walked out into the open playing fast as she swayed with the movements.

Paul's world narrowed to her.

Somewhere back in the crowded stage, someone started to play, of all things, a set of bagpipes, adding a haunting background to the tune. Another musician joined in with a drum and the crowd couldn't seem to tell if they should stare in rapt silence or dance, since the music seemed to demand both. The old upright piano joined in, and then in what should have been sacrilege among the traditional instruments in play, someone softly joined in with an electric guitar. It shouldn't have worked, and yet it meshed perfectly, evoking both a strong sense of the past alongside the present.

When the nameless goth girl lowered her bow and began to sing, Megan was fairly sure Paul stopped breathing. She looked at Bruce and couldn't help but be drawn into his grin as he watched his brother. Then he looked past her, and when she turned to see what had drawn his attention, she found his parents watching the show as well. But while his father had a simple look of appreciation, Dora was frowning at the subject of her youngest son's fascination with faint recognition. Then she shook her head as if clearing her thoughts and motioned for them to come.

"Time's up, loverboy," Jade said, noticing her parents as well.

"Not yet," Paul begged, to which his sister responded by unceremoniously picking him up and throwing him over her shoulder before starting toward the Ferris wheel that could be seen over the treetops.

Laughing at the sight of Paul hanging upside down over his sister's back as he struggled to free himself, Megan glanced back at the stage where she found the talented goth looking directly at her while she sang.

Chapter XVI: Jade Rides the Wave

Bruce drifted slowly up through disturbing dreams of darkness and monsters. He wasn't sure what time his eyes had opened and begun to track the circular path of the fan's shadow, but when the clock passed from five fifty-nine to six o'clock, he slipped out from under the blankets and knocked a book from the nightstand.

Before Megan had come, he'd never have been able to leave a book unfinished for so long. But her arrival in his life had shifted his priorities and left the book forgotten at the bottom of his backpack until the previous night.

That wasn't the only way she'd changed him. He'd stood up to bullies, broken rules and become a true part of his family for the first time in years. When he was around her, he felt like he was riding the crest of an immense wave, a wave that both excited and terrified him.

He took the book and placed it back in its proper place on the bookshelf, giving into the superstitious belief that everything to do with the book needed to be finished before he'd have any chance at winning the race. He walked silently down the hall, enjoying the feel of the cold floorboards against his bare feet.

He started the coffee pot for his parents, but felt like hot cocoa for himself. When the coffee pot gurgled pleasantly to itself, he filled the battered copper kettle that had belonged to one of his grandparents and placed it over the stove's blue flame. He found a packet of hot chocolate and sat on a stool while he waited for the water to heat.

"Can't sleep?" his father asked quietly from the kitchen doorway.

"No," Bruce said, surprised to realize that he'd felt his father's presence before he'd spoken. "Sorry, did I wake you?"

"No, I was already up."

"Why?" Bruce asked.

"Just couldn't sleep any longer. It's one of those things you get to look forward to when you get old. You get sleepy earlier every year, and you find yourself waking up earlier too."

"Dad, you're not old." Bruce assured him.

"Maybe not yet, but I'm definitely getting closer to it," he replied, taking a cup down from the cabinet and pouring coffee for himself. "Thanks," he said, nodding toward the still brewing pot.

The two of them sat in silence for a few minutes, watching the steam rise in lazy curls from the kettle on the stove.

"Dad," Bruce said.

"Yes?"

"Did you ever do anything like this when you were younger?"

"Like the race?"

"Yeah," Bruce answered. The kettle had begun to whistle softly, so he rose before it could wake anyone else and mixed the water and cocoa in a cup before sitting down with his father again.

"Not when I was your age," his father answered between sips of coffee. "But I did run track in late high school and college."

"I never knew that," Bruce said. "So, you're where I get it from."

"I'm not sure if I can take credit for that," Mr. Grimble chuckled, "I never had anything close to the natural talent you've got. Are you nervous?"

"Yes."

"Good," his father said. "That shows that you've got your mind on what you're doing, and that you aren't underestimating your opponent."

"Glenn," Bruce sneered.

"Jade told me that you raced him at school and won."

"Sort of," Bruce said, trying to figure out how to put what had happened into words. "He didn't know that I was going to come up behind him, and Mrs. Jones blew the whistle before we finished."

Bruce sipped his chocolate and watched his father take down another cup from the cabinet.

"You know that I'm not from Nickelville, right?" his dad asked.

"Yeah, you met Mom in college and she talked you into moving here after you got married."

"It's not easy moving into a small town where you're the outsider, even as an adult. "

"You can say that again," Bruce said. "Megan's having a hard time with Mrs. Jones and the rest of the kids at the Academy."

"But you made friends with her," Mr. Grimble said with a smile. "I'm proud of you, Bruce, and not just for running this race. It takes a lot of courage to stand up to someone like Jones. I know adults that steer clear of that old bat when they can. It shows compassion to put yourself into a situation like the one Megan is in when you didn't have to."

"Thanks," Bruce said, uncomfortable with the praise, especially when he felt like he was the one who should be grateful that she'd chosen to be friends with him.

"I guess what I'm trying to say is that I don't really care if you win this race today. I couldn't tell you how many I won or lost. But I remember every time I stood up for what was right, and I wish there'd been more of them. There are too many people who profit from the misery of others and

191

even more people who turn their heads the other way and ignore it. You've given me a glimpse of the man you'll be someday, and I like him."

Bruce sipped his cup, pleased and embarrassed by the words in equal measure. He watched as his father rose and filled the other cup.

"Take this to your mother," he said, holding it out. "I don't know if you've realized it or not, but she's worried sick about this race."

"I know," Bruce said guiltily. "Are you sure she's awake?"

"I'm not sure she ever slept. Tell her that breakfast will be ready in about twenty minutes. Feel free to kick your lazy brother and sister out of bed too."

Bruce carried the steaming cup past the faint glow of the curtainless windows. His feet made no sound on the bare wooden floors, but his mother already knew he was coming when he walked through the open bedroom door.

"Feeling nervous?" she asked, propping her husband's pillow behind her back.

"Bordering on terror," he admitted and passed her the hot cup.

"Thank you," she said, pausing to take a sip, "Couldn't sleep?"

"I finished my book and finally managed to get to sleep sometime after two," he answered.

"Was it good?" she asked.

"It was okay," he shrugged, sitting on the edge by her feet.

"How do you feel?"

"Besides nervous? I feel fine. You don't have to worry about me so much, Mom," he said. "I know what to watch out for. There's no tightness in my chest. I don't get winded unless I'm doing something that *should* wind me. Did Paul tell you about the other day in the woods when they were trying to catch me? They were about to pass out, but *I* was still breathing easy."

"Come here," she said, putting her cup down on the nightstand. "Who gave the three of you permission to grow up so fast? I don't like it. I've actually had nightmares where I turn around to find that my children have suddenly grown into adults when my back was turned."

He moved over and let her hug him, very much aware that she listened to his breathing as she did so.

"I'm going to go wake my delinquent sibs now," Bruce said when she'd released him. "Dad said to tell you that breakfast would be ready in a little while."

"That's good," she said. "Try not to put Jade in a bad mood this time."

"Of course not," he said with an overly innocent smile that she couldn't see in the darkened room.

The door to Jade's bedroom cracked open without a sound. A groggy, but eager Paul stood at the other end of the hallway in his flannel pajamas. Bruce padded silently down the hall and joined him.

"It's perfect," he said. "She's asleep on the opposite side. You took your socks off, right?"

"Yeah," Paul whispered.

"Good," I don't want you slipping on the floor and cracking your head on the side of her bed. On three then. One...two...THREE!"

The two of them flew down the hallway, cleared the door and jumped over the side of Jade's ancient waterbed. When they landed, it created a wave large enough to heave her over the other side.

They were laughing so hard when they slid into the kitchen that Bruce saw spots floating in front of his eyes, and Paul missed his chair when he tried to sit down.

"Leave Jade alone," Mrs. Grimble scolded when Azarich's truck pulled up into the Grimble driveway. Then she remembered what was about to happen and turned to her oldest son. "Are you sure you shouldn't ride in the ambulance with us? I forgot to look at the pollen counts."

"I'll be fine," Bruce said, climbing into the back of the truck with Jade, Paul and Megan.

"What's up?" Megan asked, noting Jade's scowl.

Paul caught Bruce's eyes and they both began to snicker.

"Laugh it up you two," Jade growled. "The only reason I haven't made myself an only child is because I want to see Glenn soundly humiliated, and they don't let girls run."

Megan looked baffled, but Jade would say no more.

Bruce was in high spirits for most of the drive into town, but not even the memory of his sister flying into the air could completely quiet his nerves. The wind whipped about the bed of the old truck, and he realized that his reason for running had changed somewhere along the way. In the past he'd dreamed of beating Glenn. Now he wanted to win for his friends and family. But that wasn't completely true either. His family would be fine if he lost. What he feared most was disappointing Megan.

For a second the sun slid behind the formidable silhouette of the Baker Hotel. Something about the sensation made him think about a bad dream, maybe not the one he'd had the previous night, but one he'd definitely had recently.

His eyes darted toward Megan, but she was lost in her own thoughts. As they passed the road that led to the Academy, her face clouded and he wondered anew about her strange behavior around the school.

194

They parked in the same field as the previous night and climbed out of the truck. The morning air was warmer than it had been for the past month, and the humidity made it feel ten degrees hotter. Worse, that same humidity would fill his lungs with moisture and take up room that he'd desperately need for oxygen. He took a deep breath and assured himself that he still had nothing to worry about.

"Where's the track?" Megan asked as they walked across the field.

"Oh, there's no track for this race," her grandfather explained. "The runners start over there between the Gateway Oaks just like they did in the old days."

Megan turned to look at the two towering trees. Though separated from the rest of the woods, these two giants projected an immensely old presence. Their branches entwined overhead, forming an arch much like the trees in the center of the courtyard.

"From there, the runners go down the road until it hits the main drive up to the Academy. They circle the school, cross the woods between the school and the Jubilee Field, then follow the same path we followed through the woods last night. A ribbon will be stretched between the trees for a finish line."

"Can we follow them?" Megan asked.

"Not really," Mr. Grimble answered. "We could follow them until they got to the school, but then we'd lose them in the woods and we wouldn't get to see who won. Most of the spectators wait here."

"Well guys," Bruce said nervously. "I guess this is it. Keep your fingers crossed for me."

The Grimbles surrounded him in a group hug, and his mother looked close to tears. Megan hugged him before he walked toward the starting line and placed a chaste kiss on his cheek that nonetheless jolted him from his nervousness. He could definitely get used to those.

195

Bruce noticed Glenn standing beneath the oaks with a group of his friends that, oddly enough, didn't include Chuck.

"Good luck, Bruce!" someone yelled from further afield.

"Put Glenn in his place, Bruce!" someone else added.

Glenn stopped relating whatever story he'd been telling and looked over at Bruce with a self-satisfied smirk that made Bruce uneasy.

The school secretary, Millie, came by with a clipboard and a bunch of numbers. She took the top one, eleven, from the stack and filled in some of the lines on the paper.

"This is your number for the race, Bruce," she said in a normal tone, looked around, and leaned closer to add, "I'll be filming the finish, so I can replay the look on his face when he loses over and over again. Let me know if you want a copy."

"I might just do that," he said, and let her pin the number on the back of his shirt with a safety pin. She walked away toward Glenn.

"Hey, watch it!" Glenn shrieked moments later. "If that gets infected I'll sue!"

The mayor stepped up to a podium that Bruce recognized from the school cafeteria's stage.

"Would the contestants please take their positions on the starting line," the mayor asked.

"Good luck," Megan called.

"Yeah, good luck you lousy jerk," Jade added.

"I'd like to bring your attention to number twelve," the mayor said when the voices of the spectators died down again. "Glenn, would you step to the front so everyone can see you? Young Mr. Floyd has won this race for the past two years," the mayor added. "Please take your positions."

The young men of Nickelville took their places between the two oaks. Bruce felt awkward, standing there while the rest assumed runner's starts.

He thought about doing it too, but didn't want to start off the race in something that felt so awkward. Instead he just leaned forward with his left leg out in front of the other.

"On my mark," the mayor said, "follow the path marked and return to this point. The one who returns first wins." He raised the starting pistol above his head and fired.

In that instant all doubt left Bruce's mind. As soon as he began to move in a rhythm that came more naturally to him than breathing, he left his fears behind along with the other runners.

By the time he'd traveled ten feet from the starting line, Bruce already led by three strides. His vision narrowed to the yellow ribbons that marked the sides of the path while the sounds of footfalls and breathing fell behind him.

This wasn't so bad, he thought. And to think he'd been losing sleep over it.

"Not too bad, Wheezy," Glenn huffed from somewhere behind him, echoing Bruce's thought.

Bruce tried to ignore the comment. It surprised him how silently Glenn ran. *Just keep putting one foot in front of the other. Be careful not to step in an armadillo hole. Worry about speed when you get to the road.*

"How long do you think you'll be able to keep up that pace?" Glenn asked from behind him again.

Just ignore him, Bruce repeated in his mind.

At last the dirt gave way to pavement and Bruce opened his strides. He risked a glance over his shoulder and saw Glenn only a few steps behind him.

"Out of breath yet, Wheezy?" Glenn gasped.

"Looks like you are," Bruce taunted and left him behind.

He still held back. Half a mile remained and Glenn trailed at least thirty feet behind him. The Academy rose over the top of the hill and Bruce wished for a light breeze.

Either Glenn couldn't come up with anything to top the taunt or he didn't have enough breath to voice it. By the time Bruce circled the Academy, he could no longer see Glenn behind him.

The marked path passed through the woods where he and Megan had walked. It wasn't in exactly the same spot, but it still felt the same. For all of its smaller size, he still sensed something vast and old there that awakened a sense of uneasy concern in him, much like he felt in situations where he might fall victim to Chuck or Glenn. Yet something here had made Megan smile.

He placed his foot poorly and almost rolled his ankle.

"Stop thinking about the kiss and watch where you're going," he huffed. It almost felt like summer or at least late spring there among the trees.

He'd never passed through Jubilee field the morning after the yearly celebration before. On some level, he'd expected to recharge himself with the wild energy he'd sensed there the previous night. But if anything, the bleached colors, muted sound and dead air of the clearing drew power from him as he ran. The carnies were nowhere to be seen, though many of the rides, booths and tents still stood amidst the trash of the previous night. And in the part of the field that the carnies kept roped off from the public, there were well over a hundred stakes driven into the ground as if to mark off new construction.

It's strange, he thought, *that they haven't already packed up and hit the road.*

Glad to be free of the deserted carnival, he entered the woods that separated him from the parking lot. He kept his eyes on the trail ahead of

198

him as the footing became more treacherous. Just before he turned the last bend in the trail, Bruce noticed someone ahead of him. Startled, he looked up just in time to see Chuck throw his closed fist toward Bruce's face.

The punch never landed. Bruce gasped involuntarily just as Chuck opened his meaty hand and let a sweaty clump of white fluff fly into his face.

As soon as that breath hit his lungs, he knew he was in trouble. His eyes watered up and his chest spasmed.

"How do you like that, Wheezy?" Chuck roared, just as something massive slammed into the bully. Bruce turned his head to follow the flight of a huge eagle as it passed. It seemed like he should remember it from someplace. Then he tripped while his eyes were averted from the path.

Bruce hit his shoulder against a tree trunk on the way down. He might have blacked out for a moment, but he wasn't entirely sure. The world spun as he tried to draw more air into his lungs.

He wasn't exactly sure what Chuck had thrown in his face, but judging from the fuzzy toad like thing perched a few inches from his nose, it had probably been hallucinogenic. The likelihood increased when it opened up its wide mouth and told him to get up before jumping into the air with the hindmost of its eight legs and taking flight with moth-like wings.

With a monumental effort, Bruce pulled his sprawled limbs back from the next county where it felt like they'd landed and tried to rise. Vertigo spun the world out from under him and he landed on his side where he could see several insect creatures with the faces of old men looking at him with concern from beneath the mushrooms where they'd been watching the race before he dropped in. Beyond them, he could see Chuck sprawled out on his back with the eagle perched on his chest, looking almost as if it were giving the boy a stern lecture.

When the monkey with the rabbit ears scurried up, Bruce decided that this party was both too crowded and too strange for him, and he closed his eyes. But the thing had other plans for him and blew some powder into his face from a pouch that hung about its torso.

"Wish…people…stop doing…that," Bruce mumbled irritably and came mostly awake.

"That's the best I can do, my Mistress," Mr. Monkey-Bunny said.

"It will suffice," a raspy voice replied, sounding almost like wind through leaves.

Bruce opened his eyes when rough hands lifted him gently from the ground on which he'd fallen, and he found himself looking into a face unlike any other he'd ever seen outside of dreams. It was female, and in its own alien way it was beautiful with eyes the swirling color of autumn leaves and tiny green vines merging with her skin. But there anything vaguely human ended as the rest of her had been formed directly from the debris of the woodland floor. Odd twigs and sprouting limbs peeked through places where he could see through her to the other side.

"Time is short, Sire," she told him, lifting him upright. "My kin and I will return you to the footrace while we speak."

"Isn't that…cheating?" he murmured as he fought to stay conscious.

"We will give you exactly the lead the coward stole from you through trickery," she said. "After that it is up to you to finish as best you can."

"Too tired," Bruce whispered as the air picked the two of them up and flew through the trees overhead. "Can't get there in time. Need Paul…"

"The time for that dream is not yet upon you," she told him. "And we near the edge of my domain. Please remember us in the days to come, and prepare for when that last drop of water falls from the tree. Now you

must make haste!" she urged, lowering him to the ground just at the edge of the trees. "The gateway will soon open for you."

Then, clearing his head with a gulp of air that fell far short of reaching his lungs, Bruce ran back into the sunlight.

Chapter XVII: Megan Breaks Free

Megan could feel an agitation she couldn't explain coming from her mother as they stood there, waiting for Bruce to come into view. It had nothing to do with the race, of that she was sure. And were it not for her mother's assurance that they had nothing to fear from the Wild Hunt, she would have sworn that the woman thought someone might find her out in the open like this.

In her eagerness to keep up with Bruce, Megan stretched her diminished senses across the field and into the woods that hid him from her view. But just as the trees shrouded her presence from those who sought her, they also hid Bruce.

Emelia stopped scanning the faces around them and placed her hand on her daughter's shoulder. With the faintest shake of her head, she told Megan that she'd noticed the girl's attempts, and that they needed to stop. Megan sighed irritably and scanned the woods with eyes alone for any sign that Bruce might be near.

A small commotion drew her attention away for just a moment when her grandfather's friends joined them. Both were out of breath, and the janitor looked as if his bad knee were bothering him today.

"Good," Mr. Green panted, "We didn't miss the finish."

The friendship forged between Megan and Bruce had drawn both their families together into something much stronger than neighbors. Win or lose, they knew this day marked the beginning of a new chapter in their lives. Warm air carried laughter through the open field, but not from the Grimbles or McGeehees. As one, they stood motionless in the humid air while tension built to the point where Megan feared something would soon break.

Azarich stepped between his daughter and Megan, enfolding them in his long arms. Emelia held her daughter's hand in her own and Megan felt, for the first time that she could remember, like a family. Nevertheless, she needed to see her friend. She needed to know he was okay.

The race covered over a mile and a half of uneven ground. Bruce was fast, but she doubted he'd break any world records in that terrain. Her antique watch showed the passage of five and then six minutes. Nine passed in agonizing silence without any movement from the woods. Mrs. Grimble chewed the polish off of all but one of her fingernails.

When Bruce cleared the woods with no one behind him, Megan's relief lasted only long enough to realize that something was terribly wrong. He filled her senses with his need to breathe, and his jumbled thoughts washed over her mind, seasoned with a taste of the woodland magic she'd felt during their walk.

Mrs. Grimble started toward him, but her husband held her shoulder.

"He knew it could happen," he whispered. "He'll never forgive you if you don't let him finish."

Megan marveled at the strength it must have taken for the woman to watch as her son labored toward them, still more than a dozen yards away. She clutched her husband's hand with white-knuckled intensity. The cheers that had begun with Bruce's appearance quickly faded into a silence in which everyone could now hear his tortured breathing.

Glenn broke free from the woods, and upon seeing Bruce still shy of the Gateway Oaks, began to sprint, putting his head down and closing the distance.

Paul began to chant Bruce's name, and within seconds the whole field rang with the sound. When his brother was within thirty feet of the white ribbon that now hung between the trees, Glenn trailed by no more than twenty.

Bruce stumbled and almost went down.

Megan stepped away from her family, reached out with her mind and willed the strength of her own body to enter his. A powerful barrier slammed down over her, cutting off her extra senses and confining her to her own body. She railed against this imprisonment, but her mother clearly intended to keep her this way until the race ended, and she came back to her senses.

But this had nothing to do with winning. Even walled off from him as she was, Megan knew something was breaking inside of him, something vital that might very well be the heart of what made him who he was. With a snarl that went unnoticed only because everyone remained too focused on the runners to hear her, Megan erupted from her mother's prison and joined him.

Emelia gasped, not only from the breaking of her shields, but at the magical shockwave that detonated through the field around them. Although it was only visible to the mother and daughter, it still sent birds flying from the trees at the edge of the woods as it continued toward the school grounds beyond.

Megan's vision sharpened, allowing her to see the individual flecks of color in each of his irises despite the distance between them. As she watched, hints of violet bloomed amidst the hazel. But the connection, strong though it was, held no power to change what had already been set in motion. Deep within her, that quiet voice asked why she did this. Why was he so important? In response, the sum of who she'd been and who she would ever be answered with such force that for the duration of a single

204

heartbeat she understood his strange feelings for her. Her awareness imprinted itself in every molecule of his being, and for just an instant, a strange feeling of completion filled her. Just as quickly it was gone, crushing her with its loss. Her lungs burned in response to his, her heart fell into beat with the power of his exertions, and energy poured out from her.

Bruce took one deep gulp of air and sprinted the last ten feet with Glenn's steps falling in his shadow. The fragile ribbon broke across his forehead instead of his chest because he was already falling when he passed through the Gateway Oaks.

The clang of a huge bell shook the very ground beneath them, making heads turn back toward the Academy. Even from this distance, Megan could feel the Dark Man come fully awake, casting his gaze in her direction. As she watched, Mr. Grimble swept his gangly son up into his arms before he could fall.

Bruce's eyes remained focused on her with a faint smile shaping his ashen lips, even as his father placed him into the ambulance.

"That bell has been frozen up solid for at least a century," Mr. Green muttered in awe.

"What have you done?" Emeila gasped, and for the first time that Megan could remember, her mother was afraid.

Unable to maintain the link any longer, Megan sagged into her grandfather's arms and continued to search for Bruce in the darkness.

Chapter XVIII: A Big Fan of Squirrels

Megan returned to herself halfway back to the house with her mother still holding her protectively. One glance at the rearview mirror told her that Jade and Paul were lost in their own thoughts as the wind whipped past them in the bed of her grandfather's truck.

Streets and houses from her mother's lost childhood slipped past, and Megan wondered what stories this place had yet to reveal. The forbidden mansion at the end of the road in particular seemed to call to her.

She felt like these past weeks had been spun from moonlight, both delicate and beautiful. She wanted to stay, but everything she touched sickened and died. Maybe it would be best to tell her mother everything and leave now. Maybe Bruce would be safe that way. But what about her grandfather? Sooner or later she'd lead the Huntsmen to Nickelville. What would happen to Azarich and the Grimbles then? The longer she stayed, the more roots she'd put down. Part of her would die when she left this behind, but at least she could move on with grace and dignity when she disappeared from their lives, not clinging to them like a spoiled child. A part of her began to understand her mother's reluctance to return to Nickelville, and more than anything she wanted to ignore it and stay anyway. Was anyone selfless enough to give up everything like that?

"So, what now?" Jade asked uncertainly after they'd left the truck.

"Come up to my room," Megan offered. "I don't have a television or computer, though."

"Your room sounds good," Paul said. "I don't feel like watching anything right now anyway."

"Me either," Jade added with a lack of direction that Megan understood too well.

Azarich and Emelia respected their need for solitude while still making it clear that they would both be downstairs if needed. For the next hour Jade laid on the bed, while Megan stared at the distant shape of the Baker Hotel from her window. Paul prowled, occasionally perching somewhere for a few seconds before resuming his measured paces around the room.

"I've always wanted a bed like this," Jade said at last. "But Mom said the hangings would hold dust and be bad for Bruce. I was mad at him for a long time because of that."

"Really?" Megan asked. "Don't take this the wrong way, but the bed doesn't seem your style."

"I'd change it up," Jade admitted, pointing to the hangings. "Those would definitely have to go. I had red velvet with black lace in mind."

"Oh," Megan said, drifting back into her own thoughts. "This is all my fault," she whispered when she could hold the thought no longer.

"What?" Paul asked, freezing in mid-stride.

"It's my fault this happened," Megan said miserably, unable to look at Bruce's siblings. The trees outside blurred, and she hurriedly wiped her eyes.

"And just how did you come to that idiotic revelation?" Jade asked, sounding at last like herself.

"I was the one who suggested he run in the race," Megan sniffed.

"Last time I checked, Bruce was a big boy and made his own decisions now." Jade said. "He even washes his hair without Mom's help."

"Yep, for at least a few weeks now," Paul added with one of his infectious grins.

"But if I hadn't brought it up, he wouldn't have run," Megan persisted.

"If you hadn't suggested it, he might not be ill yet," Paul agreed, coming over to sit next to Megan in the window, "but it would have started eventually even if he hadn't run. This way he got to race Glenn and win."

"This has happened before," Jade added. "He's had really bad attacks that put him in the hospital. I'm just surprised it came on this quickly."

"He must have gotten into something that he was really allergic to out in the woods," Paul added.

"Something that grew there since last night at the Jubilee?" Jade asked.

Downstairs the phone rang.

"Hello," Azarich's voice carried clearly up the stairs.

Silence followed as he listened to the speaker on the other end of the line. Megan felt the tension in the room thicken.

"Excellent," he continued. "The children will be glad to hear that. Jade and Paul are more than welcome to stay the night."

Megan shared a collective sigh of relief with the two Grimbles at this implication that Bruce was okay.

"Do they have any idea what brought on the attack so quickly?" he asked.

More silence.

"Is he sure?"

This time they could control their curiosity no longer. They filed out of the room and watched Azarich from the top of the stairs. Megan could feel his anger. She noticed that her mother had slipped silently in from the living room as well.

"That's despicable," Azarich said. "I might have to come out of retirement for this one, but I'm afraid Bruce's testimony might not be completely trustworthy given his condition at the end of the race. See if he can remember anything else when he wakes."

The three exchanged worried looks. This didn't sound good.

"I'll tell them," he said gravely, "Just focus on Bruce for now. Jade and Paul can stay for any length of time necessary. You've raised an admirable family, and it would be our privilege to have them stay with us."

Azarich paused once again. Only hearing half of the conversation was maddening.

"Yes, and try to get some rest yourselves. If you need us to bring up something for you to eat just give us a call. Goodbye, Ben."

He hung the old phone back up on its cradle and noticed for the first time that he wasn't alone.

"So, what's going on?" Jade prompted him.

"Come down," he said, motioning with his hands. "As I'm sure you gathered, that was Mr. Grimble. Bruce is stable, but the doctors want to keep him tonight and have given him something to help him rest," Azarich said when they were all together next to the front door. "Jade and Paul will be staying the night. I started airing out the guest rooms when we got home, so they shouldn't be too stale."

"So why did you say you might come out of retirement?" Emelia asked.

"Before Bruce fell asleep, he told his father that Chuck Baker had been waiting for him in the woods," Azarich said with a grimace.

"What did he do to Bruce?" Jade asked, bristling.

"Chuck threw something in his face when he ran past," Azarich said.

209

"Does anyone know what it was?" Paul asked.

"Bruce didn't know for sure, but he said it started his asthma attack."

"I'm gonna kill him," Jade muttered, "and then you're going to have to come out of retirement to try and keep me out of jail."

"Furthermore, there was ragweed fluff caught in Bruce's hair when they brought him into the hospital," Azarich finished.

"Oh crap," Paul groaned. "Bruce is really allergic to that stuff."

"Has Bruce ever experienced hallucinations during his asthma attacks before?" Azarich asked.

"Not that we know of," Paul said, looking puzzled. "Why"

"Apparently he told your parents an interesting tale about the woods coming alive to help him," he answered. "He said he thought he'd been drugged."

"If his oxygen levels got low enough," Paul said thoughtfully, "I guess it might be enough to make some of the stuff from his fantasy books come up from his subconscious."

Megan began to understand the traces of wild magic that had clung to him when he came out of the woods. The voice in the back of her mind whispered that she should keep this to herself for now.

"Glenn put him up to it," Jade insisted. "Chuck isn't smart enough to find his backside with both hands. There's no way he could have known what to throw at Bruce let alone where to find it."

"She's got a point," Paul added.

"That's what Doreen thought as well," Azarich agreed. "The problem is that the Baker boy's lack of intelligence isn't enough to tie Glenn to this. We'll need more."

"Okay everyone," Emelia said, herding them toward the front door. "We've spent enough time here moping around. There's nothing else we can do for now, and you children must be famished. Where do you guys want to go?"

"Gordon's is the best place to eat in Nickelville," Paul answered without thinking, and then added with a pointed look at Megan, "And best of all they don't serve corn dogs."

"Gordon's?" Emelia repeated, looking puzzled.

"An excellent suggestion," Azarich said with a mischievous grin that seemed out of place after the events of the day, pausing only to get his keys from their peg by the front door. "Maybe that will get our minds off of everything."

"That's the pizza place from the Jubilee, right?" Megan asked as they climbed once again into the back of the truck. The memory of Bruce laughing so hard just a few hours ago hung heavy in her thoughts.

"Best pizza in town," Jade answered, echoing Bruce's words from the previous night.

"They serve other stuff too," Paul added. "But most people go for the pizza."

They rode back into town in silence, each lost in their own circular paths of grief and worry. No matter how much they might want to rationalize the situation, they all felt guilty for Bruce's absence while they went to his favorite restaurant. It just wasn't fair. He should have been there with them, celebrating.

Gordan's turned out to be one of the shops nestled in the long row of neglected buildings on Main Street. But unlike most of the other businesses, it was brightly painted and looked somehow more alive. A neon sign declared that Gordon's was open, but looked out of place without the beer signs Megan was accustomed to seeing in such a place.

"Wasn't this a hardware store?' Emelia asked.

"Not for quite a while," Azarich answered, smiling again. Then he held the door open for his daughter and granddaughter. As soon as they crossed the threshold, Megan felt an awareness pass over her as if she'd tripped some sort of alarm.

Emelia shot an extremely angry look at her father, and Megan barely had time to wonder what was happening before a door at the other end of the restaurant burst open, revealing a giant of a man. As he approached, she realized that he was even larger than she'd first thought.

When she was finally able to get past his sheer size, she took in the bronze skin and black hair which he wore in a single braid down his back. Surely, he'd need to have his clothing specially made. If she was right, she could understand the work boots and the jeans, but why would someone have a t-shirt made of an elf making a strange peace-sign and captioned *Live Long and Prosper*?

"Sam!" Jade called out when she saw him, bounding up and wrapping her arms as far as they could reach around his trunk-like waist. "Did you hear about Bruce?"

"The part about him winning the race, or that he's in the hospital?" he asked in a rumbling voice that should have been incapable of expressing the tenderness Megan felt coming from him. And even though he hugged the girl in his arms back, his eyes never left Emelia.

"Both," Jade answered, releasing her hold on the big man. She wiped her eyes on her sleeve as she pulled away, having finally found the comfort she needed.

"How is he?" Sam asked, studying Emelia's face as if trying to find the girl from the hallway pictures back home.

"He'll be okay," Paul answered. "The doctors said he could come back in the morning."

"That's good news to hear," the giant replied, and there was a pause in which Megan thought he wanted to say more but didn't know how.

"Hello, Sam," Emelia said at last.

"Hello, Squirrel" he replied in little more than a whisper. "I heard you were back in town."

"Then you should have come to see me," Emelia replied with an odd expression Megan had never seen on her face before.

"After thirty years, I felt I needed an invitation," he replied. His eyes finally left her face and settled on Megan. "And who is this?"

"I'm Megan," she answered, reluctantly placing her hand into what felt like a bear trap. He shook it with the same controlled gentleness that he'd hugged Jade. But his eyes were alight with mischief, and she could feel his awareness at the edge of her mind.

"It turns out I'm a grandfather," Azarich added happily, patting the big man on the back.

"I'm honored to meet you," Sam said, reaching down to tilt her head up so he could better look into her eyes. His own were filled with an odd mixture of otherworldly wisdom and childlike innocence. Here she knew, was a man who laughed when he was happy and cried unashamedly when he was sad. "Follow me."

He led them through the crowded room, and Megan marveled that someone so unbelievably big could move with such grace that she felt clumsy just walking behind him. Corded muscle rippled beneath the fabric of his clothing, and she wondered if he was a retired football player.

Now that they were moving, she was finally able to take in her surroundings. Her eyes darted from one place to another, overwhelmed by the sheer detail of the furnishings. Extensive brickwork columns rose into exposed wooden rafters to form graceful arches over doorways and windows. None of the tables matched, though they all looked as if they'd been made by the same huge hands.

"They all incorporate parts of old Nickelville," he explained, somehow knowing where she was looking even with his back turned toward her. "The barrel in that one came from my uncle's store. The bricks in that one came from one of the kilns at the factory back when it still made bottles."

The sounds of arcade games drifted from one of the side rooms. The excitement of several people washed over her as they passed, and she realized that more of her extra senses had returned since the race.

He led them through a covered archway where the original hardware store had been joined to the building next door. The ceiling in this area had been removed to show the interior of the building overhead. The only exception was a portion in which he'd apparently set up his office. Even this had been left open, so that he could see what goings on transpired while he took care of paperwork.

"This room is for my friends and their families," he said at last, opening a door into a room unlike the rest of the place, somehow big enough to host a large party on special occasions, yet cozy and private at the same time.

The first thing Megan noticed was an upright piano against one wall with a sign that read, *"No, Sam will NOT play it again!"*

"Sorry for the chill," he apologized, crossing the room to the hearth that took up one corner of the room. A fire had been laid within, just waiting to be lit.

"Hey Sam," Emelia said, her face still colored with that same unreadable expression she'd had when they'd first seen each other. Then she tossed him a matchbox.

He caught it reflexively and glanced at the tiny worn box in his huge hand. He stared at it blankly for a moment until his mouth turned up into a grin, and he looked back up at her. Megan recognized the matchbox at once. It was the only thing her mother had ever scolded her for playing with. She'd had no idea that Emelia still carried it.

"Thanks," he said, his deep voice huskier than it had been before. Then he turned his back on the room and Megan thought she felt something happen, but she wasn't sure what. When he turned back to them, the fire had already begun to spread through the seasoned firewood.

He handed the box back to Emelia, who put it back into the inner pocket of her jacket. Then he motioned for them all to sit down at the benches that flanked two long tables.

"Whatever you want is on the house," he announced pleasantly.

"We can't possibly accept that," Azarich protested.

"You don't want to offend my hospitality now," the big man rumbled with a frown and placed his meaty hands on his hips. "Do you?"

"You always were the only person who could argue with my father," Emelia laughed. "We are honored to accept your hospitality."

Megan noticed a hint of formality in her mother's words, as if she'd said something similar many times in the past.

"But you're going to have to come over and let me feed you for a change," Azarich countered, unwilling to let it go that easily.

"That's settled then," Sam said. The frown disappeared as if it had never existed at all. "I'll back for your order in a few minutes."

"Wow," Megan said when he was gone.

"That pretty well sums up Sam Wise," Paul agreed.

"His last name is Wise?" Megan asked.

"You thought it was Gordon, didn't you?" Jade asked, pushing the menu away as if she didn't need to look at it. "Your mom was right, this place used to be a hardware store back in the day. Sam bought it when it went out of business, but he liked the way the old sign looked, so he kept both the sign and the name for the restaurant. As you probably noticed on the way in, he has a thing for old pieces of the town."

"We passed the Gordon that the place is named after on the way in," Azarich added. "He and his wife were the ones with the walkers. I used to go fishing with him until he decided he was getting too old to go out on the lake."

"Isn't he quite a bit younger than you?" Emelia asked while she looked over the menu.

"By about fifteen years," he agreed. "And Wise wasn't Sam's original surname either."

"It was Smith when we were kids," Emelia said. "But I don't remember what it was before that."

"Why does he change it so often?" Megan asked, thinking about all of the aliases she and her mother had used over the years. She hadn't even known her real name was McGeehee until she was about eight.

"Most of the Native American names we think of as normal were actually created by Hollywood," Paul explained. "Many of them didn't have last names at all until the government said they had to have them in order to be considered citizens. Quite a few drew their names out of hats. Others, like Sam, change theirs when they feel like it because they have no real ties to them."

"Mom," Megan said, noticing several pictures on the mantle of the fireplace, "Is that you?"

"Yes," her mother answered without looking. "Sam was my best friend growing up."

"He sure has a lot of pictures of you up in here to have just been friends," Paul observed, finding many more on the walls now that he knew what he was looking for.

The look Emelia gave him removed the fire's heat from the room.

"There are a lot of pictures of Mr. McGeehee, Mr. Green and Mr. Harris, too," Jade said, trying to save her little brother from premature death.

"Please call me Azarich," the old man asked.

"You do realize that your first name isn't any easier to pronounce than McGeehee," Jade observed critically.

"But why pick Wise?" Megan asked.

"It's a name from one of his favorite books," Emelia explained, apparently having decided to let Paul live a while longer. "He used to joke about changing it to Sam Wise when we were younger."

"And do you realize that in all the years since," the man under discussion announced, walking into the room, "that Bruce is the only one besides you who has ever caught the reference. Nickelville is not now, nor ever is it likely to be what I would consider a well-read community."

Mention of Bruce made them all realize how much they'd been enjoying themselves. Megan and the Grimbles fell silent. After the food was ordered, Azarich and Emelia carried most of the conversation, trying to cheer the three up again. They asked the Grimbles if they had any plans for the summer. They asked about school. But every subject led them back to Bruce, and silence still reigned when the pizza came.

Sam not only managed to carry three pizzas to the table without dropping them, but made it look as simple as breathing.

"Sorry to run," he said with a frown, "but my least favorite patrons are causing a ruckus in the other private room. "I keep trying to make them mad enough to start eating somewhere else, but they keep coming back. I guess it's the price I have to pay for being such a magnificent cook." He gave Megan a big wink and disappeared before anyone could respond.

The long and emotionally charged hours since breakfast rushed in, and they ate with little thought for anything else. Bruce had said that it was the best pizza in town. Megan would have happily told anyone who asked that Sam made the best pizza in the world. Given the fact that her mother could burn water, Megan had eaten pizza all over the country and had never tasted anything to compare to this.

When the worst of her hunger had retreated before the onslaught of so much food, Megan excused herself to find the restroom. Jade gave her an inquisitive look that asked if she wanted company, but she shook her head, not wanting to come between the eldest Grimble and the only real comfort she'd found since the race.

True to the rest of Sam's sense of humor, there were signs posted of people who clearly needed to use the restroom complete with an arrow pointing in the appropriate direction.

After she had taken care of her needs, she paused at the mirror, searching her face for the grief she felt inside. But after so many years of keeping her true feelings hidden from the world, she wasn't surprised to find little showing on the outside.

"He's going to be okay," she whispered to herself and turned to leave.

She felt the presence of someone near as soon as the bathroom door closed behind her and found Allison's gloating smile just inches before her.

"What are *you* doing here?" Allison demanded, standing so close that Megan could smell the cloying scent of the girl's perfume. "This place never was very classy, but they must be dropping what few standards they had left if they're letting someone like you in."

"Leave me alone, Allison," Megan grumbled as she tried to slip past. "I'm not in the mood today."

"Oh that's right, poor little Brucie got sick," Allison mocked, pretending to rub tears out of her eyes.

"Not before he kicked your boyfriend's butt," Megan shot back, "in spite of cheating."

"I don't know what you're talking about," Allison giggled with an airy smile.

Megan's hand shot forward of its own volition and grasped Allison by the throat. The red-head's smile disappeared when she unexpectedly found herself pinned to the back of the wall that hid them both from the room beyond.

"What did you do?" Megan whispered through gritted teeth.

"Let go of me, you freak," Allison demanded and tried in vain to break free of Megan's grip.

The overhead lights flickered and went dark. Megan felt a surge of energy flow across her arm toward Allison. The girl's eyes flew wide and Megan knew, without looking at the rich girl's newly replaced phone, that it was as fried as its predecessor.

Megan had just enough time to think that she was going too far before something deep within her, something primitive, came alive. She saw herself in the reflection of Allison's wide-eyed stare and was startled to see that not only had her eyes changed color, but they were glowing as well.

Megan's point of view reversed, and she could see herself from Allison's eyes. The rich girl's fear bathed her as the information she'd wanted unfolded within her mind's eye:

Allison, Chuck and Glenn gathered around her phone, confirming that the plants in front of them should make that obnoxious Bruce Grimble have one of his famous asthma

219

attacks...

Allison collecting more from the field behind her house...

Glenn imitating Bruce in the midst of an asthma attack while Allison laughed...

Allison explaining yet again what Chuck would have to do in order to make Bruce lose the race...

Megan pulled away from Allison's memories in furious revulsion. Her eyes focused once again on the frightened girl before her. On some level, Allison understood what had just happened.

All of Allison's dignity and haughty superiority were shed as the understanding dawned that she was no more than prey in the grip of a powerful predator. She tried once more to break free of Megan's unbelievably strong grip. Her fear flowed through the physical connection between them, and a hunger that had nothing to do with food awoke within Megan. She was torn between revulsion and terrified glee.

Pain blossomed at the base of Megan's skull, and she feared for one panicked moment that the Huntsmen had found her again.

Let her go, Emelia's voice echoed inside Megan's mind.

It took every bit of energy Megan could summon to release her hold on the spoiled girl. A wave of exhaustion rolled over her as the energy stopped flowing into her. What had she been about to do? Even with the connection broken, she had no faith in her ability to control herself and feared she might attack Allison again if she got too close.

The red-haired girl slumped against the wall. Emelia took her face between her hands and locked eyes with her.

Megan could hear whispered commands deep within the recesses of her own mind, though her mother's lips never moved. When Emelia finished, Allison stumbled away toward the other private room where her family presumably waited.

Without another word, Emelia slipped her arm under Megan's and helped her back to where Azarich and the Grimbles waited.

Megan shivered, cold for the first time she could remember.

"We need to go," Emelia announced when they got back to the table. "Megan isn't feeling well."

One look at Megan convinced everyone that it was true. She wondered what they saw when they looked at her. Some sort of monster?

"Going so soon?" Sam asked when they passed. Then he saw Megan and exchanged an unspoken message with Emelia before ushering them toward the exit.

Before they could escape through the door to Main Street, Mrs. Jones bounded into their path, dressed as usual as if she were going to some sort of celebrity function instead of lunch.

"I might have known you'd have something to do with this," the gaudy woman shrieked as she tried to grab Megan by the wrist.

Her hand was intercepted by Emelia who, in spite of the difference in their sizes, held it in a vice-like grip.

"If you have something to say, you will say it to me, Paula," Emelia growled.

"Your daughter did something to Allison," Mrs. Jones stammered, clearly not expecting this much resistance from the woman she'd tormented so often as a child.

"Megan," Emelia asked, her voice suddenly pleasant, "Did you do anything to Allison?"

"Nope," Megan lied.

"Well then, now that that's settled, we're going home," Emelia said in a pleasant voice that conflicted with the hard glint in her eyes, "My daughter isn't feeling well."

"Like anyone would believe the word of that little thief!" Mrs. Jones snarled, finally gathering herself enough to try and pull her wrist from Emelia's grasp.

"Listen to me, Paula," Emelia began, and now her tone matched her expression. "We are not children any more. More importantly, I stopped being that weak little girl so long ago that I can't even remember what she was like. You do not want to cross the woman I've become. If you don't leave my daughter alone, I will visit your evil upon you threefold. Now do I need to elaborate, or did your pathetic excuse for a brain comprehend me this first time?"

She allowed Mrs. Jones to pull away.

"You'll be sorry for this, McGeehee," the large woman said with as much venom as she could summon. It lacked much threat, however, since her voice trembled as she spoke.

"Only because I wish I'd done it years ago," Emelia purred and led Megan out into the street, then she paused, looking the woman up and down. "The years have not been kind, Paula. Now your outside matches what was always inside you."

"I *so* want to be you when I grow up," Jade exclaimed in wide-eyed admiration as they returned to the truck.

Megan rode between her mother and grandfather on the way back while she watched the Grimbles talk animatedly in the bed through the rear-view mirror. It was clear that they were discussing what her mother had just done.

She felt like she'd tried to run a marathon with a bad case of pneumonia. She'd stopped shivering, but still thought she might have a fever.

Her mother's behavior baffled Megan as they drove on. In spite of so many years of scolding Megan for losing control, Emelia seemed genuinely pleased by what had just happened. But what exactly *had* happened? Megan had never felt anything like it. She'd never seen into another person's mind before. Sure, she could often tell what they were feeling, but this was something altogether different. A part of her felt unclean for breaking into Allison's memories like that, but another part swelled within her and told her that it was good, and pleasant and absolutely what she *should* have done in that situation.

She really missed Bruce. Even though she wouldn't have been able to tell him what had happened, she knew his presence would have helped.

She must have dozed, because the next thing she knew they were parked once again in front of Azarich's house. *This time*, she thought, *I'll stay home. Bad things happen when I leave today. Maybe tomorrow will be better.*

The Grimbles gave her looks of concern as Azarich helped her up the steps into the house. Emelia, however, looked as if she couldn't have been prouder of her daughter. Did her mother really hate Mrs. Jones enough to wish harm on Allison? But if that were the case, why had she stopped it? Megan felt fairly sure that whatever came next would have been bad, possibly even fatal for the red-headed girl. Allison deserved punishment for her part in what had been done to Bruce, but surely not death? Things became fuddled in her exhausted mind, and she drifted off almost as soon as her mother led her to her bed.

Sleep well princess, her mother's voice whispered through her mind. Megan opened her eyes one last time to find Emelia smiling down at her. *You can tell me what you saw in Allison's mind when you wake.*

The last thought Megan had before she drifted away was to wonder how her mother was speaking without moving her lips, and why now, of all times, she was calling her a princess when she never had before.

The memories she'd stolen from Allison's mind tainted her dreams. Sometimes she saw them as an outsider, but at others it seemed as if she, Megan, had committed those vicious acts herself.

When she woke, the light from her window had grown dim. It was only her concern for having left Jade and Paul alone that gave her the strength to fully pull herself back toward wakefulness.

The worst of the exhaustion had receded, but she still felt that her abilities had been diminished by what she'd done for Bruce at the race, and further still by whatever she'd done to Allison.

She rose to her feet and had to steady herself against one of the bedposts. Where were the Grimbles? She felt guilty for leaving them alone for so long.

"I thought I felt you stirring," Emelia said from the doorway. "I'll help you go downstairs."

"Where are Jade and Paul?" Megan asked.

"They went to the woods for a while," Emelia said while she helped Megan down the stairs. "I get the feeling they spend a lot of time out there and wanted something more familiar for a little while."

"Good, I was afraid they might have been bored. I haven't been a very good host, have I?"

"They don't mind," her mother assured her. "I think they're going to pick up some clothes from their house as well."

"Mom," Megan said quietly, "What happened?"

"We'll talk about that later when you've had a full night's rest.

"Can we talk with our minds?"

"Try and see," Emelia answered with a smile.

Can you hear me? Megan thought with her face screwed up in concentration.

Yes, I can, Emelia replied without opening her mouth.

224

But how?

Just like we do anything else. This is a natural part of who and what we are, Megan. I've been waiting for you to do something like you did today for a long time. This is only the beginning. I'm so proud of you.

Am I some kind of monster? Megan asked in a rush. She hadn't meant to ask that question because she feared the answer. But in this kind of communication, what she thought and what she said were essentially the same.

No, my dear, you are not. If there are monsters here, then they share the Jones name. You did no lasting damage to her. By now she has convinced herself that it was all part of her imagination.

But what did I do to her?

The doorbell rang.

We will talk about this later, Megan. Now is the time for other things. You are the same young woman you were when you woke up this morning. You have not changed. You have only seen a bit deeper into the miracle that is my daughter. Take their minds off of Bruce. I sense they've got their own regrets to deal with. You will understand all of this in time. I promise.

Cold air blew in through the open door as the Grimbles carried their duffle bags in with them. A front had blown in while Megan slept, and it felt like the first breath of winter had followed the brother and sister in from the woods.

Paul helped Grandpa carry wood in from outside, and a fire soon blazed in the fireplace. They ate s'mores while Azarich told stories of his misspent youth, and at last the exertions of the day took their toll and left everyone dozing in the quiet living room while the warmth from the fire enveloped them and the sun set behind the trees.

As Megan watched the flames dance within the stone fireplace, her awareness of the room faded around her.

225

She could see the grandmother whom she so resembled sitting on the couch near the fire, sewing the quilt from her grandpa's bed.

He was watching her from the doorway. His hair was dark and free of gray.

The scene in her mind faded into one of the Academy's classrooms. A very young Paula was throwing wads of paper at Emelia.

The scene shifted again.

There were oil lamps around the room, and a fire was burning in that fireplace too. It was a warm, cozy place and Megan could smell cinnamon. A bassinet held a wiggling bundle that cried weakly. Into the room walked...

Megan jerked her eyes away from the fire to find her mother staring at her with interest.

"Okay kids," the small woman said, "It's been a long day and tomorrow won't be much better. Go wash up and head to bed."

"Grandpa," Megan asked as they all headed toward the stairs, "was the Academy around before there was electricity?"

"Why yes," he answered, puzzled. "The gas-lamp fixtures were still set into the walls when your grandmother and I went there."

Why do you ask? Emelia asked.

Not trusting this new form of communication, Megan shrugged in reply.

Chapter XIX: Last Minute Holiday Preparations

A detached part of Megan's mind knew that she was dreaming as she fell. Maybe that's why her descent felt more like an escape. The shadows around her came to life, seeming more substantial than she herself felt. Each of them beckoned to her, trying to call her back. But she had severed her ties with them, and they no longer had any power over her.

Then she became aware of a presence rushing toward her, one that she'd been waiting for.

The sunlight that streamed in from her window felt like the visual equivalent of a scream when she woke, and the entire top of her skull throbbed in response to her movements as she threw aside the bedspread and started to dress.

Why did you let me sleep so late? Megan asked her mother, unsure of the range for this form of communication.

You needed it after what happened at Gordon's, came the reply. *Everyone just finished eating. Come down while it's still warm.*

Bruce is coming home, Megan replied, dismissing the suggestion of food.

How can you tell?

I can feel him, just like we do with each other.

I see, Emelia sent and for the first time, Megan noticed that she could sense emotions with the thoughts. Her mother was worried about something.

What's wrong?

I'm making some toast for you. After what happened yesterday at Gordon's, you're going to need some energy.

Is that why my head hurts so much?

Stopping a judgment once the process has started takes a tremendous amount of power.

A judgment?

That is a discussion for another day. You have neither the time nor the background knowledge to understand what happened at Gordon's. But I promise you that you will be told everything when the time is right.

Mom, am I dangerous? Should I avoid Bruce and the others? I don't think I could live with myself if I ever hurt them.

You are very dangerous my love, but not to the people you care for. Your power merely turns evil upon itself. Your Grimbles have nothing to fear from you. They are some of the first genuinely good people I've met in a long time.

"Mom and Dad just drove up with Bruce!" Paul yelled from somewhere down below.

Megan slipped her shoes on, ran a brush quickly through her dark hair and pulled it back at the base of her neck. She tried to take the stairs at a run, but discovered she was still weak as well as disoriented.

"Thanks for letting us crash with you," Jade said, offering her hand to Azarich.

"It was our pleasure," Azarich said, ignoring the hand and hugging both of the Grimble children as if they were his own.

228

"Tell him he was amazing yesterday," Emelia said as she gave her daughter a quick hug, some toast and a glass of juice. *Take it easy,* she added inside Megan's mind.

Megan drained the glass, gave it to her mother and then followed the Grimbles out the front door. The only reason she could keep up with them as they walked was because they were burdened by the duffle bags they'd brought over. She still felt bad about leaving them alone for so much of the night.

"He's going to be really weak," Jade warned before they reached the front door. "He'll be fine, but I'm betting he looks like hell."

Megan nodded, remembering how he'd looked when they loaded him into the ambulance. Then she thought of the way he'd met her at this door the last time, and her mouth filled with a metallic taste that soured her stomach. She threw the uneaten toast into the yard for the birds.

She wasn't sure what to expect when she turned the corner and peered through the open door to Bruce's room. In spite of what his siblings had told her, she still felt responsible.

He was lying on the bed with his eyes closed when they walked in. His chest moved quickly in time with each short rasp of breath.

"Hey champ," Jade said.

"I kicked his butt," Bruce wheezed without opening his eyes, "didn't I?"

Megan felt her eyes begin to water, but pushed it back and sat down on the nearest corner of his bed.

"Yeah, you should have seen the look on his face when you broke the ribbon," Jade said in a bright and cheerful tone, though her eyes held a curious mixture of tenderness and anger.

"What's wrong, Megan?" Bruce asked and at last opened his eyes.

"Are you mad at me?" she asked.

229

"Why would… I be… mad?" he asked between gasps.

"She seems to think it's her fault you got sick," Paul said. "Something about being the one who suggested you run."

Bruce pushed himself up with difficulty and moved over to sit next to her.

"Yesterday… I beat… Glenn… even though he… cheated," Bruce said in broken gasps that made Megan feel even worse. "He's teased me… about my… asthma… for years."

She wished he would wait to tell her what he had to say.

"He and his... friends have... bullied me into thinking I'm... less than they are. I know I sound horrible... and I feel like crap... but I'm not... going to die." His smile and the energy in his eyes shone brighter.

Bruce reached out and took her hand in his own.

Power rushed through their connected hands, and her headache faded in an instant. Afraid that she was draining him like she had Allison, she mistook the surprise on his face for pain and pulled her hand from his. He took a deep, easy breath and frowned at her hand.

"You've never seen him like this before," Jade said. "He won't be running again until we have a good frost, but he's actually doing better than I thought he would be. And he'll continue to get better as long as he has the good sense to stay away from me when I'm waking up in the morning."

Bruce doubled over, coughing so deep that Megan worried that something inside him might burst. She looked to Jade for help, but Bruce's sister was smiling.

"She… She hung in the air… for a second with her arms …and legs flapping… before she fell," he gasped and started to cough again.

He was *laughing*. She reached out and took his hand in her own again, wanting to see if it helped his breathing.

"I think some serious payback is in order," Bruce said, and she could tell that he was also aware of the effect her touch had.

"I'll say," Megan agreed, starting to feel better.

"Now you're talking," Jade added.

"I've been thinking about something ever since Allison dumped ink on our stuff," Bruce said, reluctantly letting go of Megan's hand to sit at his computer. Soon the four of them were gathered before its screen, marveling at the detail that Bruce had already put into the sophisticated blueprints."

"I've got one that will work for that," Megan said, pointing at the screen without getting too close lest she fry it like she had so many other pieces of technology. "I was going to throw it away anyway."

"I can get those," Jade said. "Mom can't know though. She'll think I'm going to use them on myself. It's going to be tough getting all this ready before Thanksgiving break," she added. "It's only a week away."

Chapter XX: Emelia's Promise

A volley of cheers greeted Megan, Bruce, Jade and Paul when they climbed into the bus on Tuesday morning. Even the bus driver joined in.

Bruce enjoyed the moment, even though he had to hold onto the seat next to him while he stood. His medication left him light-headed when he exerted himself.

Paul carried a big box that held his "Liquid Viscosity" project for science. His parents had praised him because it was the first science project he'd ever made that didn't deal with fossilization.

Megan noticed that Chuck and Glenn weren't riding. All things considered, it was the best ride to school that Bruce or Megan had ever had. Everyone treated them as if they belonged. Jade and Paul had always been accepted, but Bruce's miracle seemed to have spread out to cover Megan as well.

When they arrived, they found Alan and Tom standing in the cafeteria staring up at the clear windows high overhead. The curtains that had shrouded them from the lunch-hour sun had been torn loose and shredded to lie across the tables and floor beneath. No one was quite sure how the vandal had even gotten up there.

Students and teachers who'd never spoken to Bruce before the race, now congratulated him. The usual sneers were gone, except for the one they expected at their lockers.

"Oh, nice jacket, McGeehee," Allison's shrill whine echoed down the hall.

"Thanks," Megan said, twirling like a model so the teacher's daughter could get a better look at the ragged denim. "I thought of you when I pulled it out of the closet."

Allison walked away unsure if she'd been insulted or not.

According to Bruce, this was the first time Chuck had missed a day of school since kindergarten. Without the ninth-grade bully to protect him, many believed Glenn should have an unfortunate accident before the day was over.

Even Mrs. Jones appeared subdued by what had happened. She still glared at Megan and called on her in that piercing voice. She did so, however, with a lack of enthusiasm that left Megan hoping that the worst was over.

Shortly before break, the Dark Man materialized directly next to her desk without even a hint of cinnamon. One of his hands rested on the back of the chair in front of her and the other on the one in which she sat. Leaning over her, his nose was mere inches from her cheek.

It took every ounce of willpower to resist the urge to slide out the other side and escape. But aside from her clenched jaw, she allowed nothing of her panic to show where anyone but Bruce might notice.

Several students looked up at the ceiling when the lights began to grow brighter.

Tendrils of power crept across the surface of her shields like plagues of locusts, pinching and prodding their way along as he looked for holes in her defenses.

Now she understood why her mother had been so traumatized. What had it been like to spend years fighting him off like this without anyone in which she could confide her pain?

When he didn't find any openings, he lifted his hand from the back of the bench and with one finger extended, began to slowly move it toward her temple as if to brush away a stray lock of hair.

Her eyes fell on the evil woman at the front of the room, remembering how she'd cowered when Emelia finally stood up to her. Even though Bruce wasn't touching her, he was still close enough to give her more strength than she had without him. Turning her head to look directly into the apparition's eyes, she began to push back, knowing even as she did that her eyes had changed color.

You stole my mother's childhood, she sent, her jaw tight as she stared him down. *But I am more than I seem. Leave me alone!*

The phantom recoiled as if struck, confused by what he saw in her at that moment and hopefully realizing that this prey wasn't as defenseless as he'd hoped. Then he turned away from her as if hearing something in the distance and faded away.

Megan sagged back into her seat, unsure if she should feel relief or vindication.

Mrs. Jones passed up three opportunities to call on Megan while the class read aloud from the literature book before an office aide came to the door with a note from the principal.

"Miss McGeehee," the teacher whined with something resembling her former glee. "You're wanted in the office by the principal."

Megan looked over at Bruce, who shared her bewilderment as to what might have caused this summons from the reclusive head of the school. Then, with a shrug, she gathered her things and followed the girl out the door, stopping only to get her backpack. After Allison's ink prank, she

234

didn't want to leave it behind. Then she followed the girl around the corner to the office, trying not to think about the last time she'd been there.

"Have a seat outside Mr. Hamby's office, Megan," Millie said pleasantly.

"Am I in trouble?" Megan asked, remembering the missing watch.

"I don't think so," Millie said. "Your mother came in about half an hour ago and Mr. Hamby wanted to see you."

Megan had completely forgotten about her mother's promise to speak with the principal, but it appeared Emelia had not. Remembering the last time she'd waited here, she looked around for Mr. Bob, realizing that she hadn't seen him in a while.

The door to the office opened, and Emelia McGeehee stepped out, almost as pale as she'd been when they first came to town. Behind her stood the Dark Man, clearer than she'd ever seen him. *So that's where he went,* Megan thought.

Emelia rushed past Megan without seeing her.

Millie watched her go with concern.

"Megan," she said. "Why don't you go and make sure that your mom is okay."

"Sure," Megan said with growing dread and followed her out the office door.

Emelia was halfway down the steps by the time Megan caught up to her.

"Mom," Megan called, and when her mother didn't respond, *Mom.*

Emelia jumped and turned. Her eyes darted from Megan back to the door as if she expected something to come after her.

"It's okay, Mom," Megan said, wishing that she'd said something before now or at least warned her mother in some way. "I've seen him too."

If Megan had slapped her, it wouldn't have had as much of an effect on the frightened woman standing on the steps below her as those four words did.

Chapter XXI: Empty Seat

Bruce's asthma grew worse as his distance from Megan increased. By the time Mrs. Jones sat down with another magazine, he suspected his friend had left the Academy.

"I'll bet they finally found out where she's been hiding the stuff she stole," Allison whispered loud enough for the entire class to hear when the bell rang for class to go outside.

"Go down to the clinic, Bruce," Mrs. Jones said. "I can't leave you in here alone after you've spent so much time with that little thief."

Bruce slipped from the room with as much dignity as he could in the midst of a coughing fit. His chest was sore from labored breathing, and he had to rest in the cafeteria before continuing. A part of him wanted the petty defiance of going to the library or slipping into the attic instead of the clinic as he'd been told. But his lungs burned, and he desperately needed his inhaler.

He looked for signs of Megan when he passed through the office on his way to the clinic, already knowing that he wouldn't find any. Mr. Dander's door stood open as well as Mr. Hamby's. Where had she gone?

"Where has that man gone now?" Millie asked in exasperation when she stepped out of the principal's door with a stack of papers in her hand. "He disappears almost as fast as that cat appears around my fish!"

Bruce found the clinic empty as well, so he turned on the lights, took his inhaler out of the cabinet for a long deep puff, then walked over to the cot and collapsed there, trying to recall the speed with which he'd been able to run just days earlier. Pulling his feet up and leaning back against the wall, he could just see out through the stained-glass window where Mr. Green was trying to repair a lawnmower.

"He should try to mow behind the wall," Bruce said absently when the tall grass from his memory intruded on his thoughts.

Bruce considered himself a rational person, especially for a ninth-grader. But the mystery of that hidden corner kept surfacing in his thoughts, particularly when he was separated from his friend. For reasons he didn't want to contemplate too deeply, he'd noticed he always had trouble thinking around her. Shaking his head to clear it, he turned to the problem at hand. He hadn't seen anyone when he'd looked over the top, but that didn't mean a person couldn't have been hiding close to the base of the wall or even in the tall grass. Particularly since he'd only been able to look for a second. That made him feel a little better. Just the possibility that it was nothing more sinister than someone pulling a prank on him made things easier to handle. But hadn't he seen something else? Hadn't there been something else about getting the book back?

What about the wind and the rainstorm that had only raged above the school? It was too much of a coincidence that it started the second he got the book back. What did that leave? Monsters? He didn't care what it might be, but he knew all living things had to eat. So unless Mr. Danders had been sneaking in after-hours to throw in students with low test scores, anything back there would have starved by now. Something big enough to throw a book over a wall couldn't survive on a hunting ground that small. His research on wolves had taught him that. Furthermore, judging from the height of the grass back there, it definitely wasn't an herbivore either.

Why was he worried about its diet when the big question remained? *How did it influence the weather?*

Bruce shook his head. His breathing sounded loud in his ears, and the constant effort to breathe gave him a headache.

When the end of break came, he still had no explanation for what had happened that day in the courtyard. He rose on unsteady feet and walked back through the office.

"Did Megan ever return to class?" Millie asked when he passed.

"No," he answered.

"She must have gone home with her mother," she muttered. "But she should have cleared it with us before she did."

"Her mom was here?" Bruce wheezed.

"Yes, she looked a little bit spooked," Millie answered, still irritated as she returned to her work.

When lunch came, Bruce noticed a pile of new curtains on the edge of the stage. Mr. Green stood at the top of a tall ladder, hanging a set over one of the clear windows that looked out high above. For some reason, all of the light from the unobstructed windows now converged on a single spot as if they were spotlights. But even as one part of his mind argued that such a thing wasn't possible, another part, a part he didn't recognize or understand, began to explain exactly how it had been done.

Without Megan nearby, his breathing was shallow and labored. As far as he could tell, this new medication wasn't working at all.

He took his usual seat and stared at the lunch before him without any appetite whatsoever. Mr. Green climbed down the ladder and moved it to the next window before heading to the stage for another curtain.

Adrenaline flooded Bruce's body and freed his lungs as a vision of one of the heavy rods falling flashed through his mind's eye. He flew into motion even before the squeal of twisting metal reached his ears, snatching the sour milk kid from where he stood near the wall, waiting to return his tray.

The heavy iron rod slammed end first directly into the spot where the boy had stood only a fraction of a second before, gouging the wooden floor deeply enough to hold the length of iron upright for a second before falling to its side with a loud reverberating clang. The whole cafeteria stared at them in stunned silence for a few seconds before the rest of the rods broke loose, one after the other, and fell to the ground below.

When Jade and Paul arrived, they showered him with questions. But now that the adrenaline had burned through his blood, he couldn't breathe well enough to answer. He'd studied the first rod that had fallen. Whatever had pulled it loose had twisted the thick iron too badly to be reinstalled, not that anyone would ever dream of putting them back up there now. One rod falling would have been a strange event, all of them coming down simply wasn't possible. He could hear hushed whispers of vandalism from the teacher's lounge past the roar of excited student conversation even though that shouldn't have been possible either. Something strange was going on here, and he couldn't help but suspect that Megan knew more about such things than she let on.

When the subject changed to what they needed to do in order to get the last pieces in place for their revenge on the Trio, he listened to his siblings' whispered words and tried to think about something other than Megan's empty seat. After school, he rode next to Paul in the last row since Jade had missed the bus in order to make a slight detour along the way home.

Chapter XXII: Well of Dreams

At first Megan feared that they'd leave Nickelville that very moment with only Azarich's truck and the clothes they wore. Emelia refused to speak and Megan's attempts to speak mind-to-mind met with a blank void that made her feel as if she'd been put on psychic hold while her mother spoke with someone else.

Meanwhile, her sense of Bruce grew weaker the further they traveled from the school. She clung to him as long as she could, afraid that she might never feel his presence at the edge of her mind again.

She took a deep breath and tried to slow her racing heart. She tried to focus on the faint scent of her grandfather's cologne that lingered in the cab of the truck. But thinking of Azarich only reminded her of how much she had to lose.

How long would they have before the Huntsmen caught her scent?

But Emelia drove past the turn without hesitation, and Megan allowed herself to hope. But then the entrance to Beverly Road passed as well. Megan had never been through this part of Nickelville before and soon understood why. If she'd thought that the town was a community on its deathbed, then the portion that extended beyond Beverly Road had been infected by some wasting disease and begun to rot. The road rose from the floor of the valley in which the sleepy town of Nickelville had grown. She glanced back through the truck's rear window and found that she could see the entirety of the town with the Baker Hotel rising like a dark finger toward the heavens.

Houses with broken windows and sagging roofs peeked from tall weeds. Trumpet vines held what remained of the buildings in a rough embrace, both holding them up and splitting them asunder. The road faded to little more than the memory of those who'd traveled there before.

The stress of the past half-hour drained from Megan's body, and now that it appeared they might not be leaving after all, she felt drowsy. She closed her eyes and rubbed them absently with the back of her hand.

When she opened them, hazy images overlapped the abandoned remains of the town. She glanced at Emelia, expecting her mother to react in some way since she too had seen ghostly images surrounding the Academy. But they continued on in silence.

This wasn't the same as the Academy, she realized. While the illusions at the school felt completely real, these looked tired and washed out, like photographs left forgotten in the sun.

A huge eagle unlike any Megan had seen before perched on a chimney that stood among the fallen remains of the dwelling to which it had once belonged. It watched them as they passed, but before she could mention it to her mother, it passed from sight and her thoughts as well.

At first, she could only see the outlines of cabins. But as they drove deeper into the lost community, she could see horses, cattle and other livestock as well. Then came the children: hanging from trees, running alongside young colts, and climbing across rooftops. There were adults too, but they were the faintest wisps of memory in this ghostly community. Megan wondered if the imprint left by children on a place were always more pronounced than the ones left by their elders.

242

As she became accustomed to the strange images, she realized that she wasn't seeing a group of children, but rather a single active boy who seemed to be everywhere at once.

The road led them to the remains of a large building. Here the ground rejected the intrusion of plants as if it were too hard packed from the decades in which the community had gathered there. But the lack of destructive vegetation had not saved the building from the fate of its neighbors. In the present it was a jumble of rotting beams and stone walls. In the past it had been the General Store where the community had gathered for supplies, mail and gossip.

Here she saw the largest congregation of phantoms. More substantial than the others, perhaps because they'd spent so much time there in life, Megan could tell that they were all Native American.

The young boy was there as well, walking along the wooden hitching post like a balance beam. Even at his young age, Megan could tell he'd one day grow into a big man.

"What happened here?" Megan whispered.

"The modern age," Emelia answered, much to her daughter's surprise.

"What do you mean?"

"This is where the Native American part of Nickelville used to live, long before the settlers came."

"Where did they go?" Megan asked.

"They didn't."

"Didn't what?"

"They didn't go anywhere," Emelia answered wearily. "At least not at first."

"I don't get it," Megan said with a frown. "There were a lot of people who lived here. Now it's a ghost town." Emelia looked up sharply, and her lips thinned into a pale line at mention of the word *ghost*.

"That's not my story to tell," Megan's mother answered cryptically and then returned to her silent contemplation of the road.

When it became clear that she had no intention of elaborating further, Megan puzzled over the way this strange juxtaposition of the past and present made her feel compared to her experiences at the Academy.

The abandoned road led them back into the trees, and Megan felt the now familiar awareness settle over them as they passed. What was it about these trees that differed from the ones found in other parts of the world? She felt fairly confident in her belief that they were responsible for hiding her from the Wild Hunt, but was there more? Was it a coincidence that so much of the supernatural strangeness that permeated Nickelville seemed to be concentrated around the oldest trees?

The road meandered in a series of offset circles, robbing Megan of her sense of direction. On more than one occasion, her mother turned onto a path that seemed to actively hide from Megan's sight, almost as if the path were alive and protective of its secrets.

Megan reached out with her senses at one such juncture, curious about what she would find.

"Leave the wards alone," Emelia ordered.

"Wards?"

"Protective barriers. I'll have to fix them if you push too hard."

"Like the one at Gordon's?"

"Sort of," Emelia answered. "But that one was keyed specifically to me."

"Then why did I feel it?" Megan asked.

"Because half of you is me," her mother answered.

244

"So," Megan said cautiously. "Sam…"

"Was my best friend throughout childhood," she answered, staring straight ahead as she drove.

"Just a friend?" Megan asked, remembering when her mother had asked the same question of her just a few days previous.

"No," Emelia admitted. "He became much more than that as we grew older."

The road ended at a valley clearing that reminded Megan of the one from her dream. She was glad to see no stone monoliths or steps leading down to the valley floor. There was, however, a stone ring at its center, where she somehow knew the fires of the Elders had burned for thousands of years.

Emelia stopped the truck, got out and slammed the door behind her. Meagan followed as her mother descended the slope without explanation or backward glance. This place felt unfathomably old, yet she sensed some hidden potential for youth and vitality within it that defied explanation.

Megan didn't notice Sam Wise's presence until his shadow fell across her. Such an event should have startled her, but she realized she'd been expecting him. Even so, someone that big shouldn't have been able to move so quietly. When her eyes found his, she recognized the boy from her visions.

Together they followed Emelia down the slope. Their footsteps sounded distant and subdued. The air felt sluggish against her skin, though it flowed easily enough into her lungs. Even though her vision was clear, shapes lurked at the edges of her peripheral vision, and her extra senses told her that the three of them were far from alone within the valley.

When at last they reached the bottom, Megan looked up toward the rim and marveled at the symmetrical feature and wondered if it were man made. For that matter, the whole geography of the town felt too ordered to be entirely natural.

Sam took her by the hand and showed her where to stand. When he took his own place, they were evenly spaced around the perimeter of the stone ring. Fire sprang unbidden from within, even though there was nothing there to burn.

Megan averted her eyes from its shifting depths, worried that it might ensnare her within the waking dreams that fire often brought. As she did so, she found the specters of what she thought were Sam's ancestors standing row upon row all the way back up the slopes and beyond, making it look as if she, her mother and Sam stood on the floor of a bottomless hole in time.

For the first time Megan understood exactly how small and insignificant she was. Like stars that had all but vanished except for the lingering glimmer that found its way to Earth, the entities of the past looked down upon the three of them and joined what had once been with what might yet be.

Look within the flames, Sam's thoughts commanded.

Megan jumped, surprised to find that he shared this ability. As bidden, she allowed her mind to drift through the images that danced within the fire and at once her world was aflame.

This is the Well of Dreams, he explained. *In the days of my ancestors it was a place of learning. It was here that my grandfather revealed the collective memories we have amassed since the dawn of my people, lest they be forever lost. But I am the last, and there is no one left to whom I can pass them.*

Megan experienced his grief as if it were her own through the mental bond that joined the three of them. How could a person with so much sorrow in their soul also exude such happiness and joy?

Why are we here? Megan asked.

Your mother has told me of this Dark Man before. When we were children she confided her experiences of the Academy to me and with her permission, I brought them before the few Elders that remained. I was told that there are no ghosts, only places that hold the echoes of those who have gone before. They could offer no proof as to what happens to us when we leave these bodies, but they knew beyond a doubt that we do not remain here.

If you already know that they don't exist, why are we here? Megan asked.

The faint but persuasive voice within her mind stopped her from pointing out the proof of the afterlife that she could sense in the valley. Was she imagining the multitude rising around them? She needed to stop thinking about them lest her mother and Sam sense something amiss through the bond they shared.

The elders are gone, but I can still use the Well of Dreams to examine the memories that you hold of this Dark Man, he sent.

Then what is he? Megan asked.

Some places hold memories of the events that have unfolded there, particularly places where those events caused grief or anger. It could be that your Dark Man is just the echo of some past tragedy.

"Megan and I would disagree," Emelia said aloud with a mirthless laugh that felt blasphemous in the unnatural silence of the valley.

She's right, Megan thought, *he watches me and follows me through the school. If it was just a memory, he would just stare off into space. Mr. Bob can see him too.*

Mr. Bob?

The school cat, Megan explained.

247

You have a cat at your school? Sam asked. *Perhaps your people are not as barbaric as I'd thought. It's not surprising that the animal should be aware of this apparition. No one has ever bothered to teach them that it isn't possible, so they live with their senses awake to the world around them.*

And ever since the race, Megan added reluctantly, *he's been trying to get past my shields.*

Show us what's happened, Emelia prompted, worried by this new development. *Visualize what you've seen, and we will all see it within the flames.*

Megan concentrated on the memory of being drawn back into the old Academy. The flames froze, listening to her thoughts before reflecting her memory.

Then, with a wrenching sense of vertigo, Megan lost control of the fire. It grew beyond the bonfire Sam had called and stretched in a single brilliant pillar of light up through the ring of his elders and high into the sky.

Before she could react, the fire flowed over her and filled the whole of the valley with cold flames that burned, yet did not consume.

At first, the fire surged in chaotic patterns that teased her mind to understand. Then they merged and twisted into the silent features of the Dark Man. There still wasn't any sound to this pyrotechnic display, only the roar of power in her mind.

Pain blossomed at the base of her skull, and she staggered a step toward the flame as if summoned. Outside of the valley, past the trees that hid them and into the world beyond, she felt someone become aware of her.

"They have our scent!" Emelia screamed.

Megan tried to pull away from the looming face before her, but discovered that she'd lost the power to move after that first unwilling step. She could see her hands before her where they'd risen of their own accord to block the light from her eyes. But they might as well have belonged to someone else for all the good they did her.

She could feel Sam and her mother struggling with no more success than she'd found. The pain at the base of her skull multiplied a hundred-fold, and for the first time she could sense the thoughts of the Huntsmen, which probably meant they could sense hers as well. This fire had shredded her defenses and left her mind naked to the world around her.

Megan flung her senses out across the valley in desperation and found not only Sam's ancestors, but others as well. Their essence, old beyond imagining, rose to protect the three fragile beings trapped within the Well.

Unable to move, Megan watched them through the corners of her eyes as they advanced, forcing the dark presence at the center of the flames back into whatever hell it had escaped from to come here.

But in spite of the way the Dark Man's interaction with the Well of Dreams had left her vulnerable to the Wild Hunt, Megan almost felt sorry for him in those last moments. Something in the way his luminous green eyes held hers reminded her of the way she'd felt back at the apartment.

The magical turbulence of his banishment threw the three of them several feet up the slope and for a moment, Megan could see the figures that gathered around her clearly. Many of them looked like Sam's ancestors, but there were just as many who were not.

It was these others, these men and women in strange clothing that evoked something primal within her. They knelt before her, placing one fist over their hearts and bowing their heads in supplication before returning from whence they'd come.

Megan began to retch in the dry grass. She felt bruised, burned and hollowed out inside. Yet she also felt cleansed.

"Mom," she croaked, and found that her voice now sounded normal in her ears.

Emelia crawled to her side as drained by the experience as her daughter. Sam joined them, though his pride bade him rise to unsteady feet and stagger to them before dropping unceremoniously to his knees.

"Was that supposed to happen?" Megan asked, watching as the big man gave up and fell back on the ground.

"Nope," he whispered.

"Why did the memory of the school draw us in like that?" Emelia asked.

"The school?" Megan asked, confused.

"It was like we were trapped in your school," Sam said. "And I think there was something holding onto us, something desperate in the way someone drowning will pull rescuers under the surface too. Isn't that what you saw?"

"Yeah," Megan lied quickly, laying back on the grass to hide her confusion. Why hadn't they seen the Dark Man? Did they even know that she'd had help breaking them free?

"I'm getting too old for this sort of thing," Emelia muttered, struggling to rise to her feet.

"Do we have to leave Nickelville?" Megan asked even though she dreaded the answer. "The Huntsmen know where we are now, don't they?"

"I don't think so," Emelia replied. "You weren't visible long enough for them to pinpoint our location. But they definitely know what part of the country we're in, and I bet they'll be all over the state within hours."

"What are you two talking about?" Sam asked.

"Another time, my friend," Emelia evaded. "Suffice it to say that there are people following us, and we would be in danger if we were to leave the town. I'm afraid we're going to have to stay here and let the Old Ones camouflage us a while longer. If the Huntsmen sensed Megan that quickly, then it may mean that they still remain in the area. I don't think we'd make it ten miles beyond the city limits before they caught us."

"Why is it so much easier for them to find me now?" Megan asked.

"Your abilities are awakening," Emelia answered. "You were like a candle's flame on a dark night to them before. Now you're like a spotlight."

"So I can keep going to school?" Megan asked eagerly.

"Why didn't you tell me what was happening?" Emelia asked, and she could feel her mother's hurt even louder than her voice.

"I don't want to run anymore," Megan said quietly.

"I know it's nice to have new clothes and someplace warm to sleep…"

"It's not that," Megan interrupted. "Mom, that last place almost killed you, and I was no more than a day or two away from going full blown crazy town."

Emelia nodded, reluctantly agreeing with the assessment.

"I need to know my grandfather," Megan added. "I mean, you and I love each other so much, but there's always been something missing."

"A hole where you knew someone should be?" Emelia asked, her eyes flicking to the man kneeling nearby and back so quickly that Megan thought she might have imagined it.

"Exactly!" Megan agreed. "And there's more…"

"Bruce," Emelia said, watching her daughter's reaction closely.

"And the rest of them," Megan added before her mother could make it weird. "And Tom and Alan and everything!"

"Are you sure you don't want me to homeschool you?" Emelia asked. "You could still see your friends outside of school. The Dark Man is fully awake now. Now that he can see you, it will be much, much worse than it was before."

"No, I need to be with other kids my age. I mean, I love you and Grandpa..." Megan added before her mother could take offense, "But I've never had a chance to fit in like this before. I think it would be good for me and help me blend in better in the future."

"Maybe I should go back in tonight," her mother said, frowning. "Maybe I can find a way to destroy him or at least bind him someplace where he can't reach you. I know a lot more about such things than I did when I was a student there."

"No," Megan said quickly. "I don't want to put you in any kind of danger. He never actually hurt you in any way physically, did he?"

"No," her mother answered, looking at her with concern. "But psychological scars go much deeper than anything physical."

"I can handle him," Megan promised.

"You're much tougher than I was at your age," Emelia observed.

"Now if you want to banish Mrs. Jones..."

"Don't tempt me," Emelia said with a genuine smile.

Megan could tell she'd won this battle. She wished she could find more pleasure in this rare victory, but more than anything she felt confused and overwhelmed. She was relieved that she wouldn't have to hide the Dark Man from her mother any longer, but the events at the Well had created whole new questions. Even more troubling were the thoughts she'd sensed from the Huntsmen. If they were the bad guys, then why were they so worried about her safety?

Chapter XXIII: An Unexpected Ally

Bruce took the first good breath he'd had since Megan's disappearance from class when he felt her standing outside at the curb. He told himself it was just the relief of being near her, but he knew something else was at work. And it wasn't just his breathing that improved. His senses came alive and he felt, for lack of a better word, *more* when he was around her.

He thought about their conversation on the phone the previous night, if one could call it that. Between his wheezing and the static on the line they could barely understand each other. Yet somehow it was still enough. As cliché as it sounded, the two of them didn't really have to talk in order to know what the other was thinking.

"Are you doing okay?" Paul asked when they joined her.

"Nervous," she answered with a shrug. "Today's the day huh?"

"Absolutely," Jade answered.

"What if Chuck isn't back yet?" Megan asked quietly.

"He will be," Bruce said, looking down Beverly Drive to where the bus approached. He still felt shaky, but that was probably as much from his medication as nerves.

The four of them watched it rumble down the road, bringing with it an end to all of the plans and preparations since the Jubilee. Somewhere in the back of Bruce's mind, he could hear the voice of reason trying to talk him out of this, but he found it easier to ignore now that the four of them were together again.

Bruce could see Chuck and Glenn glaring down at him as the bus rolled to a stop. Judging from the bruising around Chuck's eye, his father hadn't taken the medical bills caused by his son's prank very well. In a larger town such clear abuse would have been reported. But this was Nickelville, and the old ways still found fertile soil in which to grow.

Bruce's eyes locked with Chuck's and he could see the other boy's entire life laid out before him, from his abusive childhood all the way to the menial job and the alcoholism that would eventually kill him. He could see all the elements that had helped to shape Chuck into the person he was and would eventually become. Bruce supposed he should feel sorry for him, but still couldn't find any sympathy for the boy. Even though the world had not been kind to Chuck, the path of the bully had still been chosen of his own free will, and Bruce refused to be his victim any longer.

Then something changed in the bully's glare as if he'd remembered something, and the trajectory of his life became much less clear.

Bruce smiled brightly at his two adversaries as he passed, holding his breath as he did so they couldn't tease him about his breathing. Then he and Megan took their customary seat and chatted pleasantly about the upcoming Thanksgiving break, lest anyone hear about their plans for the day and report them.

Megan put her hand on his arm where no one could see and stared out the window when they ran out of things that they didn't really want to talk about while avoiding the one thing that they did. She only glanced at him when the static barrier slid past.

Did that seem stronger? Her thoughts seemed to echo in his mind. He nodded in response.

When the bus stopped in front of the stone steps, the riders rose to their feet and followed the other students toward the huge wooden doors.

"Look for me before you go in to be sure I've been able to plant the bait," Jade whispered in his ear. She kissed him on the top of the head, then thought better of it and punched him in the shoulder before disappearing with Paul through the crowded front doors.

Bruce noticed a strangely dressed man in the hall, but thought nothing more about it. Maybe one of the high school classes was putting on a performance or something.

The day dragged by, punctuated only by accusations of theft that for some reason made Megan laugh, further infuriating Mrs. Jones. When the bell finally rang for break, they quietly lined up with the others. Bruce could breathe with ease now due to the adrenaline that flooded his blood. He could feel it radiating from Megan as well, and he wondered how anyone around them could possibly be so blind as to not sense it as well.

Together they strolled across the courtyard toward the forbidden corner, giving everyone time to notice them.

Allison watched closely, hoping to repeat previous trouble.

Megan made a show of putting her jacket on in spite of the day's warmth.

Bruce glanced over at the empty classroom window where Jade and Paul waited. His sister gave him a thumbs up. Megan knew his siblings were there as well, even though she hadn't looked in that direction.

Afraid he'd lose his nerve if they waited any longer, Bruce led Megan into the bushes. However, as soon as they were inside, he led her in the opposite direction from his hiding spot and found a place where they could watch through a hole in the leaves.

Delighted, Allison ran straight to Chuck and Glenn, her hands flashing in many excited gestures toward a piece of denim that peeked through the bushes where Bruce and Megan had been caught before.

The Trio ran over until they were only a few feet away. Chuck crept slowly forward, hand reaching for the familiar blue cloth. Seconds crept by until Bruce could hear his own heart pounding in his ears and realized he wasn't breathing.

"Come on," Megan whispered, holding his hand with white-knuckled intensity.

"Pull it as hard as you can," Bruce urged.

When it looked like Chuck wouldn't do so, Glenn pushed him aside and did it himself. Snatching the piece of cloth that looked so much like Megan's jacket, he pulled with all of his might.

The cord attached to the cloth went taut. Water balloons flew through the bushes at the Trio's legs, bursting as they passed through the sharp edges of the holly leaves and drenching their legs in a sulfurous stench that Bruce could smell all the way from their hidden vantage point.

When two jets of liquid, one clear and the other black, shot from the top of the bushes, both he and Megan knew Glenn had pulled so hard that he'd knocked the soakers askew. Instead of landing on the tops of their heads, it was going to hit them square in the face.

As one, both he and Megan reached out with their minds, merging into one consciousness and *turned* the liquids from their paths so that they drenched the hair of Allison, Chuck and Glenn with streams of India ink and peroxide.

Suddenly exhausted, Bruce sagged against Megan as her surprised thoughts tried to untangle from his.

A stern face appeared in the bushes in front of their hole, blocking their view of the courtyard. For a second, he thought it was Mrs. Jones, but then he recognized the man he'd seen earlier. Up close, Bruce could see that his face was covered in barely-closed cuts as if he'd been thrown through a window.

The Dark Man! Megan's thoughts roared in his mind.

"Dark Man?" Bruce groaned, but Megan had already jerked him to a crawl and pushed him back toward the opening in the bushes. He could feel her fear as they fled.

When they burst free, the ghost (for he now knew that's what it was from Megan's own thoughts) was striding toward them, looking quite solid for someone who didn't exist. Megan snatched up Bruce's hand, and he could feel something flow out from him into her. Then she *pushed* with her mind.

The angry apparition grew transparent, but Bruce could feel him dig in and hold on. Thunder rolled through the courtyard and clouds began to gather overhead as the energy they expended upset the natural balance of the weather.

Using the framework of Megan's power as a guide, Bruce gathered his will and added his own strength to hers.

This time the ghost disappeared and stayed gone.

"What the...?" he stammered, almost collapsing into her.

"I'll explain later," she whispered in panic, looking around to see if anyone had noticed them coming out of the bushes.

"Are you sure about that?" he pressed.

"I promise," she said as Mrs. Jones caught sight of them, "No more secrets between us."

A short time later, Bruce, Megan, Jade and Paul found themselves sitting once again in the worn but comfortable chairs outside of Mr.

Danders's office. Each of them wore infectious smiles and broke into laughter that spread throughout the office each time it happened.

Unlike most who broke the rules, they had enough honor to take responsibility for their actions and as a result, they were prepared to suffer through whatever consequences there might be. There would be no denials or hiding from the truth. Why should they? Nothing that Mrs. Jones or her husband's supporters could do would ever be able to take away the memory of the Terrible Trio reeking of rotten eggs from the stink balloons while patches of white and black spread through their hair.

"Bruce Grimble," Mr. Dander's voice called from the open door of his office.

Bruce took a raspy breath and rose unsteadily to his feet. The adrenaline had run its short life through his metabolism, and his breathing was worse than it had been before recess. But the faster he got this over, the faster he'd be able to get close to Megan and breathe again.

"Maybe we'll get lucky and have extra days added to our Thanksgiving Break," Jade said brightly, trying to ease Bruce's worries. *Even if things go badly in there,* he thought, *it was all worth it just for the way it brought Jade, Paul and me closer together.* He marveled at how much his life had changed since falling out of the *Tribune* window.

"She's coming home," he whispered ominously and allowed his eyes to meet Megan's. He felt something huge moving beneath the surface of his world and wondered exactly how much control he had over his life. But wherever it led, he knew she would be there, and that wherever she went, he would follow.

"Close the door behind you," the vice principal ordered, not even bothering to look up at Bruce as he entered.

Bruce did as he asked, then sat down in the chair before the man could ask. He knew he'd broken the rules and that he should be punished, but that didn't mean he had to be meek or frightened. No matter how unpleasant this might be, it would eventually end, and he would still have Megan and his family when it was over.

"Do you deny setting up that contraption behind the bushes?" Mr. Danders asked.

"I designed it."

"Do you have any idea how easily it could have blinded them?" the man pressed.

"That's what the stink balloons were for," Bruce replied, seeing no reason to hold anything back.

"What do you mean?" Mr. Danders asked, leaning back into his chair with a frown.

"They hit them low to make sure they were looking down when the ink and peroxide hit the tops of their heads. We thickened each solution with corn starch to make it less likely to run down into their eyes. We also hid three sets of eye wash bottles in the bushes nearby in case something went wrong."

"So your intention was to humiliate them," he said quietly looking at Bruce closely for the first time, "not to hurt them."

"That's correct."

Mr. Danders rubbed his eyes as if he were suddenly very tired, rose from his desk and walked over to the curtained window. He pulled the drapes aside, and Bruce was pleasantly surprised to discover that they were clean enough to not add dust to the air. The garish light from the colored panes of glass painted the room in sadness. The weary man looked outside for a moment in silent contemplation.

"Did you do this in retaliation for what happened at the Jubilee?" he asked at last.

260

"Yes," Bruce answered. "We know that revenge is wrong, and I hope you're not planning on giving me the lecture about how an eye for an eye makes the whole world blind. Aside from the bills that Chuck's dad has had to pay, nothing will happen to those three. They do stuff like this to people all the time and never have anything bad happen to them in return."

"What about Allison Jones?" he asked. "I wasn't aware that she had anything to do with the incident. Was she merely collateral damage?"

"Do you really think Chuck or Glenn could have come up with that scheme on their own?" Bruce countered. "She all but bragged about it to Megan that night when they ran into each other at Gordon's. But even if she did openly admit to it, what judge would believe an outsider like Megan over the daughter of Nickelville's most powerful citizen?"

Mr. Danders snorted, then fell silent again as he continued to stare out the colored window at the distorted world outside.

"So what now?" Bruce asked, anxious to return to Megan's side.

"That thing in the bushes was quite impressive," Mr. Danders said, appearing not to have heard Bruce's question. "You also took their safety into mind, even after their disregard for yours."

"Uh," Bruce stammered, unsure of how to respond. "Thanks."

"I can't allow this to go unpunished," Mr. Danders said, turning to look back at Bruce and resuming the mask of professional indifference that he normally wore.

"No sir," Bruce agreed, relieved that the moment of judgment had come at last, and it would soon be over.

"But I also can't in good conscience suspend you and the others as your teacher has demanded while Mr. Baker, Mr. Floyd and Miss Jones go all but unpunished for what would in other towns be considered an attempt on your life."

The man straightened his tie, and walked past Bruce to open the door.

261

"Would the three of you please join us in my office?" he asked.

As the stern man returned to his desk, Megan slipped quickly behind Bruce and allowed her hand to make contact with the back of his neck as if by accident. His breathing eased at once.

"After speaking with Bruce about the unpleasant accident you four caused today, I have come to the decision that you had no intention of causing any harm to the three children who accidentally triggered your device. But by bringing such a dangerous thing into our building, you put others in jeopardy, and for that you will receive two weeks detention to be served as Mr. Green sees fit. You will report to him immediately after school, and your families will be notified. He will take you home after school today since he says he was already going there to speak with Mr. McGeehee."

Mr. Danders drew closer to them so that his next words would not carry beyond his door.

"You are all intelligent enough to know that you've made an extremely dangerous enemy in the Jones family. I would strongly advise you to leave Allison alone lest I be forced to act further in this matter. Go back to your classes and look suitably chastised if you value the well-being of your families and friends."

The four of them stared at one another in disbelief. Had they heard him correctly? Were they really going to get off that easily? More than a bit confused, but nevertheless elated, they filed out of the office and tried to follow Mr. Danders's advice.

It wasn't until much later that Bruce realized that the vice principal had never intended to suspend them even before bringing him in. Otherwise, he wouldn't have already discussed their punishment with Mr. Green before they came.

Chapter XXIV: Bruce's Hoarding Nightmare

Megan enjoyed the afternoon once Mrs. Jones took her skunk-streaked daughter away to the hair stylist in an attempt to salvage the girl's flaming locks. The substitute made no attempt to control the class, and Megan moved over to sit with Bruce since the desk benches were more than wide enough to comfortably sit two. Glenn's mother had not yet arrived, but Bruce assured her that they'd likely be able to hear her all the way to Mrs. Jones's classroom when she did. Chuck's father had taken it in stride and merely asked that the school send his son over to the gym and have the coach shave Chuck's head the way the football team wore theirs.

It was upon Mrs. Jones's departure that Megan realized exactly how much the other students hated the Terrible Trio. The entire class treated her and Bruce like celebrities; some of them going so far as to tell her how they'd never believed she was a thief and apologizing for any bad feelings. Word of the prank spread, infecting the minds of students and staff alike until most gave up any pretense of study.

When the day finally came to an end, they found Mr. Green waiting for them outside the back door of the school. His weathered face lit with a broad grin when he saw them, and he barely managed to get them away from the prying ears of other students before demanding every detail of what they'd done.

"You shouldn't have done it," he croaked, hoarse from the bellowing laughter with which he'd been seized after listening to Paul relate the whole tale twice and then demanding more detail of exactly how the Trio and Mrs. Jones had reacted. For some reason it just sounded better when the youngest Grimble told the tale.

"I'm just surprised that Mr. Danders let us off so easily," Bruce said.

"I'm not," Mr. Green countered.

"Why not?" Jade asked. "If he's secretly a nice guy, he's done a wonderful job of hiding it from the students."

"Mr. Danders might not have much of a sense of humor," Mr. Green explained, "but he has a very strong sense of what's right and wrong. I'm not saying I'd want to spend time with him outside of work, but I trust him to do right by this school and her students. That's why he's fought so hard to get rid of Mrs. Jones."

"He has?" Megan asked. She could normally read people better than that, but if what Mr. Green said was true, she'd misjudged the vice principal badly.

"Absolutely," Mr. Green continued. "Hasn't won him any friends with the school board either."

"With Allison's father heading it, I'd guess not," Jade added.

Megan didn't want the fun to end, but knew they needed to get on with the detention lest Mr. Green get into trouble for not doing his job. "So what exactly is it that we've got to do in detention with you for two weeks?"

"I'm not sure yet," Mr. Green answered, rising from the upturned bucket on which he'd been sitting and motioning for them to follow. "I just found out that y'all were going to be helping me an hour or two before you came out. I guess you can start by cleaning out this shed. It was a mess

264

when I took this job and as you can tell, I'm not the most organized of people.

They looked at each other uneasily. The so-called shed to which the janitor referred was in reality a fairly large building that stood directly behind the Academy. It had the same dark stonework as the school, but it was only a single story high. It wasn't quite as big around as the McGeehee house, but it wasn't that much smaller either. When combined with the fact that Mr. Green had been working at the Academy since before their parents were born, it made them suspect they weren't getting off so easily after all.

When he slid the door to the shed open, Megan feared Bruce might pass out, not from lack of air but because the layers of junk were too much for his abnormally ordered mind to accept.

"Have you ever thought about going on that hoarders show?" Paul asked.

Mr. Green looked mildly offended and chose not to hear.

"You might want to start off by just exploring for today. We spent most of the time yapping about your prank. Mind ya, it wasn't time ill spent in my humble opinion, but I don't see much use in dragging everything out of here on the last afternoon before Thanksgiving break just to end up lugging it all back in again in half an hour."

"I don't even know what some of this stuff is," Jade said, picking up a strange sledgehammer with one sharp edge.

"That's an adze," Paul said, glancing over at her.

"That's right," the janitor said, a little surprised that his young friend would recognize such a thing.

"I'm going to need paper," Bruce said bravely.

"Why?" Paul said, reaching into his book bag and pulling out a spiral.

"This is going to take major planning if we're going to get this done in two weeks," Bruce answered, then looked over at Mr. Green. "Can we take longer than that if we need to?"

Megan looked at her best friend with growing respect. She knew he'd refuse to put anything less than his best effort into this, even when someone who was in better health would have avoided it.

"Sure," Mr. Green said absently, digging behind his work bench for something. "Don't feel like you have to though."

"I'll come finish it by myself if I have to," Bruce said, taking the existence of this mess as a personal insult.

"We're with you bro," Jade added, actually looking as if she might enjoy the challenge that the shed presented. "What do you want us to do? You stay here so the dust won't get to you."

"Just start calling out what you see and I'll start making a rough inventory so I can plan where to put everything after the break."

"There it is," Mr. Green mumbled, spying a bucket full of plumbing supplies that was sitting on the top of an ornate pedestal. "Well, if you run into any problems, I'll be fixing a clogged toilet over at the high school end. They've probably flushed one of Gerald's hedge-hogs down it or something of the like. I just hope I don't have to go down into the crawl space under the building again. That place gives me the willies."

"Yeah, have fun with that," Jade called from the top of the old tractor tire on which she perched, "Too cool, I think I see a big geode under that table over there!"

"Of course," the older man said with a mischievous twinkle in his eyes, "If someone has to go down there it would only make sense to use one of you delinquents. You are in detention after all."

Paul stuck his head out from under a table to gauge the seriousness of the offer.

"Any exposed rock down there?" he asked.

"Pretty much all there is," Mr. Green answered. "They had to dig out the original foundation to add running water at some point. The rest of the school foundation rests on big stone slabs."

"Then we'd better come with you," Jade said eagerly. "Inventory is more your speed Bruce."

"Hey now," Mr. Green said, "I was just kidding. I'd never ask a student to go down there."

"If you're completely sure that it's not going to cave in on us, I've always been weirdly curious about what was under the school," Paul said, looking over at Bruce and Megan. "You guys won't need us, will you?"

"We're good," Megan said. "Try not to get into trouble without us," she added.

"If you're sure you two don't mind," Mr. Green said, pleased in spite of himself, "it would probably help us get out of here sooner. You can tell me more about how mad Mrs. Jones was again too."

"It's a deal," Paul said. "Just don't be surprised if Bruce has everything cleaned out and alphabetized when we get back."

Megan giggled in spite of herself, as they left.

"It wouldn't take long you know," Bruce said when the other three had gone.

"What wouldn't take long?" Megan asked, trying to figure out exactly where to start.

"Alphabetizing this place," Bruce answered without looking up from the diagrams he was already drawing in the spiral.

"You're kidding," Megan said, looking at the sheer volume of the building's contents.

"Nope," he said. "It would all go under either 'T' or 'J.'

Megan gave him a puzzle look.

"Trash or Junk," he said.

"Ha-ha," she replied, even though he did have a pretty good point. "Want me to start calling stuff out?"

"If you don't mind. I hate to say it, but even with you touching me I don't think I could handle this much dust without having another attack."

"You've noticed it too?" she asked quietly, hardly daring to speak about it aloud.

"Ever since the race," he admitted. "I could feel things better at the Jubilee when we were touching too."

"Wow," was all she could think of to say at first. "It's the first thing I've ever been able to do that wasn't bad in some way."

"How do you do it?" he asked in the quiet that followed.

"I don't know," Megan answered uneasily. It was hard for her to talk about these things with someone else. Now that she was the one with the answers, she felt torn between the past she'd shared with her mother and the future she so desperately wanted here in Nickelville.

"How can you not know?" he asked.

"It's just a part of me," she explained, afraid that once she started talking everything would force itself past her suddenly dry lips until there was nothing left of her that he didn't know and understand. Overshadowing that fear was one she couldn't consciously acknowledge: the fear of how much she wanted to let that happen.

"Hey guys," said an unexpected male voice, startling them from their thoughts. "Do you know where Mr. Green is?"

So intent on their discussion of her secret, they'd completely missed the approach of the older student that now stood in the shed's open doorway.

"He went down to the high school bathroom to unclog a toilet," Megan answered, wondering how much he might have overheard. "He thought it had something to do with a hedge-hog."

"Oh," he said, mildly horrified, "Thanks. And by the way, you guys totally get my vote for best prank of the year. Did anyone video it?"

"I don't think so," Bruce answered with a laugh that made him start to cough.

"Too bad," the boy said on his way out the door. "I would have paid good money to watch that over and over again."

When he'd gone, Megan berated herself for being so careless. After all, her entire family would pay the price if anyone but Bruce found out. Before he could say anything else out loud, she stepped closer to him and placed her palm over his left temple. His breathing eased at once.

Can you hear me?

His eyes widened and his thoughts began to mesh with hers as they had in the courtyard. With gentle yet firm force she pushed him back, holding contact with him but keeping their minds separate. Had her own mind been this open the first time her mother had shown her?

I promise I'll explain everything, but not here or now. Someone might hear us if we speak out loud, and I am too new at this to do it for very long.

What are you?

I'm your friend, she answered, *the same person I was before you knew all of this.* She stroked his cheek and turned back to the junk.

"Two broken toilets," she called out, "or should I stick to the stuff that isn't trash?"

"Everything for now," he said, taking the discovery that his best friend was a telepathic, asthma-reducing ghost magnet rather well. "We'll have to talk to Mr. Green to find out what we can get rid of before we know what is trash. I sure do hope he doesn't have an emotional attachment to all this stuff."

"Me too," she called, moving deeper into the piles. "Half a case of chalk, three bottles of drain cleaner, a box of rags, a rusty thermos that sloshes when shaken…"

"Gross," he said. "Slow down a little. I'm amazing but not supernatural."

She knew that was directed at her abilities, but chose to ignore it.

"One bucket full of assorted soda bottle caps," she drawled. "Want me to count them?"

Bruce didn't respond.

Megan looked up to find Bruce staring over the top of the spiral at something just out of her vision.

"Megan," he said uneasily. "Come over here for a minute."

When she reached his side, she realized that the Dark Man had materialized on the other side of a huge library bookshelf, peering at them between two empty shelves.

She reached down to take Bruce's hand, mentally preparing to banish the spirit again. The Dark Man, however, had other plans. He surged forward, taking the bookcase with him. The overloaded shelves held for a second before groaning in protest and toppling toward them.

Bruce grabbed Megan and shoved her to safety. A large crate full of books slammed into his shoulder, knocking him to the ground and worse yet, showering him with books, dust and a cloud of mold spores. Within seconds, he was gasping for air.

Still holding tight to his hand, Megan searched for the ghost, but he'd disappeared yet again.

"Need to get my inhaler," Bruce gasped.

"Come on," she said, doing her best to brush the dusty mess from his face, "I can't leave you alone here to go get it." His eyes traveled the shed as hers had done. He quickly pulled himself to his feet and allowed her to help him as they made their way back to the Academy.

She'd never been this close to him before, and it was hard to focus on anything with his mind so open. Furthermore, her concern kept trying to change into something else she couldn't understand, something that drained away from her like water dropped on desert sands.

She could tell he was trying not to lean on her too heavily, but the longer he went without enough air, the less choice he had. By the time Mr. Bob fell into step with them, she'd begun to worry if they were going to make it before he passed out.

A woman's screams echoed across the cafeteria when they came in across from the ornate library doors.

"Can you hear that?' she asked, worried that it was another manifestation.

"Can…probably hear her…at Baker Hotel," he gasped. "Need rest here…"

She helped him to the nearest table, planning to run and get the nurse. But as soon as she turned to go, the cafeteria disappeared, leaving her stranded in a cavernous room down which long benches had been placed. Light streamed in through the windows overhead, focusing their light on a man and woman standing in front of a pulpit. She wore a pale green gown and there were several men and women gathered around them. One of them looked a lot like Paul…

"Bruce," she called, "I can't see…"

His hand clutched hers, and the vision dissolved. They made it like this for a few steps before he swayed and almost fell. She ducked under his

271

arm and the strange fading sensation started again. His head was nodding as if he were falling asleep while they shuffled on.

"Are those two of the culprits?" an unpleasant woman screeched when they finally made it through the office door.

"Does he need his inhaler?" Millie asked, catching sight of Bruce.

Megan nodded, winded as well from the effort of helping the taller boy down the hall and actively willing his breathing to improve.

"The nurse is still here," Millie said, pointing back to the clinic door. "She'll have him fixed up in no time."

"I am going to sue their families for this," the ferret faced woman screamed.

"Will that be before or after the Grimble family presses charges for the attempt made by your son and his friend on their child's life in order to win a race?" Mr. Danders asked.

The woman shrank back from him as if struck. She held her tongue, but judging by the look of loathing she gave Bruce and Megan before storming past and slamming the door, she wasn't finished with the matter.

As soon as Megan guided Bruce through the clinic door, the overwhelming scent of cinnamon hit her, and she almost lost her grip on him in panic.

Her eyes searched the room, looking for another manifestation. She listened for footsteps. She looked for signs of the past creeping into the present. Instead she found a red candle burning on the corner of the nurse's desk.

"Well if it isn't Goose Brimble," the nurse said pleasantly.

The elderly woman walked over to the sink, took off her wedding band before washing her hands, and then stopped to pet Mr. Bob before returning to Bruce.

272

He rolled his eyes at Megan as the nurse sat down, took a clipboard from her drawer and started to ask him questions.

"How long have you been feeling unwell?"

"Are you experiencing any aches or pains?"

"Are you feeling nauseous?"

She was preparing to stick a thermometer in his mouth when Megan decided she'd better intervene before Bruce's lips finished turning blue.

"Excuse me," she interrupted. "I think Bruce came in because he needs his asthma inhaler."

"What was that my dear?" the nurse asked in a grandmotherly voice.

"I need...my inhaler," Bruce gasped.

"Oh, well of course Goose," she said, crossing to the medicine cabinet. She returned with one of Bruce's inhalers which he snatched as politely as he could under the circumstances and took an eager puff from it. Within seconds, the rapid rise and fall of his chest slowed and he breathed a relaxed sigh. Then he took another for good measure.

"Thank you," he said.

"You're welcome, Goose," she said. "You really should have your pharmacist correct your name on the label. We can't technically give you your medicine if it's wrong."

"I'll have my mom talk to him again," Bruce said, leading Megan out by the hand.

"What's wrong with that woman?" Megan asked when they were back outside.

"She's almost completely deaf," Bruce answered. "She's been working here for a long, long time. She eventually figures out what's wrong with me, even if she can't get my name straight."

They met Jade on their way out the back door.

"There you guys are," she said, relieved to have found them.

"Bruce had an asthma attack when that old bookshelf fell down and blew dust on us," Megan said.

"And mold spores," Bruce added.

"Ugh, not good little brother. You guys both okay?"

"Yeah," Bruce answered. "Just a little rough there for a while. Megan got to meet the nurse."

"Sweet, isn't she?" Jade asked Megan with a grin. "She sure likes our Goose, doesn't she?"

Back at the shed, they found a drenched Paul drying his hair with an old and questionably clean towel.

"I hope that was from the clean water pipe and not the sewage line," Bruce said, giving his brother a wide berth.

"Mr. Green hosed me down after I came up from the crawlspace. I didn't even notice all of the spiders with that amazing exposure down there. I've never seen anything like it before. Well, it was amazing until I had some sort of panic attack and thought the roof was falling in on me."

"That bookshelf didn't fall on you did it?" Mr. Green asked.

"No, it just scared us," Megan answered. "The books blew dust and mold on Bruce though and he had an attack. We just got back from the clinic."

"Did you see the books that fell out of that crate?" Jade asked, flipping through one.

"What is it?" Bruce asked, finally finding something he could see as more than junk.

"Looks like an old church hymnal," Paul said, frowning as if he wanted to say more before handing one over to his brother.

"Look at the publication date," Bruce added. "These things are just over two hundred years old."

274

"I run across old stuff like that from time to time," Mr. Green said, looking through one himself. "They must have been stored here brand new. Doesn't look like they're worn the way most of the stuff around here is."

"When are we heading home?" Paul asked. "It was totally worth going down there, but I hate wet clothes."

"That's more than enough for one day as far as I'm concerned," the janitor answered. "You two saved me hours of work. That line might have burst over the break and flooded the whole high school wing."

"Any way we could have gotten it to flood Mrs. Jones's room instead?" Megan asked.

"Don't be gettin' any more ideas," Mr. Green scolded. "You don't want to know what she's like when something puts her out like that. Anyway, I just spoke with Azarich."

"And?" Megan asked.

"Looks like Mr. and Mrs. Harris, Sam Wise, the Grimbles and myself are all going to be joining you for Thanksgiving dinner."

"Really?" Megan asked, forgetting all of the worry she'd felt just a short time earlier.

"Yep. Let's get out of here and start this break."

Chapter XXV: Big Mama Comes Calling

Later that evening, Emelia led Megan out the back door and through Azarich's porch side arboretum to the back of the McGeehee property. For the last hour and a half, Azarich and Mr. Green had been reliving days long past when they'd been the ones pulling pranks at Nickelville Academy, and Megan would have liked to hear more.

But her mother wanted to go for a walk, and with the exception of her short foray into Guarded Wood, Megan hadn't explored the property as much as she'd have liked. So they walked down to the edge of the yard which was really nothing more than the place where Azarich stopped mowing the grass and let it grow wild. When they passed through his fruit trees, Emelia realized that her daughter had never been exposed to such things. So she taught Megan to distinguish peach from plum and apple from pear without the benefit of fruit hanging from the trees.

"I never had any idea you were such a country girl," Megan said, hoping they'd be there long enough to help eat next year's harvest.

"I grew up here," Emelia said, leading her away from the orchard and down yet another path. "But I never felt like I belonged here. And I certainly don't warrant the name *country girl*. I do, however, have some extremely fond memories of picking apples with my father. And I'd eat so many plums when they ripened that I'd get sick."

"So why this sudden interest in taking walks?" Megan asked.

"It's time to start exploring your gifts," Emelia explained. "And you need a place to practice where you won't be observed."

Megan sensed the grove before they reached it, pulling at her soul the way the smell of her grandfather's cooking stoked her appetite. They'd already reached the point where the tamed land gave way to the woods, though not quite wild enough to be part of Guarded Wood yet. But the potential was there as if one day the strange wooded lands would stretch in their sleep and send a questing tendril this way.

The grove itself was comprised of a mixture of live and deciduous oaks. And although the cold nights and shortened days had already killed the wild grasses everywhere else, a clear transition marked the edge of this special place. Almost as if a bubble of fragile spring lay contained within, the ground beneath these trees was covered in wild clover and hundreds of yellow flowers.

Emelia fell silent, looking out over the grove in surprise.

"What's wrong?" Megan asked.

"These are my favorite flowers," the gray eyed woman answered, bending over to touch one as if to make sure it was real.

"They're pretty," Megan said.

"They didn't grow here when I left," she whispered, looking out across their sprawling numbers.

"And they didn't start recently," Megan observed. "There must be hundreds."

"I never expected to set foot here again," Emelia said, then shook her head. "But that isn't why I brought you here. My mother loved to spend time out here. At least that's what my father told me."

"It was hard growing up without her, wasn't it?" Megan asked.

"Even more so when I got older," Emelia answered. "Your grandfather is a wonderful man, but he knew nothing about raising a teenage girl. Esther tried to step in, but I was at a difficult part of my life, and as much as she tried to hide it, there was always the lingering feeling on my part that I was the reason her best friend had died."

"Grandma Josie?" Megan asked to make sure she knew who her mother was talking about.

"Don't get me wrong," Emelia explained. "Esther Harris is a wonderful person. But knowing that your mother died in childbirth with you isn't something that you just shrug off."

"Did you always know?" Megan asked.

"Yes and no," the small woman answered, looking down at her feet as she walked. "I noticed pretty early on that the date on my mother's tombstone was the same as my birthday, but it wasn't until I started school that I understood exactly what that meant."

"Is that when Grandpa told you?" Megan asked. This was more than she'd ever been able to get out of her mother on the forbidden subject of her past.

"He's not the one who told me," Emelia said, and Megan could feel her shields fluctuate and harden.

"Who did?" Megan asked.

"Paula."

"Why would she do that?"

"Her older brother vandalized the house of an old man who told him to stop walking through his field," Emelia explained. "My father represented the old man in court, and Paula's parents had to pay for all of the damages."

"How old were you?"

"About eight," Emelia answered. "It would still be another year before I met Sam. My suspicion is that her parents were complaining about our family during that time and the subject of my birth came up. Then

Paula told me in the courtyard. I don't think I've ever seen my father as angry as he was that afternoon when I came home crying."

They stood there in silence for a few minutes, looking at the expanse of yellow flowers before them. Megan hadn't thought it possible to hate her teacher more than she already did.

At the very center of the grove stood a strange pool of water from which a stream flowed back into Guarded Wood. It wasn't huge as ponds went, but slightly off from its center rose an island on which four stone benches had been placed, marking the cardinal corners of the compass.

"It's a spring, isn't it?" she asked.

"Yes," her mother answered.

"What is this place and how did it get here?" she asked.

"As far as I can tell," Emelia answered, "my mother created it." Then she looked out across the grove and fallen branches began to lift into the air, breaking themselves into more manageable pieces as they came whisking toward the firepit. There they arranged themselves into something Paul might have laid out for a campfire.

"Suddenly keeping peroxide from hitting the Terrible Trio in the eyes isn't nearly as impressive," Megan whispered in awe.

"But since my mother died shortly after my birth, I can't know for sure if she created this place," Emelia continued. "I do know that my father added the benches and the bridge when I was still very young."

"Grandma was like us?" Megan asked, surprised.

"Once again, I don't know for sure. But it would explain quite a bit. You see, these sorts of abilities normally show up in certain family lines. It's the responsibility of the older generation to teach the younger."

"But Grandma died before she could teach you, and Grandpa never knew," Megan added, "The chain was broken."

279

"That's right," Emelia said, motioning for Megan to kneel next to her and pulling the small box of matches she'd given Sam at Gordon's from the pocket of her long-sleeved blouse. "Do you know what these are?"

"Oh," Megan said with a grin, "I used to know what those were called, don't tell me..."

"These are an alibi," Emelia said seriously. "We don't actually need them, but it looks suspicious if someone comes up and wants to borrow your matches and you don't have any after starting a fire."

"We don't need them?" Megan asked.

"No," Emelia said, taking Megan by the hand. "Don't try to help me with this, just open your senses and feel what I do."

Then without any pomp or ceremony, Emelia reached out to the twigs in the pit with the power of her mind and caused the tinder to catch fire. It was as easy as breathing for her mother, and Megan was eager to try.

"Did you get that?" Emelia asked, quenching the flames with the same ease that she'd created it.

"Yeah," Megan said. "Let me try."

She reached out to the fire, mentally commanding it to burst into flame, but nothing happened. She tried harder, envisioning flames dancing across the charred wood, which should easily burn now that all of the moisture was gone.

Emelia began to laugh.

"Seriously?" Megan complained, flabbergasted that her mother would make fun of her like that. "What's so funny?"

"I wish you could see the face you were making," Emelia chuckled. "It reminded me of when you were filling your diaper when you were a baby."

"Mother!" Megan scolded, looking around to make sure no one had heard. As irritated as she was by her inability to start a fire, she was pleased by the ease with which Emelia smiled these days. Maybe her mother had needed this time as much as she had.

"Fire isn't something you command," Emelia said, still smirking. "It's something you call. Try again."

Working very hard to keep her expression neutral, Megan tried again with no success.

"Don't forget to breathe," Emelia suggested.

Megan asked the fire to burn in her mind, she begged it, she threatened it, but still the wood wouldn't ignite. At last she dropped to the ground with a defeated sigh and closed her eyes in exhaustion.

"Why won't it burn?" she asked in despair.

"It's a lot like walking in the woods," Emelia said, sitting down on the ground next to her daughter. "Some paths are easier to find than others. You have to be very watchful and patient if you don't want to miss the direction you want to go. Once you know the way, it's easy. But if you don't look at it from exactly the right direction, you can walk past a hundred times and never notice its presence."

"Somehow that doesn't make me feel any better," Megan muttered.

"You'll get it," Emelia said quietly. "And I suspect there is a certain amount of a mental block that you've created to keep from using your power accidentally. That's not going to be an easy thing to overcome."

"But why is this so much harder than the other things I can do?"

"Everything else you've done instinctively," her mother answered. "This is the first time you've tried to do something when the circumstances didn't demand it."

"Would this eventually happen on its own?" Megan asked.

"Yes," Emelia said. "And I'm sure you can understand why this particular skill would best be learned where there was no one else around to witness or endanger."

281

"Setting Allison's hair on fire when she's making fun of me would probably be a bad thing, wouldn't it?" Megan mused. "Can I watch you do it again?"

"As many times as you need me to," Emelia said, starting another fire without even looking at the fire pit.

"Show off," Megan mumbled, trying in vain to understand where she'd messed up. Then she noticed the box of matches sitting next to her and picked them up for a better look. Emelia watched with an odd expression she couldn't read.

"These are special to you," Megan said. "Aren't they?"

"They're the only thing I managed to hold onto from my life here," Emelia answered, taking them back. "I stole them from Sam when he was thinking about starting to smoke. They became a running joke between us."

Megan grinned at her mother until the woman started to get angry.

"Get back to work," Emelia commanded, putting them carefully back into the inner pocket of her jacket where they rested directly over her heart.

Throughout the following day, Megan felt sudden flashes of emotion that had nothing to do with what she was doing at the time. There was irritation, boredom and occasional bursts of longing that she suspected were coming from her friend next door.

The irritation and boredom she could understand after learning that Mrs. Grimble had grounded all three of her children for what they'd done to the Terrible Trio. The longing puzzled her.

She wondered if he could feel her frustration with summoning fire. After hours of practice, she could now make the wood grow warm and once she'd even made it smolder. But a full-fledged fire remained beyond her abilities, and she'd started to obsess over it.

When Grandfather asked if they wanted to go to the store, Megan jumped at the opportunity to be away from that stupid bundle of charred sticks. Besides, with the exception of the Academy and Gordon's, Megan hadn't been to many of the fine establishments that she was sure Nickelville had to offer.

The Nickelville Grocery Store wasn't as bad as Megan had expected. The entire building could have fit inside the produce section of some of the megastores she'd been to with her mother. Nevertheless, it did possess a certain charm. It had just about everything a person could want even if there weren't many options.

"I wish I'd remembered this sooner," Azarich said, frowning. "I'm completely out of practice for this sort of thing."

"It's going to be fine, Dad," Emelia said, walking along behind him with her hands in the pockets of her old jacket. "This place hasn't changed at all."

"Oh yes it has," he argued. "I don't know why they feel the need to move things around."

"Is that so?" Emelia asked, grinning wickedly at Megan.

He led them to the back of the store with an urgency that left his short-legged descendants struggling to keep up. When he got to where he was going, he made an exclamation most unlike him.

"I was afraid of this," he said mournfully. "They're out of turkeys."

He walked over to the butcher's case and rang the bell. A few seconds later a man in a bloodstained apron came out from the back. Judging by his girth, he wasn't opposed to consuming his own wares.

"What brings you in, Azarich?" he asked, washing his hands in the sink.

"I don't suppose you're going to get any more turkeys in before the big day, are you?" Azarich asked hopefully.

"I don't expect to," the butcher answered. "Sorry to let you down."

"That's okay, Richard," Azarich said. "Looks like I'll be driving a ways tonight. We're having several families over and I'll need three birds."

"You know," the butcher said, leaning across the counter and dropping his voice. "I never get my turkeys from here. If you want one that's never been frozen, go over to the Baker farm. He's got a whole flock of 'em, and the family is strapped for cash, if you know what I mean. That's where I go every year."

"Do I just drive up to their farm?" Azarich asked. "I can't say I know the family very well."

"The fruit and vegetable stand at the crossroads is theirs," Richard said. "Just stop by and tell 'em what you want. His boys are fast. They'll probably have 'em processed and ready within the hour."

"Excuse me," Megan said awkwardly. "Is one of the boys named Chuck?"

"His mama usually calls him Charlie, but I 'spose he might well go by Chuck at school."

Megan thanked him.

"It's been my pleasure," he said, already heading back to what he'd been doing before they called him to the counter.

"Grandpa," Megan said when they left the counter. "Would you mind dropping me off before you go to the Baker farm? Chuck is one of the kids we pulled the prank on."

"I thought as much," Azarich answered. "Should I talk to his parents?"

284

"No," Megan answered quickly. "We already got him back, and I think his father beats him. Let's leave it alone, okay?"

"If that's what you want."

"Hey Megan," an older girl said as she passed by.

"Girl from school?" Azarich asked, knowing full well that any girl in this town almost had to go to the Academy, but pleased that Megan was making friends.

"Never seen her before in my life," Megan answered.

By the time they'd picked up the rest of the things Azarich needed in order to feed such a large group, half a dozen students from the Academy had stopped Megan to ask how she was doing.

Sorry, Megan sent. *I'm drawing too much attention to myself here, aren't I?*

It's okay this time, her mother replied. *For a long stay it's better if you blend in. Recluses draw attention. I'm glad you're finding friends. I'm just a little disgusted with myself for not confronting Paula when I was younger. If I'd stood up to her the way you and Bruce have done, my life here might have been quite different.*

That night Megan went to sleep thinking about starting a fire in the pit behind her house. After her mother had told her about the face she made when she was concentrating, she dreamed that she was sitting on top of a giant toilet, trying to set the toilet paper on fire while her classmates kept walking by and telling her what a great job she was doing.

She woke in darkness, sensing Bruce nearby. She slipped from her bed without making a sound and crossed the room to her window. He was standing next to one of her grandfather's pecan trees, looking up at her.

Quickly gauging how angry her mother would be if she was caught slipping out of the house, Megan slid a sweater over the t-shirt she'd been sleeping in and pulled on a pair of jeans and shoes.

It was so dark in the hallway that she closed her eyes and allowed her other senses to guide her past her mother's room and down the stairs without making a single board creak.

The closer she got to the back door, the stronger her sense of him became. She turned the doorknob and slid out into the night air, so excited that she almost forgot to shut it behind her.

Then she was hugging him so hard that they almost fell off the porch. He took a deep, relieved breath and hugged her back. A jumble of emotions flowed into her from him. They were all good, but they still confused her. His mind worked differently than hers.

"Come this way," she whispered, unsure if communicating with her mind might not wake her mother this close to the house. "I missed you."

"Where are we going?" he asked, happily allowing himself to be dragged through the darkness toward the woods.

"Someplace where we won't be seen from the house."

A new moon hung above them, and there were no lights this far out in the country. Her grandfather kept a light on at the front porch, but it couldn't be seen behind the house where they walked.

"Wow," he said, echoing her own sentiments from her first time there. "I had no idea this was back here."

"But I thought you mowed the lawn during the summer," she said.

"And I'm pretty sure Jade and Paul haven't or they would have said something about it."

"It must have been warded against discovery. Watch this," she said before focusing her will on the wood laid in the circle of stones. It burst into flames without the slightest bit of effort.

"Cool," Bruce said, squinting against the sudden brightness.

"My mom has been teaching me how to do it, although this is the first time I've been able to do it properly. My abilities are much stronger when you're here. I don't know how long we can stay without her realizing that I'm not in the house anymore, so I'm going to try something else that she and Sam taught me."

"Sam?" Bruce asked. "He knows about this stuff?"

"Surprised me too," Megan answered. "Now look into the fire with me." When he did so, she caught him up into her trance and began to weave the flames.

He watched her earliest memories of being snatched up at a moment's notice to run without explanation, clutching her lost Kermit doll. She showed him the first time she'd realized she could feel the people who were searching for her. He saw the horrible places where they'd lived and the gradual skills she'd acquired as she'd grown with sensing the world around her. He learned what it was like to always be the new kid and the fear of having anyone notice that she was different. At last she showed him her flight into Nickelville with her mother's eventual collapse and the strange presence of the trees that hid them from the outside world.

She showed him that first day on the bus when he'd offered her a seat, the grace of his movements when he ran, and how hard it had been to see him stumble from the woods in the race.

She waited, afraid that he might not want to be her friend now that she'd shown him what she really was. Then, much to her surprise, he took control of the images in the fire and showed her his own earliest memories.

His experiences were all flavored with his asthma since it had been his companion since birth. He showed her the *Tribune* where his mother worked. He showed her the doctor's office where he went so often as a child and the hospital stay when he'd had pneumonia. He showed her his

287

escape into books when the fall came and put an end to his trips to the only place he'd ever felt like he'd belonged. Then he showed her the afternoon when he'd fallen out of the window and predicted her coming to Nickelville. He showed her the day the bullies threw his book over the fence in the courtyard although that memory was hazy and hard to understand.

When she saw herself for the first time in his memories, she didn't recognize herself. He saw things in her she'd never noticed in the mirror. Once again, this was something she couldn't quite grasp or hold onto.

He seemed just as uneasy with how she might receive these memories as she had been when showing her thoughts to him.

I'll never think you're weird, she sent, echoing her promise from that afternoon in the courtyard.

He hurried her along to his view of the race, where he hadn't known if he was going to make it to the finish line until he'd seen her eyes.

Then he showed her his first glimpse of the Dark Man in the courtyard of the school.

Megan wrenched control of the fire back from him, afraid that the Dark Man would once again force his way through the fire and into her presence. Then she showed him the afternoon with Sam at the Well of Dreams.

As one, they realized that Megan's mother had left the house. In just a few moments, she'd find them.

Bruce snuffed the fire with a thought.

"How did you do that?" Megan asked, knowing even as she did that they didn't have time for explanations. She didn't know how her mother would react to finding him there and didn't want to take the chance that this would land him an even longer grounding. "Go back into the trees that way," she whispered, shoving him in the direction of the deeper woods.

"Try to clear your mind and whatever you do, don't think about me or my mother until we've gone."

He'd barely made it across the bridge and out into the trees before Emelia arrived. Megan tried to look nonchalant.

"What do you think you're doing out here in the middle of the night?" her mother asked.

"I couldn't sleep, so I thought I'd come out and practice." Megan focused hard on the words and her belief in the story lest her mother sense her thoughts and see the truth she already suspected.

"Did you now?" Emelia asked, anger flavoring each word. "And how have your efforts been progressing?"

"Better," Megan answered. "Want to see?"

"With Bruce watching?" Emelia snarled. "Do you have any idea how much danger you've put him in by telling him about us?"

"She didn't have to tell me anything," Bruce said, crossing back over and taking his place at Megan's side. "I've been seeing things ever since the two of you came to Nickelville."

"You realize that we can't leave him behind when we leave, don't you?" Emelia spat at her daughter, ignoring Bruce completely. "You've condemned him to the nomadic life we've led up to this point. Is that what you want for him?"

Megan wasn't nearly as horrified by that thought as she was by how much the idea of never leaving him behind thrilled her.

"What do you think that will do to his family?" her mother pressed. "He's a minor. Do you think anyone is going to believe that he just happened to run away at the exact time that we left town? How much harder is it going to be for us to stay hidden if I'm wanted for kidnapping? What do you think that's going to do to your grandfather?"

"Hey," Bruce said irritably. "I'm standing right here. Don't you think I should have a say in this?"

Emelia shot him a withering glare that Megan could feel even in the darkened grove.

"Did you feel me leave the house?" Megan asked.

"No," Emelia answered. "I felt Bruce cross the wards."

"There are wards here?" Megan asked, looking around.

"Do you really think I'm going to be side-tracked that easily?" Emelia asked, closing her eyes in frustration, taking a deep breath and opening them again. "But there's nothing to be done about it now. Yes, there are wards here."

"Why didn't I feel them like the ones at the Well of Dreams?"

"These are only designed to watch," Emelia said wearily, her anger slowly fading.

"Can I learn to make them too?" Megan asked.

"Not yet, you're still having trouble with the basics."

Megan reached down, took Bruce's hand in her own and called flames that roared the air above their heads before snuffing them in an instant.

"I wonder," Emelia mused, staring at the flames with surprise. "Bruce, see if you can call them back."

He called them back without effort and Megan tried to suppress her irritation.

"Megan," Emelia continued. "Move away from Bruce and try to extinguish the fire."

Megan tried, but could do little more than diminish their intensity.

"Bruce?" Emelia prompted.

He tried, but without even as much effect as Megan caused.

"I'll be damned," Emelia laughed. "Bruce, come here for a minute."

290

He looked uneasily at Megan.

"Oh come here," Emelia ordered. "I'm not going to hurt you."

Bruce crossed the distance between them and reluctantly took Emelia's outstretched hand.

Emelia's eyes widened in surprise as she looked into his, and she let his hand drop.

"What is it?" Megan asked.

"Your young friend is an amplifier," her mother answered.

"What does that mean?" Bruce asked, backing away from Emelia.

"You can amplify the abilities of people who are gifted," Emelia answered. "And you absorb their gifts as well. This changes things."

"What do you mean?" Megan asked, taking Bruce's hand again without consciously doing so.

"I don't know yet," Emelia answered. "But it does explain a few things. I notice he isn't having as much trouble breathing now either. That's not a coincidence is it?"

"That's why I don't want to be away from him for too long," Megan answered.

Emelia thought this over for a moment then bent down to pick up a flat stone from the ground at her feet. She closed her eyes for a moment, and Megan had the oddest sensation that her mother was somehow probing the rock for something.

"This should do," the woman said, opening her eyes and motioning for them to come closer. "Bruce, I want you to let this rest in your open palm."

Bruce shrugged and did as she asked.

"Megan, I want you to place your hand over his, entwining your fingers with the stone between your palms."

Megan also did as she asked.

Emelia then placed both of her own tiny hands around theirs and closed her eyes in concentration. There was something familiar about this, a warmth gone as fast as it had come.

"Both of you relax and open yourselves up as much as you can to this. I'm still not up to full strength, and it's going to be hard enough without you resisting."

Then the stone grew very cold within their hands, as if it had been emptied of all the heat that the day's sun had left within it. Before they could get used to the change, it started to pull something from them and grew warm.

"There," Emelia whispered. "That should do."

"What happened?" Bruce asked.

"Let your hands separate. Bruce, you keep the stone," Emelia ordered. "Now step away from each other."

They did as she asked. At once, they realized that they still felt the bond as if they were touching.

"That's so cool," Megan said in awe. "Can you still breathe better?"

"Yeah," Bruce answered. "I can. Do you still feel stronger?"

In answer Megan made the fire flare and die.

"Excellent," Emelia said wearily.

"What did you do?" Megan asked.

"I can boost the bond between the two of you fairly easily, but unlike Megan, I can't sense Bruce from a distance. I need a focal point to find him unless he's nearby. The stone now serves that purpose. As long as he has it on his person, I can hold the link between the two of you open."

"Thank you," Bruce said. "Can I keep it in my pocket or does it have to be in contact with my skin?"

"Your pocket should do fine, but let me see it for a second," Emelia added as an afterthought.

292

Bruce reluctantly handed it back to her, and Megan immediately felt the bond weaken. With a sudden flash of light that left a blue smear across her darkened vision, Emelia created a hole through the center of the stone.

"Now you can thread a string through it and make it into a necklace," Emelia said. "Keep it safe and don't lose it."

"Trust me, I won't," he said.

"In the wrong hands it could lead someone directly to Megan," Emelia said gravely. "I'm trusting you more than I've ever trusted someone outside of my family with this."

"I promise I won't let you down," he said, holding it tight.

"Good," Emelia said. "In time the two of you will grow into your abilities completely, and you won't need it any more. Now, with that taken care of, why don't we get young Mr. Grimble back home before his own perceptive mother discovers his absence and decides to ground him for the remainder of the time he has left in this world? I trust the two of you have no further reason to be sneaking out in the middle of the night? No need for me to take this discussion into directions that would greatly embarrass and humiliate you both?"

"No ma'am," they quickly replied in unison.

"Good," Emelia said pleasantly, "and before you realize that you can communicate through the bond the stone creates, just remember that it's passing through me. You'll be able to do so from a pretty good distance without it as you grow stronger, but for now it's channeling through me. Consider this your only warning that the line is bugged and Big Brother, well in this case Big Mama, is listening."

Chapter XXVI: Megan's Matchmaking Mishap

Although Bruce had come to know and love his brother and sister more than he would have thought possible over the past weeks, sometimes they still found ways to annoy him to the breaking point. Now was such a time.

In an anti-rhythmic pattern that set his need for order and symmetry on edge, each of his siblings was bouncing a tennis ball against the wall in the hallway.

If that wasn't bad enough, it was also making it difficult to eavesdrop on the conversation his parents were having down the hall.

Ever since Megan's mother had created the talisman that he now wore on a leather shoestring around his neck, his senses had grown steadily stronger, and his health had improved. His mother attributed this improvement in his asthma to the new medications his doctor had prescribed, but he knew better. He had, after all, been flushing them down the toilet since he'd realized they were interfering with his ability to feel Megan.

"Okay, okay," he heard his mother moan when he concentrated. "I admit it, they're driving me crazy too."

"It's not like they weren't provoked," his father reminded her. "And to be honest, I'm rather proud of Bruce for sticking up for himself."

"Me too," she admitted in a whisper, "but I would have preferred it if they hadn't included the Jones girl in their prank."

"I don't know," Mr. Grimble chortled, "maybe it's time someone stood up to that family."

"Don't even joke about that," she scolded, "we might not work for the Jones family, but they control every aspect of this town. You are a public servant after all."

"Maybe so, but I'm still proud of them. Have you seen the schematics Bruce had on his computer?"

The movement of a tennis ball as it flew at him from the doorway snapped his attention away from his parents' conversation. He reached up and caught it without looking up.

"Nice," Paul said in surprised admiration.

"Let's build a treehouse," Jade said, pushing Bruce over and sprawling across his bed. "Why is your bed so hard?"

"Probably because it's not made out of water," Paul answered.

"A tree house?" Bruce mused.

"Yeah," Paul added, motioning toward Bruce's computer. "It was so much fun designing the prank. As long as we're stuck in the house, we might as well fill the time with a dream or two."

Bruce shrugged then crawled over Jade to get to his desk.

"Mom and Dad probably won't let us build it," she yawned before looking around his bed, frowning and getting up abruptly. "Gonna go get more pillows. How can you make a proper nest in your bed with just two pillows?"

"Aren't we a bit old for a treehouse?" Bruce asked Paul when she'd left.

"Who cares?" Paul asked, turning to go. "I'm going to get the chair from my desk. Need anything?"

"Nope," Bruce said, lacing his fingers behind his head as he faced the blank screen. "Problem is, we probably need to know how the tree is shaped before I know where to put the supports."

"Let's just worry about what kinds of things we want to put in it for now," Jade suggested, her voice muffled by the armload of pillows she was forcing through his narrow door.

"I think there were some shows about this on one of those DIY channels a few weeks ago," Paul called from down the hall. "I'll bet you can find clips from them online."

By the time their parents came in to investigate the ominous silence that had descended upon the Grimble home, the children were so engrossed in their plans that they didn't notice.

"This had better not be something that I'm going to have to apologize to someone's parents about," Mrs. Grimble said, trying to sound stern.

The three of them jumped, and so did Megan next door, even though she had no idea what had startled her so.

As the dust from the box Megan was carrying drifted up into her face, her thoughts drifted as always to Bruce. The steep steps made it difficult to see over the Christmas ornaments she carried, but her extra senses steered her straight, especially with Bruce amplifying them.

When Megan carefully lowered the box to the floor in the kitchen, she was surprised to hear her mother humming in the dining room. The haunting melody evoked a sense of great age and power in Megan. She couldn't remember hearing it before, and yet it felt as if she almost knew the words that should accompany it. As she followed the melody, her mother began to sing in a language Megan didn't recognize. She had a beautiful voice, though it had been many years since her daughter had heard her sing. Perhaps it had been one of the songs her mother had sung to her when she was still young.

Transfixed, Megan barely noticed that her grandfather had joined her until he placed his arm gently around her shoulders.

"I've waited too long to hear her sing again," he whispered so that only Megan could hear. "Your grandmother's voice was just as beautiful."

Without warning, Emelia turned toward the front door, smiled and dropped the cloth she'd been using to polish the silver. She practically flew toward the door and was waiting for Sam before he rode up in an old, but well restored sports car. Megan watched them through the window, pleased by the changes she'd seen in her mother and deciding that a little bit of happiness and security weren't a bad thing.

When the two of them walked through the front door, Megan could tell that they were communicating mind to mind.

"Guess what," Azarich said, oblivious to the conversation he'd interrupted, "I just found an old trunk filled with letters dating back to my own grandparents. The one I looked at was talking about a hermit in the woods. Want to come up and have a look?"

"Thank you," Sam replied," but I actually came to speak with Megan. I've been thinking about adding some new video games to the arcade at Gordon's, and I wanted to get the perspective of what teens outside of Nickelville look for these days."

"That's fine, old man," Emelia said, linking her arm with her father's. "I'd love to see what secrets lie in our family's past."

"Megan and I will walk out back," the huge man called after them as he led her toward the back porch.

"Uh, Sam?" she said quietly.

"Yes," he said in that deep voice she so enjoyed.

"I'm not sure I'm a good person to ask about video games."

"Why not?" he asked. "Don't you like them?"

"No, I love video games," she replied sheepishly, "It's just that they usually catch on fire or blow up when I play."

"Truly?" he asked, "And why should that be so?"

"Electronics don't get along very well with me," she answered, "It's even worse when I get excited."

"How strange," he murmured thoughtfully. "I've never heard of that happening with our gifts before. Of course, electricity was a new thing back in the days when my ancestors were at the height of their power. My meager talents may not be strong enough to cause any interference."

"Where has the rest of your family gone?" Megan asked.

"They all passed on or moved away," he replied in a way that made Megan remember the debilitating sadness she'd felt from him at the Well of Dreams. "The young ones left to find better lives, leaving the old to carry on the traditions of our people. Of those who stayed, only my parents produced offspring. Then they were killed in an accident with a drunk driver while I was very young." Sam remained silent for a moment. "I've always found it ironic that people accuse us all of being alcoholics. I'd never even heard of alcohol until a white man who'd attempted to drown his sorrows in a bottle ended my childhood."

"That's awful," Megan whispered, horrified.

"My grandfather raised me after that."

"And the rest of your people too," Megan added.

"Has your mother spoken of this?" he asked softly.

"No," she answered, listening to the voice in her head that said now was the time for this to come out. "When we were in the ruins of your town, I could see images from the past all around us. There was a little boy everywhere, and I finally figured out it was you."

"Would you mind showing me this some time?" he asked, motioning for Megan to sit on a fallen log. "It would be nice to see this through your eyes and perhaps glimpse once again things that I have forgotten."

"You miss them, don't you?" Megan asked.

"In every waking moment, and in most of my dreams as well," he answered.

"So it's not weird that I can do this thing with seeing the past?" she asked, not sure how to comfort him.

"Unusual," he said, "But not particularly uncommon among my people. I do not have it myself. I would suggest that this could very well be the cause of your experiences at the Academy."

"No, this was different," she interrupted before he could continue. "At the Academy the Dark Man can *see* me. Your village was just faded images."

"And your mother tells me that you and Bruce were able to change the path of the liquids in your prank so as to protect... What is it your mother said you called them?"

"Terrible Trio," Megan answered with a grin.

"An apt name," he agreed. "So is it true that you moved things with your mind?"

"Yes," Megan answered.

"Another gift that is perhaps more rare," he said. "By the way, thank you for the laughter you gave me when Emelia told me about your prank. Those three are not among my favorite customers."

"You're welcome," she said. "Do you mind if I ask you something?"

"Of course not," he answered.

"Did you teach my mother how to use her abilities?"

299

"Yes and no," he answered with a frown. "When we were young, I taught her what I knew. She was the only person I had met who was both my age and shared my abilities."

"I know how that feels," Megan said, thinking about how dependent she'd become on those qualities in Bruce.

"We were both ten years old when I first saw your mother," he said. My grandfather had business in town that day, and I was sulking because he made me wear shoes."

Megan smiled. He was a great story teller. So good in fact that his words were summoning images in her mind like a fire.

"I was sitting on the corner, thinking about throwing one of my shoes down the storm drain and telling my grandfather it had been an accident. Then a voice from above told me that she wouldn't advise it. Next to me stood one of the older trees in town. I knew they had an awareness of sorts, but I'd never had one speak to me before. As you can imagine, being so young and coming from a background so full of strange occurrences, I addressed the tree in the language of my ancestors, and it *laughed* at me.

"She was in the tree," Megan giggled, "wasn't she?"

"To this day she still calls me *Silly Boy Who Talks to Trees* when we speak mind to mind," he said in the song-like voice of thunder laughing. "And as much as it bothered me then, it is the name I cherish most of all the ones I've worn."

"So what happened next?" Megan asked, feeling like a little girl asking for a longer bed-time story.

"When my grandfather came out, he found my shoes hanging from a tree branch, but no sign of me."

"Where did you go?" Megan asked.

"I followed her here," Sam answered with a grin. "I hid out at the edge of these woods for three days, and she snuck food out to me."

"What about your grandfather?"

"You mean the whole community," he said with a wry smile. "When I finally got homesick and went home, I discovered that everyone had been out looking for me, and there were posters of me across Nickelville."

"You must have been in serious trouble," Megan said in awe at the thought of what her mother would have done if she'd disappeared for three days at the age of ten.

"No one raised a hand to me, but their disappointment still burns all of these years later. I never did anything like that again."

"But you still came back to see her?" Megan asked.

"Nothing could keep us apart. I was half wildling in those days, and I've often wondered how many of the Goatman sightings from those days were caused by my travels to get here."

"Goatman?"

"Local Bigfoot legend," he explained.

"Is that really a thing?"

"Who knows," he replied with a shrug. "I've been far and wide without seeing it, but as we of all people know, it is easy for some beings to stay hidden when they wish it."

"You said yes and no about having taught my mother," Megan prompted.

"When your mother left Nickelville to go to college," Sam said, his thoughts distant, "she and I were matched in abilities."

"But when she returned?"

"My meager abilities are a trifle in comparison to hers. Furthermore, it is not just the strength of her abilities that has changed."

"What do you mean?"

"The flavor of her presence has changed," he answered, sounding as if he too were trying to reason through this change. "Now they feel old

301

beyond her years. When she left, she was a timid girl around everyone but me, haunted by her experiences at that school. Most of what we knew was either pieced together from what was passed down by my people or things that we had learned through trial and error. But now her abilities are like the hard-won discipline of a soldier, battle hardened and honed to deadly precision."

"Do you think she learned that on her own?" Megan asked.

"No," he replied quietly. "Such skills are not learned in the way that we learned, at least not in a single lifetime. Someone has taught her things I cannot even imagine."

"Who?" Megan asked, suspecting the answer already.

"That I do not know," he said with a sigh, "but a strong male presence permeates her."

"Could it be my father?" Megan asked.

"That would be my guess," he replied. "But she will not speak of the years in which she was lost to me. It would also explain why your own abilities are so strong."

"I'm strong?" Megan asked, surprised.

"Far stronger than I am," he assured her. "For those who can see such things, you're quite dazzling to look at in fact."

"And Mom?"

"Let me just say that I am glad to be called her friend. I do not believe that I would survive long should she consider me an enemy. And her power pales in comparison to yours, even though it is highly unlikely that you have reached the peak of what you are to become."

Megan had never thought of her mother in that way before. If they were so powerful, why were they running? How strong did the Huntsmen have to be then? If her father had taught her mother, then who had taught him?

"How could she let herself get caught up in something like this?" Megan asked.

"Sometimes the heart chooses a path for us, and nothing can change its mind," he explained. "It doesn't care much for logic or reason. But for all that, strangely enough, more often than not the heart proves to be wiser than our minds. We're just too stubborn to admit it."

"So where do Bruce's abilities come from?" Megan asked, uncomfortable with where her mind jumped at the meaning of Sam's words.

"Another puzzle in these troubling times."

"He saw me coming before I got here," Megan elaborated, hoping that Sam wouldn't notice her blush.

"He saw an event before it happened?" the big man asked.

"Yes, is that bad?"

"No gift is bad in and of itself, but I am troubled by the number of abilities that seem to have focused on the two of you. Prophesy is one of the rarest of gifts and often appears before times of great turmoil."

"Something bad is coming, isn't it?" Megan asked.

"I do not know the answer to that question, but I am reminded of an old saying among my people. We are given the strength to weather any storm, but beware the days that provide us with the need to be so strong."

"I'm afraid," Megan whispered.

"As am I, little one," the big man admitted. "But events on the horizon are not events at hearth and home. We must not let what might eventually come to pass take away from what is now at hand. Tomorrow will be a good day, and we should not allow speculations of the future to take away the fellowship of friends and family. Let's go back, and I'll go spend some time with Bruce. As one of my most avid arcade supporters, I suspect he will have more input on the subject that originally brought me here."

"He's grounded until tomorrow," Megan told him sadly.

"Then I will ask him after our wonderful meal on the morrow."

"She liked the flowers by the way," Megan said, suspecting that he had something to do with them.

"What flowers?" he asked.

"The yellow ones at my grandmother's grove," she answered.

"Oh," he said wistfully. "I'd forgotten. Are they still growing well?"

"There are hundreds of them," she answered with a grin.

"I planted some every year on her birthday," he admitted. "Every year for the first twenty that she was gone."

"Why did you stop?" Megan asked.

"I guess I figured if she hadn't returned by then, she wasn't ever going to come home," he replied.

"You did all of that just to impress her if she came back?" Megan asked.

"No," he answered, not looking at her this time. "It was a coincidence that those are her favorite flowers. It's an old tradition among my people."

"What were your people called?" Megan asked.

"We never had need of a name," he answered. "and by the time it became fashionable for the Anglos to take note of us, we were all but gone."

"I'm so sorry, Sam," she said, putting her small hand on his huge one. "What was the tradition?"

"During times of turmoil, when we were forced to part ways," he replied, looking out toward the woods. "Families planted those bright yellow flowers as a beacon so that the warriors would be able to find their way home."

"Hurry up in there," Jade yelled through the bathroom door at Paul. "If you comb your hair any longer you'll wear bald spots into your head."

"Be nice," Mrs. Grimble yelled from the kitchen.

The toilet flushed, the water ran in the sink for a moment before Paul opened the door.

"My locks are already perfect dear sister," he said with a malicious grin. "I just needed to clear the pipes, blow the ballast…"

"Holy mother…" Bruce gagged, pulling his shirt up to cover his nose and mouth.

"It's about time someone realized my divine worth," Mrs. Grimble said on her way past. "Please use air freshener Paul," she added. "That really is quite wretched."

"Dad," Jade yelled, "Paul stunk up the bathroom again!"

"I'd rather he did it there than somewhere else," Mr. Grimble called from the kitchen where he was taking the last of his famous homemade dressing out of the oven.

"Cover me," Jade said, grimly facing the offending bathroom door, "I'm going in."

Bruce sighed irritably and went to go sit in the living room. At this rate, it would be another hour before they went next door.

"Oh stop looking so gloomy," his mother teased when she saw him. "It's not like we have to drive an hour to get there."

He grunted in reply.

"Fine then," she said with a smile, "go next door, and see if they need any help getting things ready."

Bruce was out the door so fast he could barely hear her laughter even with his heightened senses. He might not be able to run yet in spite of his improved breathing, but he did walk very fast.

Halfway to Megan's house he felt her mother become aware of his approach almost as if he'd crossed some invisible boundary. It had taken him a few hours to realize he could feel her in the background of this new link with Megan. To be honest, he found it a bit unsettling, particularly when he realized how much his reaction amused her.

Megan burst from the front door of the house, rounded the corner at a dead sprint that would have made him think something was chasing her were it not for the smile on her face and the delirious happiness she radiated through the bond they shared.

It was the first time he'd ever seen her wearing a dress. Folds of green fabric flowed behind her as she ran, and he had only a second to think that she looked like a dark angel falling from the heavens above before she knocked him from his feet. In the back of his mind, Emelia was laughing.

"Sorry," she giggled, helping him up. "I couldn't help it."

"No problem," he laughed, trying not to cough. "Jade's my sister. I'm no stranger to being tackled."

Sam's delivery truck pulled up next to Mr. Green's just as the two friends walked up, hurriedly catching up on what had happened since the night in the grove.

"Need any help?" Megan asked as the big man began to unload chairs and tables from his truck.

"No, I've got it," Sam replied, carrying a table under his arm without effort. "It still feels strange not to be cooking on Thanksgiving," he said.

"It's your turn to enjoy the food that other people have cooked for a change," Emelia said, grabbing a chair to carry inside.

"I never cook anything," Mr. Green said, retrieving a dolly from his vehicle. "Why doesn't anyone ever ask me to cook?"

"Because you're one of the only people I've ever met who cooks worse than I do," Emelia said, stopping to kiss him on the cheek. "We still love you though."

"Really?" Mr. Green asked, looking hurt.

"I'd love to try your cooking sometime," Megan said, pausing to kiss him on the same cheek her mother had.

"Me too," Jade said, choosing to kiss the other cheek as she passed with a pan of their father's dressing.

"Don't forget me," Paul added, shrugging as he followed this apparently new tradition. "Any cool rock formations at your place?"

"Whatever you do, don't let them anywhere close to your yard with a shovel, pick-axe or wheelbarrow," Mr. Grimble said, walking past with bread. "And sorry, Alan, but I'm not kissing you."

"The holes they dig require work permits from the county to repair," Mrs. Grimble added, also forgoing the show of affection.

Bruce watched the people around him move in a harmonious blend of work and good-natured banter. He wanted to help, but in spite of the necklace, his body still hadn't recovered, and he tired quickly.

"We can go inside," Megan said, dragging him by the hand. "Grandpa needs help."

They found Azarich in the kitchen, taking pans of candied yams from the oven. He had a slightly flustered expression on his face, but still took the time to pull off one oven mitt and shake Bruce's hand in greeting.

"So you're the one who stole my helper!" he said.

"What can we do?" Megan asked.

"Think you can get the turkeys out of the smoker out back?" he asked.

"Probably," Megan said. "Any specialized equipment necessary for the task?"

"Not really," he said, taking a heavy wooden spoon from the counter. "Just stick this into the body cavity between the legs and lift it off the rack."

"Got it," Bruce said, taking the offered spoon. "What do we put them on?"

"Take three serving platters down from the cabinet," Azarich said, nodding toward it as he opened a can of cranberry sauce.

Megan grabbed the plates and led Bruce out the back door and down the porch to where her grandfather's brick smoker sent lazy tendrils of smoke into the cool autumn air.

"Those smell great," Megan said when they opened the smoker door. "I wonder how they taste."

"Like heaven," Bruce replied, maneuvering the first turkey onto its platter. "Azarich smokes turkeys for all of his friends at Thanksgiving and Christmas. I don't think I've ever eaten one that he didn't cook, but this is the first time I've eaten one at your house."

"That's surprising," Megan said, taking the turkey laden platter from Bruce while he loaded the second. "What did he do on the holidays?"

"He and Allan usually go fishing," Bruce said. "We always invited him over, but he never took us up on it."

"That doesn't seem like him."

"It doesn't sound like him now, but he's changed since you and your mother came. He was always nice, but there was a sadness in his eyes, even when he smiled.

What will happen to him if we have to leave? she thought, not willing to voice it aloud.

Let's hope that doesn't happen for a long time yet, he sent in return. *I'm not eager to leave my family either. Who would have thought that I'd ever hesitate to leave this town? I guess Azarich's not the only one who's changed.*

"Let's come back for the last turkey," Bruce said out loud. "I don't want to take the chance of dropping it."

Paul opened the back door of the house and yelled, "Deserts just got here. Eating in five. Are you guys ready to give us the birds?"

"These are really heavy," Megan called. "Will you get the last one?"

"I don't normally tolerate the bird from anyone," Paul grinned, "But for you my amazing lady, I'll make an exception."

"Even if I'm not a goth musician?" she asked.

"Not everyone can be perfect," he called back over his shoulder as he went to go get the turkey.

Inside they passed Mr. Harris and his wife Esther. Both carried pies and cakes. Jade followed them, carrying plates of fudge and cookies.

"How much food are they all bringing?" Megan asked. "I don't think the lunch ladies cook this much food for the whole school."

"I'm not sure you can legally call that stuff they serve at the Academy food," Jade said, sneaking a cookie from the table.

"How about quasi-nutritional food-like substance?" Paul asked, lugging the turkey laden platter.

At last the tables brought in by Sam were laden with food, and extra chairs lined the long table in the seldom used dining room, a remnant of days past when the McGeehee family must have hosted the entire town.

"Cool," Jade said in approval. "No kid's table."

"Kids table?" Megan asked.

"Most tables aren't big enough for the extended family, so the kids end up at a card table somewhere. Moving up to the adult one is like a rite of passage," Paul said, sounding once again like an encyclopedia.

"Oh," Megan said. "It's always just been Mom and me at a cafeteria somewhere."

Azarich cleared his throat at the head of the table, and everyone moved to join him around its edge.

"Would everyone please join hands as we pray," he asked.

With Megan's delicate hand on one side and Sam's gigantic one on the other, Bruce felt oddly unbalanced. He was accustomed to the jolt of electricity that came from physical contact with Megan, but this was new. Their linked hands created a strange sense of immersion that made him feel like only a small part of a greater whole yet somehow magnified into something greater at the same time.

Sam caught his eye and shook his head so slightly that no one else would notice. Yet in that minute gesture, he told Bruce to stay inside his own head and resist the temptation to explore the thoughts of those around the circle.

Everyone bowed their heads.

"Dear Lord," Azarich began, "We have so much to be thankful for this day. Health, even though Emelia and Bruce both gave us a scare."

Megan squeezed his hand on one side and so did Sam. Several fingers cracked in protest, but it was a nice gesture all the same.

"Friendships have been rekindled after long years of separation. New friendships have formed and drawn neighbors into something that feels more like family. And after so many years of fervent prayer, you have not only given my daughter back to me, but you have made me a grandfather as well. Please help us to use these gifts to further your glory. In your name we pray, Amen."

Silence greeted this closing to the prayer, and everyone hesitated to release the hands of those around them lest the feeling of fellowship be lost. When at last those long seconds ended with the breaking of the chain, the sensation faded slowly like the transition of a flame to glowing ember and then a wisp of scent on the air.

"Let's eat," Azarich said happily, his eyes moist. "Load up, there's enough for everyone to come back for fifths."

Bruce squeezed Megan's hand before leaving her side, suspecting that she and her mother wanted to spend a moment alone with her Grandfather. He knew that the three of them were holding each other close, each saying their own personal thanks.

"Hey Alan," Azarich said when they'd finished, looking down the table at his friend, "I'm surprised I haven't heard you ringing that big bell at the Academy. I know you were always tinkering around with its mount trying to figure out why the clapper wouldn't move."

"You know," the old janitor said, stopping in mid-bite with a fork full of turkey, "It's already frozen up again. It's the darndest thing. I've cleaned and lubricated every part of that beast that could possibly be stuck and it just won't budge. I'm starting to think that maybe a bird ran into the rim at just the right angle or something."

"It was probably just some foolish teenager meddling with something that she should have left alone," Emelia said while Megan gave the table her undivided attention.

"Bruce," Mr. Harris said, standing next to him at one of the serving tables, "Have you ever met my wife, Esther?"

"No," Bruce said politely, shaking her aged hand, "But if she had anything to do with all of these marvelous looking desserts, I'm glad I'm meeting her now!"

Mrs. Harris beamed with the praise.

"Is this the young man who helps you shelve the books?"

"It's the only way your husband will let me repay him for getting me out of Mrs. Jones's room so often this year," Bruce answered.

"Terrible woman," Mrs. Harris said with a comical scowl and patted him on the back with a frail touch.

Unbidden, the knowledge that there was something wrong with Mrs. Harris came into Bruce's mind. Confused, he mumbled agreement and filled his plate before returning to his seat at the table.

Jade and Paul were deep in conversation with Mr. Green when he sat down. From the occasional bits that drifted over the buzz of the others, he suspected they were trying to talk him into letting them go back under the school with better equipment this time.

His father and Azarich were talking about the plans to build a treehouse, and his mother was talking to Mr. and Mrs. Harris about the *Tribune.*

You didn't have to wait for me, Megan thought when she sat down beside him.

Sure I did. Do you sense something wrong with Mrs. Harris? he sent.

No, why?

I felt something when I touched her. I think she might be dying.

Really? Megan turned to look at the elderly woman and studied her for a moment. *She looks old and frail, but I don't feel anything life-threatening about her.*

Bruce is right, Emelia interjected, startling both of the young people who thought their conversation had been private. *Something is wrong with her.*

Are you feeling it through her body or are you seeing her future? Sam asked while talking to Jade about the things they might need for the tree house.

How can you talk and think something different at the same time? Bruce and Megan asked in unison.

Emelia laughed out loud and flashed a smile of contented enjoyment to her father while thinking, *Close your mouths and keep chewing. Your mothers taught you better manners than that.*

313

Admit it, Megan sent, *you're showing off. Now how do you do it?*

It's not as hard as you might think, Sam sent. *Though it does take some practice. You think of things while you're talking all the time that don't come out of your mouth. What we're doing is similar. We're just allowing the thoughts under the surface to be sent while we talk out loud.*

So which is it Bruce? Emelia asked. *Are you sensing something within her body or are you seeing her future?*

I'm not sure, Bruce answered. *Can you tell what's wrong with her?*

Not without looking deeper.

So why don't you look deeper? Megan asked.

That would be an invasion of her privacy, Sam answered. *Even if she wouldn't know we were looking into her thoughts or the inner workings of her body, it still wouldn't make it right. I suspect both she and Mr. Harris know something is wrong. There is a hint of sadness in his eyes that isn't normally there in spite of how much he and his wife are enjoying themselves.*

"I'm amazed you were able to get this many turkeys on such short notice," Mr. Grimble said. "They were out when I went to the store last week and weren't sure if they'd get more before today."

"I bought them from the Baker farm," Azarich replied.

All five of the Grimbles froze, and Megan realized she'd forgotten to tell Bruce about that in her summary of all that had happened since leaving school.

"Are we sure they're not poisoned?" Jade asked, studying the drumstick she'd almost finished closely.

"I only spoke to the mother," Azarich said, "But she was very polite and told me they really appreciated the business. And right before I left, she told me she was sorry about the ruckus her youngest caused at the school. She also added that if she could find a way to keep him away from

314

that *red-headed she-demon*, she thought he might turn out okay. When I apologized about his hair, she just laughed and said they'd all thought it was funny. So funny in fact that it finally got him out of the doghouse with his father."

"We're still cleaning the shed though," Bruce said firmly.

"This is going to be the best punishment ever!" Paul exclaimed, causing the entire table to fall silent. The silence made the sound of Jade slapping him across the back of the head seem that much louder.

"What was that for?" Paul asked, rubbing the back of his head. "All I said was..."

Then he saw his mother frowning.

"Nimrod," Jade muttered under her breath, shaking her head in disgust.

"What I meant to say," Paul began slowly.

This should be good, Sam thought.

"Was that I am so lucky to have a chance to learn from my mistakes."

Bruce didn't think his mother had blinked once during this whole exchange.

"And that we will never ever do anything bad again," Paul finished in a near-intelligible rush before shoving a big piece of turkey into his mouth and staring at his plate.

"So tell me more about this tree house," Azarich said, drawing all eyes toward him before anyone but Bruce noticed Mrs. Grimble's smile.

"The three of them have been holed up there in Bruce's bedroom on that computer making plans," Mr. Grimble answered. "We were a little bit worried about what they might be getting up to after the whole incident at the Academy."

"But you agreed that it might be best to give us something to occupy our creative little minds," Jade drawled, spearing another drumstick after apparently deciding that it wasn't indeed poisoned.

"I'm still not entirely sure," Dora began uneasily.

"You don't need to worry about my breathing. That new medication is working miracles for my asthma." Bruce lied, heading her off before she could fixate on that excuse again.

"Boy's got a point," Mr. Grimble added. "He doesn't usually get better once he's had an attack until we have a good frost that kills all the pollen-producing plants."

"But how much is lumber going to cost?" Dora asked, shifting tactics.

"There's a whole shed full of lumber that never got used from when we were going to replace the porch at our place," Mr. Harris offered.

"You sure you won't be needing it?" Mr. Grimble asked.

"Positive," Mrs. Harris answered. "It's just going to waste out there. My brother and I had a treehouse when we were kids. We built everything from soap box cars to rope swings over ponds. Most of my best childhood memories came from the things we built. Please take the lumber and make something worth remembering."

"I'm not sure," Mrs. Grimble stammered, surprised by the support her children were getting from everyone present.

"Dora," Mrs. Harris said, taking her hand in her own. "Sure, sometimes what they build won't work. Sometimes they'll fail and sometimes they'll fall. But they'll learn more from their mistakes than they will from their successes and grow up to do so much more than most folks do these days."

"She's right," Sam agreed in that hypnotic voice of his that made you want to listen to him no matter what he said. "They could learn a lot from such a project. How many people pay hundreds of dollars to have repairs made on their homes and machines that they could easily do themselves for pennies on the dollar?"

"And I've got all the tools they could possibly need along with the experience to make sure that it comes out all right," Mr. Green added.

"Please Mom?" Jade asked, managing to look pathetically cute even with her multi-colored hair.

Mrs. Grimble looked around the table in exasperation, trying to hold her ground before throwing her hands up in defeat.

Excited cheers greeted this surrender, both from the children and from the adults as well.

"This isn't going to be like that first pinewood derby is it?" Paul asked his father pointedly.

What's he talking about? Megan asked.

Dad gets a little over-involved sometimes. When Paul was in Cub Scouts there was this race where the boys were supposed to make their cars from a block of wood and race them on a track. The boys were supposed to do all of the work, but Dad stayed up all night and had the car finished before Paul even touched it.

Mr. Grimble looked sheepish.

"Can we use any of the old junk in the storage shed at the school?" Jade asked.

"I don't see why not," Mr. Green said thoughtfully. "Why, what did you have in mind?"

"How about that toilet with the busted tank?" Paul asked eagerly.

Mrs. Grimble didn't have time to react before Jade slapped him across the back of the head again.

No one wanted the meal to end, which might account for how miserably full they all felt by the time the last mouthfuls were swallowed. And although they spoke nothing about the sense of family, of friends and the fellowship of community, it laid the foundation of everything that transpired there.

Although Megan still lacked any true control of her ability to see the past, she thought there might very well be layers to the laughter that stretched back through the many generations of McGeehees that had broken bread at that table.

They might have all been under Azarich's roof, but no one listened to him when he tried to keep them from cleaning up. With the precision of a military campaign, they divided up the tasks and left the house looking as good as it had before they'd come.

Goodbyes were said, and at last even Bruce reluctantly returned to his home.

"Come over and look at the plans we've made," Jade pleaded.

"I'd like to, but I promised I'd help put up Christmas decorations," Megan told her happily. "Apparently it's a McGeehee tradition."

"Really?" Paul asked. "I don't remember Mr. McGeehee ever decorating before.

"He always had the most impressive display when I was a kid," Mrs. Grimble said drowsily, uncomfortably full and in need of a nap. "He stopped after we graduated from high school though. My father used to drive us to see it. That's part of the reason I wanted to build our house over here."

"That's when my mother moved away," Megan observed absently.

"Yes," Mrs. Grimble yawned. "Tell your mother and Grandfather again that we are so happy to have spent the holiday with you. I'll have Bruce bring your mother's story back tomorrow after I read it."

Then they were gone and the house seemed too quiet after all the conversation of the day. Yet it didn't seem empty, for when Megan concentrated she could feel the echo of the strong emotions the day had created and knew that they'd remain there for years to come.

"Ready to put the lights up?" Emelia asked, carrying a large box.

"Are you sure those things are going to work?" Megan asked. "They look really old."

"We'll get them to work," Emelia answered with a wink, and Megan feared there'd probably be another lesson in using her abilities before the night was over.

She wished Bruce had stayed.

"There must be enough to cover the whole roof," Megan groaned, when at last all of the boxes had been brought out.

"That's right," Emelia said pleasantly. "Help me stretch these out so we can check them."

When the strand was free, Emelia took the plug in her hand, glanced back at the house to make sure that Azarich was still inside, and lit the strand using only her abilities.

"Wow," Megan whispered. Without hesitation, she reached out to the strand closest to her and allowed the power of her mind to flow down its length.

Later, after they'd cleaned up the melted wiring and picked up all of the glass from the exploded bulbs that they could find, Emelia told her daughter that she could carry the remaining strands up the ladder. While Megan did this, her mother scurried across the roof, checking to see if the nails that held the lights in place needed maintenance.

"Sam said you liked to climb when you were little," Megan said, trying to distract her mother from any more snide comments about electricity.

"He told you how we met?" Emelia laughed. "That's good, he used to be too embarrassed to talk about it."

The front door of the house opened, and Azarich stepped out, holding a coil of rope in one hand.

"Are you sure that you ladies don't want to go pick out the tree?" he asked.

"Nope, we're having some good old-fashioned female bonding," Emelia called down to him. "You know, boys, shoes and that sort of girl talk."

Megan snorted. She couldn't think of a single discussion she'd ever had with her mother that could have been considered "girl talk."

"Well, be careful then, and I'll be back soon," he called, crawling into the cab of his truck. "Save some energy for decorating the tree!"

"We will," Emelia called back, her eyes never leaving Megan. "Although your granddaughter puts far more energy into the lights than is necessary."

Megan winced.

"Mom," she asked when he'd left.

"Yes dear?"

"I don't want you to take this the wrong way," she started.

"Well," Emelia said, sitting on the edge of the roof and getting a better look at her daughter's face. "This doesn't sound good."

"No, it's okay," Megan said awkwardly. "I just wanted to tell you that I like you a lot more in Nickelville than I did before."

"Thanks," Emelia said, raising an eyebrow. She could communicate whole conversations with that eyebrow.

"You're just a lot more open here," Megan explained. "Almost like you're a completely different person."

"This place and these people bring back much of who I once was," Emelia said. "Running for so long and pretending to be someone else put me into a kind of trance. I feel like I'm waking up after a long sleep."

"I didn't know you could sing," Megan said.

"Everyone can sing."

"Not like you," Megan said, wanting to communicate something important and feeling that she was doing a bad job of it.

"Well, thank you again," Emelia said, eyebrow going into overdrive.

"You don't think," Megan tried to say casually, "That this happy new you might have something to do with a certain giant we know and love?"

Emelia forced a laugh, looking away with a frown.

"Did you ever think about marrying him?"

Her mother stayed quiet for a long time, staring past Megan at the trees beyond their property. Just when Megan decided that she'd gone too far, her mother answered.

"He was going to ask me," Emelia whispered.

"When?" Megan asked.

"The first Christmas after I left. I was supposed to come home, but something came up," she answered sadly.

"What was it that came up?"

"A dream," Emelia replied absently, almost as if she were in the dream of which she'd spoken.

"You didn't love him?" Megan asked.

"That was never the problem."

"Then why?"

"My path led away from this town, at least for a while. Sam couldn't follow where I needed to go."

"Where did you go?"

"College."

"Sam couldn't follow you to college?" Megan asked. Sam seemed so well educated, she just assumed he'd gone himself.

"Sam couldn't leave Nickelville, and he is completely self-taught. I think that's why so much of his speech sounded old-fashioned even when we were kids. The books he read on his own aren't widely read by anyone except college professors. But he's the last of his people. There are things on his land that no one can have or know about. He's bound to this place."

"Did you meet my father at college?" Megan asked.

"Yes, although he wasn't a student there."

"Oh my god, he wasn't your professor or something like that was he?"

"Nothing like that," Emelia chuckled. "But you could certainly say he was different."

"What was he like?" Megan whispered. This was the most she'd ever heard on the subject.

"Complicated."

"Was he handsome?"

"Yes," Emelia answered with a wistful smile.

"What happened to him?" Megan asked, holding her breath as she waited for an answer.

"That, dear daughter, is a tale for another day."

"It's not too late for Sam," Megan blurted out. "He still loves you."

"I know," her mother said, climbing back to the task of the lights and turning her back on her daughter in what was clearly a dismissal.

"Do you know what the flowers in the grove were for?" Megan asked.

"I remember the tradition," Emelia answered, her shields wavering enough that Megan could tell she'd been thinking about this already.

"What if he could leave with us this time?" Megan asked.

322

"It just can't be," Emelia muttered, walking away across the roof.

"He would understand about what we're running from," Megan snapped, starting to become angry.

Emelia didn't answer.

"You're being selfish," Megan shouted, knowing she'd gone too far, but not caring. Emelia stiffened at the words. "He's waited for what? Thirty years for you to come home? Yet you won't even entertain the thought that he could make you happy!"

"How dare you call me selfish," Emelia whispered, but with a mental echo that almost made Megan lose her grip on the ladder. "You have no idea what I have given up in order to protect your future."

The lights along the entire edge of the roof began to glow. Tendrils of power arched from the brass fittings in the windows, and the branches closest to Emelia began to wilt.

Launching herself from the ladder to stand defiantly before her mother, Megan felt her own anger begin to interact with her surroundings.

THEN TELL ME, Megan thought, feeling a certain guilty glee when her mother winced. *STOP KEEPING ALL OF THESE SECRETS AND START TRUSTING ME.*

"It has nothing to do with trust," Emelia tried to explain, bringing her anger under control and pulling her power back into the confines of her own body. "There are things that you are not ready to know. If I tell you too soon, it will change the delicate balance of what is to come. You're not ready yet."

"I'm never going to be ready enough for you, am I?" Megan shouted back, not ready to end this confrontation now that it had started. She had so many dark emotions inside that she wasn't sure if she could stop now that they were finally coming out. "It's never going to be the right time."

"Oh, the time will come," Emelia said, walking toward her daughter until their eyes were only inches apart. "That moment is bearing down on us, and I don't know if you are going to be ready for it when it does."

"Then why aren't we doing more to prepare for it? Why won't you tell me who the people who are following us are?" Megan asked, feeling the last of her energy ebb and the real reason for this whole outburst coming to the surface. "Why are we different from everyone else?" She asked, trying not to cry. "Why am I so different from you?"

"Different from me?"

"The way I get caught in fire when you don't. I mean, I think I almost *ate* Allison. Why can I see the past?"

"I can see the past at the academy too," Emelia said, her motherly instinct starting to surface now that she sensed her child was hurt. "And Allison deserved to be judged."

"No, I can see Sam's village the way it used to be and all the people he grew up with. I fry electronics when I get upset and *my eyes glow purple when I'm mad.* What's wrong with me?" she sobbed.

Emelia drew her into a tight embrace.

"I promise you that this will all make sense one day soon. I remember being young, and I know how hard it is to be patient, especially when you're under pressure," Emelia assured her, stroking her daughter's dark hair. "For now, focus on controlling fire and moving objects with your mind. You and Bruce both. The control you develop in those skills will translate into the others as they materialize."

"But what about Sam?" Megan sniffed.

"I am not free to love him beyond the bounds of friendship," Emelia said sadly, "No matter how much I wish it could be otherwise."

Megan let the last of her anger and tension drain away.

324

"You'd better go call your boyfriend before your grandfather comes back with the tree," Emelia advised. "He felt this all the way over at his house, and he's worried."

"He's not my boyfriend," Megan snapped.

Emelia laughed.

"He's not," Megan repeated stubbornly.

"It would be better if he wasn't," Emelia said. "We'll get the decorations done on the inside tonight, and you can spend the day with the Grimbles tomorrow if you'd like. Please try to calm down before you use the phone," she added. "I'll need it to still be working when I call Sam. I don't think I want to explain what this was about mind to mind with him just now."

Chapter XXVII: Dealing with the Dark Man

Before the sun came up on Monday, Megan found herself awake almost an hour before her alarm. Such an early waking would normally have annoyed her, but she was anxious to find out how well her strengthened bond with Bruce might affect her experiences with the Dark Man. She threw off the covers, stretched and went in search of her grandfather, who she could feel downstairs in the kitchen.

The old coffee pot was percolating merrily when she walked into the kitchen on slippered feet, tying the belt of her new robe around her waist to ward off any unwarranted concerns Azarich might have about her in the morning chill. She took down two cups from the cupboard, filled them with the dark aromatic liquid and added cream and sugar to them both.

On her way to the door she noticed a ring of old skeleton keys hanging on a hook.

"Hey Grandpa," she said quietly, slipping out the back door, holding the handles of the steaming cups in one hand while she closed the door with the other. "Mind some company?"

"Of course not," he said, taking the offered cup and scooting over to make room for her on the porch swing. "What brings you from your warm bed so early this morning?"

"I just woke up early and thought I'd come see what you do before we get up," she said, sipping the sweet coffee.

"You're going to think me a doddering old fool," he said quietly in the early morning silence, "but for a second there I thought you were your grandmother."

"You're not old," Megan said, lowering herself onto the swing next to him, "I just look an awful lot like her."

"I'm afraid I've been old longer than you've been alive, sweet girl," he said, sipping the coffee. "You make it just like your mom does."

"So what are you doing out here?" she asked.

"Waiting for the sunrise."

"Do you come out every morning?"

"Ever since I married your grandmother," he answered. "It was how we started each day. I'd start the coffee pot, she'd come out after me when it was ready."

"You still miss her," Megan whispered, leaning her head against his arm.

"Just as much as I did when she first passed. She was my best friend after all. It's been five decades since she died, and I still catch myself thinking that I'm going to tell her about things that I've seen or thought about," he said. "See how the sky is getting lighter?"

"Yes," she answered. "How much longer?"

"Not long. There are a lot of clouds this morning, and the wind is stronger up where they're floating," he said, pointing to a swirling mass toward the horizon.

"Is it going to rain today?" she asked.

"Tonight would be my guess," he answered.

They watched in silence as the morning crept closer. At first Megan wondered what the purpose of watching the sun rise on a cloudy day could be, but as the clouds grew lighter, they shed their dark hues for shades of red, pink and purple.

"Is it always like this?" she gasped, her eyes darting across every swirl of color, trying to take it all in before it faded.

"Not always," he answered, pleased by her reaction. "But the clear days have their own beauty too."

"What causes all the colors?"

"Sadly enough, pollution," he answered, staring at the sky. "When I was a boy, sunrises were seldom this pretty."

"So it's a bad thing?" Megan said.

"Few things in this world are purely good or bad," he said, looking from the brightening sky to his granddaughter. "Sometimes we get hung up on the right and wrong thing so much that we forget that most things are both. All we can do is try to maximize the good and hold back the bad."

Megan nodded, still watching the upheavals of colored light and shadow on the horizon and wondering if he would mind if she started coming out every morning to watch it with him.

"Oh," Azarich said, shifting his cup to the other hand and reaching into the front pocket of his shirt to hand her a small photograph. "I found this last night."

She took it from his hand, expecting to find another picture of her mother as a little girl or perhaps a picture of her grandmother here in this house. But the photo was of something else entirely.

It was clearly a wedding, but a wedding unlike any she'd ever seen on television. Her mother wore a white dress that Megan suspected was old fashioned long before the picture had been taken. In shock, she realized that it was adorned with the looping patterns she'd drawn since she was old enough to hold a pencil. What did this mean?

"So he's?" Megan whispered, afraid that her mother might wake if she spoke any louder.

"Your father," Azarich finished. "This is the first time you've seen him, isn't it?"

"Yes," she answered. "He was handsome. You were there?"

He nodded.

"That was the last time I saw her before the two of you turned up at Carson's," he added sadly. "You might not want to let Emelia know I gave you that."

"I won't," Megan said, taking one last look at it in the morning light before tucking it into the pocket of her robe and giving her grandfather the hardest hug she'd ever given.

"Take it easy," he said, laughing. "These old bones break easier than they used to. Are you hungry?"

"Yes," she replied, silently thinking that nothing bad could possibly happen on such a magical day.

"Want to help me cook breakfast?"

"Sure," she said reluctantly, "but I've never really cooked anything that didn't come out of a microwave before."

"That's probably for the best," he said with a mischievous smile.

"What do you mean?"

"Well, there's only one person you could have learned to cook from," he answered.

"Oh," Megan said, catching on.

When her mother made it downstairs half an hour later, it smelled just as good as it normally did when Azarich cooked by himself. But both he and Megan were covered in flour and laughing hysterically about some joke that wasn't funny enough to repeat.

They tried to stop when they saw Emelia's sour expression, but that only made it worse.

"Do you guys think Mr. Green would let me blow out some of those formations I saw under the building?" Jade asked as the bus rumbled down Beverly Road on the way to the Academy.

"You're not serious," Megan replied.

"Somehow I doubt anyone's going to let us rig explosives under the school," Paul said sadly.

"Not to mention a really bad idea with all of the sewage pipes down there," Bruce added.

Outside, clouds thickened and darkness overcame what remained of the colorful sunrise, plunging Nickelville back into night. Flashes of lightning lit the sky with increasing regularity and thunder rattled the windows of the bus.

Megan frowned, thinking about the way it resembled the times when she and her mother had been hunted.

What's wrong? Bruce asked.

This storm doesn't feel natural, she replied.

How can you tell? Wait, do you think they've found you?

She shrugged, taking comfort in the way his shoulder felt against her own. Now that they had the stone that hung around Bruce's neck, they didn't need to be so close, but for reasons she didn't understand, she had no desire to stop.

As they drew closer to the school, the weather grew worse.

Downtown lay deserted around them, giving Megan the impression that others could sense something unnatural in the storm as well.

The bus pulled off the main road and began its final approach to the Academy.

What the hell? Bruce sent, panic flavoring his thoughts.

330

The woods around them teemed with movement as the supernatural creatures she'd seen that first day fled as far as they could get from the school. A brutish mass that looked a lot like a mossy boulder without a discernible front or back waddled past on short, bowed legs. Colorful birds with entirely too much plumage to fly sped past, and things moving too quickly to focus on jumped from branch to branch after the rest.

They were real? Bruce sent. *I thought I hallucinated the whole thing.*

They showed themselves to you? Megan asked, mildly irritated that they hadn't done so for her.

They did a lot more than that, he replied. *I couldn't have made it out of the woods without their help. But if they're scared of that thing in front of us, I'm afraid of what's going to happen when we hit it.*

Megan followed his eyes through the windshield to where they normally felt the static barrier. A wall of multicolored flame crossed the road ahead of the oblivious driver and stretched out across the boundary between the field and the woods on either side as if a giant had pulled a rainbow, burning from the sky.

Bruce snatched her hand up from her lap and braced for impact as they sped toward the flames. The nose of the bus slid without resistance through the wall of energy that crept down the aisle toward them.

Gasps and muffled exclamations escaped the people who passed through it.

Then it flowed over the two of them and Bruce clamped his eyes shut against what they knew was coming. Though it looked like fire, it felt like thousands of angry insects crawling over their skin.

As Megan watched, the stone leapt from under the collar of Bruce's shirt and might have left him completely were it not for the leather shoelace on which it had been threaded. He reached out and snatched it back, holding it tight in his fist.

331

From the direction of the Academy, something stirred.

"Don't touch anything metal," Paul called out, his voice somehow reaching everyone on the bus. "I think we may be passing through an unevenly charged place where lightning is about to strike."

Everyone on the bus reacted by pulling feet and hands from the exposed metal skin of the old bus. Even the bus driver looked reluctant to keep her hands and feet in contact with the instruments she needed to guide the vehicle.

What was that? Bruce asked. *I've never been able to see it before.*

I think it was a ward, she sent. *My mother can make them, but they're not anywhere near that strong. One thing is for sure, he knows we're coming.*

Great, he thought, scanning the Academy ahead for any signs of trouble.

Lightning bleached the world white for a second as the bus pulled up at the foot of the stone steps. The immediate blast of thunder shook the bus on its suspension and caused most of the riders to cover their ears.

"Everybody off as quickly and orderly as you can go," the bus driver yelled over the rain that now pummeled the metal roof mere inches above them. "Don't run, the steps are going to be slick. But it's safer inside the building than it is out here."

She didn't need to repeat the command. Younger students from the front of the bus flew toward the entrance the second she opened the folding door.

"No pushing," the driver yelled again, looking anxiously toward the sky through the windshield. In the last few moments it had taken on a sickly green tint that made Megan extremely uneasy.

One moment Megan was looking down the aisle of the bus, and the next, everything was engulfed in roaring flame. She'd seen this place before in the fire on the night of the race. The Dark Man stood outside the door.

Reaching out with her hands, Megan shielded the entire bus, trying to keep him out.

Bruce's hand locked over her shoulder and shook her gently. With that contact, the flames died around her and she found herself standing once again in the aisle of the bus.

She hurried to catch up with the people ahead of her.

"Everything okay?" Jade asked.

"Yeah," Megan said. "I just don't want to go inside."

"I second that," Paul said. "I never saw anything like this described in my weather merit badge."

Just as Megan stepped down into the door-well of the bus, the floor beneath her lurched forward, and she sat down hard. A wrenching sensation flowed out from her chest and she heard Bruce gasp over her shoulder.

The bond just broke, he thought, farther away than he'd sounded just seconds earlier. *The stone burned me too.*

Transparent flames danced up the rail next to her as the vision tried to reassert itself. The Dark Man stood at the bottom of the steps looking at her through the open door, but her shield held, although only barely.

"Here, let me help you," Bruce said, reaching down and putting his hand under her elbow to help her up.

Once again, the flames died away.

"How weird was that?" Jade asked. "It felt like someone hit us from behind."

Before they could respond, the rain deepened from a heavy shower into a full downpour. Sleet joined the rain only to be followed by hail.

333

"How bizarre!" Paul yelled from the seat near a window, where he'd moved to get a better look.

"You guys had better wait until this passes," the driver warned and closed the door.

While they waited, the roar of the rain and the impacts of the hail grew more intense. The pieces of ice that fell from the sky overhead passed the size of golf-balls and continued to grow.

As soon as Bruce let go of her arm, the fire started to come back. The Dark Man stood outside of the door again, untouched by the rain and hail.

Megan reached over and took Bruce's hand in her own. His eyes widened and she followed his gaze to where the Dark Man had been.

Can you see him?

Only for a second after I touch you, and then he fades away. Why can't I see him unless I'm touching you? I could do it before your mom made the stone. Why not now? Did you see the fire?

Yeah. Why isn't the stone working?

Don't know, but this is just like that day in the courtyard.

A ball of ice the size of a softball hit the windshield. The glass fractured, but held. More hit the top of the bus and it started to dent inward.

"Get down on the floor," the driver yelled above the explosive impacts. More windows cracked.

He's angry that we're blocking him out, Megan realized, huddling in the floor behind the driver's seat with Bruce.

"This is so cool!" Paul yelled, still standing.

Jade pulled him down and tried to stuff him under a seat. The space was too small, but that didn't, however, stop her from trying harder.

The pounding slowed and then stopped. The rain continued a moment longer before it too gave out, and in the ominous silence that followed,

Megan could feel Bruce's heartbeat through the hand she held close against her.

"Cool?" Jade yelled in astonishment at Paul, then slapped him across the back of the head. "Am I the only kid in my family that doesn't have brain damage?"

"Hey," he said indignantly. "If I've got brain damage it's from you doing that all the time."

Megan reluctantly let go of Bruce's hand. The flames didn't return, and she let out the breath she'd been holding.

Where is he now? Bruce asked, scanning the windows.

Tired, she thought and hoped it was true. The Dark Man had exhausted himself for the moment, but she knew he'd be back.

"Is everyone okay in there?" Mr. Harris yelled from outside.

"Yes," the driver yelled back, trying to open the doors, which were now bent inward as if something had tried to force its way in.

With a groan of protesting metal, Mr. Harris wrenched the door open and climbed the steps.

"Just the four of you?" he asked, scanning them for injuries.

They nodded. Even Paul began to realize how close they'd come to being hurt.

Mr. Green whistled from the front steps when they approached the doors. As soon as everyone was clear of the bus, Megan felt a weight lift from her mind as she released the temporary shields she'd created and every window in the bus collapsed.

It looked worse from the outside. There were so many dents in the roof and hood that the bus had a lumpy, misshapen appearance to it. Glancing around, she realized that the hail had only hit the bus. Everything else was wet but otherwise unharmed.

Now that the freak storm had passed, Mrs. Jones and Mr. Danders stepped from the front doors. The teacher's gaudy red lips were curved in one of those sickening smiles she reserved for moments when she punished Megan.

Mr. Harris, Mr. Green and the Grimbles flanked Megan like an honor guard.

"Well, well, Miss McGeehee," Mrs. Jones squealed in delight.

"Mrs. Jones," Mr. Harris began, "These children have just been through a horrible ordeal. You can't possibly expect…"

"When I want your opinion, librarian, I'll ask for it. Right now I want my property returned."

"Not this again," Bruce snapped. "What has she supposedly stolen now?"

"Were the two of you in the clinic on the Friday before the break?" Mr. Danders asked, looking as if he wanted no part of the whole situation.

"Yes," Megan said, not understanding where this was leading.

"Do you recall when the nurse took off her wedding band to wash her hands?" he continued.

"Now wait a minute," Megan said, anger overcoming her attempt to remain calm. "You're not seriously accusing me of stealing a little old woman's wedding ring, are you?"

"And my watch," Mrs. Jones added gleefully. "Between the two you might have stolen enough to be classified as a felon."

"Come on," Jade yelled defiantly. "Things have been disappearing all year."

"She's not even around when most of the stuff goes missing," Paul added. "What is she? Magic?"

"She was, however, present when both of these items disappeared," Mr. Danders said unhappily. "She's already been warned."

"So now what?" Megan asked with resignation. She was having trouble taking this seriously after what had just happened on the bus. Even without the bond she was pretty sure that she and Bruce could keep the Dark Man at bay until the end of the day when her mother could repair it.

"You'll have to spend the day in the isolation room," Mr. Danders said.

"Until the sheriff comes in to start a formal investigation," Mrs. Jones giggled.

"That's hardly fair," Mr. Green said, surprising them all. "The sheriff is Mrs. Jones's brother. He's not exactly an unbiased party."

"Do you want to return the items, Megan?" Mr. Danders pleaded.

"Where's this stupid room at?" Megan asked, holding Mrs. Jones's eyes with her own cool gaze until the teacher noticed that she and Bruce were still holding hands.

"Public affection is not allowed here," Mrs. Jones crooned.

Reluctantly, Bruce released her hand, and Megan knew at once that the Dark Man wasn't as tired as she'd hoped.

The construction of the Academy was now complete in the past world that overlapped Megan's vision of the present. Inside the front doors, she could see that the paneled walls shone in the light from gas lamps, and everything looked the same as her first vision in the hallway.

Vertigo brought bile up from her stomach, and she could taste the coppery blood in her mouth as she bit her tongue to steady herself. The people around her faded into the future, and she feared that she was being sucked away from the present to be trapped inside the dark world where *he* lived.

In panic she groped for Bruce's hand.

He gasped, suddenly drawn into the spectral world of the Academy with her.

Tell Mom and Grandpa that I love them, she sent desperately, then released her grip on his hand. She cared too much about him to bring him into this.

She could see and hear the real world around her, but it felt less and less real as the seconds ticked past on her antique watch. Mr. Danders asked her to follow him. Bruce tried to resist, but with the bond severed, his asthma was building toward an attack by the second.

The Grimbles went to their classes, but her grandfather's childhood friends, Mr. Green and Mr. Harris, stayed with her until she stood before the door to the isolation room.

"Are you sure that there's nothing you want to tell us?" Mr. Danders asked.

"That Mrs. Jones is the most petty, immature and irresponsible person I've ever met, and even Chuck Baker would make a better teacher."

Without waiting for their response, she placed her hand on the polished brass doorknob and found it warm in her hand.

"This is it," she whispered, unsure if the shadow people around her could hear. If there was a reason for all that her family had suffered through, it must be to prepare her for this moment. She took the painful memories of a life spent in hiding and armored herself with them. She calmed herself with thoughts of the Grimbles. She took courage in the memory of her mother's rich laughter at the carnival and the haunting melody she'd sung preparing for Thanksgiving. But most of all, she took strength in the image of her father that she'd slipped into her hand on the way down the hall. Something dormant flared within her, and she was ready to face him.

The door swung inward on well-oiled hinges. Inside stood a table surrounded with chairs. It was beautiful. Carved images like those on the library door and the foyer walls led her eyes to the other end where the

Dark Man sat, waiting. She noticed, in spite of the pristine condition of the room, that there was a musty smell like the basements of some of the buildings she'd lived in.

The lock behind her clicked, leaving Megan alone with her worst nightmare.

Bruce glared at Mrs. Jones through the first lecture she'd given in months, hearing nothing of what she said. She smiled a wicked little smile while she pranced around the classroom.

He looked up at the clock again. Mrs. Jones smiled even wider.

Bruce found a place on his desk where he could focus his eyes and not be disturbed by the deranged woman in charge of his education.

He pulled out a paper and wrote:

Items Missing:

1) Watch

2) Ear ring (why just one?)

3) Wedding ring

He stared at the list. He knew of other things that had disappeared, but none of them had been valuable. He racked his brain for things common to them and could only link them by the fact that they were shiny.

People present:

1) Megan

2) Myself

3) Mrs. Jones

4) Mrs. Howie

People present in each occurrence:

1) Megan

2) Myself

Nothing else came to mind. There were no other common factors between them.

What about the ghost? The Dark Man had been present in the courtyard when the watch was stolen, although Megan hadn't acted like he was close enough to take something. Could he be present but not show himself to her? What if it was the ghost? They couldn't exactly tell Mr. Danders that the thief was the spirit of a dead kleptomaniac.

He'd been running his left hand over the grooves in the desktop where someone had carved their initials. Things like that always bothered his sense of order, as well as his dislike for things that had been poorly done. But now while his anger and helplessness to protect Megan boiled over, he noticed that something had changed.

Lifting his hand, he found that not only was the damage to the desk repaired, but the finish looked as if it were no more than a few days old at most where he'd been touching it.

Puzzlement gave way to irritation, and he crumpled the paper and threw it into his desk. Mrs. Jones smiled again. He wondered if anyone would help him hold her down while he shoved it down her throat along with a few of her fashion magazines.

As pleasant as that thought was, it soon gave way to the memory of the bus. It bothered him that the Dark Man seemed to have complete control over the weather around the school. How much energy had it taken to bring down hail of that size? Bruce knew that it took time for ice like that to form. Had the Dark Man known he would need the hail in advance? Could he see the future too? Did his reach extend miles into the sky where the ice had formed?

Bruce thought about these questions, and didn't like what they suggested. He scanned all of the information in his mind about ghosts and realized that these abilities suggested that the Dark Man might not be a ghost at all, or at least he wasn't *just* a ghost. But if that was the case, what *was* he?

Megan took the seat opposite the Dark Man, wondering how much of her surroundings were present in the real world, and how much of it had been put in her mind by him.

"You could have hurt us if you'd wanted to,*"* she said.

"That was never my intent," he replied in a voice that was surprisingly pleasant to hear. "It's extremely difficult to reach you from where I am. The power I expend not only taxes my limits, but also makes it difficult to do anything with any degree of precision."

"What about the curtain rods in the cafeteria?" she asked.

"Sometimes it's hard to control which parts of your world I interact with," he explained. "I dislike the way they block the light. The way it flows in brings me peace. It reminds me of better days."

"Why me?"

"I've been waiting for you for longer than you can imagine," he answered. "I need you to finish this."

"Finish what?" she asked.

"I can't hold this long enough to tell you," he explained. "Will you allow me to show you?"

A part of her wanted to lock her shields down and block him out. She sensed that he'd depleted most of his energy breaking through the bond she shared with Bruce. But another part of her noted the way his feelings felt at the edge of her mind. She sensed nothing sinister in his intent. Before she could second-guess herself, she nodded and lowered her shields.

341

Images began to flow into her mind, forcing their way into the dark recesses and blinding her to the world around her. Unafraid for the first time in her life, she surrendered to the flood.

Bruce listened to the thunder roll outside and knew it signaled the approach of another storm. He shifted uncomfortably in his seat and wondered if it was natural or not. He prayed the Dark Man was too tired from the destruction of the bus to find Megan, and that this was just an aftershock of the earlier storm.

Images from the woods played across his mind's eye as he tried to come to terms with what he'd seen. The only reason he'd handled what happened during the race so well was that he'd truly believed that he'd hallucinated it all. But now he knew better, and it honestly wasn't the discovery that things like dryads and pookahs were real that bothered him the most. It was the knowledge that he'd apparently been living alongside them for his entire life without noticing. It was enough to shake his entire understanding of reality.

Glenn and Chuck walked through the classroom doors together. Wet spots on their shirts told Bruce that the rain had returned.

Thunder rattled the building, much closer this time than the last.

"Mrs. Jones," he said, raising his hand, "May I go to the restroom?"

"Do you really think I don't know what you have planned?" she giggled. There was something so reptilian about the laugh that it turned his stomach and made the need to go real.

"I need to go to the restroom," he repeated.

"Well then," she purred. "You won't mind if Glenn comes with you?"

"As long as he doesn't have to stay in the stall with me," Bruce taunted. The class laughed, Glenn turned red and Mrs. Jones stopped smiling.

"He'll tell me if you try anything."

"Of course," Bruce said. "But what if he can't keep up? I don't suppose Chuck has any more ragweed?"

The class erupted into laughter again, and the red splotches on Glenn's face grew darker.

"Just go, Grimble," Mrs. Jones said in a low voice that silenced the class, "before I change my mind."

Bruce strolled from the room, wishing that he could have thought of a way to insult Allison as well.

Rain beat against the colored windows that lined the hall. Another burst of thunder shook the Academy.

"Better be careful," Glenn growled from Bruce's side while they walked. "She's a powerful person in this town."

"No one in my family works for her husband. She can't hold jobs over me like she does your dad."

"Leave my dad out of this."

"Or what?" Bruce said, acting as if nothing were out of the ordinary. "Chuck isn't here to protect you. I may be having asthma problems, but the moment the adrenaline kicks in from fighting, I'll be back in top shape until it's over. And given how you've bullied me for so long, I'm not sure I'd be able to stop once I start."

Glenn didn't respond.

"From your silence I guess you read that the same place where you found out how to rig the race."

"Just take your dump so we can get back to class," Glenn snapped.

Bruce strolled into the restroom while Glenn thankfully waited outside.

Mr. Bob, who'd been in the stall, darted between Bruce's legs and out through the open bathroom door.

"Stupid cat," Bruce muttered then froze with the words still fresh from his lips. His needs forgotten, Bruce knocked Glenn over on his way out of the bathroom.

"Hey, where do you think you're going?" Glenn yelped and took off at a sprint toward the classroom.

Bruce didn't answer. He hoped that Glenn would lead Mrs. Jones to the isolation room and not to the office.

Chapter XXVIII: Mysterious Mr. Bob

Lightning arced across what Bruce could see of the sky through the high cafeteria windows which had until recently been curtained. Thunder followed an instant later, speeding his steps as he worried anew what might be happening to Megan in that locked room.

"Can I help you?" Millie asked when Bruce walked through the office doors.

"Yes, I need to speak with Mr. Danders."

"May I ask why?"

"I think I know where to find the stolen things," Bruce answered.

"I was hoping to see you," Mr. Danders said from the doorway to his office.

"You were?" Bruce asked.

"It's hard to say something that you know will get your friend in trouble, but you're doing the right thing."

"It wasn't Megan," Bruce said.

"Really?" Mr. Danders said, frowning. "May I ask who it was then?"

"I'd rather not say until I make sure that the things are where I think they are. Can Mr. Green open the lock on that old wardrobe in the library?"

"Why would he need to do that?" Mr. Danders asked.

"Because Mr. Harris lost the key a long time ago."

345

"Then how would you know that the items are there?" Mr. Danders asked.

"I don't know for sure, but the thief might have access to it."

Bruce tried not to shift from foot to foot while the vice principal studied him silently.

"Come with me," Mr. Danders said at last.

Bruce followed him to the janitor's closet where Mr. Green was repairing the caster to one of the library shelving carts.

"Mr. Green," the vice-principal said. "Bring what tools you'd need to open the old wardrobe in the library."

"Sure," the janitor said, giving Bruce a curious look.

The three of them walked across the cafeteria and into the library where Mr. Harris stood behind the counter, reading the newspaper when they came in.

"Can I help you?" he asked.

"Is that the wardrobe you're talking about?" Mr. Danders asked Bruce.

"Yes."

"Mr. Green?" Mr. Danders prompted.

Mr. Harris came over to watch, but asked nothing else while Mr. Green slipped a small screwdriver into the space between the old hinges and started to gently tap the pins out. After several minutes of work, the last fell with a ping to the ground.

"Well Bruce, here's your chance to clear your friend's name," Mr. Danders offered, making a sweeping gesture toward the wardrobe.

Bruce stepped forward and slowly pulled the door free. Most of the space was filled with old books and papers. But the bottom left side, surrounding a hole where Mr. Bob had entered hundreds if not thousands of times, was a pile of glittering objects.

Soda tabs, tin foil, and other shiny bits of metal made up the bulk of his hoard, but there were a few valuables as well. After digging for a moment, Bruce came up with Mrs. Jones's watch and the nurse's wedding ring.

"Brilliant," Mr. Harris breathed behind Bruce. "Who would have ever suspected that he was keeping all of that stuff in there?"

"Who?" Mr. Danders asked, turning his bushy unibrow into a child's drawing of a seagull.

"Mr. Bob," the librarian answered with a laugh. "He's been sleeping in there ever since he showed up at the Academy."

"Do you mean to tell me that a cat has been stealing all of the things that are missing?" Mr. Danders asked.

"How did you figure it out?" Mr. Harris asked Bruce.

"Mr. Bob likes to follow Megan around," Bruce said. "He's been there every time something's disappeared. I was trying to figure out who could have taken all of the stuff, but Megan and I were the only two people who were there every time. It completely stumped me until I saw Mr. Bob earlier and wondered if he'd knocked the ring down the sink. Then I remembered that he was sitting there with us when the watch disappeared too."

"Megan is a fortunate girl to have you as a friend," Mr. Danders said. "Let's return these things to their owners and release Megan from isolation."

Megan floated through dreams of a past not her own, drowning in the depths of something utterly incompatible with her mind. At first the transfer of his memories into her mind had gone smoothly, giving her the faintest outline of a man named Jacob Routh, whom the women of her family would later know as the Dark Man for the style of his clothing.

But then something had gone horribly wrong. An image spun away from its intended destination, disrupting the coherent flow and making it impossible for her to understand what he tried to show her. What felt like the history of the world poured down on her, quickly submerging her sense of self in this alien persona that threatened to drown her.

By the time he realized what had happened and stopped the flow, it was too late. All he could do was halt the process and hope for the best.

She felt as if she were drowning. Something was changing the way her mind interpreted the sensation and making her feel like it was actual water that filled her lungs and dragged her down into the depths. Her struggle became less urgent, less important in the face of such soul-weary exhaustion.

Then a hand closed over hers and through that tender contact her strength returned. Instinctively understanding where the visions ended and she began, the presence lifted her up, back to the place from which she'd come. She felt his lips graze her forehead as he carried her back ashore. She whispered his name as she opened her eyes...

"Welcome back," Bruce whispered. "Are you okay?"

"My skull feels about ten sizes too small for my brain," she answered, disoriented and aware that it felt like her nose had been running. She ran the back of her hand across her nose since she didn't have anything else, and it came away slick with blood.

"Here," Mr. Green said, pulling a surprisingly clean handkerchief from the pocket of his work-stained overalls. "You'll want to pinch your nose shut with that until it stops."

The stone is working again, Bruce thought.

He had to show me something, and we kept blocking him out when we worked together. She sent. *So he broke the bond until he was done.*

"What happened?" Mr. Harris asked.

"I must have nodded off and hit my nose," she lied with a dismissive shrug. "It was so nice in here with the rain coming down outside."

"Why don't you take a minute to collect yourself," Mr. Harris said in a fatherly tone that made Megan wonder if he and his wife had any children.

So he's not bad? Bruce asked, skeptical. *What about the bus this morning?*

Powerful use of abilities messes with the weather. She answered. *For some reason he felt he had to get through to me today.*

You mean that storm was just a side effect of how much power it took to separate us? What about the bookshelf he tried to crush us with?

He has trouble focusing from where he's at. He knocked it down by accident while trying to reach me before we blocked him out again.

What did he show you? Bruce asked.

Too much to explain, she answered. *Remember when your computer was taking a long time to process the information you gave it for the prank?*

Sure, he thought, *but what does that have to do with anything?*

My mind is trying to sort through everything he showed me. I've got about a million thoughts and memories in my head that aren't mine right now.

While the bleeding stopped, Bruce explained the role Mr. Bob had played in their problems at the Academy. After proving that she could stand unaided, Mr. Danders agreed that she could return to class.

"Let's show that hag I didn't steal her stupid watch," Megan said.

This time it wasn't just Mr. Green that pretended he couldn't hear.

349

"Mrs. Jones," the vice principal said from her classroom doorway.

"So you found him," Mrs. Jones said, glaring at Bruce until she noticed Megan standing there as well. "What is *she* doing out of isolation?"

"Bruce has something for you," Mr. Danders said.

Bruce walked up and handed her watch back to her.

"So she decided to come clean," Mrs. Jones said, casting a lofty glare at Megan.

"It was in the old wardrobe in the library," Bruce said, "where Mr. Bob put it after he ran off during recess."

"You expect me to believe that a cat stole my watch?" she said, turning from Bruce to the vice principal, "Mr. Danders, surely you don't believe this farce. He and that McGeehee girl must have slipped the missing items in there and then made up this story to get out of trouble."

"The wardrobe has been locked for years," Mr. Danders said with the first smile Megan had ever seen on his lips.

"Then how did the cat put it in there?"

"Through a hole in the back," Bruce said.

"And how did you find it?"

"Mr. Harris told me that the cat sleeps in there while we were helping him the other day," Bruce said. "You know, the day he took us because your daughter had vandalized our lockers."

"How convenient," Mrs. Jones hissed, ignoring the accusation.

"I think you owe Megan an apology," Mr. Danders said quietly.

"I will do no such thing," Mrs. Jones spat.

"To refuse would be to open yourself up to lawsuits," Mr. Danders said. "I trust you remember what her grandfather's profession was before he retired?"

Anger radiated from the foul woman in waves. The class watched her glare at the ground in front of her, pouting like an overgrown child.

"I'm sorry I accused you of stealing," Mrs. Jones said. She didn't sound very convincing.

"Well," Mr. Danders said, wringing his hands in the symbolic gesture of leaving the whole business behind, "since that's done I can go back to my office and get some work done." He turned and walked toward the door. "Oh," he said, turning back to the class, "Good job, Bruce."

Bruce went back to his seat still enjoying the ease of each breath thanks to the adrenaline and restored link with Megan. Better yet, his smile infuriated Mrs. Jones as much as her own had sickened him earlier.

"Get your library books out and read quietly until lunch," Mrs. Jones snarled. The class hurried to do what she asked.

Jade and Paul were already sitting at their customary table when Megan and Bruce got there. Bruce handed Megan a sandwich, and she threw her lunch bag into the trashcan next to the table without bothering to open it. Her mother had taken over the making of Megan's lunch now that she was feeling better, and not even Jade wanted it any more.

"How are we supposed to break you out of prison when you're already out?" Jade asked, surprised to see her friend.

"I figured out who took the missing stuff," Bruce said, pride showing while he hovered protectively near Megan.

"Cool!" Paul exclaimed around a bite. "Who did it, Sherlock?"

"Mr. Bob," Megan answered and then helped Bruce tell the story. It helped with the flood of images that still pulsed inside her head.

"Man, what I wouldn't have given to see Jones apologize," Jade said. "I never could stand that woman."

"I don't think she liked you much either," Bruce said, "The first thing she asked me when I got to her class was if I was anything like you."

"How did you answer?" Paul asked.

"I just shrugged and tried to blend into the woodwork…" Bruce said, trailing off as he looked toward the stage.

Megan followed his eyes and found the Dark Man standing there, watching. He seemed diminished by what they'd tried to do. Diminished and concerned.

So we're sure he's not a bad guy? Bruce asked.

Creepy, but not bad. She answered. *I hope he doesn't want to show me anything else. My brain is full.*

I think he wants us to follow him into that closet, Bruce thought.

Why not? She sent. *After all, how much worse could our day get? When your day starts off with the storm of the century and includes having a ghost shove a few million images directly into your brain, everything else should be easy.*

The bell rang, and students started back to class. Jade and Paul bid them farewell and left the cafeteria while Bruce and Megan lingered behind. When they reached Mrs. Jones's room, Bruce took her by the hand and pulled her into a group of older kids who were walking toward the high school side of the building.

She wondered why he was taking the long way around, but assumed he knew what he was doing. When they came to the cafeteria door opposite from the one that they normally used, she realized he'd placed them next to where they'd seen the Dark Man only moments before.

Just as he started to open it, they heard Mrs. Jones somewhere nearby.

"Why should I come to the office with you?" Jade asked with an air of belligerence. "You're not my teacher anymore."

"You'll do as I say if you know what's good for you," Mrs. Jones snarled.

Cracking the door slowly open, they saw Jade arguing with their teacher. The Terrible Trio were there as well, however, only Chuck was turned in their direction.

How did she realize we were missing so fast? Bruce asked.

I'll bet the Trio noticed us when we broke away from the class, Megan thought.

"Where did they go?" The nasty woman bellowed.

"I don't know," Jade drawled slowly as if she were talking to a slow child. "They're in your class. Shouldn't you be the one who knows where they are?"

This comment didn't sit well with Mrs. Jones, who took a menacing step closer to Jade and momentarily blocked Chuck's view. Bruce opened the door and Megan slipped into the cafeteria behind him.

If only Mrs. Jones would stay there for a few seconds longer, Megan thought.

Three feet from the door Chuck caught sight of them. Megan froze, waiting for Bruce's long-time bully to sound the alarm. But even though he clearly saw them, he turned toward Jade as if nothing had happened. Bruce opened the door, and they slipped inside.

Inside, shelves lined the walls, and a workbench took up the back wall. And although the Dark Man had disappeared, they both heard the sounds of footsteps overhead.

Bruce climbed up onto the table and pulled down a retractable ladder that Megan would have otherwise missed. It had a weird lump of metal tied to the end of the cord.

"What's up there?" Megan asked.

"The attic," he answered, swinging his leg up and climbing the first few steps. "It's where they keep the old textbooks and props from school plays. It's really a cool place."

"No one will look for us up there?" she asked.

"I don't think so. Sometimes I come up here when my Mom says my asthma is too bad, and I have to stay inside. I'm supposed to stay in the clinic, but Mrs. Howie drives me nuts sometimes. Just make sure that you walk quietly. The classrooms run beneath us, and we don't want someone to tell Mr. Green that there are rats up here."

"Are there?" Megan asked.

"Are there what?" Bruce asked, peering down at her from the open trap door.

"Rats."

"Not that I've ever seen."

"I can handle mice, and I can put up with snakes if I have to, but rats really gross me out," Megan said, pulling herself over the edge into the attic.

"They're not so bad," Bruce said.

"You've never woken up with them in your bed with you," Megan replied.

The roar of the rain on the slate roof overhead filled the dark space before them where one small window looked out over the parking lot. Huge timbers rose from the sides of the room, meeting high overhead. Crossbeams bridged them, supporting the roof with a long line of capital letter A's that probably ran the length of the school beyond the room in which they stood.

Even though they could see the window, too many boxes had been stacked within the space for them to possibly get over to it. Luckily, a path had been left open to the door for the next room.

"Let's go a couple of rooms over," Bruce suggested, heading for the door that stood on the opposite side of the room. "I don't think anyone will look for us up here, but let's not be standing by the ladder if they do."

"Sure," Megan agreed.

The next room held the props that Bruce had mentioned. Trunks full of old clothing and costumes stood open from the rummaging of Academy students from years past to be used on the school's small wooden stage. An old bicycle hung upside down on the wall with the meager light from the room's single window glowing through it. Beside it stood the Dark Man.

"Now what?" Bruce asked, not at all pleased to be alone with the specter in such a creepy place. "Why doesn't he just tell us what he wants?"

"I think it drained him too much," she said quietly. "He used too much of his power to separate us. Then he used almost everything he had left trying to show me."

As if in response, the ghost nodded before walking through the wall into the next room. Megan looked at Bruce, shrugged and walked toward the door. "So now he's going to try and show us."

"Careful," Bruce said quietly. "It might creak."

"Do you really think anyone is going to hear it over all of this rain and thunder?" she asked.

"Why chance it?"

Their fears proved unwarranted though since the door swung silently open to reveal another room full of boxes and furniture.

These new rooms had two windows, one opening outside the Academy and the other down onto the courtyard below. In the first of the courtyard windows, Megan could see the nearest bell-tower. As they followed the Dark Man through several more rooms in silent succession, the crates were replaced by boxes. They must have come to the end of the school because the next door opened from the right side of the room instead of directly across from them as all of the others had. The dust on the floors grew deep and spongy.

"Try not to stir it up," Bruce said, frowning at the floor.

At last they came to a room without a second door. The crates in this room were huge, leaving Megan to wonder how they'd been brought up in the first place.

The Dark Man disappeared into the crates on the wall to their right.

"Well, I guess that's the end of the road for us," Bruce said, disappointed.

"Let's have a look around anyway," Megan said, her earlier fear gone.

"Why not?" he asked with a shrug. "Can't say that I'm particularly eager to get back to Jones's class."

They had to be careful not to get splinters from the old crates while they pushed them over a tiny bit at a time. The rain fell even harder now, and Megan wondered if the Dark Man was helping them yet again.

When at last they moved the crates far enough away from the wall, Megan squeezed in.

There's another door back here, Megan sent.

Can you open it? Bruce asked.

No, it's locked, she sent.

Clearing her mind of everything except the lock, she probed its pieces until she understood how it worked. Then with all the concentration she could muster, she pulled Bruce's mind into the trance and unlocked the door.

"Are you ready to find out what's hidden back here?" she asked.

Chapter XXIX: The Hidden Room

The hinges creaked in protest when Megan pushed it open. Dust fell from the ledge above the door and Bruce started to sneeze.

"Sorry," he whispered. "I hope they didn't hear that downstairs."

"It's okay," she said. "What do you think this place was?"

"I don't know," He said, following her into the dimly lit room, "But I don't think anyone's been up here in a long time. There aren't any footsteps in the dust."

Rows of what looked like church pews leaned against the wall. Stacks of crates filled most of the room, making it look like a maze. They stayed close together while they searched, careful not to become separated.

"The top of that crate looks loose," Bruce said, pushing one of the lids aside.

"What's in it?" she asked.

"Books," he said, pulling one out and flipping through the faded pages. "It's an old Bible."

"The crate's full of them," Megan said. "I wonder what all of these are doing up here?"

"Beats me, but remember the old hymnals in the storage shed? Let's see if we can get into any of the others."

In the corner of the room, an old cross stood in the shadows, cobwebs trailing down in wisps from the ceiling to the floor.

"It's beautiful," Megan said when a flash of lightning lit the room for an instant. She pulled the webs away and blew some of the dust free so that she could see the carvings that covered the wooden surface.

Something about the cross triggered a flow of images in her mind.

He carved this himself, she thought. There was more in her head about the cross, but she still couldn't pull it into focus.

Who did? Bruce asked.

The Dark Man.

When they walked around the next corner, they came face to face with the ghost.

At first the Dark Man stood, looking out the window toward the courtyard. Then he turned and looked at Megan, who was tempted to take hold of Bruce's hand.

As they watched, the lid of a crate they'd been unable to open slid aside. An old leather-bound book rose from its depths and floated over to where they stood. With a thump that could surely be heard downstairs, it fell to the dusty floorboards at their feet before the ghost turned to look once again down into the courtyard.

The sound of someone walking on the wooden floorboards in the next room stopped them short.

"Bruce? Megan? Is that you thumpin' around up here?" Mr. Green called. As quietly as they could, the two friends crept over to a dark corner and waited.

"All right, you might as well come out and show yourselves," the husky voice came again. "It's not safe up here, 'specially during a storm like this one. So you'd better come down."

They stood motionless behind the crates, hoping that he wouldn't see their footprints in the dust.

"Oh well," they heard him say. "Must be rats again. I guess I'll go on down and get the traps ready. Must be big ones this time. Could have sworn it sounded like a couple of kids." The footsteps grew fainter, and Bruce let out the breath he'd been holding.

"That was close," Megan whispered. "I wonder why he didn't check in here."

"He may not know about this room," Bruce said. "He's been here a long time, but I suspect this room has been closed off longer."

"Is it another Bible?" Bruce asked when Megan reached down to pick up the book.

"I don't think so," she said. "It's handwritten. Looks more like someone's journal to me."

"Can I see?" Bruce asked, moving closer to the window and the meager light that flowed through it, but not close enough to put him within easy reach of the Dark Man. "I think you're right. The first entry is from May 13, 1817. This thing is older than the town."

"What does it say?" Megan asked.

Bruce cleared the dust from his throat.

I built our house out of materials that were left over from the building of the church. It doesn't look like any of the other houses in our little settlement, but Sorina likes it. She told me today that I'm going to be a father. I hope we can fill this whole church with the sound of our children!

"Well, he sounded happy," Megan said. "Whose diary do you think this is?"

"Let me see," Bruce said, flipping through the faded pages. On the very last page, he found what he was looking for. "It's signed Reverend Jacob Routh."

"That's the Dark Man! He was a preacher?"

"Looks that way. You don't usually think of preachers being that happy about things, Bruce said, returning to the book.

Sorina has me worried. She caught sick last week and isn't feeling better yet. We thought it was just a bad vapor, but that

361

*would have passed by now. If she doesn't get better by tomorrow
I'll call on Doc Campbell.*

"Did she get better?" Megan asked, hoping that this might unravel some of the information he'd given her.

"I'm looking," Bruce said. "This one is from December of the same year."

*Doc Campbell can't help my Sorina. She is very ill now, and
we both fear for the unborn child. I spend the days comforting her
as best I can and the nights praying by her side. Please, God,
don't take her from me.*

"Go on," she said.

"Oh, this is terrible," he said. "His wife died a few hours after she gave birth. The baby didn't last much longer. The last thing she said to Jacob was that she wanted to be buried in the place where they first met."

"Why did he want us to have this?" Megan asked, thinking about the house she'd seen in flames. She thought about the quilt and the weak cries from the bassinet. She'd heard a baby crying more than once at the Academy.

"She's too weak," Megan whispered, remembering.

"This is interesting," Bruce said. "Jacob built a huge church to surround the place where he met the woman he would later marry. Apparently, she said she wouldn't marry him unless it was in a church, so he built one and became its first minister." Bruce flipped to the last few pages. "Since Jacob and Sorina didn't have any surviving children to pass his land on to, he left the church to be used by the town as long as they kept up the graves. It also says that if they should fail to do so, the deed to the land would be given back to her family, the Kennemurs." Bruce looked up at Megan. "Well, that's it. I wonder what happened to the church and why everything ended up here."

362

Free from the fear that she'd held for so long, Megan walked toward the window and looked past the Dark Man into the walled-off portion of the courtyard.

"What's wrong?" Bruce asked, seeing the way she stiffened when another flash of light lit the courtyard below.

He came over to the window and looked down through the rain to the area he'd only glimpsed from the top of the wall. The stone he'd seen in the center of the clearing was a cross. Wild roses climbed the base and bloomed in the damp air. At first, he didn't realize what it was, but then another flash of light showed him more: a name that was carved across the top: Routh.

"This is his church," Megan said, remembering how the cafeteria had looked in the vision while she'd taken Bruce to the clinic. "And those are the graves of Sorina Routh and her child."

Chapter XXX: Lost in the Shadows

A bell rang nearby as the older students moved on to their next class. The first time Megan had heard it, she'd thought it sounded more like an old church bell than a school bell. She'd been right. It was a church built by a man to convince a woman to marry him, a man so full of that grief that he'd lingered on after death to make sure his promises were kept.

"What do we do now?" Bruce asked.

"If we get this journal to my Grandfather, I'll bet he can do something about it."

"They're already looking for us downstairs," Bruce said. "Do you think we could hide it until the end of the day?"

"I'd rather not take any chances of anyone from the school finding it," Megan said. "You realize what the walled off graves mean?"

"The city has forfeited its ownership of the Academy to that family he mentioned," Bruce answered. "That must be why he's trying to get the journal to us."

"You know this place a lot better than I do. Do you have any idea how we could get out without being seen?"

"Not really," Bruce said, "There are only two doors out of the building and one ladder leading down from here. The back of the school would probably be better, since I doubt we could pass by the office without being seen."

"How did they get all of that big stuff up that little ladder?" Megan asked.

"I was wondering the same thing myself," he murmured absently.

"Let's get going," she said, clutching the journal close.

Careful not to make more noise than necessary, they slid out from behind the crates that hid the door to the forgotten room. Overhead the sound of rain falling on the roof continued.

"If we can find Mr. Green first, he might be able to smuggle us out with the trash or something," Megan suggested. " Maybe he's still in the cafeteria cleaning up from lunch."

"Let's hope so," Bruce said.

Checking each room as they went, the two retraced their steps toward the ladder room. Outside, the storm raged on.

Megan climbed down the ladder as quietly as she could, then placed her ear against the door to see if she could hear anything on the other side.

Let me see the journal, Bruce sent.

Megan pulled it from the waistband of her pants. Bruce pulled a trash bag from Mr. Green's workbench and wrapped it thoroughly in layers of plastic before handing it back.

Megan gave him a questioning look.

We're going to get awfully wet out there, he thought. *It will fit in my pocket if you want me to carry it.*

Megan nodded in response and then opened the door a crack to peer outside. Mrs. Jones had probably taken Jade to the office by now and Mr. Green had moved on to his duties elsewhere.

Let's go, Megan thought, walking quickly into the open.

You know, we might have a better chance of getting out the front door now that I think about it, Bruce thought.

Why?

Whatever reason Bruce might have had become unimportant when the scarred carnie from the Jubilee unexpectedly pulled back the curtains on the stage.

Bruce grabbed Megan by the arm and dragged her back into the janitor's closet.

"What are you doing?" Megan whispered in despair. "We should have made a run for it. Now we're stuck in here."

"We wouldn't have made it," Bruce said, frowning. Barely pausing to think, he took several wooden poles out of a trashcan and used them to wedge the door shut behind the heavy workbench.

"How do you know?" she asked.

"I just do," he said.

"Did you see it?" she whispered, panic rising.

"Yeah," he mumbled. "Up is the only way we can go that doesn't lead to something bad."

For the second time in an hour, the two of them made their way up the ladder and across through the maze of rooms, this time making no effort to be quiet. A muffled crash below told them that the carnie was coming for them again.

Megan cast a glance over her shoulder as they passed through one of the doors. She closed her eyes in concentration.

"What are you doing?" Bruce cried. "We don't have time…"

With a crash the door slammed and locked.

"Good idea, Bruce said, grabbing her by the hand. "Now let's *go!*" Soon they were in the older rooms with the deep dust on the floor. Fresh puffs of dust rose with each footstep, and Megan realized that she had to do something if they were going to have any chance of losing the carnie.

"Go ahead of me," Megan said, pushing Bruce through the door and shutting it with him on the other side.

Megan concentrated on the stale air in the room around her. In seconds the dust was scoured from the floor to hang in a dirty fog across the room. Holding her breath, she followed Bruce and locked that door as well.

"He's not slowing down very much," Bruce wheezed as they ran, "And we're running out of rooms."

"If you've got any ideas, now would be the time to speak up," Megan gasped, starting to tire as well.

When they came to the hidden room, Megan repeated the trick with the dust, hoping to hide the door. Once inside, she turned to Bruce with fear in her eyes.

"This door opens inward," he said. "We can barricade it from the inside. Help me move that crate over the doorway."

They struggled to move the heavy wooden box, but only succeeded in moving it a few inches before they heard the man enter the next room.

"That's right," Megan heard the man say loudly. "I followed them up here. They haven't exactly been quiet and all of the dust in the past few rooms has been disturbed. And it looks like they've found their way into the barricaded area. You'd better call in…"

For the first time in her life, Megan reached out and intentionally fried something electronic. But in her excitement, she blew out the main breaker to the entire school, plunging the lights in the parking lot into darkness.

Spreading her feet apart and focusing all of her will on the crate, she was rewarded by a screech of scraping wood as it slid halfway across the doorframe.

Not to be outdone, Bruce knocked the pews over and slid them against the door as well.

"Let's see him get through that any time soon," Megan gasped.

Bruce sat down hard on the edge of one of the pews. Megan joined him.

What now? He asked. *I don't know who he was talking to, but it's clear he was calling for reinforcements.*

What happens if he catches us? Megan asked.

Bad things, but I can't see through them to see exactly what.

In a flash of lightning, they noticed that the Dark Man had returned. As they watched, he walked toward the wall to their right and passed through a table pushed against the wall on which the paintings that had once adorned the walls of the church leaned.

It turns here! they thought in unison.

No longer trying to hide their passage, they found that the door wasn't even closed and that they could crawl under the table on which the paintings rested. The next room was completely empty as were the ones after that.

"Another ladder," Megan whispered, overwhelmed with relief when she saw the familiar shape rising in the darkened room.

"And a freight access, " Bruce said with a frown and pointing toward a large square opening in the floor over which a block and tackle had been mounted.

"What's wrong?" she asked, slowing along with him.

"I thought I knew the whole school layout downstairs, but I don't know any place where that ladder could lead."

"We'll figure it out as we go," she said, grabbing him by the hand and leading him down.

The room below had no windows and was so dark that they quickly became disoriented.

Find a door, Megan sent, not wanting to take a chance that someone outside would hear.

That's what I'm telling you, he sent back, *if there was a door I would have seen it before now and known about the ladder. I think this room is walled off to hide the church stuff upstairs.*

So we're still trapped? She thought, wanting to cry. They were so close to getting away, how could it end like this?

Light flared next to them as the Dark Man appeared, holding a mass of green flame in his hand. He pointed at the wall closest to Megan and it swung outward.

Standing outside the opening were Allison and Glenn.

"Mom!" Allison screeched down the hall toward her mother's room.

That call was never heard though, at least not by Mrs. Jones. The rain outside, which had grown harder all morning, turned into a deluge. Lightning flashed and thunder drowned out Allison's call.

The Dark Man faded out then reappeared, looking nothing like the sad phantom Megan normally saw. Towering above the terrified teens, he let out a low howl that built into an ear-splitting screech. Then he moved toward them.

Glenn turned and ran into the girl's restroom, knocking Allison aside in his haste to flee. The door slammed shut behind them just as an explosion shook the floor. It merged almost completely with the thunder overhead. Water gushed from under the door and covered the wooden floors.

Jacob Routh turned toward them, returning to normal as he faded from view.

"That's all he had left," Megan whispered.

"There you are," the carnie yelled from the top of the ladder.

Together they raced for the back door of the school. Doors opened and heads peeked out as they ran past with the carnie close behind. Megan already had her hand stretched out to grasp the handle to the back door

369

when it opened to admit a policeman with a striking resemblance to Mrs. Jones.

Bruce grabbed Megan by the shoulder and dragged her into yet another supply closet. Completely out of options, he locked the door with a thought and sunk to the ground in exhaustion.

In darkness that smelled of bleach, they held each other while the sheriff and the carnie began to beat on the door. In seconds someone would bring the key.

Megan's thoughts were no longer rational. She'd been hunted for most of her life and now she'd been caught. In terror, she reached out as she'd done at the Well of Dreams, seeking any aid she could find.

The world twisted around them, and then they weren't in the closet anymore.

The sky overhead spread a blanket of uniform gray as far as they could see. Completely devoid of clouds, it also lacked sun, moon or any other landmarks. Cold burned exposed skin and seconds stretched into hours. Jagged rocks rose from the frozen ground like the broken fingers of giants, providing just a tiny bit of shelter from the cold.

Already oxygen-starved, Bruce sagged against Megan, losing consciousness almost at once. Working solely by instinct, she wove her power about Bruce in a cocoon of warmth she didn't need. But even so, she couldn't hope to maintain it for long.

"Help!" she screamed, but the wind stole her voice and carried away her pleas.

Two figures formed within the darkness, indistinct at first then growing more defined as they approached. Of equal size and stature, the two women could have been sisters.

Still clutching Bruce against her, Megan found herself looking into the picture on the fireplace mantle. She took her grandmother's hand, and Sorina Routh wrapped her arms around Bruce.

At first nothing happened. The destination at the other end wouldn't solidify. Then Megan's searching mind found a clearing full of yellow flowers, and in her heart she could feel them calling her home. The cold world twisted around them, funneling them back to Nickelville.

With a sickening thud, they splashed into the fire ring in her grandmother's grove. Their frost-covered skin steamed in the sudden warmth and Megan's vision snuffed out altogether.

Chapter XXXI: Reverend Routh Remembered

As Megan crawled through strange dreams filled with dusty rooms and carved wooden crosses, she became aware of the warm presence of her mother. Bruce was near as well, but she could tell from the flavor of his thoughts that he still slept.

As pleasant as the moment was, it didn't last. Memories began to return, many of them not her own. She tried to sit up, and pain twisted thorny vines through her every joint and muscle to blossom behind her eyes.

Bruce lay next to her on Emelia's bed, his hand enfolding her own. She wasn't sure if they'd sought each other while unconscious, or if her mother had done it to strengthen their bond while they healed.

Megan tried to speak mind to mind, but the pain flared, and Bruce moaned in his sleep.

"Grandpa isn't here yet," Emelia told her. "You can speak out loud."

"What happened?" Megan croaked. Though little more than a whisper, it still pounded in her head.

"You traveled through the shadows," Emelia answered, stroking Megan's eyes and forcing them to close. There was a mixture of pride and anger in the words. "And you must promise me that you won't try to do it again."

"What?" Megan asked, unable to formulate a better question.

"You pulled Bruce with you into a space between this world and the next," Emelia explained quietly. "It's a way to travel great distances in an instant. But for a novice like you, the danger of being trapped there is too great to risk. I'm frankly amazed you made it out alive, let alone where you were aiming for."

"Had help," Megan whispered.

"What do you mean?" Emelia asked.

"Grandma guided me to her grove," Megan whispered, listening to the voice that said her mother wasn't quite ready for Sorina Routh yet. "And Sam's flowers."

"Are you sure?" Emelia asked in awe.

Megan nodded, starting to drift away again. Bruce's rhythmic breathing called her back into the world of dreams. But the voice in her head wouldn't let her sleep just yet.

"Journal," Megan winced. "Bruce's pocket."

The motion of her mother searching his pockets made the world lurch unpleasantly. If this was what it felt like to have a hangover, Megan decided she had no need to ever drink alcohol.

"Okay, I've got it," Emelia said, "what's so important about it?"

"Jacob Routh's," Megan murmured sleepily.

"And who is he?" Emelia asked, turning the book over in her hands. "It looks old."

"Dark Man," Megan whispered.

Emelia hissed in revulsion and dropped the book on the floor next to the bed.

"Good guy," Megan whispered, slipping away. "Grandpa needs to read it."

Then she was gone again.

Bruce woke with a start when Sam lifted Megan from the bed and carried her to the next room.

"Bruce?" Emelia whispered in his ear.

"Yes," he mumbled, already starting to drift off again.

"Your parents are at the front door."

Bruce opened his eyes and wished at once that he hadn't.

"We have to tell them the same story about what happened," Emelia pressed, "and right now I don't know what happened myself. Megan is too weak from what she did to get the two of you here, and I'm afraid I'm going to have to see what happened through your memories. Unless it is something you think your parents can hear?"

"Not even close," he croaked. "Go ahead."

"This may hurt a little bit," Emelia warned, "I'm sorry."

Though he sensed she was trying to be careful, he also knew she was in a hurry. Downstairs someone opened the front door for his parents.

It's a rare young man who would give his girlfriend's mother a chance to rifle through his thoughts, Emelia sent, trying to distract him from the pain.

We don't like each other that way, he responded.

You can't lie mind to mind Bruce, Emelia whispered through him then withdrew from his thoughts.

He didn't have the strength to argue.

"They didn't want to get Mr. Green or Mr. Harris in trouble by involving them," Sam told his parents as they came up the stairs, "and made it all the way to Gordon's in the storm."

As soon as Bruce saw his parents, the desire to tell them everything grew almost too great to bear. One look at Emelia told him that she and

374

Sam would understand if he did. But even though he couldn't explain how he knew that nothing good would come of opening his parents' eyes to this strange new world through which he and Megan traveled, it was still the truth. For a while at least, his destiny lay on a different path from theirs, and this realization haunted him far worse than anything that had transpired at the school.

"Why did you leave the Academy?" Mrs. Grimble asked softly, holding his hand as if it might break.

"I wasn't feeling well at lunch," Bruce said, ignoring the pain in his head and rising up on his elbows.

"Asthma?" his father asked.

"No, nauseous," Bruce lied. "Megan was going to help me to the clinic, but that strange man from the Jubilee started chasing us."

Keep it simple and as close to the truth as possible, Emelia advised. *You're exhausted and not thinking clearly. Elaboration will only make holes in the story.*

"Why would he do that, and what was he doing at the Academy in the first place?" Mr. Grimble asked.

"I've been trying to figure that out as well," Sam said. "He's been poking around town a lot since the Jubilee."

Azarich walked into the room carrying the journal.

"Did you read it?" Bruce asked, easily distracted in his exhaustion. "Do you know about the graves?"

"Graves?" his mother asked, the journalist in her catching the scent of a story.

"I'll tell you all about that in a minute," Azarich said, placing the journal on the nightstand as he came to stand next to Emelia. "Let's hear what Bruce has to say first."

"The man chased you out of the building?" Mr. Grimble asked, angry. "What were the teachers doing while this was going on?"

"Mrs. Jones had her brother, the sheriff, and the Terrible Trio looking for us too," Bruce said, losing steam and wanting nothing more than to go back to sleep.

"And you went into the school's attic to hide from them?" Emelia prompted when he paused.

"Yeah," Bruce whispered, leaning back again. "Although Chuck saw us and didn't tell so we could get to the access ladder." His head was pounding fiercely.

"Megan said that there's a hidden series of rooms up there," Sam said, coming to the rescue.

"They found the journal in the one that overlooks the hidden part of the courtyard," Emelia added.

"Good heavens," Mrs. Grimble said, her hand covering her mouth. "You don't mean there are graves back there?"

"Bingo," Bruce whispered, hysterical with exhaustion.

"They found another ladder down and slipped out the back of the school," Sam added.

"How did they make it all the way to Gordon's without being picked up?" Mr. Grimble asked. "And why aren't you more wet?"

You made ponchos out of trash bags, Emelia sent. *You cut through the woods to town to avoid the sheriff.*

Grateful, Bruce relayed what she said. He was too far gone to come up with anything that quick on his own.

Bruce realized that his father was staring down at the floor where his shoes rested, far too clean to have traveled through the woods in a storm.

Damn his keen observations, Emelia thought.

"Why wasn't I invited to the party?" Megan said from the doorway, distracting everyone from the awkward matter of the shoes. She looked terrible, and if she felt anything like Bruce did, he was amazed that she could stand. Of course, if Azarich had already had a chance to read the journal, maybe they'd been out longer than he thought. "Come on Granpa, tell them about the journal."

Everyone turned an expectant eye on Azarich, while Sam led Megan over to sit on the edge of the bed.

"According to this journal, the school was originally a church built by a man named Jacob Routh," he said.

"One of the town's forefathers," Mrs. Grimble added. "Strange man from what the town records say about him."

"I wouldn't know about that part," Azarich continued, "But to make a long story short, he gave the church to the town on the condition that they promised to maintain the graves of his wife and newborn son."

"I've always wondered what was back there," Mrs. Grimble added. Bruce had no doubts that this would be the front page of the *Tribune* before the week was out, at least the parts they could tell.

Downstairs, someone opened the front door.

"We're up here," Azarich yelled, making both Bruce and Megan wince.

Mr. Green and Mr. Harris walked through the door of the crowded bedroom, scanning the room anxiously. Jade and Paul trailed after them, and Bruce was touched by how relieved they looked when they saw him.

"Thank God you two are okay," the librarian said.

"You gave us one hell of a scare," Mr. Green said. "Sorry for the language," he added. "We would have been here sooner, but most of the cars in the parking lot wouldn't start after that lightning storm. Blew the fuses out on just about everything."

Emelia raised an inquisitive eyebrow toward Megan.

"To bring you up to speed," Sam said, "They ended up in the Attic at the school…"

"I knew it wasn't rats!" Mr. Green yelled, once again making Bruce wish everyone would just go away and let him sleep.

"And found out that there are graves behind the wall in the courtyard," Emelia added.

"That I didn't know," Mr. Green muttered.

"And the school used to be a church that will revert back to some family since the graves weren't maintained," Bruce finished.

"I did a little bit of checking to see if the part where it talks about the Academy reverting," Azarich said.

"And?" Megan asked.

"It's true."

"But is that really going to change anything?" Megan asked. "What we need is a way to get rid of Mrs. Jones, not the school."

"That's the interesting part," Azarich said with relish. "I called a friend of mine at the Nickelville Historical Society to make sure. Sorina's sister was married to the first mayor of Nickelville, a man by the name of Beverly. A generation later, the family had a big falling out over two deaths in the family and split. When they did, one side took up the Kennemur name again while the Beverly line died out completely."

"How's that interesting?" Jade asked.

"You see, I happen to know that there aren't any Kennemurs left around here," Azarich continued, raising the family eyebrow at Jade in mild irritation. "The last Mr. and Mrs. Kennemur had a daughter, so the name wasn't carried on."

Azarich's childhood friends looked as if they'd been the ones who'd seen a ghost.

"Get to the point," Mrs. Grimble said impatiently.

"The last Kennemur girl's name was Josephine. She was a beautiful woman," he said. "The most beautiful I've ever seen."

Emelia's eyes widened.

"Okay," Megan said, "Everyone here acts like this means something. Would you mind letting Bruce and I in on the secret? We're not exactly at our best right now."

"She was your grandmother," Grandpa said.

"That would make me…" Emelia stammered.

"The rightful owner of Nickelville Academy," Sam finished.

Chapter XXXII: Revelation and Resignation

Like everything else in Nickelville, the courthouse had been built to suit the needs of people long dead. Rows of wooden pews groaned under the unaccustomed weight of full capacity. Before the night was over, it looked like the citizens of the town would be standing in the aisles and peering in the windows. Megan was glad they'd arrived early and gotten a pew to themselves since the two families plus their friends took up quite a bit of space.

"I don't like this," Emelia murmured. "Dora, are you sure the Academy was opened while Tony's great grandfather was mayor?"

"Yes," Bruce's mother answered absently as she motioned for one of the *Tribune's* photographers to get a better view before the courtroom was too packed to move. "I spoke with him on the phone and tried to set up an interview. He was angry, but didn't seem particularly surprised to hear that there were graves in the courtyard."

"You think he knew about them?" Megan asked.

"Someone maintained that wall," Mr. Green answered. "And it wasn't me. I came back from summer break one year to find the whole thing had been replaced."

"All the teachers thought it was odd," Mr. Harris added. "We asked about it from time to time and were told politely but firmly to mind our own business."

"Here they come," Jade whispered.

Megan followed her gaze and found Mrs. Jones and her daughter following a sour looking man in an expensive suit. Something about him made her uneasy, though she couldn't place what it might be.

No love was lost on these three, and from the expressions mirrored all across the room, Megan doubted that there was much respect either. But there was a great deal of fear: the kind reserved for dictators in third world countries.

Megan still felt the effects of what she'd done to escape from the school. Having so many people pressed in around her, broadcasting emotions in a steady roar, made her stomach contract into something with jagged edges that seemed to be cutting through her control of her abilities.

The current mayor, who Megan recognized from the start of the Jubilee race, stepped up to the microphone to address the crowd. She felt a small surge of energy escape her control.

The sound system belched feedback, causing everyone to wince. Bruce laid his hand over hers, dampening the effect of her tension on the electronics.

"Ladies and Gentlemen," the mayor began when silence resumed. "Thank you for coming out tonight for this emergency school board meeting. Before we get started, I assume everyone has read today's editorial on the matter at hand in the *Tribune*?"

Murmurs of consent filled the room.

"Then I would like to thank Mrs. Grimble and her staff for, as always, being so diligent in keeping the citizens of our town apprised of any situations that arise."

The citizens of Nickelville applauded, though Mr. Jones looked less than pleased. Megan was tempted to probe him from where she sat.

"Are there really graves at the Academy?" a woman shouted.

381

"I'm afraid so," the mayor answered.

"What are we going to do about it?" a man yelled out. "It's just not right to have graves in a school where children are supposed to be learning."

Cries of agreement drowned out whatever the mayor said next.

"Which is exactly why they were hidden," Mr. Jones said, rising to his feet and approaching the podium where the mayor stood.

"The council will now hear Mr. Tony Jones," the mayor said, practically tripping over himself to get away.

Now the game starts in earnest, Sam thought.

The entire room hushed, waiting to see what would happen next.

"Good people of Nickelville," Mr. Jones purred, drawing them in despite their dislike for him, "Yes, the Academy holds a less than savory secret. But this information was not held from you in order to cause you harm. Please let me explain how we came to be where we stand today. Over ninety years ago when our town was much younger than it is now, a fire claimed the original school building. Our town did not have the resources to build a new one, and we were not willing to send our children forty miles by wagon to the nearest school. What were we to do?"

Megan had to admit he was a good speaker.

"My great-great grandfather, who was mayor at the time, suggested that we use the abandoned church left in the town's care after its builder died," he said with a sadness that almost seemed genuine.

"Once again," he continued, "What were we to do?"

For the first time since he'd started talking, the crowd found their voice and began to answer with cries of "Use the church!"

"Exactly," he said with a dismissive smile. "But my ancestor didn't want the innocent children of this town staring out the window at a graveyard while they studied."

Mr. Jones unhooked the mike from its stand and moved down the aisle toward Mrs. Jones and their daughter.

"If I had to make the same decision, I'd choose exactly what he did," he said, motioning for Allison to join him. "My own daughter goes to school there, and I would have spared her this knowledge if I could. What purpose does it serve? Why did the corner of that courtyard have to be exposed, I ask? It doesn't make any difference in the grand scheme of things, so I say let's let it remain hidden and go on with our lives."

The room broke into applause as Mr. Jones returned the mike to the mayor and took his seat once again.

"Thank you, Mr. Jones," the town's supposed leader said, returning to the podium. "The council would now like to call Mr. Azarich McGeehee."

All eyes turned to Megan's grandfather as he rose from his seat and walked with the vigor of a much younger man toward the podium. Megan wondered if she'd ever be that brave.

"Hello everyone," he said with a pleasant smile that cut through tension and worry in the room like a lighthouse on a stormy night. "I'd like to thank Tony for explaining how the final wishes of a dying man were ignored while the graves of his wife and child were hidden away and neglected."

Shocked silence greeted this statement, made worse by the pleasant tone of the man who spoke it.

"As you all know from reading that fine article written by Mrs. Dora Grimble, the deed of the Academy was given to the town of Nickelville on the condition that the graves it contains were maintained in dignity and respect."

"Now there's no need," Mr. Jones interrupted.

"I'm afraid there is, Tony," Azarich said with an edge to his voice that made Megan realize that the cheerful man she called Grandfather had more depth than she'd realized. "But before we go any further I want to put to rest any fears that the good people of this town might have about the school being closed. In spite of the breach of contract that has, as of today, placed ownership of the Academy in the hands of my daughter, the oldest remaining descendant of the Kennemur line, she is willing to allow the town to continue to use the building free of charge as long as certain conditions are met."

Azarich gave the citizens a moment to digest that information. Many of them looked visibly relieved, knowing that the McGeehees would never ask anything unfair of the town.

"And what might those conditions be?" the mayor asked.

"First of all," Azarich said pleasantly, "The wall comes down and the graves are given the respect they deserve."

"Is that really appropriate?" Mr. Jones interjected.

"Children see people die several times a day on television and in their video games," Azarich countered. "Do you really think two tombstones are going to scar them emotionally?"

Mr. Jones nodded and opened his hands in a gesture of good-natured defeat.

"Is that it?" the mayor asked.

"No, there is one more term that my family and I would like to discuss in private," Azarich said, for the first time showing a hint of tension in the wrinkled lines around his eyes.

"With me?" the mayor asked.

"No," Azarich answered. "With Mr. Jones and his family."

Megan felt like throwing up.

"Then I say we adjourn for a short break while the two families meet," the mayor announced, clearly pleased to be left out of whatever was about to transpire.

Emelia rose silently from the pew, leading Megan by the hand toward the door that stood behind the long tables where the council members sat.

What is he doing? Megan asked.

I'm not sure, but it will all work out okay. We have nothing to fear from the Jones family at this time, no matter how powerful they may think they are. They may control most of this tiny little town, but as you and I know, Nickelville is but a small part of the greater world.

As soon as the door clicked behind them, the pleasant façade that Mr. Jones had displayed dissolved into a mask of angry resentment.

"How dare you dig up this town's dirty laundry to make a point," he snarled. "You're lucky we didn't slap her and that Grimble boy with a criminal trespass charge for going up there in the first place. I hear she's been a problem since she got here."

"And where did you hear that?" Azarich said, still smiling. "I was under the impression that discipline matters were protected under federal privacy laws."

"Give the lawyer act a rest," Mrs. Jones snapped. "We're not afraid of you. I'm perfectly within my rights to speak with my husband about my days at work."

"As long as you don't use names," Azarich said. "The problem here is that Tony isn't just your husband. He's also the chairman of the school board. Much of what you told him probably dealt with the unfortunate thefts, which I might remind you, were not committed by my granddaughter. It's not a stretch to call that slander."

"What about what they did to my hair?" Allison screeched.

"An unfortunate accident according to the school," Azarich said smoothly. "Your parents are more than welcome to try and sue for damages. It doesn't, however, change the problem we just discussed."

"Well, I'm not apologizing again," Mrs. Jones snapped, crossing her arms in defiance.

"No one is asking you to," Azarich said. "We're asking you to resign from the Academy."

Everyone in the room stared at him in shock.

"You're not serious?" Mrs. Jones snarled in anger, her face turning an unpleasant shade of purple.

"Oh, I'm afraid I am," Azarich said pleasantly.

"This town is not going to bow to blackmail," Mr. Jones snarled. "What you're doing isn't legal."

"Oh, I wouldn't say that," Azarich replied. "If she doesn't resign, I'm not going to close the school. I'm going to request an inquiry. As I'm sure you know, our state requires that all teachers hold a valid teaching certificate in the subject that they teach."

"Well," Mrs. Jones said evasively, "certain allowances were made…"

"In which you were given two years to complete the certification process," Azarich prompted. "Had you fulfilled those requirements, you would have been required to take additional training each year to maintain certification. It's been twelve years Paula, and you've never taken a single educational class. As far as your record shows, you don't have a single required qualification to teach."

"That's hardly a reason to demand her job," Mr. Jones said, with much less bluster than he'd given just moments before.

"There's also the issue of bringing in that gentleman who chased Bruce and Megan from the school grounds. Who is he, and have his credentials been checked according to school policy to allow him to wander freely around the school?"

"Mr. O'Toole has nothing to do with this," Mr. Jones said, looking uncomfortable.

"Then why was he there?" Azarich pressed. "And what about Sheriff Pullen? Do we really need to look into the circumstances surrounding his rise to that position?"

"You're behind this, aren't you?" Mrs. Jones whined, turning toward Emelia. "You were always jealous of me."

Emelia laughed.

"So you admit it?" Mr. Jones demanded, happy to turn his attention from Azarich's argument.

"I think you've got things turned around," Emelia said. "She's been jealous ever since you started paying attention to me at the Academy."

"Liar!" Allison screamed. "Why would my father ever lower himself to your level?"

"Ladies," Azarich said in that pleasant tone that upset the entire Jones family to no end. "Let's not forget why we're here. Not only does Paula lack the credentials to teach, but she's been doing a very poor job of it. Her test scores have been far below average for her entire career. Furthermore, I have it from several sources that she's failed past students purely on the basis of their parents' standing in the community."

"Who is committing slander now!" the unpleasant woman jeered, voice breaking in anger. "You just wanted to get us in here so you say these things without witnesses."

"No, Paula," Azarich said, "I brought you in here so you could save face and make it look like it was your idea to retire. As much as I might dislike the way your family has used its power in this town, I see no reason to air your dirty laundry for the whole town to see."

Mr. Jones lost some of his resentment at these words, and his wife saw the change in him at once.

"You're not seriously going to go along with this?"

"I told you repeatedly to finish your certification," he said at last. "It's your own laziness that's to blame here, Paula. If he had brought these things up out there, we'd be facing a full investigation. You've hated that job from the start anyway."

"I'm not quitting just because these common, low class blackmailers say I should," Mrs. Jones squealed.

"Fine, then you'll be fired before the week is out," Mr. Jones said with resignation. "People will laugh at you every time you leave the house and I'll be inclined to join them."

Mrs. Jones looked from her husband to the McGeehees, fury radiating from her in such force that Megan started to get a headache. Without warning, the woman launched herself at her.

Megan effortlessly caught both of the woman's outstretched wrists, looked into her eyes and felt the hungry thing deep within her come alive with the contact.

She made no attempt to hide the glow of her eyes as the woman's thoughts flooded over her since she knew that her grandfather wouldn't be able to see her face at that angle. The force within her began to feed, but unlike the incident with Allison at the pizzeria, this time Megan stayed in control.

"You'd hate for us to find those allergy searches that your daughter made on your classroom computer," Megan said in a voice deeper than her own. "I know for a fact that the Grimbles would press charges and sue if they found out you had something to do with the attack on their son. Who knows, by the time it was all done, they might be the richest family in the county instead of you." Shutting down the hunger within her, she mechanically released the woman's wrists and stepped back.

"She's a witch!" Allison squealed, eyes wide.

388

"Name-calling is the sign of a weak mind, Allison," Emelia said, taking Megan by the hand and leading her toward the door. "I assume we're done here?"

Silence.

"Good," she said with relish. "Father, Sam has invited all of us over to Gordon's for dinner. I think that would be the perfect ending to the day, don't you?"

Without waiting for a response, she led Megan out the door and into the company of friends.

Chapter XXXIII: One Less Mystery

In the week that followed Mrs. Jones's resignation, Mrs. Wesson came in as the new ninth grade teacher. For the first time since the year started, abundant laughter and learning filled the classroom.

Well, almost everyone laughed more. Allison and Glenn found it difficult to adjust to the new rules and jokes that were played on them as the result of their bizarre story about being chased into the girl's restroom by an angry ghost. Allison withdrew from the school a few days later, presumably to be home schooled by her mother.

As only word can spread in a small town, everyone was informed one Saturday of the need to help renovate the hidden corner of the courtyard. Generations of Academy students showed up to help tear down the wall, as did Sam Wise, who'd never set foot within its walls before. When it fell, the citizens of Nickelville looked in at the century-old subject of childhood curiosity.

The three old men outworked everyone else even if Mr. Green did on occasion seem distracted by an older woman with badly dyed red hair. When the timbers came down at last, a stone cross emerged from the tall grass. Roses wound around its base and climbed to its top. When the volunteers began to cut the waist-high grass down, a smaller, second grave was found. Upon closer inspection, they found elaborate inscriptions carved into the bases of both.

Here lies Sorina Kennemur Routh, beloved Angel who graced this world
for too short a time.

Here lies Jonathan Routh, the light of his mother's eyes.

They searched for a third marker, but found the rest of the corner to be empty.

"That's weird," Megan said. "I thought Jacob would have been buried here too."

"I'll do some checking into the town records and see what I can find out about that," Mrs. Grimble said. "Who knows, there might be another story in it. See you at the *Tribune* on Monday," she said to Emelia before leaving. "Coming Bruce?"

"Mr. McGeehee said he'd bring me home," Bruce answered, his asthma now in full remission.

A low iron fence replaced the wooden wall, found at the back of the school's shed by Megan and her friends while finishing up their detentions with Mr. Green. Mr. Harris fastened a plaque to it with a brief description of the events that led to the small cemetery's discovery. This description, of course, said nothing about the spectral Dark Man.

When at last the work was done, the citizens of Nickelville took one last look at the stone cross and went back home, glad to have at least one less mystery in their lives.

Mr. Harris brought his wife up when all was done, and she shared fresh cookies and lemonade around. Mr. Green, dirt clinging to almost every inch of his body from the day's work, stood with them, admiring the fence.

"This is one of those times when I can still feel Josie here," Grandpa said.

"And Carl," added Mr. Harris. Megan looked forward to hearing more stories about their lost friend, and knew that she now had plenty of time to do so since she and her mother planned to stay.

Handshakes were exchanged, and the old friends left the courtyard where they'd played as children, leaving Bruce and the McGeehees alone in the school that they technically owned.

"I'll go warm up the truck," Azarich said, walking slowly away and looking once again like her caring grandfather and not the iron-willed lawyer that he'd been at the school board meeting. "Come on Bruce, let's give them a moment alone."

Just before the mother and daughter turned to go, Jacob Routh, no longer known as the Dark Man, appeared. Megan was glad he did. She didn't want to remember him the way he'd looked in the hallway when he'd chased Allison and Glenn.

"I've never seen him smile before," Emelia said and put her arm around her daughter, something she had done more since returning home than she had in the previous fifteen years of Megan's life.

Thank you, he said without voice and then slowly faded away.

About the Author

Tom Barnett was a sick kid who escaped into fantasy books at a young age. As he grew, his asthma got better, but his love of reading never diminished. After three decades of leading teens toward a love of reading in which the stories of Nickelville have been percolating in the back of his mind, he's finally set them free.

Tom currently teaches middle school English in the Dallas area where he lives with his wife and children. He is also owned by several cats, one of which may or may not be the oldest creature in the universe.

www.ingramcontent.com/pod-product-compliance
Lightning Source LLC
Chambersburg PA
CBHW030546260626
47157CB00006B/2207